AUĒ

Becky Manawatu (Ngāi Tahu) was born in Nelson, raised in Waimangaroa, and lived in Germany and Italy before returning to the West Coast with her family. *Auē* is her first novel.

AUĒ

BECKY MANAWATU

SCRIBE

Melbourne | London | Minneapolis

Scribe Publications
18–20 Edward St, Brunswick, Victoria 3056, Australia
2 John St, Clerkenwell, London, WC1N 2ES, United Kingdom
3754 Pleasant Ave, Suite 100, Minneapolis, Minnesota 55409, USA

First published by Mākaro Press 2019
Published by Scribe 2022
Reprinted 2024
Copyright © Becky Manawatu 2019

Typesetting by Paul Stewart and Scribe

Printed and bound in the UK by CPI Group (UK) Ltd,
Croydon CR0 4YY

Scribe is committed to the sustainable use of natural resources
and the use of paper products made responsibly from those
resources.

978 1 914484 67 4 (UK edition)
978 1 922585 29 5 (Australian edition)
978 1 964992 05 1 (US edition)
978 1 922586 35 3 (ebook)

Catalogue records for this book are available from
the National Library of Australia and the British Library.

scribepublications.com.au
scribepublications.co.uk
scribepublications.com

to Mum
and in memory of Glen Bo Duggan

BIRD

I am drowned.

My heart expands as if preparing for flight, but doesn't lift off. And now in its hush, like the beatless whoosh of a planing bird's spread wings, what I have done swells. Greater than the very sea we've drowned in.

Ārama

Taukiri and I drove here in Tom Aiken's truck. We borrowed it to move all my stuff. Tom Aiken helped. Uncle Stu didn't. This was my home now.

Taukiri said that – 'Home now, buddy' – but he wouldn't look at me. He looked around me, at the toaster, at a dead fly on the windowsill, at the door handle. He said something dumb, 'You'll love it, there are cows.'

You're an orphan. I'm leaving. But cows.

He carried boxes into my new bedroom and pretended not to notice I hadn't said a word since he'd packed up our house in Cheviot and driven me here. To Kaikōura. To Aunty Kat. To a place we sometimes visited but never stopped the night. He put the bed against the wall and the toys on the shelves, and lined up some of the books just like before. Not all of them. He left some of the books in the box, then he lifted it with a grunt and shoved it in the wardrobe.

'Look after them for us,' he said.

I didn't answer. He didn't care.

Taukiri looked around like he was happy now. 'Just the same. Good eh.'

He didn't say it like a question, so I kept my mouth shut.

'I'll be back as soon as I can, okay?' But something in his voice didn't sound like him.

I followed my brother outside. The others followed too. Tauk kissed me on top of my head then got in his car. He looked at the steering wheel, looked at the road ahead, plugged his phone in, scrolled through, hit the screen. Music roared from the car. Snoop Dogg.

Aunty Kat came over and folded her arms. Tauk turned the song down before Snoop said the 'N' word. Beth and Tom Aiken were there too. Tauk stared at Beth, then her dog, Lupo, like he was actually leaving me with them and not with Aunty Kat and Uncle Stu.

'Be good,' he said.

'The driving. That coast, Taukiri,' Aunty Kat said, her arms still folded, 'just go easy.'

I hadn't said a word in so long because I was afraid of how I'd sound. I hoped it would stop him, me not talking. Worry him a bit. But even when I didn't say goodbye, he left.

He turned up Snoop Dogg as he drove off, which stung a bit.

We stood in the driveway. Me and Beth. Aunty Kat and Tom Aiken. Lupo was wagging his tail because he thought it was a happy thing. He didn't know about goodbyes. At least this time I had a chance to say it. I just couldn't. Uncle Stu wasn't outside with us. He was drinking beer in front of the TV in the lounge of my new home. He'd had a long day, Aunty Kat said.

'You and your brother look so different,' Beth said as Taukiri's car disappeared into the dust cloud it made for itself. Lupo had run off behind the car, chasing the spinning wheels, but then he'd seen a butterfly and decided to follow that instead.

Taukiri and I didn't look different. We looked exactly the same. But I wasn't talking yet, so I couldn't argue with Beth.

'You both have those eyes, though,' she said, looking at mine. 'But yours are sad. His are angry.'

Tauk's car was on the main road. His surfboard on the roof made it look like he was just going to the beach for a surf, but something in my tummy told me it might be a long one.

'He's an idiot. You're better off without him,' said Aunty Kat, and she stomped off to the house.

Tom Aiken put his hand on my shoulder. 'He'll be back. Before you know it.'

I hoped he'd come and take me away from this shit-hole. I'd never used the word 'shit' before, but my mum and dad were dead and my brother just drove off with his guitar and surfboard, listening to Snoop Dogg, so there was no one around who'd care if I said 'shit-hole', or even the 'F' word. It was weird. I didn't think I was happy about it. I'd heard Taukiri swear before, but not around me or Mum and Dad.

Only when he was hanging out with his mates and he thought none of us was around to hear him. It's actually funny how much you learn from hearing things you shouldn't. I never thought my brother was much of a troublemaker, but I'd heard Nanny say he was. He sure was.

When Taukiri was gone we went to the bush to play.

I dug a hole in the dirt while Beth swung on a branch.

'I dare you to eat a worm,' I said. It surprised me that my voice sounded totally normal.

I flicked the dirt off a worm I'd found and hiffed it at her.

She caught it in one hand. 'Right,' said Beth, and she popped it into her mouth. Even let it dangle there a bit. It was wriggling around, but she didn't care. She sucked it up so slowly I nearly puked. I told her to stop, so she spat it out. A bird swooped down from the trees and snatched it up.

'Lazy bird,' Beth said. 'That worm was dug up.'

I decided to make a rule for myself – if I said a swear word, I'd have to eat a worm like Beth did.

We went to the swamp. Lupo started barking and Beth told him to shut it. When he stopped we heard a noise. A scuffle then a cry, like something was being hurt.

Beth pointed to the flax bushes, 'Is that mum weka teaching her baby a lesson?'

There were two wekas busy doing something terrible.

'That's not what mum wekas do. Is it?'

Beth shrugged. 'Let's see.'

We walked closer. The strange cry got loud. The wekas were using their beaks to tear at the thing that was making the sound.

'Bastards got a baby rabbit,' Beth said.

In the muddy edge of the swamp there was a baby rabbit with skin hanging off, and legs going ways they shouldn't, and the tiny bottom jaw torn away. It was crying like a baby. The wekas kept going at it with their beaks, their wings back behind them like seagulls do at washed-up fish or chips.

'Oi!' Beth yelled, and she ran towards them. They moved away, but not far. The baby rabbit tried to jump but it moved like it was made of the insides coming out of its belly. Its face fell into the swamp, and

7

we watched it try to get air by lifting a nose out of the muddy water as if it was the heaviest nose an animal ever had.

Beth ran to it. She took her jersey off and scooped the muddy, blood-covered baby into it. The crying stopped.

'*Shhh*, I got you. Those bastards. Eating you alive!' Beth turned to where the birds were watching, grunting like winged lions. 'Bugger off.'

'What should we do?' I asked.

Beth opened her jersey and we looked inside at the rabbit. Its back was like luncheon sausage, the face was half gone and the tiny top teeth were all that was left of its mouth. The legs had turned under, as if they were only fur now. Just soft fur and meat with no bones inside. It made me think of a toy, a toy made yuck for halloween.

Beth opened the jersey some more, and out the side of the rabbit's belly a little bit of a yellow-bag thing was poking, and a fringe thing with teeth made from skin.

I threw up.

'You weirdo,' said Beth. 'We need to help it.'

I wiped my mouth, 'We can take it home and get some bandages. Plasters.'

I swallowed back more throw-up.

'No,' Beth said. 'We need to help it die. It's probably wishing it was never born.'

'Rabbits don't wish.'

'What would you know, townie?'

Cheviot was actually country as, but I didn't get into that with her.

'If it can wish then take it home, bandage it, plaster it.'

'It'll be dead. Go get me a rock.'

Lupo followed me, sniffing around, wagging his tail the whole time. I found a big rock, and when I got back with it Beth put the baby down under a tree on a thick root.

'Give it.'

I gave her the rock.

'Don't look if you don't want,' she said. 'Ready?' she said to the rabbit, which didn't answer.

She lifted the rock up and I kept looking. I wished I hadn't. Lupo barked and Beth wobbled. The rock came hard down on the rabbit's back legs, making it cry like it had before, only more squealed.

The wekas started to grunt again.

Beth was crying. 'I missed.'

Lupo barked. I kicked him in his guts to shut him up. He yelped.

Beth picked up the rock that had a bloody brown-and-yellow slick over it. The baby rabbit's eyes said it was ready. Beth brought the rock down again. Right on its head this time. She sat down on the ground and looked at her hands. There were a few little smudges of blood on one palm. I sat beside her.

'Are you okay?'

She didn't answer, then stood up. 'Don't kick my dog ever again, townie.'

'Sorry … I …'

'You what? Wanted to help? I didn't need it.' She dragged her hand across her wet eyes. 'This is a farm. And that was just a rabbit.'

She bent down and rolled the rock away. I looked at the squashed meat and guts and fur.

'Now you bastards can have the damn thing,' Beth said, walking away. The wekas tore away pieces of rabbit and ran into the bush.

She stormed off towards her house, with Lupo behind. I followed too, but she didn't want me following her because she turned and stuck her tongue out. I stopped at the barn and cut across the paddock to my house.

To *my* house, like Taukiri said.

I went straight to the bathroom to wash my hands. I looked in the bathroom cabinet and found a box of plasters. I put one on my thumb, which felt good. So I put one on my knee too. Then I put one on my forehead, and another one on my other knee and one on my wrist. I wrapped one around my other thumb and I put one on the back of my neck, one on my chest and one on my cheek, and I put one over my belly button, and when there were no plasters left I stopped searching for places I was sore.

❧

Uncle Stu grunted like a weka through dinner, chewing at the bones of the pork ribs Aunty Kat had made. He pushed his chair out, making a loud squeak when he had finished and kissed Aunty Kat's head with grease around his mouth. He hadn't noticed that it was my first night eating dinner with them and no one said a thing about the plasters that weren't covered by my clothes. But what was the worst was Uncle Stu left his knife and fork leaning on his plate like he wasn't finished eating and walked off.

My dad always lined his up in the middle of the plate, then took it to the kitchen. And if he'd kissed Mum with grease around his mouth, he'd have made a joke of it, and Mum would have laughed. Aunty Kat had closed her eyes and made her lips into a line.

After we ate I went to the bathroom to brush my teeth but couldn't find my toothbrush. We'd left it behind in our bathroom. The one at our house. Taukiri packed, so really it was his fault that I had no toothbrush.

There was a soft toy on my bed. It looked like a baby rabbit before it was ripped to pieces and squashed by a rock. I threw it onto the floor. I climbed in my bed and tried not to look at it.

Aunty Kat came in to say goodnight.

'I haven't brushed my teeth,' I grinned wide to show her. 'Tauk didn't pack my toothbrush.'

'We'll grab one tomorrow.' She looked at the toy on the floor, 'You don't like soft toys, huh?'

'Not that much.'

'I'll try to remember you're not a little boy anymore. Sorry.'

I had a strange feeling, like when you're in a deep bath and you pull the plug but don't get out, just sit there getting heavier and heavier until the last bit of water twists loud down the drain.

Aunty Kat patted my head. 'I suppose you're also too big for goodnight kisses?'

I said, 'Uh huh,' even though I wasn't.

She turned off my light and went into the hall. She put her hand on the hall light switch. I bit my lip.

'I hope you don't mind if I leave this on,' she said. 'Easier for Uncle Stu to find his way downstairs in the morning.'

'That's okay. If it's easier,' I said.

She left, but I didn't think I'd be able to sleep, because I had meat between my teeth.

We are on a beach. Beth is holding the baby rabbit. It is in one happy piece. The beach is the same one where Taukiri was found. Bones Bay. A secret place. Up till now only three of us knew about it. Koro knows and he is in my dream. I am happy to see him. In my dream he is in one piece too.

We're sitting around a campfire. Beth makes me and Taukiri laugh a lot, and I feel happy. Then we see something moving in the water. It swims towards us. It feels like something bad is about to happen and I'm scared. Beth and I cuddle into Taukiri. The rabbit too. Taukiri makes us all feel safe. Two figures come up out of the water. We soon see it is Mum and Dad. They come up the beach. They sit down by the fire. We all stay very quiet, like stones. Taukiri still has his arms around us; I can feel his fingers pressing deep into my arm. I ask Mum and Dad where they've been. They don't know.

We go back to being quiet, but the roar of the sea is loud, and Mum and Dad are shaking and their skin is almost blue. They look like themselves. Alive. Just cold. Mum sits by Koro and puts her hand on his leg.

Nanny arrives. She's wearing her favourite pearl earrings. She walks to Taukiri. They frown at each other. Tauk gives her a pūkana and I think she's gonna belt him. But she says, 'You left this behind,' and swings his bone carving in front of her. We both have the same one. It is our thing – the bone-carving warriors.

'I wanted to,' he says.

I look down for mine and it's not on the string around my neck.

There's a toothbrush instead.

I woke up. Tried to go back to my dream to yell at Taukiri for saying he'd left his bone carving behind because he wanted to. But I just stayed there in my new room, with my eyes scrunched tight and furry

11

teeth. A storm was crashing around outside, and rain was thuck-thucking on our tin roof, and the only thing I liked about all the noise the storm was making was it kept all those nasty birds quiet.

By the time she was talking to me again, Beth was making the place less of a S.H.I.T. hole and I was getting good at spelling swear words. A week after the baby-rabbit thing and the me-kicking-her-dog-in-the-guts thing, she arrived at my place while I was outside making a gun from a stick and said, 'It's pretty cool how close we live to each other eh?'

I'd tried to count the steps from my door to hers three times already, but every time I'd got distracted by a pūkeko or a weka. And if it wasn't one of those birds that walked around like they owned the place, a cow would distract me, or I'd think I saw something shiny, like a pearl, and I'd have to stop and check what it was. Pick it up. Drop it again. Then I lost count. I didn't know if I agreed with what Beth said – that we lived close. I thought if we really lived close, I wouldn't forget so easily which step I should be counting.

Beth told me her mum had died too, so we had that the same. She was lucky, though, because she still had her dad. We were gonna ask if we could be brother and sister, which made me less sad that my real brother had left me there.

My aunty said Taukiri was probably never coming back. She said he would probably find his crackhead mother and they could ruin their lives together. I reminded her our mother was dead and she wasn't a crackhead, whatever that was. She said nothing. I couldn't believe she was so stupid that she forgot her own sister died. We'd all gone to the tangi. I'd watched Aunty try not to cry while Taukiri played his guitar and sang her favourite song 'Tai Aroha' – and not just because it had her name in it – for everyone.

I was going to be Beth's brother, and then when we were old enough we'd change from being brother and sister to husband and wife, and we'd move to Auckland and buy a smart car. Beth said a smart car would be the best idea because parking in Auckland was supposed to be a B.I.T.C.H. A real S.H.I.T. of one. Beth swore a lot. It was lucky she didn't have a rule about having to eat a worm every time or she would probably have turned into a bird herself.

Beth reckoned we only needed to have a smart car because we were not going to have kids. She said even though we'd be husband and wife she didn't want to do what husbands and wives did to have babies. And she was right. It was disgusting. Lupo would fit in the smart car perfectly.

I liked Lupo, even though I'd kicked him. He was definitely dumb but really funny. Especially when he was chasing things. Normally whatever he was chasing outsmarted him.

My favourite thing about Beth was that she was a chatterbox. Aunty Kat and Uncle Stu didn't say much funny stuff, only 'do this' or 'do that'. Sometimes Aunty Kat asked, 'You okay, boy?' It was nice when she asked, but I thought she liked it best if I just said yes, and so I did, even when it was a lie. I wasn't happy about lying either, or at least no one noticing it. Mum would have seen it. Stopped me in my tracks. I would eat a worm if I told a lie too, like my swearing rule.

To help.

To help me be a good orphan.

We were getting homeschooled together. Beth was supposed to start school last year but her dad forgot or something. Or maybe she'd tried it and got sent home too often for bad behaviour, so Tom Aiken decided she could learn at home. Something like that.

Beth changed her stories a lot. *A lot, a lot.*

My aunty offered for her to do some learning with me. The school was ages away, and counting the steps there would be really impossible. Aunty Kat said she wasn't expecting to be raising a child out here in the wops. We should be grateful, she said.

It made me dizzy when I had to sit and learn the same things as before, when I felt like I didn't need all that stuff anymore. It annoyed me that most of the time it was like nothing had changed. I liked that we used to learn Māori at my old school. I was one of the best in the class because Mum had already taught me and Taukiri how to count. She'd taught us the colours, some songs and every night we said a karakia.

Nanny said things too.

When I used to visit she'd come to the door and say, 'Haere mai,

13

haere mai, Ārama.' And if I brought something awesome like the picture I drew at school of a taniwha she'd clap her hands and say, 'Tino pai rawa, my moko!' Sometimes Tauk made her mutter, and shake her head and say, 'Whakamā, whakamā.' And 'Kei te pēhea koe?' she asked me all the time, like *all* the time. And she didn't care that I always answered the same, 'Kei te pai ahau, Nanny,' even when I wasn't.

Taukiri once told me that it was okay that I didn't know how to say anything else, because that's all people wanted to hear anyway. And now I knew that was true.

Aunty Kat said she wouldn't be teaching us Māori.

'How could I? What do I remember? When do I use it?'

'You're brown,' Beth said.

'And?'

'Mum knew some. Nanny and Koro know heaps,' I said.

'Living in a fairy tale,' Aunty Kat said.

Beth sat up straight. 'That'd be cool.'

'Cool?' said Aunty Kat. 'With all the wolves and mean stepmothers and the dilemmas.'

'What's a dilemma?' Beth asked.

'Two choices with equally shitty outcomes.'

'So don't choose one. Stay put.'

'That's a choice too.' Then Aunty Kat said nothing for a bit. 'Maybe when Nanny's not so busy she'll teach you some Māori. I lost mine.'

In our classes Beth learned to write a lot more than her own name and words like cow, cat or P.I.S.S. and S.H.I.T.

My aunty didn't understand how Beth had so much to say about things when she hadn't been to school. Beth said her own aunty sometimes phoned her from Auckland and talked about life in the city, and that's what got Beth talking. Aunty Kat said that was bull S.H.I.T. and the reason Beth had so much to say was from watching too much TV. Beth got sulky and didn't talk for the rest of our lesson. But she came bouncing back, happy as a bird, the next day and acted like she hadn't been peed off at all.

Later, when Aunty Kat was making a coffee, Beth whispered, 'I'm still mad at her, but I really want to learn to write so I can get a big office job with my aunty in the big city. Then we can buy our smart car and apartment.'

I knew what an apartment was, but often Beth thought she had to explain everything to me. She said an apartment was houses stacked onto each other like boxes until they made a big tall building. In an apartment you could never be lonely, and if you ever ran out of anything you could just go ask for it from your neighbours. Which did sound cool. But when I got to thinking about it, I realised being in the bottom box, or even somewhere in the middle, would be C.R.A.P. because another box, and another, and all its stuff, and all the people inside, would be between you and the sky all the time.

I liked just having our tin roof between us and the sky. Sometimes at night it was scary to hear a storm, but I thought it was better being able to hear it. To know it was there.

Having more neighbours would be cool though. We just had Tom Aiken and Beth. Before I moved here we lived in Cheviot and I could walk to school, or to my friend's house if I wanted to. Even to the Four Square for a lolly. Everything was close enough. Just a walk. And while I took it, I could still see my house when I turned back. A few other kids lived on our street. I sometimes wondered if they missed me. I sometimes wondered if they stopped at our old door and hoped I'd run out.

At night I missed Taukiri's bedroom more than I missed my own. Sometimes I think I missed it more than I missed Taukiri. I definitely missed it more than I missed Nanny – and that was also a lot. I wanted to feel the way it felt to be in his room.

Night-time was the hardest for me. Without Mum and Dad. Without Taukiri just down the hall. Aunty Kat read to me, but it wasn't the same. It was like eating sugar when you want a lolly. That's what I could compare it to because when I asked Aunty if we could go for a drive to buy a bag of lollies, she laughed, and said there was not a chance. She told me if I needed a sweet that bad I should eat a bit of sugar. So I did. I sat on the kitchen floor with a bag of Pam's sugar and shovelled spoons and spoons of it into my mouth. Then I lay on the couch with a sore tummy and head for the rest of the day. And it didn't even taste good.

Nanny kept a jar full of lollies at her house. Sometimes she even had bags of Eskimos or Pineapple Lumps. It was strange I hadn't seen her since I'd been at Aunty Kat and Uncle Stu's. When I had my real life – not this one that felt like something I might wake up from – I saw my nanny at least once a week. She came for dinner all the time and always brought me a pressie. I could call her day or night for anything, she said. Since I came here I've called her house one hundred times already to tell her she needs to get Taukiri to come back. But she doesn't answer.

I called Taukiri's cellphone three times the day he left. I called it three times the day after, and I've called it at least three times each day since. It only rang twice. Now it goes straight to answerphone. 'Sup, this is Tauk's phone. Don't check voicemail, so send a text.'

I didn't tell Aunty Kat I was calling Tauk though. If she saw me using the phone she just sighed. 'Nanny's busy, Ari. Stop calling. She'll call you back when she can.'

My mum used to say things happen in threes. Once I fell off my bike three times in one week. 'Everything happens in threes, be more careful,' she'd said. But that was just on the second crash, so I was never sure if I crashed the third time *because* of the rule of threes, or if I just wanted to get the last one out the way.

Mum kissed me and put plasters on the five places I was bleeding and I put one more on a bruise.

I thought of Taukiri away from here, driving his car whenever he wanted, music so loud. He'd left a long time ago already, he must've made it safely to wherever he'd gone. But I couldn't help going over things that had already happened, trying to figure out what had been done in threes and what hadn't.

Mum was dead. Dad was dead. Did that mean someone else had to die too? Or could that rabbit count as the third?

Today, I counted up seventy-four plasters left from the box of a hundred I found, and told Aunty Kat we should always keep more than one box in the house. We lived in the wops, after all. It seemed like she didn't hear me so I snuck into her handbag and put 'plasters lots' on her grocery list.

Taukiri

I am outskies, offskies, goneskies. Save your tearskies, Ari.

I drove down the driveway of Aunty Kat's farm with my windows up. First Snoop Dogg, then NOFX's 'Eat the Meek' vibrating the whole car, roaring in my ears, in case Ari yelled for me to stop. And I didn't look in the rearview mirror. The dog barked and chased me down the driveway.

Ari would be all good with Beth and even though Uncle Stu was a real prick, Tom would be there. My brother would be better off without me. There was something he didn't know. He didn't know I was trouble and that bad things happened to the people I loved.

I drove away with the windows up to keep out the smell of the sea.

I was glad to be heading north, not south. Glad not to pass Ōaro or Claverley. Glad to head inland first. Wondered if I'd made the right choice. Then 1814 started up with 'Whakahonohono Mai'. I cranked it. It was too easy to leave like that.

Music loud. Windows up. Easy as. That town, that cunty sea, easy as to leave. Ari was harder, but what was done was done.

My hands trembled on the steering wheel. I was worried I'd forget to hold tight. My heart beat faster when the road cut towards the sea, when a car came towards me, when I remembered I was in a heavy, heavy machine, and heavy, heavy machines could sink like stones.

When a song came on with a miserable beat, I hit next.

Mum and Dad used to love driving us south, to Ōaro, to see the Haumuri Bluffs, then driving on until the land opened out again at Claverley – and though we couldn't see Bones Bay from the road, Ari and I always knew it was there. We'd nudge each other. Grab our bone carvings. Seals would leap from rocks and Ari would point and I would look but miss seeing them. Pretend I had. And when you

17

looked out as far as you could, you believed in taniwha and that it might be true your tīpuna followed stars to find their way here.

Kaikōura was always a disaster waiting to happen. Volatile, exposed. That's why you lost your breath there, that's why you took your eyes off the road. That's why your grip of the steering wheel loosened without your realising it had.

Ari's fingers turning, spinning the bone carving, his chin quivering. *What you gonna do, Tauk? What you gonna do?* It overwhelmed me, drowned me in a lime sea. He was better off with Aunty Kat.

Surfing used to empty my mind. As it turned out, almost dying did too. The sea was a bitch, a monstrous bitch. My lungs had burnt, and every time I thought I'd got the air I needed, I was hit again. In the mouth, against the back of my throat, and so far into my nose it stung my brain. The water was black and bigger than anything else. I'd prayed, dumb-arse I was. Held my bone carving, prayed and trod water.

Driving north, I had my guitar in the backseat, and my surfboard on the roofrack to sell in Wellington. I would have done anything possible to surf once. Loved it, loved the sea. I'd wag school, forget a job Dad wanted done, steal a bike to get there quicker. Not now.

Dad taught me to drive in this car, not my real dad. My real dad died when I was little. I hardly remembered him. Only his eyes and his hands and sometimes his voice. A story or two. That might seem a lot to remember about someone, but it wasn't because I hardly cared that I remembered those things. I didn't tell the stories.

At the ferry terminal, waiting to drive aboard the Interislander, I was shaking. I was afraid to cross that water.

Then I remembered the pills I'd stolen. I'd seen Aunty Kat throw some back a few times during the tangi, and later I'd gone to her bathroom and pocketed the lot, stashed them in the chocolate box Ari gave me for my birthday.

The pills helped – blunted the edge.

Picton grew smaller, slowly at first. Then I must have blinked and it was gone and I was annoyed, like when you're posting a crack-up Snapchat story – one where your mate's crashed out and your other mate's shaving that guy's eyebrow off – and you're on one per cent and about to send it to all your friends and your battery dies.

A woman came out on deck and stood close to me, even though there was no one else around and plenty of space. She had a doughy face and small eyes. She was wearing a really ugly purple windbreaker.

'Don't mind me, I just find it so lovely out here. You too?' She lifted her chin and her throat rippled in the wind.

I coughed over the side, but nothing came up. Not a single grain of ghost sand.

'Oh you poor thing,' she touched my back.

I flinched. 'Don't,' I said, then walked inside.

I went to the bar. The bartender had thick purple lips like they'd been sucked on or punched. He was wearing a white shirt with the sleeves rolled up.

'I'll grab a beer, bro.'

I thought he might ask for ID, but he didn't. He didn't speak, either, didn't move, just looked at me like I was an idiot.

Finally he sighed, 'Just any old beer then?'

I looked at the taps. 'That one. Monteiths. Lager.'

He poured the beer. The froth spilling from it, he set it in front of me. 'Ten dollars, thanks.'

'You're joking?'

'Yeah, nah. Not at all.'

And that was when a call came from Aunty Kat's landline. I ignored it, took ten bucks out my wallet and sipped the cold beer until my phone stopped vibrating.

It sprang to life again and my head started to spin.

'You must have a magic phone,' said the bartender. 'Hardly anyone gets signal here. Don't worry, it'll be dead soon.'

'What?'

'The coverage.'

The boat swayed and I felt a cold sting, close under the skin of my face.

I grabbed my phone and raced outside. The woman in the purple windbreaker was still there. The phone started buzzing in my hands again, and the metallic smell of the sea stung me in my nose, in my throat, pressed itself into my head until I felt like I'd bleed from my

19

ears, and the woman was right in front of me now, looking at me, and her eyes were bloodshot as if she'd been crying. My phone vibrated again and I took it out of my pocket and threw it into the water, went back to the bar and drank my ten-dollar beer.

It was amazing to be on another island. I felt separated from all that had happened. *That* was there. *They* were there. And I was here. And between here and there was enough water to swallow it all up. I'd told everyone I was leaving to find my mother, my birth mother, who deserted me. But I wasn't. I didn't give a fuck about her. She was a bitch for leaving me. I hated her, and I always would. And if we crossed paths I would tell her the woman who raised me was dead, so now I was motherless.

My birth mother might be further north than Wellington. Te Kūiti probably. Tom Aiken said I might find her there. Though he hoped not, he hoped she was somewhere else. Tom Aiken gave me money. He said to go find her and bring her home. I'd told him I would. I'd try. I needed that money, but I didn't need to bring her back anywhere. She could stay wherever the fuck she liked.

Somewhere round that harbour I found a place to park my car, down a gravel road, beside an abandoned house. The windows of the house were broken, and the door hung off its hinges. I stood in the doorway and took a look inside. In one corner there was a pile of rubbish bags stacked on top of each other, a sour smell. There was a rustle and a scurry then a squeak. A cold dark that trumped the night outside. Near the door was a wooden table. On the table there was a dirty cup, a plate with a spiderweb clinging to it. The floor had been ripped out in patches and the walls had been partially removed so that wires hung from the exposed frame of the house. The scurry again. Another squeak.

I'd sleep in my car. Park between the house and the low scrub so no one saw me. If it cost ten bucks for a beer up here, I wasn't going to survive long on what little money I had. I definitely couldn't afford a bed anywhere.

I'd try and sell my board as soon as possible.

The first night sleeping in the car was hard, because I couldn't leave the door open. The smell of the sea got in when I opened it. That smell that pressed up into my brain and made my eyes water. And the sound, the hollow pulling and pushing that made my ears ache.

My legs and neck were sore in the morning from sleeping curled up in the backseat.

I drove around job hunting. One guy at a scallop-shelling factory wanted my phone number. He looked a little sorry for me when I told him I didn't have a phone. I'd had a number, Facebook, Snapchat, Instagram. I'd posted photos of Ari and me. People liked the pictures of us on the beach, especially the one after we'd been swimming, holding up our bone carvings in a cheers.

And my friends would've been messaging me. 'Bro how are you?' 'Sup?' 'Keen to go out bro?' 'What's going on ya stuck-up egg?' And those messages were going into an abyss and I gave zero fucks. They could drift out to the Kaikōura Canyon for all I cared. That place like a hungry mouth, flicking out its tongue against my back, wanting to swallow me whole. A mouth as deep as twelve footy fields. And I had escaped it, and all I planned on doing with my second chance was to escape some more. But to do that I needed money. I needed a job.

I let the guy feel sorry for me.

He had long blond lashes, freckled skin and a shaven head. He held his mouth in a thin line like he already knew I'd disappoint him.

I let my face muscles slacken. Made sure he knew I was someone he should feel sorry for. I milked this as much as I could. Without words. Without saying it all out loud. Telling the story would be cheating and I drew the line there. I should come back after Christmas, he said. And though after Christmas seemed a long way away, it was something.

Afterwards I went to a public library.

I took a book from a shelf and went to a couch and sat down. The softness – the way it gave way, just barely, beneath me – made me feel heavy. My arms, my legs, even my belly. I looked at the book to keep myself afloat. The book was called *Stitches* by David Small. I opened it and there were hardly any words, just black-and-white pictures. One was of a small boy, disappearing into a sheet of paper, first his head, then his torso, then his whole body was lost.

I kept turning the pages and found it was a story about a boy who loses his voice after an operation to remove cancer from his neck.

I touched my neck and found the string of my bone carving there, and I felt heavier still, but now in smaller parts of me, like my toes and eyelids. I turned back to the page where the boy was disappearing into the sheet of paper. I had an urge to take the picture. To keep it. There was no one around so I slid the book between my legs and started to tear the page from the book. Tiny bit by tiny bit. So slowly that only I could hear the tearing.

I liked the quiet ripping sound and the small secret and taking something that wasn't mine. Liked ruining the book for the next person.

I left the library. Found a Four Square and bought a Coke. Drank it and the bubbles stung my raw throat, still so raw from all the sea and sand I'd swallowed up. Walked into the city. I found a bench and sat on it to listen to a guy thumb bar chords and sing.

He was decent. A lot of people were listening to him play. People danced and threw coins into his guitar case. I stayed until he finished and then flicked him a dollar coin.

'Chur, bro,' he said.

The evening began and the smell of the sea came into the city. There were other evening smells: beef chargrilling, onions and spices frying, and I could smell the sea creeping into the city too. It was stronger than all of them. I went to the train station and caught the Hutt line. When I saw a guard making her way through the carriages checking tickets, I walked to the last carriage. The train stopped and I got off. I walked an hour or more then caught the train back.

In the car I took the stolen page out of my pocket, and I thought more about the book in the library missing its page than the picture itself. I found a blue pen in the glovebox and drew music notes on the sheet of paper the boy was disappearing into.

The next afternoon I went back to the bench where I'd heard the busker. He was there again.

My money was running low but I'd bought two bottles of Coke. I'd slung my guitar over my shoulder when I left the car, without really thinking about it. When I arrived at the busker's spot I gave him the Coke, then sat down and listened. After a few songs he came over, clacked his bottle against mine.

'Thanks, bro, just what I needed.' He nodded at my guitar, 'You play too?'

'Yeah. A bit.'

He opened his palm, smiled. Waited for me to strum a chord and prove I didn't just carry around a guitar to look cool. I played 'Tai Aroha' first. My mum's favourite song. One she taught me. But he couldn't join in, so I finished it quickly and got into the opening chords of Herbs' 'Dragons and Demons'. The busker nodded then, tapped his foot, began to sing the words, and soon enough we were jamming together. People gathered – some danced and threw coins. A girl whistled. A man filmed us on his cellphone. I was loving it – best I'd felt in weeks.

When we stopped the busker counted up the money in the hat.

'Shit! Good Saturday,' he looked at his phone, 'and it's not even two yet.' He gave me a handful of coins and a five-dollar note.

'We had something going, bro. I'm Elliot.' He stuck out his hand.

'Taukiri.'

'See you next week, Taukiri?'

'Bloody oath.'

He capped his head and walked away. I counted thirteen dollars. I put seven in my chocolate box and hid it in the boot of the car.

I came across a post office. I went inside and walked up to the counter. I pulled the stolen picture, tattooed with music notes, out of my pocket. I wrote on it: 'Sorry, Ari.'

The man behind the counter had hound eyes and a black goatee.

'I want to post this,' I said to him.

He slid a single envelope across the counter.

I wrote Ari's name and Aunty Kat's address on the envelope and put the picture inside it. I licked the sticky bit at the back.

'Old school,' the post office man said, smiling. 'They don't need to be licked anymore.'

I felt my cheeks get hot.

'Normal or fast?' he asked.

'Is there slow?'

'Ha. No.'

'Normal then.' I paid and left.

I went to a café and ordered a roast pork sandwich and ate at the tables outside. A small boy was sitting at a table across from me with a woman who had long blonde dreadlocks. She was wearing a low-cut singlet and had an angel tattooed across her upper chest. Gravy dribbled down the boy's chin, and he didn't even notice, just kept eating.

'You've got gravy on your chin,' the woman said, scratching the inside of her elbow.

He wiped it off with his sleeve.

'Not on your sleeve,' she said, but he just carried on eating. Like it was the best sandwich he'd ever had. Like he was thinking, Fuck the gravy on my chin, the gravy on my sleeve, everything in the whole world that wasn't this sandwich. That was how Ari ate too. With his tongue out like a dog, thinking about nothing else. If there was gravy dribbling down Ari's chin, and he noticed it at all, he'd try and lick it away. He'd lick it from his neck if he could …

I drove back out of the city. I turned at the gravel road. At the end of it, near the sea, I parked between the abandoned house and the scrub again, turned off the car. In a weird way, this car parked beside a broken-down house was home now.

The sea was close enough for me to hear the constant hit and pull and drag she made at the shore, but I slept with my car door open this time. I didn't curl up. I extended my legs and let my feet hang out. The songs I'd played on Cuba Street were still in my head, washing away the sound of her singing.

I could often hear Mum – I often felt her – but not Dad. I wondered if that was because we got Dad's body home and not Mum's.

I was so long in that water. After that long it gets right in.

I am in a white room, covered by white sheets. The only colours I see are Ari's green eyes, crimson-rimmed, watching me try to spit up something that isn't there. Ghost sand.

Ari runs his hand along the side of the bed, up and down, back and forth. He must hope I will wake and fix everything. I see that in the quiver of his chin. And he says: 'Mum and Dad are dead.'

Hard, deep crying has turned his irises the colour of bright limes, and he is saying, 'Mum and Dad are dead. They're dead. They're dead. And I thought you'd die too. I thought you'd die too and I'd be left all alone.'

He stops running his hand along the bed and grabs his bone carving. But all I can do is try to spit up the ghost sand.

Bone-white bluffs crumbling down on me.

Close my eyes and try to stay on the road, away from the bull kelp, writhing, ready to take hold and squeeze like tentacles. Try to claw my way to shore.

The road, just a ledge, between walls of earth and the wide, stony-toothed, monstrous mouth of the sea.

I am in a white room, covered by white sheets. I'm waking.

Ārama

I got up extra early this morning, hoping that if Uncle Stu saw me, he might take me for a ride on the four-wheeler, and then to help milk the cows. I had on my gumboots and an old T-shirt I didn't mind wrecking, but when he came downstairs he didn't even say good morning. He just looked at me sitting at the kitchen table. Didn't make himself a coffee. He just walked out the door.

I got myself some Weet-Bix. I was sad Aunty Kat didn't have a tin of peaches in her cupboard and she only had white sugar. I liked brown best. It was so C.R.A.P. eating Weet-Bix alone at the table when I could have been burning around the farm on a four-wheeler, or cruising in a tractor, or something cool like that.

Aunty Kat came downstairs. I kept eating.

'Ari,' she said.

I looked at her and she smiled, then she leaned down and wiped my chin. 'Milk all over your face.'

I stuck out my tongue and licked my lips.

'Hurry along, we're going to town.'

Then I was glad Uncle Stu hadn't taken me with him to the milking shed. We were going to Cooper's Catch for a feed of fish and chips, Aunty Kat said. And I had two bucks to spend at the dairy. If Beth didn't have any money I had enough for us to buy a one-dollar mixture each. We'd drink L&P with our lunch. We both thought it was way better than normal lemonade.

Aunty Kat was wearing earrings and something that made her eyes look pretty. She didn't look so tired. She smelled like Palmolive shampoo and not like cow dung. She looked more like Mum.

It was really warm, and Beth had on shorts and purple sandals. She was standing in her driveway. She had brushed her hair and her toenails were painted bright yellow. Lupo was with her.

'Yes, I've been waiting to go for a cruise to town in this poo-brown Cortina,' Beth said, climbing in. 'Don't worry, I'll be back,' she said to Lupo.

Beth pointed her finger out the window at him like it was a gun.

'Chick, chick, boom,' she said. And he flopped on the ground like he was dead.

Me and Aunty Kat cracked up.

'It's the only trick he knows,' Beth said. 'Dad taught it to him so he could play with me when he's too busy, which is always.'

'Look. Sit, Lupo, sit.' He didn't sit. 'Chick, chick, boom,' and he flopped on the ground. 'Dongi dog.'

When we drove by Mangamanu we saw heaps of surfers out in the water and, it was a little dumb, but I started looking for Taukiri.

Beth said, 'You know some kid was surfing out there and a shark came at him.'

I kept searching the water. Beth grabbed my hand. 'But guess what? That kid had his wits about him. He punched that shark right in his nose!'

Taukiri, I thought.

'But you know what happened next,' she dropped her voice to a whisper. I looked away from the car window, and into Beth's lowered eyes. 'That kid, that kid … he had a *knife* in the leg of his wetsuit.'

'Who surfs with a knife?'

'*This* kid, listen … this kid punched that shark so hard on the nose it rolled upside down, and its huge white belly was facing the sky.' Beth paused, looked out the window, then she leaned back to me again. The car was snaking along the road. 'So that kid, took out his knife and made a big slice down the shark's belly.' Beth sliced the air with her hand and waited. The road was getting snakier. 'And then, you wouldn't believe it, but with all the guts, all the hanging bits, and all the blood, hundreds of fish swam free.'

'No.'

'Wait, here's the best bit! A *seagull*, its feathers covered in blood, not a bit of white left on it – climbed out. Mangled leg. One eye. It climbed up out of that turned-up shark and flew off.' Beth let go of my hand. 'Flew off at an angle, all over the place, probably smashed right back into the water and ended up drowning anyway. But still.' She sat back, grinning. 'Awesome.'

And that's when I ruined the whole day by throwing up all over her purple sandals and painted toenails.

Beth shrieked. She went white in the face, balled up her fists and smacked me right in my cheek. Then she looked down at the puke on her feet and between her toes and cracked up laughing. Aunty Kat yelled at me for making a mess in her car, then at Beth for telling stupid stories.

'She punched me in the face,' I yelled.

'You're not bleeding,' Beth said.

'Say sorry,' said Aunty Kat.

'Sorry for punching you, you weirdo townie,' Beth said, still laughing.

Even though I was angry she'd punched me, I laughed too. The smell of my puke stayed with us all day even after Aunty Kat had tossed Beth's sandals in a bin. Aunty Kat bought Beth new sandals from the St John store and that made me happy because that's sort of what my mum would have done.

Beth complained. 'Mine were new.'

'These are new, to you,' Aunty Kat said.

'Mine were purple.'

'These aren't.'

'These are too big.'

'They're the size that match your mouth.'

Beth seemed happy with that.

Town was decorated cool-as for Christmas. It was when I saw the snowmen painted on the shop windows and people walking around in jandals and shorts that I remembered Christmas was coming. It was really weird that I had forgotten. I never forgot Christmas. That feeling it normally gave me in my tummy had never let me forget before.

Then I remembered something. Something Taukiri told me before he left: Tom Aiken had a gift for me, from him.

Aunty Kat was different away from the farm. She still looked like

28

she was ready to growl, or clip ears, but she was friendly.

Some people stopped to talk to her and asked her how she was doing, and then they'd look at me and smile. Not with their teeth, though, only with the corners of their lips up. It felt like those smiles were fakes.

Every time someone smiled at me I looked at my feet, or my lunch, or my fingers. My mum wouldn't be happy with me if I gave someone the bird for smiling at me like that, so I didn't, at least not so they could see. When Aunty Kat stopped to talk to a kuia on the street, I hid behind my aunty and pretended to be shy. When she said, 'Oh, he's gone all shy. Come out, tama,' I pulled the bird into Aunty Kat's back. Beth saw me and covered her mouth with her hands, then we both started laughing hard out. Aunty Kat looked embarrassed because the kuia's face went red. We were laughing so much, until Aunty clipped my ears and said that she'd change her mind about stopping at the dairy.

I'm glad she didn't.

At the dairy a lady served us. She smiled at us with her nice teeth and gave us each free Chupa Chups with our one-dollar mixtures. She laughed when Beth told her the story about the shark.

I tried to open my Chupa Chup. I tried to bite through the plastic but it wouldn't come open. I kept nibbling on it.

'Kat, honey,' the dairy lady said to Aunty, 'you need a night out.'

'That's the last thing I need right now.'

'What, Stu being Stu again?'

'No, no. Just. *You know*,' said Aunty Kat, and she looked at Beth and me.

'We'll get a babysitter. Here. The kids can all sleep here together. They'll love it.'

'Yeah, Aunty,' I said.

'That would be cool,' said Beth. She winked at me, a real quick wink, and whispered, 'All the lollies we can eat, Ari.'

'You need a night out,' Beth said, and elbowed me. I was still trying to open my Chupa Chup. Beth snatched it from me, set her teeth on it and tore the lollipop free from the plastic. She handed it to me.

'Eeww. My spit was on that.'

'*Eeww*,' Beth copied me. 'Your aunty needs a night off looking after you eh?'

'Yeah, Aunty Kat. You do,' I said, sucking on my Chupa Chup.

'Okay, okay. I'll talk with Stu.'

The dairy lady leaned to Aunty Kat, 'You tell *Stu* …' and the nice smile was gone from her face.

'He's been good lately. Don't worry. It won't be a problem.'

The dairy lady still didn't smile, 'You tell Stu …'

Aunty Kat laughed, 'I will. I'll tell him.'

I wondered what Aunty Kat should tell Stu. It would probably be something he wouldn't hear anyway.

They decided to make the night out in a couple of weeks' time. 'After all the fuss of Christmas,' Aunty Kat said. And I hoped there would be no fuss for Christmas. I didn't feel like fuss.

I saw some plasters on a shelf, grabbed three boxes and took them to the counter.

'We have plasters at home,' Aunty Kat said.

'I used them all.'

'On what?'

'Lots of things,' I said. 'Anyway they're on your list.'

Aunty Kat pulled out her shopping list. I saw my writing 'plasters lots'.

'Now you can cross it off.' I smiled at her.

The dairy lady put the plasters in a bag. 'They're on me. Buy me a beer one day, Kat.'

We ate our dollar mixtures on the drive home. The dairy lady's kids were probably allowed dollar mixtures whenever they liked, Beth said. I said probably not but they would have got them more often than we did, and I bet they never had to eat a teaspoon of Pam's sugar when they had a craving for a lolly.

We got home and I went to the bathroom and looked in the mirror to see if I had a mark on my face where Beth had punched me. It felt quite sore when I touched it, but I couldn't see anything. I put a plaster on it, though, to be on the safe side. I put two of the boxes in the bathroom cabinet and took one and slipped it under my mattress for emergencies.

Beth was tired and grumpy at class the next day. Aunty Kat smelled of cow dung again and had no pretty stuff on her eyes. She got peed off because Beth had forgotten almost everything we had learned last week. I was peed off because Beth wasn't making any jokes, and learning was more fun when she was being funny. She didn't even get snotty with Aunty Kat. And I really loved it when Beth was being smart to her, though I didn't show it because I didn't want my ears clipped.

Aunty Kat noticed Beth's bad mood too because she gave a big huff and started going through the sounds letters make together. Beth perked up.

'S and L make the *ssslll* sound. S and H make the *ssshhh* sound,' she said. 'Sllloppy shhhit. Like what landed on Dad's head this morning.'

Aunty Kat growled at her for swearing, then she laughed too.

At bedtime, I couldn't get to sleep after Aunty Kat left my bedroom. Tauk had set everything up here just like they were before but it looked different. Even the things looked like different things.

Then we are at the dairy in town and my mum is selling us the dollar mixtures instead of the lady. I am so happy to see her. But Beth and I still have to leave with Aunty Kat. I can't understand why. I tell everyone I want to stay and live at the dairy with my mum, but even she just smiles at me.

'I want to stay here with you, Mum,' I say.

She hands me a packet of plasters and a Chupa Chup.

'Use these. Goodbye,' she says.

And then I'm in my new bedroom and it's made of whale ribs that let the night in. And when I try to sleep, I look up through the ribs at the moon and I can't.

I woke up but scrunched my eyes tight, so tight my head hurt. I tried to shut out the white moonlight coming in the window. And as I lay there wide awake with my eyes scrunched shut, it seemed like even Beth, on the next farm, might not be real at all. Even though I knew I could watch the lights of her house from my window.

When I opened my eyes again I saw my old room around me, and I had to blink and blink to find a tear in the wallpaper and the shape of the light shade that made this room different to my old room.

I got out of bed and my feet on the carpet made me get a yucky, walking-in-the-swamp feeling in my legs, and I thought something might snatch me at my ankles and pull me under the bed, so I ran quickly to the window, and only when I saw the shadow of the bush outside and the moonlight instead of the streetlights and the sound of birds that liked night-time I knew I was not in my old room, and I knew I had woken from a bad dream but not from the one I wanted to wake from because there was still no Mum and Dad, no other bed to crawl into. There was no Taukiri.

Across the paddocks and past the trees, a light was shining at Beth's house. I went back to bed, taking two steps and then leaping like Sonny Bill Williams so that whatever was under my bed couldn't get me. I pulled the blankets up over my head and stayed awake all night long.

On Christmas Eve, Tom Aiken and Beth picked up me and Aunty Kat to go and cut our Christmas tree. They already had theirs.

'Why'd you take so long to get one?' Tom Aiken said.

'Just busy,' Aunty Kat said, 'and to be quite honest, we're not feeling very Christmassy.'

'Too bad,' he said. 'Know the perfect place to get one. An old mate won't mind.'

Even though he said 'old mate', Tom Aiken still put us on lookout. He told us to stand out by the gravel road and yell if we saw a red truck coming.

Beth asked, 'Are we stealing? Because if we are Santa might see and then we won't get any pressies.'

Tom Aiken told her to relax. He was only worried that maybe the old mate might have forgotten that he didn't mind us taking a tree.

Beth looked at him like she didn't believe a word he said. I pretty much trusted Beth's face and anything she had to say more than anyone else.

Aunty Kat went and helped Tom Aiken, while me and Beth watched out for the mate who might have forgotten that he didn't mind us cutting down one of his trees. The sun was burning down on us and I was feeling so tired from the brightness. Beth looked up at the sky, and said: 'You know what, Santa, I'm just doing as I'm told, and that's good.' She punched my arm. 'That's good, right?'

I liked being able to help Beth feel better, because even though she didn't realise it, she made me feel better all the time.

I folded my arms and looked down the road and said, 'If I still had a dad who told me what to do, I'd do what I was told and I wouldn't care what Santa thought.'

Beth slapped my back. 'Yeah,' she said.

We looked out for the red truck. Then Tom Aiken yelled, 'Come on, guys. Let's go, let's go!'

We ran up to Tom's truck and jumped in, and we sped off with a brown-green tree bouncing along in the trailer.

'Dad,' Beth said, 'it looks dead.'

Tom Aiken laughed, 'What did you expect? I wasn't going to steal one of his good ones.' And Aunty Kat said not to worry, because she had some white paint at home.

'Yes,' Beth yelled, and started singing, that she wanted a white Christmas, that she dreamed of a lovely white Christmas.

'Why don't you get one off your own farm, Tom?' Aunty Kat asked.

'Where's the fun in that? I mean, who is going to remember that story. We're making memories.'

And we all sang at the top of our lungs while Lupo went mental.

Christmas morning was S.H.I.T.

I woke up and the house was quiet, because Aunty Kat had gone to help Uncle Stu do the milking. I decided to pretend it wasn't Christmas at all.

You wait for Christmas, you count sleeps for Christmas. And I hadn't.

I got up and went to the bathroom and found things to plaster. I put my hand over my chest to find my heartbeat, then put about six plasters over the loudness.

Taukiri

I woke because it was hot in the car. Yesterday, I'd stopped at a supermarket and bought a loaf of bread, some marge and a jar of Marmite. I added a dozen beers to my trolley. And I needed a new toothbrush.

I went to the toothbrush aisle. First, I picked up a green one, but that was the colour of the one that always showed up in our bathroom for Ari. Just showed up. One blue, one green. Just showed up.

Some things I should have told Aunty Kat: Ari has a green toothbrush and a new one should just appear when he needs it. He likes brown sugar on his Weet-Bix. He has nightmares and he will need another bed to crawl into when he does.

I bought a yellow toothbrush. And a box of beer. I shouldn't have bought the beer because I had hardly any money left. I was down to coins and not many were gold.

Christmas lunch was Marmite sandwiches and beer on the beach.

One year Ari got a box of chocolates, and when the box was empty, he cut out photos of me and him, pictures of waves and surfboards and a guitar and glued them to the box to give to me for my birthday. That empty chocolate box was the best present I'd ever been given. Well, best homemade one. Mum gave me Dad's old guitar for Christmas last year. I had all that with me now. The guitar. The chocolate box. My beers.

I walked down to the beach. Got the closest I had been to the sea since Bones Bay.

Tom Aiken said I should have waited till after Christmas. 'Stay,' he said. 'Spend Christmas, then go.'

I sat on the beach and strummed the guitar.

After a song or two I stopped playing and took my shoes off. The beer made me brave. I put my feet into the sand, and let it squeeze up between my toes.

I walked towards the sea and stopped where it could have touched me. I sculled my beer and threw the empty bottle into the tide and yelled. 'You're not fooling me. I hate you.'

I put my sneakers back on, and walked up to my car. With my back to the water, after throwing my bottle and yelling at it, I felt like the sea might follow me and eat me up in one huge foamy mouthful. But when I looked back, it was pulling away in a sad grey murmur.

In my car, I took off my shoes and rubbed every grain of sand out from between my toes. I put on clean socks and cracked another beer.

Ari would have opened his present by now, I thought. And even though I hardly gave a shit, I hoped he liked it. I hoped he'd find someone to teach him to play.

Ārama

The lounge smelled like paint, not like Christmas – which was good. Aunty Kat had covered the tree with white paint, the whole thing. To be honest, she'd looked a bit nuts painting and painting every inch of it when only parts of it were brown. When it was dry, Aunty Kat and I'd hung fairy lights and tinsel on the branches.

The house was so quiet it couldn't be Christmas.

I waited for Aunty Kat to come back from milking, and we opened the presents while Uncle Stu was showering. One present said: *Dear Ari, Love Aunty Kat and Uncle Stu* and inside was a remote control helicopter. I was used to hugging whoever I got a pressie from, so I was glad Uncle Stu wasn't there.

My pillowcase had chocolates, socks with fire trucks on them, felt-tip pens, a colouring book and a rugby ball. Santa still found me, which almost made it feel like Christmas, but I didn't let that feeling get too far in. Uncle Stu decided he would go to some hunting buddy's house for Christmas. That was good. He put a crate of beer in the back of his truck and left. Aunty Kat phoned Tom Aiken and asked if him and Beth would like to come for a barbecue.

'We have lamb and sausages, and I made potato salad,' she said. 'No, I haven't made a pav.'

An hour later they arrived. Beth brought the doll she got from Santa.

'I don't think Santa knows me that well, bringing me a dumb doll,' she said, holding it in both arms, close under her chin.

Tom Aiken had a big pavlova covered with whipped cream and fresh blackberries.

'Wow,' Aunty Kat said.

'It's a supermarket job. Beth decorated it.'

'It looks lovely.'

'I've got something else,' he said. 'I'll just go to the truck.'

I could see what it was even though it was wrapped up in paper with snowflakes on it.

'It's from Taukiri,' Tom Aiken said, 'He asked me to give it to you.'

I snatched the present and bolted upstairs. As I ran I heard Tom Aiken laugh and say: 'Thought he'd be excited about that one.'

It was big and I tripped on the stairs and fell. When I fell the present made a hollow sound like it had something to say, something deep like *fee, fi, fo fum*. Then it sighed.

I dragged it up the rest of the stairs and set the pressie down to open my bedroom door. I hauled it into my room. I didn't look at it and I tried not to listen, shoved the present from Taukiri under the bed.

Then I went to the bathroom, took off my socks and wrapped plasters around my two small toes because I'd hurt them running up the stairs.

Tom Aiken cooked the sausages and lamb chops on the barbecue. We ate lunch and it was delicious, so delicious it almost felt like Christmas, with the creamy potato salad and salty pink slices of lamb with crispy fat on the outside.

I thought of how often Uncle Stu sat down for dinner and was disappointed with it, and how it seemed dumb of him to go when he knew he would have nothing to complain about this time. Or maybe he would? It was better without him, which again felt like a Christmas miracle, but I decided to pretend there was no such thing as a Christmas miracle. And it was good he didn't get to enjoy the lunch. Which was probably a bad thought to have but I didn't care.

Aunty Kat brought out Tom Aiken and Beth's pavlova. Me and Beth stuffed ourselves with it. It was soft and crispy and creamy, and though the berries made me suck my tongue, it really was the best thing I'd eaten ever. After lunch Tom Aiken and Aunty Kat went and pulled a black plastic sheet from the tin shed by the house and put the hose on it for me and Beth to slide down.

Tom Aiken decided we needed the best slope, so we all hiked up to the slopiest paddock. Aunty Kat and Tom Aiken sat at the top with a chilly bin of beer between them, watching me and Beth run barefoot up the hill and slide full pelt down the black plastic. We had the big hose Tom Aiken used to clean the cowshed spraying full bore on it, and Beth poured out a huge bottle of Budget dishwashing liquid over it and the black sheet foamed up. We slid down over and over again, and laughter buzzed in my bones and tummy like bees.

We played until it was late, because different birds started to make different sounds, and different shadows fell on the ground. And our fingers were like soggy walnuts.

It was not Christmas. It was just a hot summer day having fun with Beth. We got some pressies and had a yummy lunch. And I'd got the best thing ever: a promise from Taukiri that he was coming back. He'd never want anyone else to teach me to play the present stuffed under the bed. That meant he had to be coming back sometime soon. When that happened I'd pull the present out and we'd open it together.

Unless it was a trick.

Unless Taukiri found a box shaped like a guitar but inside the box was something different. No, Tauk wasn't that mean. And the present made noises.

It wasn't Christmas. It couldn't have been. Nanny never called.

I was the mail collector. Mostly I collected boring letters with typed-up names and see-through windows for Kataraina Te Au or Stuart Johnson. I liked having a job, but most things I brought Aunty Kat made her frown and sigh.

One afternoon I opened the mailbox, and there were the same boring ones, three of them. Telecom, Kaikōura District Council, Farmlands. But there was another one that had handwriting on it.

I ran up the driveway, waving it in the air.

Running into the house, I banged into Uncle Stu.

'Sorry,' I said.

'There any mail?'

'Yes, look,' I said. 'For me. From Tauk.'

He snatched the other envelopes from under my arm and opened one.

Felt him expand, his teeth pressing together. Felt the air turn to tiny splinters that get into your fingers and toes and have to be poked out with sewing needles.

'Why *you* need a letter?' he said.

He slapped a sheet of paper against my chest. It was covered in numbers.

'You don't need no letter.'

He ripped Tauk's letter out of my hand and walked outside with it. I followed, but I couldn't shout *give it back*, because I hadn't been able to breathe in the air that he'd made sharp with all his splinters.

He took a box of matches out of his pocket, took a match out and struck it against the box, then set the envelope on fire.

'No, no, no,' I said. 'No.'

'All the phone calls you made.'

When it was mostly burned he tossed my letter and its scaly black ash on the ground.

He walked away, got on his four-wheeler and tore off. I looked at what was left of the letter and saw two legs disappearing into ash. Nothing else. Had Taukiri drawn me a picture? Had he written anything? When was he coming back?

I closed my mouth and held back words that stung my gums and tongue, the back of my throat. I chewed them like they were a mouthful of tiny splinters and tried to swallow them.

I went to the bathroom, took two plasters out of the box in the cabinet and went to my bedroom. I lay down on my bed. I put four over my mouth, and then I closed my eyes and put the plasters over them too. Held the tears right in.

When I heard the four-wheeler arrive back home, and the door slam, I just lay straight and still. And when I heard what he started to do to Aunty Kat in their bedroom I used the rest of the box of plasters on my ears. But I still needed a pillow, and even when I had the pillow over my head I could hear his yelling. Thumping. Aunty Kat crying.

In the morning Aunty Kat wasn't in the kitchen. There was a note on the table that said she had to help Uncle Stu all day and I should eat breakfast and then go and play with Beth.

Beth was busy hanging laundry on a clothes horse. She was home alone too.

'No class today,' I said.

'Fine by me. I got better things to do,' she said, and carried on hanging up laundry.

After that we went to the bush to build a hut with some ponga fern. We built it like a teepee and tied it at the top with rope. Inside the hut was damp and our bums got wet from sitting on the ground. Beth found some logs to use as seats and a wooden beer crate from the house to use as a table. She also went and got an old glass milk bottle. She filled it with weeds and put it on our table. It was nice. I told her we should pretend we were Eskimos and this was the house that we'd made ourselves from the ribs of a washed-up whale. That was a game me and Taukiri had played at Bones Bay sometimes.

When we got hungry Beth said we could go make some lunch.

Her house was nice. She had empty beer bottles and jam jars everywhere filled with flowers and weeds. The house didn't smell as much like cow dung and hay as Aunty Kat's and Uncle Stu's. It smelled lemony, like a mum lived in it. Which was strange because one didn't.

Beth took margarine and a block of cheese out of the fridge. She made us sandwiches as quickly as my mum or Aunty Kat would have. She washed two apples and put them on the table with our sandwiches. She poured us two glasses of milk and wiped away crumbs. She looked like a dwarf, because she was moving like an adult but she was too short to be one.

Lupo came into the kitchen. He had a swollen muzzle.

'Caught another bee, did you, dongi?'

He flopped to the ground. Beth wet a tea towel and put it on his muzzle.

'Bloody dumb dog. Don't chase bees.'

She took a big bite of sandwich, chewed and opened her mouth.

'Eeeww,' I said.

'Townie.'

'Dirty country kid.'

'Lupo is a dumb dog eh?' Beth asked me, like she really wanted my opinion.

I leaned down and patted him. His fur was the colour of Caramello chocolate and he had really soft ears and a black mark like a cross between his shoulders.

Beth kept talking. Food in her mouth. 'I mean, how many times do you have to get stung by a bee to learn not to chase them? Not to catch them with your mouth.'

'He's just playful, just kind, makes him forget about stingers.'

'Yeah, and being playful and forgetful is good, because then Dad doesn't want him on the farm. Said he'd shoot him if I didn't love him so much. I told him I'd run away if he shot my dog, and never come back. Run all the way to Auckland and I'd never miss him.'

'To your aunty?' I said.

'Yeah. Apparently I lived with her for a bit. After my mum ...'

'Do you remember?'

'No. But it was probably awesome.'

Beth said we should watch a movie and I thought that was a good idea. We were talking too much, and when you talk too much you normally hear and say things you'd rather not.

She opened a cupboard and pulled out a movie called *Django Unchained* and put it in the DVD player.

'This is my favourite movie,' Beth said. 'But don't tell my dad. He said I'm not allowed to watch it, which made me watch it.'

The movie really scared me, but I had to pretend it didn't, because Beth kept looking at me, saying, 'Scared shitless, aren't you, townie?'

There were a lot of really terrible words in the movie, and a lot, a lot, a lot of people murdering other people. When a man tied a black woman to a tree and took out his whip, I pretended I needed to go to the bathroom.

Beth said, 'Okay, I'll pause it. You don't want to miss this, Django's about to make this guy pay.'

'Tired of watching TV.'

'Ha. I get it. Couldn't watch all of it the first few times either. Some parts I still can't stomach. It's rough, kiddo. She's a dog-eat-dog world. Let's go play Django instead. We can try watch some more tomorrow.'

I was Django because I was Māori.

I wished I looked like I was Māori. Like my mum. Like Tauk. I mean, I *looked* like Tauk but I didn't have his skin. Then I felt bad, because I looked like my dad, and how would he feel if he knew that I wished I didn't look like him?

'Sorry, Dad,' I said very quiet, so Beth wouldn't hear.

But she must have because she put her hand on my shoulder. 'I'm sorry he's dead. I'm sorry they're dead.'

'Yeah.'

Then she picked up her gun, which was a stick, and stuck it my back. 'Now. Hands up, Django. Yar my slave.' And for a second I wondered if it was still Beth behind me.

I replied: 'Now don't shoot me like a dog in the street.'

And Beth grinned. 'Like the sheriff?'

'Exactly,' I said.

I decided Beth was the best friend I'd had, even though she was only eight-and-a-bit and I was eight-and-a-half and she was a girl.

'Should we play with your doll?' I asked her.

'Yes, let's put her in the hotbox,' she said. 'She is Broomhilda, your Broomhilda. And you must rescue her.'

'You should be the doc.'

'We need a baddie. I'll be Monsieur Candie. Try not to be offended if I call you a nigger – remember I'm just playing my part.'

'I don't think you should say that, Beth.'

'It's just a game. It's just a word.'

But I knew it was a bad one because Mum used to growl at Tauk when he played music with it. Plus it made me feel strange.

'Still,' I said.

'Fine.'

Monsieur Candie fed a black man to a pack of dogs. Django was watching, Django didn't wince, because he was pretending to be brave, playing a part. After we rescued Broomhilda from the hotbox we fed her to Lupo, who only licked her, which I was happy about. Me and Beth probably wouldn't ever pretend that we were a mummy and daddy and baby, like normal kids would playing with a doll.

We got hungry again and walked back to her house for a second lunch. While we were eating another cheese sandwich in the kitchen, Tom Aiken came home. He said hi to us both, and Beth told him we were a slave and a slave driver. 'Like you are,' she laughed. And Tom Aiken kissed Beth on her head then walked over to the couch and slumped into it.

Beth made him a cheese sandwich. He ate it fast, then burped really loud. Me and Beth cracked up. He drank a glass of milk that left a big milk moustache. Beth rolled her eyes. Tom Aiken picked up a book and started reading, but pretty soon he fell asleep. Beth took away his sandwich plate. While she was in the kitchen I walked over to the couch to look at him.

I could tell by the soft sound of him breathing that he'd never burn someone's letter.

I stared and stared at him. Beth's dad asleep on the couch made me want to cry, but I held it all in as hard as I could. I pulled a blanket over Tom Aiken, and I held it all in.

I counted the steps back home. Think I got to a hundred and eleven before a rabbit leapt in front of me.

At the farmhouse the table was set for three. It always made me sad to see Aunty Kat's table set for three. Uncle Stu called Aunty Kat a useless C.U.N.T. at tea-time. His toasted sandwich was a bit burnt. I'd never heard that word before, but I could tell it was a bad one because even the pot plant on the windowsill seemed to stop what it was doing. And I got that strange feeling again.

Aunty Kat looked at me, then at Uncle Stu, and she left the table. She came back with a fresh golden-brown sandwich. Her eyes were swollen, like her lip.

I was glad when she came back to the table because being alone with Uncle Stu was pretty bad, and he hadn't talked to me since he burned Tauk's letter. Being with him made me miss my dad so bad.

After he finished his toasted sandwich Uncle Stu spoke.

'So,' he said, almost smiling. 'You'll be on your own a bit more now.'

He stood up and left.

'He fired a farmhand today,' Aunty Kat said. 'To save money. I'll be helping him and won't be teaching you. We're just a walk away, though, if there is any trouble. And you can play with Beth. She's used to being alone. You'll be fine. You will really be fine. We'll sort something out.'

I couldn't tell if Aunty Kat was actually talking to me or not, and I stopped listening. I thought about how many terrible words there were, and how when they were let loose in the world, they sucked up all the air around them.

Jade and Toko

Toko and Jade met at a beach party. Jade was there with her cousin Sav, who was in love with a boy called Tommy, and she'd convinced Jade to sneak away with her. Sneak away from their men to attend an aunty's tangi. But they drove right by the town where the tangi was to be held, and as they passed the turn-off that would have taken them to the place they had said they were going to, Sav crossed her chest and said, 'Life's for the living. Drive on, baby, my aunty would want it.' Then, laughing, 'Dirty little slut she was, God bless her.'

Jade was new to the small group that spent every summer weekend at the beach beside a bonfire, smoking, drinking, and playing music. Sav was a regular blow-in. Arriving, she hollered, 'Look who's back, e hoas! Check it out. And now it's a party.'

There was a guy there playing a guitar and singing. His T-shirt was white, his voice was beautiful, his eyes were shattering.

His dark skin glistened in the firelight.

His smile in the night was wicked.

A lovely kind of wicked.

Jade heard the guy with the white T-shirt, wicked smile and shattering eyes say, 'She's mine.' And even though Jade had spent a lifetime feeling claimed by men and wishing she wasn't, she didn't mind.

Something about him made her want to party.

His good smile, not broken from gear, made her feel as if she were poised at the edge of a deep and swift river – a river almost, quite possibly but possibly not, too wide to leap – with nothing but a desire to cross it.

She stood to dance. With her eyes closed, she swayed. She lifted her arms above her head, so high she felt the sea air on her stomach, and danced without fear of unwanted attention, of asking for it.

Toko sang Eddie Lovette's 'Just One Look'.

He sang so loud, with such control and strength that she felt the earth give out beneath her.

Later there were only a few people around the fire, their hands above the remains of it, drawing away the last heat from the embers.

A blanket fell on her shoulders. She hadn't noticed him stop singing. Or she might have, but in case he was watching her she had danced anyway. Lifting the blanket up, spinning it above her, her toes dug into the sand, she turned to face him.

'Where you from, girl?' he said.

She spun once more, and laughed, 'Hell.'

The House was Jade's first home. That's where her mum, Felicity, satiated a craving for drugs and non-conformity. Felicity had never held a job longer than a sniff but had found herself at home at the House. And Jade's dad, Head, was the Pres.

Jade was spoilt, Felicity said. 'Straight up. You one lucky mob kid.'

Felicity and Head loved Jade. Some days they fed her before she went to school, and sometimes she went in op shop-clean clothes. Sometimes, after she was combed free of them, she had no kutu eating her scalp, laying eggs in her long dark hair. Sometimes Felicity was sober when Jade came home, and there'd be a leg of mutton roasting in the oven and a stack of plates and a pile of cutlery in the middle of the cleared-especially table. The spotting knives out of sight.

And no matter what, every morning Jade was told she was loved. Even if the day turned to shit, she started her day *loved*.

There were people who passed through the House who cared enough too.

'Come have a kai, bub.'

'Here's fifty cents, bub.'

'You wanna sip of my beer, bub?'

'If you wanna puff on this smoke, you gotta smoke the whole thing. That'll learn ya.'

Soon after her eighth birthday a man with a nose like a fat roasted yam and a neck like a bull said, 'You wanna go for a drive, bub?'

'Where to?'

'The beach.'

'I've never been to the beach,' she said.

'Aw, fuck me. Today's your lucky day.'

Jade had gone to find a towel. There were no clean ones, so she took a sarong Felicity had bought from an op shop. She wrapped it around her shoulders and skipped to find the man. Her father was standing with him. 'I got no towel, but this,' and she held up the sarong and spun around.

'What's that for?' Head asked.

Jade pointed. 'He's taking me to the beach.'

'Really? He didn't say.'

Head grabbed the man's shoulders and headbutted him in his roasted-yam nose. Blood sprang from it. Head smacked him in his big belly. And when the man doubled over, Head kneed him in his face. Head told Jade to go to his Mustang. Felicity stumbled from the House and climbed into the car too. Jade's mother stunk of old pyjamas and gin.

'Chee-hoo, bub. Your dad's taking us to the bloody beach. How about that?'

Head came from the House with a red bed sheet. 'Here, my queen,' and he handed it to Felicity. 'To dry yourself with.'

'You think I'm getting my junk out at the beach in the sun? Ha!'

Jade was glad that the man hadn't taken her. It was a long drive, took them all afternoon and night. After a KFC dinner, Jade slept. By sunrise the next day her legs and neck ached and she'd had enough, and then she saw the sea. For the first time. And because it had been such a long journey, it was so special to see the sea and she was glad again the man hadn't been the one who brought her to it.

On the beach, Felicity sat sullen under the bright sun, sharkies on but squinting, and Jade went to the shore and touched the sea with her toes, then walked further, until it was over her ankles, wading further and further until it was at her armpits, and she had to leap to keep the water from touching her neck and face. Because that would be too much, to get sea in your face on your first trip to the beach.

Head took off his jacket and T-shirt. Jade thought his tattooed torso made him look like a god. He rolled up his jeans and kicked sea water at his daughter's face. 'Duck under, go on,' he said.

Felicity took off her pyjama bottoms and top and walked to the water's edge in her underwear. 'Got your junk out, missus?' Head said, kicking water at her then.

Felicity ignored Head and walked into the sea, a grimace pressed on her face. She dunked herself under, like someone had pushed her head and was holding her down. She came up, eyes wide, gasping. She walked back to her spot in the sand and wrapped the red bed sheet around her like it was a dress. But she stumbled in the folds that gathered at her feet like a sea creature.

'Come back in, Mum,' Jade called.

And she walked back to them and into the water, Head watching her like she was floating up a church aisle to him.

'You a queen,' he said.

'Piss off, Māui,' she grunted. The red sheet swam around her.

She leaned close to Jade and said: 'That was the first time I put my head under, into the sea, bub. It was nice. Think I wanted to stay under. Wanted to become that mermaid.'

'From our book, Mum?'

'Yeah, bub. Learn to read that for me eh?'

'You can't be her. She's white, Mum.'

Felicity walked further into the sea then. 'Ha. True. But fuck it.'

A few weeks before, Jade's teacher had arrived at the House and asked to come in. Jade couldn't believe it when she saw her at the door because she looked like a movie star. Straight shiny hair, pink cheeks, curled-up lashes. Jade'd grabbed her hand. 'Come, come,' she pulled her, 'come and see my bedroom.'

Felicity frowned, held Jade's arm. 'She's got better things to do, don't you, Mrs Teacher?'

'Miss Matt,' she replied. 'And I have time.'

Jade didn't like Miss Matt after the visit. For one she wouldn't sit on her bed, two she wouldn't stay for tea and three she made Felicity cry. Felicity cried for almost two days after Miss Matt's visit. Cried and cried and stayed in her bed. 'Things got to change,' she howled.

Head put a wall up through the room. He painted Jade's side yellow and Felicity bought pictures from an op shop and hung them.

Miss Matt visited again. She brought a huge cardboard box full of books.

Felicity opened the box, and her eyes had gone all round and bright when she saw *The Little Mermaid* on top. She sat on the edge of the bed and opened the book and ran her hand over the pictures. 'I remember this,' she said. And she sat there so long, so quiet, running her fingers, like she was running them through the mermaid's hair.

The quietest Jade had seen her mother – until the beach.

Felicity walked further into the sea, letting the red bed sheet soak up the salt water, and Jade looked at her mum's turned back, mottled with acne scars, stretched places, until it looked torn to silver white like the underbelly of a kahawai, and Jade felt like she suddenly had a very important job to do. Learn to read *The Little Mermaid*. For Felicity. It had always been stories that kept them safe in the House. Legends. The legend of Head.

The legend that held the dogs at bay.

Years later Sav had told it to Jade like a fairy tale.

'Once upon a time, three gangsters were driving through the night, with a bootload of weed, and not a gram of crack left to smoke in their pipes. They were almost home …'

When their car broke down in the countryside they started to walk.

'Ahhh, to walk in the countryside on the gear,' Sav said.

On their journey they came across a tent. Inside it they found a woman and a man. They dragged her from the tent. The man too. They kicked him half to death. They raped her.

'Ah, the countryside,' Sav said.

Two rapists were not deterred by her screaming. Her wish for home. Her bare heels kicking, clicking, not once, not twice, but at least three times.

The third man had not raped her though. He ran to a farmhouse, broke into it, and made a phone call to the House. He told Head what was going on. Told his Pres what was going on in the countryside, with the cows and sheep and industry all around.

Head took a gun – from a locked box, in a locked drawer – and got in his Mustang and drove to the countryside. He pulled up in his car, got out and shot one rapist in the foot. The other ran at him, but tripped on his trousers and fell face down in the rich countryside dirt. Head turned him over and kicked him in the crotch.

'Before that night, nothing so terrible had ever happened in the countryside,' Sav told Jade.

Head kicked and he kicked, and he stomped on the rapist's crotch.

Did he give mercy?

'Yes, yes he did,' Sav said.

But when he looked down at the poor woman on the ground, he thought of you, Jade, and the day he took you to the beach and you had spun under the sun with your sarong in the sky. In that fleeting moment, he'd seen you as a little woman and outside, breathing in the sea air, he'd understood better who he was, what he was, and so he swiftly tooketh his mercy away.

Stomped again. Ignored a brother's prayer, some half-arsed karakia. And he stomped.

He carried the woman, then the man, to the Mustang. He drove them to a hospital, left them on its steps. He got in his car and honked his horn. Not once, Jade, not twice, but at least three times. He drove to a payphone and he called the po-po and told them where they could find the rapists, the animals with the other animals in the countryside. Box and lock, he told the po-po.

'I know what you're thinking, Jade,' Sav said. 'Why is she with him? But look at the bright side. I get to be here with you. I look after you, because your father isn't here anymore. And on the beach that day, without the walls of the House around him, you spinning under the blue sky, he finally understood – he was born to be your father.'

And Jade had let loose one or two tears and told Sav her version of the story.

The phone had rung. Head had come into the bedroom and got his gun. Felicity had begged him not to leave with it, not to go out and do anything stupid. He told her to shut-the-actual-fuck-up. And because that was what she did best, she obliged. She crawled into bed and cried until he returned, with his trousers and boots covered in blood, his hands shaking, tears running down his cheeks.

Head had sat on the edge of the bed. Felicity left the room. When she returned she took the gun and wiped it with a flannel.

She boxed and locked it.

Then she wiped Head's face with the flannel, helped him out of his bloody boots, his bloody trousers, his wet shirt. She took his hand and led him out of the sleeping room. When they returned he was wearing cleaner clothes and Felicity hadn't asked one question, because that was another thing she did best.

And Jade had learned what love was.

Love took off the bloody shirt and boots, it silently led people to bathrooms and turned on taps for them so they could rinse their bloody palms. It didn't ask questions. More importantly, it boxed and locked the gun.

The years after that night must have been the best of Jade's and Felicity's lives. Property of a feared man. A ruthless man, possessing the only thing that mobsters might fear: a few unwavering principles. Felicity was no longer House property, she was Head's, and Head's alone.

Felicity and Jade. Queen and princess. Of mongrels.

Despite his few unwavering principles there were nights when Head's troubles forced him to tear up the earth beneath him. Or the walls. And the people. Just to see better, just for a moment's fucken clarity. Just to see who, where, what the fuck he was. Sometimes he'd get drunk. And he would tear their sleeping room apart and throw Felicity across it. Smack her. Sometimes Jade copped it: 'What are you looking at?' Or, 'Go on. Get the fuck out.' And Jade would go outside and cuddle into a stolen blanket and try to sleep against the concrete foundation of the House until morning, when Head would find her and croon sorrow and gush tears so much sweeter than any predictable, rage-less man could ever conjure.

He would pick her up, and carry her inside.

But his patriarchy was tested again and again. And each time the legend of Head was pressed at, prodded, questioned, it weakened a little, losing its structure, its bones, until it became a myth.

Jade's lips and legs, and eyes too, too sweet for such a place, started to draw the dogs, mongrel-eyed, sniffing. And the fractured knuckles of wisdom Head had pocketed over his troubled lifetime were the first bones they cracked their yellowed teeth on.

The young guitar-playing man on the beach, though, was white-toothed and sea-eyed. And when she laughed and told him she was from hell, he didn't find it funny.

Taukiri

I washed where and when I could.

Yesterday I went to a camping ground. The bathrooms had showers that ran when you put a dollar coin into a little silver box. I was glad, because it made me feel like I'd paid for what I used, though I knew that wasn't quite true. There was a laundry and I needed coins there too. I had three pairs of jeans, a couple of trackie pants, four boardies and four T-shirts, one jersey, two hoodies, a pile of undies and some socks. They'd already lasted me longer than was cool. I used some coins to do the washing.

Each day it took over an hour to walk as far as the train station from where I was parked. I'd pay for the odd train trip, steal the odd one. I walked a lot, looking for a job. Some nights my legs ached badly.

It was after Christmas so I was going back to the scallop-shelling factory. I hoped it'd go well at the factory. It was probably good I couldn't afford a razor. The hair on my face had almost grown evenly, and I looked a bit older than I was.

When I got there I saw the freckled man with the sandy-blonde buzz cut I'd talked to last time. He was wearing gumboots and overalls and hosing down big plastic bins. I waved out to him. He looked up but didn't stop what he was doing. He didn't recognise me. I put my hand down and walked across the wet concrete. He continued his hosing, no expression on his face.

'I'm Taukiri, I was here last week.'

'Right,' his face lifted a little, lifting mine. 'The kid. You have a beard,' he laughed. He hosed down the large bins. I ran my hand over my face. I must have looked embarrassed.

'It's good. Girls must love it.'

I shrugged.

'You said to come back.'

'Yeah. Yeah, I suppose did.'

I turned a coin in my pocket. And stared at him. I widened my stance and didn't move a muscle. He turned his back to me, and started stacking the clean bins into each other.

I didn't blink. He looked over his shoulder, looked from my skate shoes, up to my eyes. And back down to the shoes.

'Look. Kid.'

I dropped all bets on the sad card I had hoped to play. I stopped turning the coin in my pocket and strode towards the stack of plastic bins and picked them up. All of them. My biceps shaking under the weight of them.

But I stopped it. Stopped the shaking.

'Where do you need these?'

His gumboots slopped through the puddles as he led me inside the factory. And I let the stack down slowly, calmly, like I could have carried them forever if I was paid to.

I busked with Elliot most nights and worked in a factory shelling scallops most days. There was a shower complex for staff members. I was just as grateful for that as the pay packet I collected weekly.

We worked long hours. I was happy that I finished early enough to shower the shellfish smell off me and get to Cuba Street before Elliot was ready to start. Sometimes he started without me.

'Cheers, bro,' I'd say, 'for warming up my crowd.'

Scallop shelling gave me too much time to think. I tried to stop myself, but as I pried the scallop meat from shells, standing on the cold concrete floor of the factory, they came. The father and mother who began my life. I tried not to remember them because I confused them with stories I had been told, or photos I'd seen. I was sure I remembered a song that my father used to play on his guitar, with me sitting on his lap. But then I heard it on the radio and it reminded me of Mum, so I couldn't remember who the memory belonged to.

I guessed it would be this way for me and Ari. We would look for pieces of everyone we'd lost, in mirrors and crowds.

That's how Ari would come to feel about me – that he'd lost me and had to search for me in places where I wasn't.

He'd get over that though. It'd get easier.

Elliot helped. I liked to busk with him, play the guitar and sing with him. Sometimes people loved our music and stopped to listen, like they did at that first jam session.

Once a group of men walked by and I heard someone say. 'Oh look, a bit of Māori-oke.'

And everyone laughed, and Elliot told me not to worry about dickheads like them.

Sometimes uni students would sit around, maybe listening, eyes closed, nodding their heads and smoking. Once or twice people even danced. That was cool.

Often I'd go to Cuba Street but Elliot wouldn't be there. Once I played anyway. Opened my guitar case and started. People walked by, didn't stop, hardly listened. One boy wearing a superhero cape and gumboots – looked about a year younger than Ari – grabbed his mum's hand and begged for money to give me. She gave an embarrassed smile and pulled out a coin. He snatched it and charged towards me, waving it, flipped the silver coin in the case.

'Cheers, dude,' I called to him as he sprinted back to his mum, almost tripping on his gumboots, his cape rippling out behind him like a wave.

After busking, walking home, Elliot would often ask me questions, and I'd say, 'Bro, I don't want to talk about it. I just want to forget.'

The first time I said that he walked me to my car, pulled some tablets from his pocket, set them on the bonnet, crushed them, raked the powder into a line and told me to snort it. So I did.

Then he took me to a party.

'Are you forgetting, bro?' he'd asked me later, when we were in a shed, sitting on busted couches, fairy-lights strung up above us, people talking, whispering, laughing. Our guitars had started playing themselves and a girl beside me was kissing my neck. She put her hand under my T-shirt. Asked me what my bone carving meant.

She asked me again, 'What does it mean?'

Like she cared. I told her it was a gift from my koro. Then I kissed her to shut her up. To make sure she didn't ask again. To make sure we didn't start to talk about our lives, feelings, futures.

The air smelled like stars and pot.

'Forgetting, bro?' Elliot asked again.

'What? Forgetting what?'

And he'd laughed, but I didn't know why.

The girl licked at my neck like the sea, and I hated her and wanted her for it. I didn't ask her name because I couldn't have cared less.

Ārama

Aunty Kat was taking me and Beth for a picnic at the waterfall.

'There is the best swimming hole in the world,' Beth said, 'You just have to watch out for grandaddy eels who might think your toes are little saveloys, because little saveloys are their favourite food.'

Uncle Stu was supposed to come, because it was his day off, but he was going to the Craypot with Tom Aiken instead. Tom Aiken normally spent his day off with Beth, but there was a pool tournament on and he was the best player in Kaikōura. He might come home with a trophy. That's what Aunty Kat said when she saw that Beth was sad about her dad not coming – she said he would probably bring her home a trophy.

'I don't want a piece-of-shit trophy,' Beth said.

Aunty Kat ignored her swear word. I'd told Aunty Kat I'd had a S.H.I.T. sleep, and even though I'd only spelled it, she'd clipped me around the ear.

The drive to Smithy's waterfall was bumpy and the car filled with dust because Lupo goes mental if the window isn't let down. The stupid dog yelped every time a piece of gravel hit the bottom of the car. When we parked the car and opened the door Lupo jumped out and ran off into the bush. Beth said he knew the way so well because Tom Aiken brought Beth and him here all the time.

It was so hot and I really couldn't wait to get into the water. All I could hear was the sound of the waterfall and grass swishing at my legs. I snatched a piece and put it in my mouth like Django would. It made me feel like I didn't have a worry in the world. No Uncle Stu, no dead Mum and Dad, no brother I wanted back.

Beth walked up beside Aunty Kat and grabbed her hand. At first Aunty Kat looked surprised, but then she gave Beth's hand a squeeze.

Aunty Kat was so different away from the farm and Uncle Stu. More like my mum.

Beth and I both had rugby shorts to swim in. Mine were Canterbury Crusaders ones and hers were plain black. Aunty Kat had a purple swimsuit and a towel around her waist. Normally she wore old T-shirts with holes in them and stained jeans.

We left our picnic basket and bags on the riverbank, at the bottom of the waterfall.

I took off my T-shirt.

'Wow,' Beth said, stepping closer to me. 'That's amazing.'

I touched my bone carving. 'Taukiri has the same. It's whale bone.'

I could see she'd never seen something like it before. It made me proud to have something that could make Beth stop talking.

'It's the sea,' I told her. I wanted to tell her more. The story Tauk had told me, but it didn't come. Just sadness. Just wishes. Just *come back, Tauk*.

She blinked. 'Come on,' she said.

Beth said we should climb up to the swimming hole. The way up was steep, but Beth knew every free root to grab, every rock strong enough to hold us, and every branch to reach for.

Lupo beat us up. Dongi Lupo. He made his way under the gorse and blackberry. When we got to the top Lupo was looking down at the swimming hole, wagging his tail, tongue out, thick globs of dog saliva falling from it.

Beth scrambled up a tall boulder leaning out over the swimming hole and dive-bombed into the water. Aunty Kat went next. The boulder was high, so I started walking into the water from the riverbank. It was colder than I thought. Jumping in would be easier.

Beth told me to climb the rock with her. It was then that I remembered I hadn't packed any plasters, which was really dumb of me. I wanted to run home and get some. Just in case.

'Come on. What would Django do? He'd manu.' Beth said.

Then she started singing it, clapping her hands. 'What would Django do, do, do? He'd manu, nu, nu, nu.'

Aunty Kat said we could jump in together, because the boulder was big enough for us all to stand on. In the water I thought I saw

Mum's face. Aunty Kat counted to three and we all leapt high up into the air, so high, and Lupo barked, and a cloud covered the sun, and we fell – legs up, bums down, we fell – and the cloud moved over the sun and the world was suddenly bright again and we all did the best ever manu. Tauk would have thought so too. He loved doing manus. I couldn't wait to bring him here. It could be our new secret place, like Bones Bay.

Jade and Toko

He ran his tongue up the birds tattooed on her ribcage. Her mouth open wide she took in a bellyful of air and held it inside her, opened her legs and touched herself. This feeling of wanting to fuck just as much as the person she'd fuck was new. She'd never wanted Coon; he'd snared her. This man, this man was licking her, kissing her, swallowing her, consuming her, and yet she felt like a musical note ... a lyric ... let loose in the world, unable to be grasped or captured by anyone. Not ever again.

'I can't,' she clawed his back, tried to tuck her abdomen under her ribcage, 'I can't do this.'

He understood, and stopped torturing her. Gave her what she was asking for, what she deserved, what she wanted.

She woke alone in his bed, and fantasised about making a confession.

You rooted someone else, Coon could say, as he always did.

Yes, she could reply now.

Yes? He'd prod.

Sure have, she would say.

Hope it was worth it, slut. Smack!

Sure was.

Jade had only said no once. The next day Coon had been sorry for what he'd done. His sorry had been sweet and more like love than anything she ever saw in him.

There was saying no and not being heard and there was never having been up for it.

Toko's bedroom was simple. Besides the large bed, there were only two pieces of furniture: a wardrobe and a bedside table with a lamp on it. On one wall there was a clock.

She liked his sheets. It felt good to be naked between them.

She heard him padding up the hall. The door opened. He was wearing a towel. He walked to the bed and sat on the edge.

'Thirsty?' he asked. 'It's a dangerous thing.'

'That's deep,' she said.

'We in deep all right, girl.'

A slice of lemon bobbed in the glass; her heart bobbed at his kindness.

The sound of the sea nearby promised green. She was used to angrier colors, dirtier ones. Blood-red and bruise-black stains. Sounds that promised stains upon the stains.

He took her empty glass, set it on the floor, took off the towel and climbed back into their wrecked bed.

Sav found Jade at Toko's house a day and a half after the beach party. Jade was sitting in a deckchair in the sun. Sav sat down opposite her.

'He gonna find you, hun. For sure. It's a mess, babe, but you gotta come back. Don't make me go back without you. He'll kill me. We will get out. We'll sort it. Come back this last time, and we'll make a plan.'

Jade thought of letting her cousin go back and explain. He might let it be. Sav might be fine. He might just be sad, angry even, and that'd be fair enough.

Coon might drink it out. Get himself wasted. Yell. Punch things, people even. Maybe cry some actual tears. She knew, though, that her being dead would be better than just gone, just packed up and left. *Yeah, nah, nah, nah, nah, nah,* Coon would think, *no way.*

'Last time, I promise,' Sav said. 'We gonna make another life. I promised Head I would get you out. But we can't do it like this.'

'When did you make that promise?'

'He was dead, and I was drunk, but still, it counts. Probably more.'

Jade said goodbye to Toko. Made herself seem a real free spirit.

'Was fun,' she said, 'should do it again sometime.' And she felt like a fake, using words she had heard used in movies. Doing and saying things she knew would be done and said better by princesses in books. *Should do it again sometime.* Cue: *Flick hair. Bat lashes. Sashay away.* She had no idea who she was, but it was not the girl she was pretending to be.

Truth was, she had already imagined their babies, and washing their sheets, and picking his T-shirts, jeans, underwear – hers too – off the floor when the bed was too far.

They needed to go though. Sav was right – Coon would find her. So they did.

They got in the car and left.

'Remember, hun, we were at my aunty's tangi in Christchurch, all right? Don't mention Kaikōura. The dumb-arse Hash is, he'll still put two and two together.'

'He'll make five, and then you'll be in more shit.'

'Babe, it's not funny. I know it's shit.'

'It is.'

'But it's the life we chose.'

'You chose.'

'Yeah I chose. It's fucked up, babe.'

'It is.'

It was a long, painfully long, painfully quiet trip after that. Sav drove and Jade slept. Then Jade drove and Sav slept, and they didn't stop for food the whole way.

They could joke, though, that was what kept them going. Their freedom was laughter.

'Shit, what you going to do back with Hash? He gonna give you as much lovin' as Tommy?'

Sav laughed, slapped the steering wheel.

'You're a mean bitch, you know that. Head sure munted Hash. It was no story.'

'First-hand proof?'

'It's ugly, babe.'

They laughed until they cried. They laughed until the tears became real tears. They cried over their own powerlessness, as they slowly, and seemingly by choice, propelled themselves towards the House.

Enough, they said to themselves. That was enough.

Sav said: 'Good thing Coon had the landline cut.'

'No it's not.'

'If he hadn't, my aunty be ringing up, asking me why the hell I wasn't at that tangi when she funded the trip.'

'She sure funded something.' Jade smiled.

Sav touched Jade's hair. 'Minx.'

It was raining when they pulled up at the House.

Jade thought of a place where coming in from the rain might feel good. Like coming home. She'd not come home from the rain since Head was killed. Ever since, she'd been crawling blind through its gummy mud.

Sav walked to her room and closed the door. The smell of the house bothered Jade most. When she walked in, it came at her.

It was quiet, and she began walking around to find the reason. The lounge was piled with crates. The floor was sticky. There were cigarette butts, roaches. Half-eaten takeaways. Wrappers. Piss. She wondered if Coon and Hash were on the hunt, on the mish, to bring the little sluts back. She worried for Toko, but there was nothing she could do.

She decided to clean her bed sheets.

There was a mountain of washing in the laundry that smelled of mould.

The machine smelled worse. Jade used a bucket and some soapy water to clean it up. Then put her sheets inside to wash.

With the machine running she went to work. She found some dishwashing liquid in the kitchen. Better than nothing, she thought. She started in the lounge. There'd been a party. Some drinking and drug-taking. Maybe a punch-up. Maybe someone ended up with his teeth kicked in, which would explain the pieces she found in her cloth.

There'd been some sad version of a party.

Jade tried at least. She scrubbed at booze, dirt, blood, urine and vomit for two hours. The smell, loosened from the wooden floor and carpet, only furthered itself into her skin. She hardly ever got a real chance to clean up between parties. It wasn't worth the trouble. But wondering when Coon would come back – and in what state – she was glad for the distraction.

Jade moved from one shithole room to another. Picking up things. Wiping. Sweeping. Opening windows. She went out to bring her sheets in, hugged them to her chest and looked for something. Something new. Something promising. But still found the House. Inside, she spread them out on the bed, climbed in between them, closed her eyes and fell asleep.

When she woke the house was dark, and she heard voices. Shouting. Clinking. Laughter. Bass. Drums.

She heard Coon. Her body became tense and she curled her toes against the soles of her feet. Wide awake, she listened. Waited.

The noise moved to the street. She heard bottles breaking on the concrete. Then her door swung open and Coon staggered into the room.

'Baby, you miss me, baby. I'm home.'

Jade, confused, didn't answer.

'You mad, baby? Oh, baby. Don't be mad. We been on a run. Three days, no sleep. Farrr. But the gear we got, baby, the gear. We gonna get rich. I'm gonna buy you things. So many things. Farrr.'

And she felt terrible that she'd been such a slut, made such a fool of him, while he was working to make their future full of things.

'There's some kaimoana in the fridge for you. Know how you like that shit.'

He dropped beside her and fell asleep.

She got out of bed, put on her sneakers and went to the kitchen. A monumental mess, like she hadn't cleaned up. Broken glass on the floor, vomit in the sink. It smelled of smoke and weed and sick and beer and rancid oil and disease. She opened the fridge. A bottle of tomato sauce, an old cabbage, the bony carcass of a cooked chicken.

And there, stashed in the back so no one would steal it, a Filet-O-Fish. Suddenly ravenous, she grabbed it, unwrapped it, wolfed it down, so quick her chest hurt.

She went back to bed.

He'd pissed himself. And the strong stench in the room made her feel deep pity for herself and for him. She who'd cleaned the sheets, and he, who might, depending on his mood, wake to feel embarrassed.

Taukiri

Our busking almost took us to the beach last night, a crew in tow. It was someone's idea, an idea I immediately hated, and I told Elliot I hated it. The streetlights above us had come on, making yellow moons on the grey concrete. An American tourist had said in her accent – which made her sound like she had seen the entire world, and this was just another island on her list, her tanned arm hanging around Elliot's neck, capping her head with his busker's hat – 'Let's go to the beach.'

'Shit idea,' I said to Elliot. 'Let's go somewhere else.'

'Where?' said the American, with a careless laugh. 'Where, could be better than the beach?'

'Was I talking to you?' I said.

'It's all right, bro.' Elliot kissed her cheek. 'Baby. I have a million places better.' And his hand ran up under her shirt.

'A million? Like to see you try and show *me* a million places I haven't seen.'

'A million, I promise.' And he pulled something I was coming to have on-sight reaction to. A wicked desire for.

We swallowed tablets. 'Don't worry, bro. I got you,' Elliot whispered with the first lifting of my bones and muscles and organs. My heart enjoying the lightness of barely beating.

'Remember,' she whispered, already removed from the energy-filled, storm-to-the-beach trooper she had been, 'A million things.'

At a house, after the American girl had stripped her clothes off and passed out in his lap, Elliot and I sort of talked.

'Not feeling much eh, bro. Give me another one.'

I crushed it, snorted it, and he fell asleep.

I tried not to mind that I was not sure where we were.

We had walked. I remembered that. And Elliot had used a key to get inside. It must be his house! We had eaten chips, and the American girl had started to dance and had taken all her clothes off.

I was glad to know it was probably Elliot's house. Is that what he had said? 'Let's go to my house.' I wasn't sure. But I was pretending not to care. The white wallpaper was peeling in the farthest corners, and the ceiling was high like a church.

We were on a floor in front of an empty fireplace. And then I saw a bird perched on the hearth. It cocked its head and looked at me. Blinking eyes like Ari had when I woke in the hospital. The tail was fanned out behind it.

'I have tried to save so many of you,' I whispered, and the little bird seemed to listen with its whole tiny being. 'Only succeeded once. Ari and I. With a tūī. You know any tūī? Nah, you a pīwakawaka. You too cool for other birds.'

The pīwakawaka cocked its head the other way.

'You a reckless bird,' I said, 'coming inside like this.'

Elliot snored. The American girl had put her head on his lap, her chest still bare. I took off my hoodie and hiffed it over her. I turned back to the bird.

'Is your name Ari?' I said to the bird.

I stood and the bird flew at my face, then began flitting around the room. It crashed into the window, then a mirror, into a wall, flew so close to my head I felt its feathers slice across my neck.

I picked up a hearth brush from beside the fire and threw it at the stupid bird. Just missed. The brush hit the wall with a loud smack that echoed around the high-ceilinged room. The bird cut across the room again, hit the window once more before falling to flounder on the floor.

I went over and opened the window. Shooed the bird towards the opening.

'Fly free.'

Hands, I saw, flying off into the sky, then wild flowers, and books. I saw, I saw a book flying off into the air. And I thought of the stories I had, which I'd not told.

I rushed to my guitar lying on the ground, and sang to fight off the crushing weight on me then.

Elliot stirred as I sang – I heard him moving – but I held my eyes closed. I felt a hand on my shoulder. I opened my eyes and there was another girl, not Elliot's girl. This one had brown eyes and a freckle on her eyelid.

'A pīwakawaka got in,' I said.

She sat down in front of me and crossed her legs.

'That's not good. Keep playing though. Keep singing.'

I closed my eyes again, and sang. Then paused, with my eyes still shut. 'Where am I, pretty girl with a freckle on her eyelid?'

'My house.'

'And who are you, pretty girl with a freckle on her eyelid?'

'Megan. My name is Megan.'

'I think I will call you pretty girl with a freckle on her eyelid.'

'That's okay with me, but please … not when my boyfriend is around.'

'No. Never in front of him. But every other chance I get.'

I opened my eyes.

'You're good,' she said.

I looked around the room, 'Did we make this mess?'

'Unless I came home in the middle of the night, wasted, and undressed that girl, while throwing chips and shit everywhere, then yes, it was you guys.'

'That there,' I nodded towards the hearth brush, 'was the bird's fault. And she was having fun. But I will own up to the chips.'

I collected the hearth brush, found the shovel and began to sweep chips from the floor.

The pretty girl with the freckle on her eyelid stayed sitting, cross-legged, watching me.

'You're Taukiri.'

'That's me.'

'Do you want to know how I know that?'

'Sure.'

'I'm Elliot's sister.'

'What do you do when you not being Elliot's sister?'

'I take photographs.'

'Of what?'

'Things.'

'Like people? Like weddings?'

'More like parts of stories,' she rubbed her hand down her shin, 'I like stories. Elliot told me yours. Well some of it …'

I kept sweeping. Though there was nothing left to sweep.

'It's a sad story,' she continued.

'I suppose it is.'

'You must feel very lonely.' And her voice echoed, and bounced off the walls like she was tricking me, and actually *she* was the sea, in human form, come to see for herself the pain she had caused me. The freckle on her eye starfished out and the sun began to move over her face like it does below the surface of water.

I dropped the brush to the floor, 'Nice meeting you.' And I walked out a door, which led to a hall, which led to a kitchen without a door. I walked back down the hall, passing the starfish-freckle girl, her hair moving above her like seaweed. She said as I passed her, 'That way.'

I stepped out into the day. The full, piercing light of day. How had morning come already?

I heard a plane taking off, a car roaring up the hill.

I walked downhill, past the wooden houses which all looked like Megan's place, my body feeling too light. Why was I walking so easily? What had I forgotten? What had I neglected?

'Shit,' I said. I had left my guitar in the lounge, propped against the sofa.

I headed back up the hill. The clouds were rushing fast across the sky, and the sun was making a last attempt to burn everything on earth before the black clouds could stop it.

I jogged the last few metres to Megan's and found my guitar leaning against the front door, as if it had run outside and was waiting for me like a kid left behind. There was the chip in the varnish that had always been there, but now it looked like a small starfish.

Grabbed the poor guitar.

Distant thunder. Back down the hill to the city hoping I'd find my car. Sky filled with storm.

Heart was pounding, wanted my car like I once wanted a craypot buoy, or a piece of driftwood. Land. Rain cut the warm morning, came in a wave, like the sea had been lifted to be dumped, heavy on a burning earth.

A kid, who looked exactly, I mean *exactly* like me, was laughing. He said: 'There's the guy who drives round town with a surfboard on his roof to look cool.'

I gripped my guitar tighter. It seemed to squeeze me back, afraid. Afraid of the water. I wanted to smash that kid who looked exactly like me right in his exactly-like-mine face. Smash him with my guitar for hassling me, but he flew up into the sky. 'Hahahahahahahahahahahahahaha,' he called.

To the library. Told my guitar to be quiet, but a note rang out, shaking the books from their shelves.

'Ssshhh,' I said, but we were told to leave and had to run out into a rain, full of starfish and salt. A Neptune bolt.

And more Neptune bolts.

I emptied a rubbish bag onto the street, split it open with my nails and everything inside spilled like fish guts onto the watery pavement. I wrapped my guitar in slimy black plastic, profanities spitting at me from behind its duct-taped lips. When I finally found my car, the door opened for me, like it was awaiting our getaway.

Stan Walker was driving. He was playing Soundgarden's 'Black Hole Sun'. I was grateful to Stan for driving me. I looked at his neck. 'Whakamā' his tattoo said.

'It means beautiful,' Stan said, and I wondered why he was lying to me.

'Play me something of yours,' I said.

'Sorry, bro. Can't find my stuff. Put it in the backseat, now it's gone.'

Chris Cornell was sitting there instead, his goatee growing long like he'd eaten magic beans. He looked like a god. Tangaroa. But he was wearing Nanny's pearl earrings.

'Oh, these,' he said, when he saw me staring at them. 'A Scottish sailor gave them to me when we fell in love.'

We were getting away, at breakneck pace.

My surfboard turned into a fin to help us sail through the city quick as a fish.

They found balance again. Sun and sea. Sea had stopped pouring from its ancient beds into the sky, and sun stopped being a black-hole cunt, burning everything, and when the car stopped beside the abandoned house, I heard the birds making noises that promised peace and harmony and other bullshit.

Parked between the old house and the low scrub, I closed my eyes in the backseat of the car with my wet clothes still on.

There was a price for emptying your head. It emptied, euphorically, on the going out, sure, but all the junk flooded back eventually. Only more broken than it was before.

I slept in a puddle on the backseat.

Then I am trying to get to work, but my bones and muscles can't work out who should be in charge and lean on each other like they're drunk men. All the scallops I should shell are swept into the corner of the factory by a man with long sandy lashes, wearing gumboots and overalls. The scallop meat rots and I twirl coins in my pockets. And eat Nanny's pearl earrings. To dust. To ghost sand. And I cough and cough and cough.

Ārama

We were going to sleepover at the dairy. Me and Beth were so excited. Beth was wondering exactly how many lollies we would be allowed to eat. She guessed one hundred. I said, no way. I reckoned forty max and I didn't think I'd even had that many in my whole life, so that was a lot. Tom Aiken would go with Aunty Kat, and Uncle Stu too.

I didn't think Aunty Kat was really happy because she wanted to go just with her friend. Me and Beth really didn't care. We were just so excited to be going for a sleepover at the dairy. I hoped the kids that lived there were nice. The dairy lady looked nice. She had a friendly smile, so I thought the kids would be friendly too. If you could eat junk food and lollies whenever you wanted you would probably always be friendly.

After lunch I packed my old schoolbag. The last time I packed my bag was when Taukiri drove me here from our house.

When I opened it I found all the photos I'd brought with me of Mum and Dad. I sat on the floor looking through them. There were a lot. Even some of Mum and Dad when they were much younger. I think before I was born. In an envelope was another small bundle of photos that I hadn't seen before but I must have just thrown in from Mum's stuff.

There was a picture of Taukiri as a little boy, maybe a little younger than me. He was with two people I didn't know. The man looked like my mum. It must have been her brother who died. I think he died in some sort of fishing accident. I remembered his name. It was Uncle Toko. He looked so much like my mum. They were twins. It was cool that my mum had a twin brother, but I wished I'd met him. The woman with them was pretty. She was much smaller than Uncle Toko. She was tiptoeing, and wrapping her arms and legs – her whole body, even her grinning face – around him in so many places, like she was a vine.

Taukiri was little, and he was up on Uncle Toko's shoulders. I wondered if Tauk remembered Uncle Toko.

I put all the photos in the front pocket of my schoolbag and carried on packing my things for the sleepover. I packed my Crusaders rugby jersey to sleep in, a pressie from Dad. I packed underwear, a hoodie and some trackies. I threw in a torch, my toothbrush and a box of plasters with seventy-eight plasters left in it.

We weren't leaving until after dinner, but I was ready and I was so excited. After I finished packing I went over to Beth's place to see how her packing was going. She had already put her bag at the door and her doll – name of Broomhilda – was poking out the top. I felt better that I had packed my plasters when I saw Broomhilda.

We decided to go for a walk on the farm, hoping to make the day go a bit faster. Lupo came with us. Me and Beth hiffed sticks for him in the paddock. After a while he got tired and gave up chasing them.

We went climbing in the hay shed between the stacked-up bales. They were stacked like apartments on top of each other. We pretended this was our apartment building, and we crawled around between the bales. We found pathways and cubby holes. We visited each other in each other's cubby holes, to borrow stuff, like DVDs and toothpaste.

Beth came to my cubby hole. 'Got any whisky? I'm all out,' she said.

'Sure thing, Doc.' And I grabbed her a bottle and she unscrewed the lid and drank straight from it, then handed it to me. I took a sip.

'Let's go make some trouble, Django.'

'First tell me the story of Broomhilda again, Doc.'

'Okay, Django. Well, Broomhilda is the daughter of a god. And she disobeys her father and so he puts her on a mountain, and surrounds her with a circle of hell fire, and she must be rescued by a hero strong enough and brave enough to go through hell fire and slay a dragon.' Beth took another scull of whisky. 'Shall we go rescue her, Django?'

'That's a good idea,' I said.

'But first you'll need some Dutch courage,' and she handed me back the invisible bottle.

'What's Dutch courage?'

'Dad gets it from beer when he's afraid to enter pool competitions. He plays best when he's three or four beers deep. Any more and he's buggered, any less and he's just hopeless from nerves.'

I took a swig. 'Your dad tells you a lot of things.'

'I also listen in on stuff. Now pack the whisky and let's go.'

Off we went with our Dutch courage to be brave in the hell fire and the dragons, and to save Broomhilda, while hiffing sticks for Lupo.

Afterwards we needed to cool off so we took Lupo back to the river for a drink and to put our feet in. We sat on the rocks with our bare feet dangling into the rapids while Lupo walked up and down, dragging his tongue along the water, sometimes biting at it.

Cows came from the paddock above to drink at the river. They didn't get bothered by Lupo who wagged his tail when he saw them and was leaping around making a dumb yapping noise. The cows just kept licking the river, looking at him across their cow noses like he was the most boring thing they ever saw.

Watching the cows drink made me remember something Taukiri once read me from a fact book: 'Did you know cows make almost fifty litres of saliva a day? That's like fifty milk bottles.'

'Really? That's cool. I wish I could do that.'

'Yeah, me too.' Though I wasn't sure why.

'It's not cool your uncle lets these cows down here. My dad said.'

'Why?'

'Bad for the environment, or something.'

One cow did a S.H.I.T. in the water.

'Remember when we found that rabbit?' Beth asked.

'Yes.'

'That rabbit's mum and dad were probably dead.'

I ran my thumb along the rock, until it hurt enough that I'd be able to put a plaster on it when I got home.

'Let's go to my place and watch *Django*.'

'Why do you like that movie so much?'

'It's a dog-eat-dog world and we gotta stay ahead of the game.'

'That's not how the world really is.'

'Isn't it? Like I said that rabbit was probably an orphan, like you are. Like I sort of am.'

We went to her house. Beth put *Django* on.

'Where were we up to?'

'The bit where a black woman was tied to a tree.'

She fast-forwarded and pressed play. 'This is our class now, Ari. Let's watch the best bit.'

Men were riding horses with white cloth masks, holding sticks that were on fire. They were galloping and shouting the 'N' word.

'Why is this the best bit?' I asked.

'Watch.'

The men with white masks started to argue about how they couldn't see properly in their masks, and Willard got upset because his wife, Jenny, was the one who put the eyeholes in the masks, so he rode away.

The men in the masks wanted to make the 'N' word and the 'N' lover pay.

Django and the Doc were hidden in the forest and when the men with white masks arrived to make them pay, they realised they'd been tricked.

'*Auf weidersehen*,' Doc said, then he shot a wagon and it blew up and all the white-masked men and their horses went flying.

Beth cracked up, she slapped her hands on her thighs, then made a gun with her finger. '*Auf weidersehen*,' she said. 'Chick, chick, boom.'

We walked over to Aunty Kat and Uncle Stu's place to see if Aunty Kat was getting ready to go yet. Uncle Stu's work boots were at the door. His truck and the four-wheeler were parked at the shed, which meant he was home.

Something smashed and Uncle Stu was yelling. We walked around to the side of the house to wait until the yelling stopped.

When it had been quiet for a while we went in.

Aunty Kat was on the kitchen floor picking up pieces of broken plate and scooping up mashed potato. Beth crouched beside her and started helping. Aunty Kat kept her head down.

'Are we going soon, Aunty?' I asked.

'I'm a bit tired. Maybe another night okay?'

'We already packed our things though. We waited all day.'

'I know. And I'm sorry. It's just been a long day. I'm not much in the mood anymore.'

Uncle Stu walked into the kitchen. 'You're not going anywhere,' he said, then walked out.

I saw Beth ball her fists up. Twist her face. Lift her shoulders. Her jaw shook a little.

I ran out the back door. I ran and ran. I ran to the hay shed and climbed up into the hay bales and hid myself way up between the roof and the highest stack. I pulled handfuls of hay from the bales and made a nest of it around me until I was sure no one would ever find me. I lay as still as I could, only taking in tiny breaths so the hay covering me barely moved. It got hot and I wanted to take a big deep breath of fresh air, but more than that I wanted to never be found and to never see Uncle Stu ever again.

Light came in through old nail holes in the roof where there were no nails anymore, and there was a lot of dust, but the hay smelled good, and I was hidden high up against the warm tin roof and wooden beams.

I fell asleep in my nest of hay. When I woke up I was itchy all over and my mouth was really dry. I felt so thirsty. My face was sticky from tears and dust was glued to it. My eyes itched. Outside it was getting dark. No light was streaming in through the nail and rust holes anymore. I heard a sniffing, and rustle in the hay, and then I felt something wet on my toes. I jerked my legs up. Then the wetness wiped at my face. Lupo. A light shone into my nest of scratchy hay.

'You in there, Ari?' Tom Aiken.

'Ari, come out.' Beth.

'Mate, you gonna get bitten by bugs sleeping up there. Come down.'

I peeked. There was Tom Aiken, Beth beside him.

'Jump down, bud, I'll catch ya.'

I pulled back into my nest.

'Come on, bud. Let's go home.'

'I don't want to go home,' I yelled.

'I don't mean *home* home. I just. I just mean let's go eat roast chicken. Roast chicken in the oven at our house. Which is another one of your homes. Our house is yours.'

I didn't answer.

'Did I mention roast chicken, no vegetables? White bread and butter? Ice cream for desert? Did I mention that you can have a sleepover and we can watch a movie and eat some junk food?'

I didn't answer, but my mouth watered, and my back was suddenly real itchy.

'Come on, bud.'

I asked, 'What about L&P?'

Then Beth yelled out. 'We have a Sodastream maker!'

I peeked again. 'Can I really sleepover?'

'Sure can,' he held up my schoolbag. 'Your aunty already dropped off your stuff.'

That was sad, I thought, like she'd given up.

I leapt down. Tom Aiken caught me. Then he squeezed me. He squeezed me tight against him and it made me feel like I was L&P being poured too fast into a glass. I was spilling out. My face was sticky from dried-up tears. It felt all rough and dirty.

At the house Beth said, 'Come on, Django.'

I followed her.

In the bathroom she wet a flannel. 'Clean your face, then you will feel a million times better.' I did and she dusted some hay off my back. Then turned on the tap again. 'Wash your hands,' she said. I did. The water was cold and made everything feel better then. At least with the cold water rushing over my hands, watching dirt rush down the drain, it felt like you could start fresh whenever you wanted.

'Can you get my bag?' I said.

Beth brought my bag and I got into my box of plasters. I put one on my elbow where I'd scratched myself crawling in the hay bales.

Tom Aiken was buttering bread. The kitchen smelled good and when he opened the oven, the smell of herbs and fat and hot food rocketed out with the sound of the chicken's skin sizzling. Beth took plates from cupboard and set the table for three, salt and pepper in the middle, alongside a tower of buttered bread. Tom Aiken took out the chicken then stabbed it with a knife. 'Done,' he said. Beth made cola with the Sodastream.

Tom Aiken said, 'Now this night is going to be better than a sleepover at a dairy.'

'Because of chicken?' Beth said.

'I said *going* to be.'

'Keep talking.'

'Ice cream.'

'Whoop-dee-doo.'

'Movie and junk food.'

'Not bad. But not exactly better than sleeping over at a place with all the junk food ever.'

Tom Aiken looked up into his head then. He didn't have another thing. 'The last thing will be a surprise,' he said.

The sandwiches were soft and salty and because the chicken was still warm the butter melted and the bread went all gooey. We didn't talk much while we were eating. Tom Aiken washed his food back with beer, and me and Beth washed ours back with cola.

In the lounge after dinner Tom Aiken went into the DVD cupboard. I saw inside. I saw the pile to the side, away from the others, but not well hidden. *Django Unchained*, *Kill Bill*, *Lucky Number Slevin*, *Blood Diamond*, *Snow White and the Huntsman*.

Tom Aiken reached for one from the front pile. 'This one?' he said, holding up *Alice in Wonderland*.

'No, that's for babies,' Beth said.

'You used to love it,' Tom Aiken said.

Beth went into the cupboard and pulled out *Hunt for the Wilderpeople*. 'This,' she said, and gave it to her dad.

Hunt for the Wilderpeople was sad. Ricky Baker had no parents, and when he finally decided he liked his foster mum, she died and she was the best. And I thought, how bad was his luck, how unlucky do you have to be?

Ricky Baker wrote haikus.

His haiku about maggots was cool, and his one about Kingi who was a wanker and how Ricky Baker wanted him to die. In pain. Which I thought was a pretty bad thing to admit to.

We ate heaps of junk. So much until my teeth hurt and I was thirsty.

After the movie Beth said, 'Now for the grand surprise, Dad?'

Tom Aiken searched his head again. 'A haiku competition.'

'Dumb,' Beth said.

'Hang on,' Tom Aiken held up his hand, 'And the winner gets a spin on the four-wheeler.'

'In the dark?' Beth asked.

'In the dark,' he said, grinning. 'Now you have five minutes to write a haiku.'

We grabbed pens and paper and took them to the table. 'What are you writing about?' Beth asked.

'Tauk. And you?'

'A wanker.'

Tom Aiken came into the kitchen and opened another beer. 'Right,' he said. 'Haiku time.'

Beth went first, holding up each finger with each new sound.

'Stu-art John-son you / are the ug-li-est farm-er / hope cows shit on you.'

Tom Aiken spat out some beer, 'Beth, that's not nice,' but he said it in a high singy voice so I could tell he actually liked her haiku. Beth could tell her Dad liked it too and she looked down at the paper and smiled proudly at it, like she'd already won the four-wheeler ride, even though she probably got to go riding all the time.

Tom clapped. 'Right, Ari's turn.'

'Tau-ki-ri wrote me / a let-ter and it said he's / on his way home-home.'

Beth and Tom Aiken didn't say anything. I explained my haiku. 'I'm home-home now. Like he's home-home to me.'

Tom Aiken clapped. 'And the winner is Beth-Ari. Ari-Beth. Both you poets.'

And I frothed up again. Because we were going on the four-wheeler.

It was dark outside. The grass was wet and the air heavy. Still warm but heavy. Tom Aiken got on the four-wheeler and turned the key and it sprang to life. He looked at me. 'You first,' he yelled. I got on the back and wrapped my arms around his waist. His stomach was a bit soft but I could almost get right around. He smelled like dirt and hay and chicken and beer and sky and rivers and mountains. 'Ready?' he said, and I nodded into his back.

And we were off and we were speeding fast over dips, up and down. Pebbles and dirt sprayed into my bare legs, stinging them. I was a bottle of L&P shaken and shaken and shaken and opened and fizzing then just going, just going off. Bees buzzed in my bones and I closed my eyes and listened to the growl of the four-wheeler. Should I let go? Should I hold my arms out and fly?

I loosened my grip, just a bit, just a bit, then we sped up, hit a bump, and I flew out of my seat a bit and thought I'd fall off but I gripped onto Tom Aiken tight again, tighter than before.

Back at the house Tom Aiken took the roast chicken from the fridge. He pulled a bone from it.

'Wishbone,' he said. He put it in the windowsill. 'I'm going to let it dry here, for you guys. Then you can wish on it next time you have a sleepover. This is also your home-home, Ari. Now, another movie before bed?'

'Really, *really*?'

'Yes, but Ari's choice.'

I wanted a real kid's one. A cartoon. Colour. 'The Alice one,' I said.

I wasn't surprised that Beth's favourite part was when near the end the queen ran around saying, 'Off with their heads.'

At bedtime Beth skipped ahead singing about people losing their heads for painting the roses red. The moment she opened her bedroom door I realised I'd never been in there before. It was pink. It had lace curtains. There was a doll's house. Her duvet was purple and she had a unicorn-shaped lamp on a small table beside her bed.

Broomhilda was on her bed, and Broomhilda had a teacup in front of her. There was another teacup on the bed, like Beth and Broomhilda had drunk tea together. Without me. Like this was her secret life. Unicorns and lace and tea parties.

'It's pink,' I said.

Beth punched my arm. 'And? Got a problem?'

'I mean. It's nice.'

'Tip and tail?' Beth said, leaping into bed.

I dug my PJs out of my bag, and quickly put them on, then crawled

81

into the bed beside Beth. I snuggled right up against her. Pressed my back against hers, my head on her pillow.

Tom Aiken laughed. 'I wouldn't tip and tail either. She got stink feet.'

He turned off the light. 'Night, Beth-Ari. Night, Ari-Beth,' he said, then laughed. When he left, Beth told me she had another haiku.

'Tell me it,' I said.

'Boun-ty on your head / Stu-art John-son you wank-er / Hope you die, real soon.'

'I'm tired, Beth,' I said.

'You mean, Doc.'

'Yeah. Go to sleep, Doc.'

'It's a good one though, right?'

'Yeah. It is.'

I felt bad that I liked the haiku so much.

Jade and Toko

Sav told Jade she wanted to run away. And, in the same breath, said why she never would. Hash was nasty. 'Just as nasty as Coon, only secret about it,' she said.

But the one-mores were piling up. One more beating, one more toke, one more drink, one more shot. It was something of a dying.

Sav said she'd realised it had been a bad idea to come back.

They should have stayed in Kaikōura, taken the risk. It was Sav who'd said: 'Don't make me go back without you. He'll kill me.' But now it was Jade who getting on while Sav suffered. Their suffering had always circled the others, like they existed at opposite ends of a karmic wheel.

Sav was pregnant and everyone would know it wasn't Hash's. Roadkill Rapist was his nickname. Hash came back to the House after Head was shot. Point-blank.

Coon had walked Hash into the House, his hand on his shoulder, and said – in front of Jade – 'He's dead. Welcome back, brother.'

Sav had been with Hash as long as she could remember. Though Sav often said she couldn't work out where it began, or when it became so prisonlike. And now she was pregnant.

What had Hash expected? She was and always would be just a slut. *Girls gotta do*. But lately she was passing up the drugs she had once loved, needed. At parties she filled beer bottles with water, and passed morning sickness off as another hangover, 'Faarr, gettin' too fucken old for this eh,' she'd say, to no one. And Jade would try to guess her age. She was easily old enough to be Jade's aunty,

Sav had a jagged beauty, which had hooked Tommy, who was some years younger. She was a Māori Mrs Robinson with affiliations, but no one sang to her that they'd like to help her learn to help herself.

Sav had made herself a dodgy appointment when the boys had a run. A big boys' mission. They were bringing in some new shit – even newer to them than meth – and this shit was hard to get. Coon was breaking ground. An entrepreneur. Unlike Head, so stuck in his ways. Jade had encouraged it, 'You're gonna be a king.' But she knew the gang – the game of gang – was already destroying itself. Smack would save them a drawn-out version of the inevitable. Coon would get him and his dumb entourage hooked, and bring them down.

Meth spurred on their violent tendencies. Heroin, Jade hoped, might just fuck them up, make them broke, maybe even make them dead. Jade saw an end. She and Sav just needed to ride it out.

On the way to the dodgy appointment Sav had stopped, touched her flat stomach and said to her baby cousin, 'There must be another way,' and they'd turned and walked back to the House.

'We could fly off – to Aussie or, I dunno, London.'

'We'll be lucky to get a bus ticket to South Auckland,' said Jade.

Freedom twirled in their heads, like sarongs in the sky and coins in pockets.

Jade saw freedom once. Like it was a tangible thing, like it was the heel of Santa's foot going up the chimney, and she was pointing and saying, 'Look, it's real. It's really real.'

It was when Head was shot.

A prospect was boxed and locked.

And after her father's tangi, on her first day out in the stark brightness of the world, she'd been waiting at the bus station, crying. She had a small bag between her feet and she had *almost* enough money for a bus ticket in her pocket. He'd found her, not by accident. Sought her out, head cocked, looked at her, innocently surprised. Pleased with himself for, so unexpectedly, being at the right place at the right time.

'Don't leave Felicity alone. Not now, not yet,' he said.

'Soon, then.'

'Yeah, soon.'

Without a second thought she returned to the House.

Up the chimney it had gone. She was almost fifteen years old.

'I'll look after you both,' he said.

And he did. He took good care to make sure her mother stayed addicted to what he could afford. Mostly glue. Eventually, Felicity stopped looking out of her eyes. But the night after Head's tangi, Jade was in the bed she had somehow, and so suddenly, come to share with Coon, like some sort of deal had been made – in some sort of fine print, some language she knew the words of, yet could not work out what they meant when they were put together in such a way that wanted intentionally to confuse.

It was the same bed Head and Felicity had shared.

Why am I in here? she thought.

Her mother had moved to a different room, a smaller one, less queen-like. And eventually to another house, sometimes the open air. For sometimes she punished herself with homelessness. Because despite the way she stared into nothing, drool on her chin, Jade knew Felicity saw Coon. Felicity saw right through. She saw what he would do to her daughter without Head around. But the slow-healing wounds, so many of them, were gumming over each other. Jade knew those gummy scars had made her mother weak, her movements slow, like she was wading through silt. Gluey silt. So she couldn't stop him. And she would rather not see what she'd done. How her choices had decided her daughter's lot.

On the bed Coon took Jade to, there were blankets. A red bed sheet, faded to pink. The same place Jade had tucked her knees under her chin to hear Felicity's version of stories. Sometimes Head had listened too. Together the three of them had leafed through books. The ones with Māui catching the sun, or finding his mother, or defying things.

Jade knew Felicity was making up the words, because they sounded like her words, and not the words she'd heard at school.

'And then Māui, gotta rope and he said, "Oi, you dumb Sun. We got shit to do, slow your arse down." "Make me," Sun said – cheeky cunt he was.' And every time she got to the end of the book she'd say, 'Tū meke, Māui, now we have time to do all the many, many things we wanna do today. Like take a hit from a bong.'

Felicity smiled at Head, but he didn't always smile back. He looked at Felicity and he looked at the book, and he knew there was something he was being denied.

Jade had wanted her father to defy things too. She saw that Head was inspired by Māui, but there was something else, the thing that stopped him becoming Māui. The wish that someone had read those stories to *him*, before tucking *him* into bed. And he would huff and stand. Shrug on his leather jacket and leave the room like he intended to defy, like he was a Māori warrior. But on the street, in the real world, he realised they were just stories. The sun couldn't be slowed. Never had been.

He let the rage he was defying, was roping up, tear from him, and inflicted it on anyone who so much as looked at him like he should be better than he was.

But sometimes instead of going out into the world to prove himself, he'd stay home and take out *The Little Mermaid* from the box, because he'd heard his queen tell his princess that she must learn to read it.

They'd sit on the bed and he'd teach her. And he was better at teaching than Miss Matt. Head made Jade feel like they were working the words out together. Miss Matt made Jade feel like she'd been done an extraordinary favour. That Miss Matt had been so generous, Jade could never repay her.

So Head taught his little princess. Because though he couldn't read those Māui books in te reo, he could read the Pākehā ones too easy. Stumbled on a word here and there, but mostly, too easy. If he couldn't give his queen jewels he'd make sure she got the story she wanted. And stories were more precious than pearls or diamond necklaces, brooches or ruby rings, or so he told his daughter.

'Stories are knowledge, knowledge is power and one day we'll take our power and rule something better than this House.'

'And then will you buy us necklaces and rings and diamonds and other pretty stuff?' Jade asked.

He laughed. 'Too easy.'

'Promise?'

Head held up his pinky, and Jade twisted hers around it like a beansprout on a beanpole. 'Promise,' he said.

When at last Jade could do it, she read to her mother. Slowly at first, then clearly, and confidently until sometimes it seemed to Jade that Felicity could no longer bear listening to how swiftly she was being outgrown.

Lying there on the sheet faded to pink, Coon whispered into Jade's back: 'You should know, your old man didn't see it coming. Wouldn't have felt it. From behind, yeah, single bullet. That kid. Some fatherless little fucker.'

Coon had touched her so softly. And as Jade lay there, her eyes closed, she wondered if he thought she was asleep while he whispered into her back. Or if he didn't care that those words might hurt her. But his soft hand as he spoke of the violence that ended her father's life reminded her of something. The only type of love she knew. Fury then remorse and forgiveness. And she hoped Coon knew how far his fury should go to create a perfect equation of those things. An equilibrium they could measure love by. A trinity. Love, as she'd learned it.

No questions asked.

She had one thought, one question she kept locked and boxed. Where was the gun that killed Head? Was it his gun? Was it now Coon's, just like she was now Coon's and the bed was now Coon's and the red bed sheet was now Coon's?

The gang didn't have guns.

They had baseball bats they didn't play baseball with, crowbars they didn't use for prying things open. Gaffs they never took sons eeling with. Hands to make fists with, boots to kick with. But no guns. Guns were just something they saw in the gangs on TV, and wondered, like children do, how it would be to have that toy. To make playing gang feel more real. Head's death had been a ledge from which she could have flown, but Coon had been there. He had called her back, cupped her in his hands and offered her back the only life she knew.

She learned quickly that he could be mean: 'I'll kill you if you ever try to leave me.' But he was also sweet, he was also vulnerable: 'If you ever leave me, I'll kill myself.'

Sav wanted a rewrite of the deal.

She prayed to God to pluck her up and place her back down – somewhere better, somewhere sunny, somewhere she could swing her child around until the world became a blur.

A good old-fashioned tangi was most often Sav's escape. An actress, she wailed over cousins she'd never met. She said, less than prayerfully: 'God's a greedy bastard. How could he take her? Doesn't he have enough?'

Jade couldn't work out if she should be in awe of, or disgusted by her cousin's ability to fake mourning. Until it gave Jade an escape or two from the House, she was sure it should have been the latter. After that, Jade accepted Sav's defence: 'Girls gotta do, babe, what girls gotta do.'

And Sav would reapply her mascara. She'd smack her freshly painted lips together. Look in the rearview mirror and pinch her cheeks. She'd put something happy, something 'road-trippy,' into the player.

She was a survivor. She found means and ways of making life work for her. Of getting back to Tommy. Without anyone getting hurt.

But that felt forever ago.

Looking at her now, Jade doubted pinching her cheeks would even draw blood to them.

'Have you called him?' Jade asked.

'No, I'll just arrive one day. One fine day, babe.'

'Call him.'

'I'm scared.'

Jade called Tommy herself. She walked to a pay phone close by, and called him. He answered on the second ring.

'This is Jade. Sav's cousin.'

'Everything okay?'

'She's pregnant.'

Tommy said nothing. Then, 'What should I do?'

'I just thought you should know.'

'I suppose I should know.'

'I better go. Like I said, I just …'

'Tell her everything's gonna be fine.'

'I will.'

Jade hung up the phone and became filled with regret, became heavy with it. Over what, she wasn't sure, but she was sure they shouldn't have come back.

A week later and they'd heard nothing from Tommy.

Sav's belly became more difficult to hide, even in baggy hoodies and sweatshirts. She'd got skinny. And had given up trying. Couldn't bear the secret, wished to be released from it, whichever way that would come.

Jade was killing herself thinking, trying to figure out what to do.

They were to celebrate Jade's birthday, Coon had decided. They would have a birthday party. He'd never used the phrase birthday party before. But this was to be a party.

'Hell, yeah, how old you gonna be, girl – twenty, twenty-one?'

'Eighteen,' she said.

Coon was off his face. He'd given Jade money to go buy herself a dress for her birthday party. 'Let's party like we're fucken royals,' he said. 'Get yourself a dress, girl, and one for Sav.'

Jade had put the money away for a few days, and thought some more on it. At last, she stormed to Sav's bedroom. Money for dresses in her fist.

Sav was naked, asleep on her bed.

Sav was skin, bone and baby.

Jade threw a blanket over her.

'You wanna get yourself killed, girl – what you thinking?'

Sav didn't reply.

Jade watched Sav's belly rise and fall, softly and slowly, and as it moved, she understood something. Sav's baby – despite its mother, despite her surroundings, and despite what it unknowingly grew towards as the meat melted from its mother's bones – would grow and grow and grow, like it was a magic bean, unfurling, reaching up to the sky where bloodthirsty giants lived. *Fee, fi, fo, fum.*

The womb was a golden deceit. The baby was both worlds away from, and already imprisoned within, the House.

She imagines what it feels like in a womb as she sits beside Sav and runs her hand over her cousin's forehead and into her greasy hair.

Sav opens her eyes, 'I'm very thirsty.'

Jade goes to the kitchen. She finds a glass. She cleans and dries it. She walks outside.

She makes her way to the fence which separates the House from another house, possibly a home. The people in it probably hate the House, but they are beggars not choosers. Jade almost feels sorrier for them than for herself.

Not that she indulged Coon by letting him near her pain, but if she had, Jade could have screamed and screamed and no one would've come. Neighbours.

There's a branch that hangs over the fence, though, and Jade plucks a lemon from it.

She takes it back to the House and to the kitchen.

She finds a knife and slices the lemon into small rounds.

She fills the clean glass with water from the tap and drops lemon slices into it.

In Sav's room Jade crouches beside her. 'Open your eyes.'

Sav doesn't stir.

'Please, open your eyes.'

Sav opens her eyes. Stares at Jade like they're worlds apart. Opposite ends.

'Drink this,' Jade says.

Sav takes it; she drinks.

'What am I doing?' Sav whispers, panicked. 'I'm going to lose my baby.'

'Your life.'

'Throw me that hoodie.'

Jade pulls an oversized hoodie over Sav.

Jade shows Sav the money that Coon gave her for dresses. 'We're getting you a bus ticket out of here, babe,' she says.

She counts out forty dollars. Coon's grand gesture. Dresses for princesses. Forty bucks worth of dresses. For sluts.

'Coon will kill you.'

'He won't.'

'He'll hurt you.'

For a moment, Jade doesn't reply. Then, 'He might. But compared to what'll happen to you? Come on, we're going, we can say we're going shopping for dresses. You will go up north. For now. Then south. Not right away, but soon.'

Jade packs a bag for Sav and throws it out the bedroom window. The girls walk slowly through the House. Jade puts her head into the living room – the room which a family would have used for living type things, but here other things happened – and unwillingly, accidentally, locks eyes with Coon. She fears always the emptiness of them. The commonplace 'not looking out' that she saw more and more often at the House.

'Going shopping,' she says, and turns quick on her heels.

'Get here.'

She keeps her back to him. 'For the dresses, Coon. You told me to shop for dresses.'

'Get here.'

Jade turns.

He stares empty-eyed at her. His two-day-old dress-shopping suggestion lost in the disconnection of his mind. In the mess of firing neurons, which spark from frayed ends. A time-bomb. A tick-tock. Tick-tock. The mouse ran up the clock.

'You got money?'

'You gave me money.'

'Lying slut.' Tick.

'But Coon.' She tries to soften the edge of her voice, the clawing of it, the escape in it. '*Baby*. You gave it to me.'

'You no princess here no more. Money for dresses. Ha. Get here. Give it.' Tock.

Sav whimpers. Jade kicks her. Warns her to stay quiet. She walks to Coon and takes the slut money from her pocket.

'Here.' She gives it to him.

Coon has an idea. His face lights bright when he has an idea. He looks surprised and pleased with himself.

It evokes something in Jade which resembles love for Coon. *Love for Coon*. Like it's a phenomenon, a myth. Had there ever been such a thing? Was that why she tried? That dark undercurrent of wonder, worry even, that there had never been *love for Coon*. And that undercurrent pulled her under, almost drowned her, time and time again.

She can feel the fool in her.

She can feel the fool that wants to take Coon into her arms.

And at the same time wants to kick in his brains.

Do it! Kick in his brains!

But Fool-Jade unfolds her hands to him.

As something mean unfolds in Coon's meth-head.

Some mean thing.

Tick.

Tock.

'You want your money? Earn it. Dance for the boys.'

Jade doesn't move. 'Don't need it.'

'Dance, bitch,' and he hurls a full beer bottle against the door. It smashes and the brown liquid bursts out. Stains upon stains. Sounds make promises of things to come.

'Don't need the money. Don't need a dress.'

'But the boys need dancing. Don't you, boys?'

His boys don't move and nor does Jade.

Fool-Jade is gone.

Smart-Jade takes over. She won't indulge him. She imposes stillness on her body. The toleration of imposition is something she has mastered.

She won't give him a twitch. *No love for Coon.* He stands and walks towards her. Tries to lure her to a place where she should fear him. Where no one can help or hear her. Not Sav, not God. Not the neighbours.

Sav whimpers again behind the door. Coon cocks his head like a puppy. Tick.

'Is that you, Sav? Come here, baby,' Coon says, as he looks at Jade. 'Ah. Yeah! A dancing partner. Come on. Something to loosen you up.'

He takes hold of Jade and Sav. His fingers dig into the flesh of their arms. He leads them to the couch.

Needles are spread out on a coffee table in front of it, like toys.

Toys that make all they exist for feel more real.

To make their game of gang feel more real.

He pushes the two women down between two mongrels who are barely conscious. Coon is the only one awake to play, who hasn't taken his hit. If Jade had walked in just a few minutes later she might have found a different scene. She might have found Coon feeling the only love he ever knew. Love in his blood. Warm and beautiful.

Needles were new toys.

This Sunday afternoon, a treat – something that made Coon feel like he was the king of something – smack.

'Who first?' Coon sniggers. Tick.

Afraid, Smart-Jade pushes Fool-Jade to the stage.

Don't worry. I'm here, Smart-Jade says. *You just need to do the talking.*

'You, my king. You first.'

Everybody plays the fool.

'No, no … pretty women first.'

He hands her a belt. Tock.

Jade hopes stalling might give Sav a chance. To not have to put this shit in her blood. Not put this shit in her baby's blood. She begins wrapping her own arm.

'Sav first. Greedy bitch,' Coon slaps Jade's face. Either way, it would have been wrong. Had she wrapped Sav's arm first, he'd have said, 'You first.'

Coon wraps Sav's limp arm. She has already disappeared, like she'll be back, like she's out to pick up sugar to make Sunday pancakes.

Jade prays for colours. Whites and lemon yellows, and the green of the sea. She presses the needle into Sav's arm and tendrils of bloody smoke curl into it. It's very black, what she's done.

She drops the needle to the floor.

'You now,' Coon says.

As Jade begins to wrap her arm, a smell, so sweet, soaks the air. It makes her sick. Blood spreads from between Sav's legs, onto the Sunday afternoon sofa.

Sav looks dead – she looks like a dead woman with a bellyful of a secret.

'What the fuck?' Coon lifts Sav's shirt and reveals the truth. *Fee, fi, fo, fum.*

93

He crouches, cocks his head, takes Sav's face, softly, so softly in his hands. 'You been teaching your baby cousin how to work the system? Huh? Huh, Sav? Teaching Jade how to make a fool of her man?'

He rises, twisting Sav's hair around and around and around his hand, then pulling, pulling her to stand. Lifting her up, up, up, like a puppet. 'Farrr. Sav's slut class,' he says, turning to Jade, 'And? Are you an A student?'

He tosses Sav to the floor. Blood pools around her.

The scent of it. Tick tock.

Then, he takes the first swinging boot to Sav's belly. Boom. Boom. Boom.

Jade falls to her knees. She tries to block the blows, absorb them, take them for her cousin. They get stronger, swift. They move from Sav's belly, to Jade's splayed hands. Her face, her belly too. Sav's thighs. Jade's chest. Jade's head. Sav's belly. Jade's tail bone. Sav's belly, Sav's belly.

Sav's belly.

Hands, legs, hearts.

Three hearts.

Two stopped beating before he was done. Before he said, 'No place for a kid. You know that.' People had come into the room having heard terrible noises. A young fatherless prospect, tattooed up his face with some wretched affinity, had run in yelling, 'Oi, man. Fuck. It's enough.'

And it was.

Jade opened her eyes, reached out, pulled at her cousin's arms. 'Let's go. Let's go. Sav. Sav. Shopping.' Though she hurt, though she hurt all over. Though she felt broken to her core.

Coon fell into the sofa, looked down at the mess he had made.

At leisure, but grunting, heaving, he wrapped his meatless arm, pressed the needle hard into his veins, and lay back.

'Let her sleep that shit off, you dumb bitch. She's in no state for shopping.' Then, eyes rolled up in his head, face loosening from skull, he whispered, 'Sorry about ya dad, Jade. Seen it in that kid's eyes,

94

yeah, and when I said to him, "You put that bullet in his head, son," he pressed on the trigger, real quick, hoping it wouldn't be the last time that I'd call him son. Son. Yeah. I seen it. I seen it. Fatherless little fuck. Yeah. They the easy ones to teach our ways, those fatherless bastards. *Shoot him, son.* I whispered right in the kid's ear. Bang. Dead. And I am king! King Coon. Yeah.'

He closed his eyes. Let the Class A love flood through his veins.

It was impossible for Jade to run. Tail bone that felt like a mesh bag of smashed glass marbles. Leg didn't want to hold her, wanted to let her fall, wanted to keep her in the clouds with giants. Clawed out. Fingertips bleeding. Clawed out. Out of the House and under the Sunday sky.

Shrugged people off, away. 'No. No. Too late. Too late. For. Your. Help.'

And when they didn't listen, she shouted, 'Fuck off.'

She made it to the street. Passed out on the footpath. She woke and saw a face. And the face was a man's and it loomed over her. The man was unimpressed with what he'd seen. She thought she saw judgement. 'Why would someone stay here?' she thought she heard him say. And she thought someone had replied: 'Not now, Toko.'

Were they talking about her?

Then Sav was laid beside her. And a man was breathing into Sav's mouth and pumping her chest with his hands. 'I'm here, I'm here. Wake up.'

Once upon a time there were two damsels in distress …

Toko and young Tommy had arrived minutes too late. For one of them at least, and just in the nick of time for the other.

Perhaps they'd sat in the car summoning the courage to enter the House longer than they should have. Perhaps they'd stopped for a pie on the way. Perhaps they'd gone to the pub for a quick drink to help them face the danger they doubted they'd face at all.

'It can't be that bad,' they might have told themselves. 'I mean, wouldn't they have left already if it was.'

But, koo-koo-ka-choo.

Taukiri

I woke cold, body aching, mouth dry.

I woke and wanted to watch Ari sprinkle brown sugar over his Weet-Bix, so I bit down hard on my tongue.

Where was I?

The room smelled of wood. The sun came through a square of sunlight. I was in a low single bed. It had yellow sheets and a duvet with Chewbacca printed on it. My guitar was on the floor. It was wrapped in a plastic rubbish bag. Why did I do that? And where was I?

The room had something, maybe a woody smell, which reminded me of the high ceilinged room I was snorting up in, what, a night ago? Two nights ago? Life felt chopped, and scrapbooked. Cut and glued, placed randomly.

Yesterday, I thought. I woke in a room where a bird asked questions with its eyes before the room filled with the sea, and I must have experienced some sort of weird trip-out as I ran over town with my guitar, trying to hide from either a burning or a flooding. Or was it both?

My head hurt.

I felt for my bone carving. It was still there.

I heard a creaking, and there she was again. Pretty girl with a freckle on her eyelid.

The freckle wasn't a starfish anymore.

She sat on the bed and I sat up.

'How you feeling?' she asked.

'Fine, a bit yuck, but fine. Just trying to work out how I got here.'

'I followed you.'

'Why?'

'You were so out of it when you left. I followed you to that house

96

and you fell asleep in your car, drenched. So I drove you here.'

'Thank you.'

'Elliot will drive me to pick up my car. I had to leave it. It would have been impossible to move you.'

My grey hoodie and jeans were folded on a chair.

'How did I …?'

'Elliot helped me,' she said.

'Megan?'

She nodded.

'You take photographs?'

'Yes.'

'You didn't tell me what of.'

'I'm sort of a cop. But I only take photos.'

'Of like, crime scenes?'

'Sometimes. Or accidents. The odd publicity event.'

She looked at the carving on my chest. I took it in my hand.

She opened her mouth to ask something, but stopped herself. Then she walked out, closing the door behind her.

Needed more sleep. Less light. Another me.

The door opened again, and there was a louder creaking than before. Elliot was standing beside the bed.

'Bro, you freaked me out. And Megan is flipping at me, and Jason, man, Jason's pissed.'

'Who's Jason?'

'My sister's boyfriend. Where I get my shit from, our shit. All the shit that keeps all your shit at bay comes from Jason. So yeah, good one.'

'Sorry.'

'Bro, you probably lost your job. You been in bed two days.'

'I know.'

'It's all good. You can help us. When he cools down.'

I swallowed. My throat was bone dry. 'Cool,' I said.

'I'll let you sleep.'

'Bro, my guitar?'

Elliot picked it up. 'What were you thinking? Running around in the rain with it. It's pretty scratched, and dented as. You're a neglectful musician.'

I sat up. 'Could you pass it? And my T-shirt.'

He passed them to me. 'You're a shitty, shitty neglectful musician, a liability of a friend, but certainly, your majesty, anything else?'

He handed me the guitar and it made a hollow, sulky sound.

I put on the T-shirt. 'Cheers, bro.'

After he shut the door behind him I spooned myself against the guitar's cool rosewood arch.

Ārama

Me and Beth were playing in Tom Aiken's truck.

Well, I was first. I was sitting in the driver's seat making *vrrrooommm* noises, and banging on the horn, and I had my arm resting on the open window, my elbow out, just like Tom Aiken always did.

I yelled out to Lupo, 'Get in behind!' and he looked at me, with his head cocked, and then got distracted by a bee that needed chasing and ran off. Beth came out the house and asked me what I was doing.

'Aunty Kat sent me over because Uncle Stu is in a bad mood. He needs quiet.'

'Are you that loud?'

I shrugged, then beat down on the horn hard, and went back to making *vrrrooommm* noises.

Beth hopped in the passenger's side. 'What are you doing?'

'Just playing.'

'But farm vehicles are not toys. And you're too big to make *vrrrooommm* noises.'

I stopped. I felt a bit stupid. 'Yeah, I know.'

Beth started cracking up. 'Just joking,' she said and buckled up her seat belt. 'Let's go to Auckland, Django!'

'How will we get across Cook Strait?' I asked.

'What's that?'

'The sea between the North Island and the South.'

'Oh.' She looked embarrassed, but she shook it off, like only Beth could. 'When you press this button our car turns into an airplane,' and she pressed the play button on the stereo.

'Let's drive to see Taukiri.'

'Okay. Go.'

Beth pointed to something then threw her arms in the air. 'Watch out, you gonna crash.'

She made a screeching sound with her mouth.

'Good one. We're dead now, dummy. No Taukiri for you. Never get to see him again.'

I fake-laughed. I knew what she was trying to do. She could be mean like that sometimes. She liked to see my eyes water. She got a kick out of it. Probably because I showed her up knowing what the Cook Strait was and all. Her aunty obviously hasn't told her about that yet, and her stupid *Django* movie could only teach her so much.

Then she said, 'You know, I can actually drive this truck.'

'Don't lie,' I said, my hands still tight on the steering wheel, 'You are way too small. You can't even reach the pedals.'

'Well, when I sit on Dad's knee I can drive it. I can even change gears.'

'Really? Show me.'

'Dad's not here.' I knew she felt like she needed to prove it to me. But she really didn't. I believed her. I was just teasing.

'Can I sit on your knee?' she asked.

'I don't think it's a good idea to drive the truck without your dad.'

Beth got out the truck. Now I'd done it. She saw I was a bit scared and that always got her going. If I was scared she wasn't, and if she was scared I wasn't. It didn't normally go that way round though.

She climbed in my side, sat down on my knee and put both hands on the steering wheel.

'Okay, so when I say release the accelerator, and press the clutch, you do that, okay, but nice and slow. And if I say brake, brake.'

I looked at my feet, 'Which is which?'

'Clutch, left. Brake, middle. Accelerator, right. Got it?'

I put my foot on the left pedal. 'Clutch,' I said. Beth nodded.

I moved my foot to the middle one, 'Brake.'

Beth nodded. I moved my foot to the far right.

'Accelerator.'

'Belts on, we are good to go.' She laughed, as she put her hand on the gear thing and turned the key. She said Tom Aiken always left his keys in the truck.

'Accelerator.' I pressed my foot down. The truck sounded angry. 'Release accelerator, slow! Clutch.'

And Beth, one hand on the wheel, one on the gear, moved it until the truck sounded happy again.

'Good!' she shouted, and then we shot forward, and the truck shook like it was a wet dog and stopped.

'Stall,' she said as she turned the key again.

We started over, but every time on the first gear change we made the truck choke and shake until it turned itself off.

'I really can do this, Ari,' she said, looking at me sadly.

'I believe you. Anyway, I think it's me, with the accelerator and clutch thingy.'

'Oh,' she said, still looking sad. 'That's the part my dad always does. Maybe that's the hard bit.'

'I don't think so. I think it's just you guys make a good team.'

'Yeah,' she perked up. 'We probably do. And me and you are a good team at other stuff. Should we go play Django?'

'Sure, Doc.'

We got out of the truck, and Beth yelled out to Lupo, 'Come on boy, come on!' and Lupo came bounding to us, as we headed over to the farm to play.

When I went back home, I couldn't hear Aunty Kat. There was a plate on the table with a sandwich. And a note: *Eat something, and take yourself to bed. Not feeling well. Love Aunty Kat.*

I ate my sandwich alone at the table. I could hear myself chew, which I didn't like. I turned on the TV because it was so early, and watched *Shortland Street*. Aunty Kat didn't have Cartoon Network like I had in my real life. Mum never used to let me watch *Shortland Street*, but now I've seen most of *Django*, who would care what I watched on TV for the rest of my dumb life?

After *Shortland Street* I went upstairs, brushed my teeth and put my pyjamas on. I did it all quite slowly, hoping that before I actually got to bed, Aunty Kat would come out of her closed bedroom to say good night to me. But she didn't.

I turned off my light, then had to find my way to the bed. I hit my shin on the corner and reached under the mattress for my emergency box of plasters. I plastered my shin and some bruises on my knees and elbows. They weren't bleeding, but still – they felt better plastered.

I stared at the ceiling. I'd sleep if Taukiri was against my back holding me close to his chest. They were always the best sleeps. After a bad dream I would creep to his bed and whisper, 'Taukiri, can I sleep with you?' And he would just throw open his blankets and tuck himself and the blankets around me. A couple of times, though, I woke up in Taukiri's bed but I couldn't remember getting there. Couldn't remember a bad dream. And I'd ask him, 'Did I have a bad dream last night?'

He'd say, 'Yes.'

But sometimes it sounded like he was lying.

I didn't really understand the word 'orphan' until I became one. The first time Tauk brought a baby bird home, he said we had to help it because it was an orphan. I asked Mum what that meant and she said it meant that the bird had no mummy or daddy. I don't remember feeling any more sorry for the bird after she said that. Most birds seem fine on their own. Most animals seem fine on their own, and I thought probably such a terrible thing had never happened and never would happen to a kid.

Taukiri was a real D.I.C.K. for leaving me. He should've known I wouldn't be happy with Aunty Kat and Uncle Stu. If it was a good place he would have stayed too, but he left, he left with his guitar, and somewhere in some stupid city he was playing songs I couldn't hear. No one played songs here. No one listened to music or told stories. They didn't even realise not doing those things made them bad people. The worst thing was I didn't think Aunty Kat was a bad person, she was just a ghost of a person, and I knew why. Uncle Stu made people doubt they existed, and when you doubted you existed long enough, you started to disappear.

Maybe the day my family stopped existing, I did too.

Was I just a ghost haunting the wrong house?

Crying in my old room felt different to crying at the farm. On the farm it scared me to cry, because no one might stop it. Even if they tried. That left it to me. I was left to me, and that's what it meant to be an orphan.

When you doubted you existed, it was impossible to trust yourself in your own hands.

That bird was lucky Taukiri picked it up. He was a D.I.C.K. for leaving me. He wouldn't do that to a stupid bird who didn't even know it was an orphan. I thought I might be starting to hate him. Trying to go to sleep with hate inside me was hard.

I fell asleep though.

I knew because when I woke up the sun was already in the window, and I heard Tom Aiken downstairs talking to Aunty Kat. He'd come to see if Aunty Kat needed anything from town. I went downstairs and asked if I could go for a ride with him.

Aunty Kat said no at first, but Tom Aiken said it would be good because I could give Beth some company for the trip.

Tom Aiken said I could sit in the front, and asked me to find a CD from the glovebox to play. He had all the same music as my mum and dad, and suddenly I was a bit scared to hear those songs. Beth asked me to put on Queen – 'Bohemian Rhapsody'.

As soon as I heard it I knew it was meant for me.

It was asking the same questions I was. The right questions, the ones that everyone who got old forgot to ask. Was this the *real* life? Or was it just a stupid, stupid fantasy?

A weird-as game?

That was the song. A story and a play and music. Loud, loud music. It made me feel like I was flying and then like I was underwater, like way, way underwater. The beat picked up and the words, they were terrible and sad and angry but then so high and happy.

Beth pretended she was holding a guitar and was picking it and head banging, and she mouthed the words, and she yelled at me. 'Drum, townie!' So I started to drum. We guitared and drummed and head banged and pianoed. Tom Aiken, too, tapping the steering wheel and head banging and smashing his fist into the air. Beth yelled, 'Here's the best bit.' And when the guitar shocked up the hairs on my arms, Beth closed her eyes and was guitaring hard out. Then the song slowed up, and Beth put her guitar down and pianoed and there was a final clashing sound and we did the clashing together.

We sort of stayed on the silence when the song finished, like we were floating on the sea, nothing but sky above us.

Beth sighed. 'Ahhh, that was fun,' she said.

'You're a weird kid,' Tom Aiken said. 'Isn't she, Ari?'

'What? It's decent music,' she said.

'What music do you like, Ari?' Tom Aiken asked.

'Tauk's.'

'True. He's good. How's your present going then?

'What present?'

'The one,' and he looked in the rearview mirror at me, 'the one I gave you at Christmas.'

'Oh, yeah, that. Under my bed. Waiting for Tauk. I'll open it with him. In case it's a trick.'

'A trick?'

'Yeah. A trick. Like when you wrap presents in big boxes, but there's really there's more boxes inside, boxes and boxes, smaller and smaller, and a small present when you wanted a big one. You can do that with shapes as well. Which would be mean of Tauk – but you never know. Maybe it's a guitar-shaped box. Though I kind of already know it's not a trick because it was already making noises when I hid it. You just never know, you know, with presents.'

'If you change your mind, we can unwrap it with you,' said Tom Aiken.

'It's okay. I'm going to wait. Shouldn't be long now.'

When we got on the gravel road, Tom Aiken complained that his seat felt strange, like someone else had been sitting in it.

'How'd you know?'

'Just do. I can just feel that someone else has been sitting in my chair,' he roared like a bear. He pulled to the side of the road.

'Right, let's show him how it's done, little lady!' And Beth squealed, as she rushed up front and jumped into his lap.

'So, buddy,' Tom Aiken said, looking back at me, 'what I noticed you might have been doing wrong yesterday, when I was spying on you …'

'I knew it,' Beth yelled. 'I knew you didn't just feel that someone else had been sitting in your chair!'

'I did but I also saw you. Because I was spying. I am always spying, even when I'm not.'

'What the hell does that mean?'

'Watch your language. Anyway, what I noticed, Ari, is that you were probably not taking your foot off the clutch slow enough, and not pressing on the accelerator fast enough. Which is why you stalled. Come, jump up front, and watch my feet.'

I scrambled to the front as the truck started moving along the gravel road. Lupo was nutting off.

'Wind the window down, would ya, for that dumb dog? I swear … If you didn't love him so much …'

Beth slapped her dad.

'Watch, Ari,' said Tom Aiken. 'Watch my feet.' I watched his feet, and he seemed to move them opposite ways but at the same time. One up, one down. 'Always smooth, you see?'

I nodded, and the truck sounded happy with the two of them. Beth steering the wheel and changing gears, and Tom Aiken moving his foot up and down.

'Good. Wake me up when we get to town.' Tom closed his eyes, and pretended to snore, then pretended to wake suddenly as me and Beth cracked up laughing.

In town Tom Aiken got us something to eat at a café. It was pretty cool to be eating out and we were allowed to choose anything we wanted from a glass cabinet. I chose a mince pastie and Beth got a potato-top pie. Tom Aiken had a cup of tea and a sausage roll. A lot of people said hi to him. A lady came to talk about us starting in school. She was real nice. She had blonde hair and red lipstick. She said she would get some information for Tom. It was probably best to start as soon as possible. *Get back to normal.* Tom Aiken agreed, but said it was just a shame there was no school bus that passed by our way, to make it easier. The lady asked for his phone number, so she could let him know about the bus. She touched his shoulder.

'Was lovely to see you again, Tommy.'

People kept coming to say hi to Tom Aiken, and all of them called him Tommy and started talking about things that made him look at me and then look at them, and suddenly it would seem like no one knew what they should say anymore.

Tom Aiken went up to the counter to ask for paper bags so we could take our food away, 'Come on,' he said, 'let's go park at the seal colony.'

We drove down the main street, then out to the Seafood Barbecue at Jimmy Armers Beach. I opened the window and could smell fish being fried in garlic butter, and it made me hungry again.

'Can we get fish?' I asked Tom Aiken.

'Got worms, boy?'

'What?'

'Nothing. Sure.'

Tom Aiken parked the truck by the caravan. 'You two go. I'll wait,' and he handed Beth a ten-dollar note.

We went to the counter. A tall skinny man with long dreadlocks and skin the colour of Milo leaned towards us. His white apron was smeared black with pāua.

He grinned as we walked towards him. 'Out for a date, huh?'

'Piss off,' Beth yelled, folding her arms. 'Guess you don't want our business.' She waved the ten dollars in the air. 'We were gonna buy a whole crayfish, but probs won't now.'

The man smiled. 'I'm sorry. That was rude of me.'

'You should be. Now, what are we having, Django? My shout.'

I looked at the list of things we could choose from written on a whiteboard. *Pāua pattie $10, Grilled fish $7, Scallops $8, Whitebait pattie $8, Crayfish $25 +*

I nudged Beth and pointed. She looked at the board, pressed the money into her fist, twisted her lips.

The man leaned forward. 'Can I tell you a secret?'

We stepped closer to the counter. 'Honestly, the last time we got fresh crayfish was a week ago. We're still selling it off to the tourists who don't know any better, but I'd be embarrassed to sell it to you two. I bet you know your kaimoana.'

Beth beamed, then leaned closer. 'I didn't want to say anything, but I thought I smelled something a bit rank.'

He nodded slowly, 'Look, I'm going to be honest. The best thing we got at the moment is fresh tarakihi. How about that?'

'Sounds good.' Beth nudged me. 'Okay?'

'I wanted fish anyway,' I said.

The man grilled the fish in garlic butter and made a half sandwich each, instead of one, so we didn't have to share.

'Enjoy,' he said, handing them to us carefully. He took Beth's money from the counter and slid her back some coins. She winked and left them on the counter. 'Shout yourself a beer. For your honesty.'

He laughed, shook his head. More people came up behind us with backpacks on. We started back to the truck. Beth yelled out to the new customers. 'I highly recommend the crayfish,' she said to them.

It was magic to eat fish sandwiches so close to the sea, with gulls squawking, the water hitting the rocks and all the salt in the air.

After we ate, Tom Aiken took us to the seal colony. There we could see the mountains on both sides of Kaikōura.

'This is the best spot to understand what a peninsula is,' Tom Aiken said.

'What's a peninsula?' Beth asked.

'Just land. Land almost completely surrounded by water. Except for one piece, one small bit, which connects it to the rest, and that little bit is all that's stopping it from being an island.'

We looked out the car window, where the seals were lying in the sun and on each side of us were mountains, and everywhere else was sea.

What would happen if there was an earthquake strong enough to break the land away? Or if the sea rose up quick and suddenly that tiny bit of land stopping us from being an island was swept away?

On the way back home, when we got to the gravel road where our driveways met, Tom Aiken pulled over.

'Your turn, kid,' he said, turning to me.

'Really?'

'Come here – jump on my lap.'

I climbed over.

'Can you see out the window?'

I looked over the steering wheel. I could just see above my hands. 'Yup.'

'You're pretty tall, buddy. Just like your dad.'

I didn't mind Tom Aiken talking about my dad.

'I'm here, bud. I can grab the wheel anytime. And look, I can even do the brake, you know, just if you forget or something.'

I let out the excited laugh-bubble from my tummy.

'Ready. Let's go,' he said. 'Turn the key.'

I did, and the engine made the best *vrrrooommm* sound.

We moved. Beth giggled.

'Let's go home,' Tom Aiken said.

'To your house?' I asked.

Tom Aiken nodded.

I held the steering wheel tight and drove us *home*. I drove us all the way *home*.

Tom Aiken taught me to drive a car – I couldn't do it by myself yet, but with a few more runs on Tom Aiken's lap I'd be good to go.

We played at Beth's, until Tom said he better take me home. I felt more at home at Beth's place than I did in a house that I had my own bedroom in.

Tom Aiken and Beth took me home-home.

The table was set for three.

Maybe a sandwich alone, listening to myself chew, was not so bad.

Tom said dinner smelled good, and I begged Aunty Kat to let them stay and eat with us. Tom Aiken said no, Aunty Kat said yes, Uncle Stu arrived and didn't seem to care either way but opened a beer for Tom Aiken, which seemed to convince him. Suddenly, with Beth and Tom Aiken at the table, there was a feeling in that house, like it wasn't the worst place on earth.

Until it was again.

Uncle Stu scrunched his face into a nasty pout while he listened to Aunty Kat and Tom Aiken talk.

'How good was that beach in summer?' Tom said.

'Then Jade arrived,' Aunty Kat said.

And they stopped talking.

When Tom Aiken started clearing up dishes with Aunty Kat, Uncle Stu's face got the nastiest, and he started making weka grunts which I knew he was going to turn into mean words.

'You been workin' all day, Aiken. That lazy bitch hardly does a thing.'

'Stu!' Aunty Kat yelled. 'The kids!'

'Come on. Take a joke, Kat.' Uncle Stu leaned back in his chair. 'You wanna help her, Aiken?'

'I'm fine, Tommy.' said Aunty Kat. 'Sit, have a drink.'

'Yeah. *Tommy*. Why don't I call you Tommy? Kat calls you Tommy. Have a drink, Tommy.' And Uncle Stu shot a beer across the table.

Tom Aiken looked at Aunty Kat. Then he sat back down and opened the bottle and lifted it to his lips. Aunty Kat tried to move around the room invisibly. I knew that movement, because I did it too. Ari moved like that when it was better to be Ghost-Ari.

It only made everything worse though. When you're a ghost it was hard to hold solid things, like plates, and that's probably why Aunty Kat dropped one.

Tom Aiken reached to catch it. Uncle Stu took a drink and watched Tom Aiken move towards the falling plate. But it smashed on the floor. Uncle Stu laughed.

'Tommy, Tommy,' he said, shaking his head. And the way he said Tom Aiken's name made it the worst place in the world again.

Tom Aiken came over to talk to Aunty Kat the next day. He waited until Uncle Stu was out on the farm. He had good news. We were getting a school bus, he said. We should have had one out here for ages, the lady had told him. There were five kids being homeschooled: me and Beth, plus three brothers and sisters who lived even further away than us.

And from now on we could all go to school on the bus.

'And Kat,' Tom Aiken said, 'about last night, at dinner … there's something else I want to talk to you about.'

'Great,' she said. 'Wow, school!' But she didn't look in his eyes. 'You reckon Beth will go all right?'

'She struggled once or twice before. But with all you've done for her, Kat, I reckon she'll do all right.'

So Beth had tried school.

And all I could think about was school.

I ran to my room and got out my schoolbag – the one we'd packed to come here. I opened it up, and found the photo again. The one of us. There we were. Me, Taukiri, Mum and Dad.

In my hands.

Forgot, then, why I was in my room. Had come up here happy about school? *Tom Aiken had news? Good news? I was happy?* A really bad feeling then, like a baby bird would feel falling from its nest, falling away from its mummy and daddy and hitting the ground. I had nightmares like it, this feeling. In the nightmares I knew the ground was coming, and knowing it made my body ache. But you just fall and fall, aching all the way.

I grabbed my bone carving and closed my eyes. I said, 'Come on, Tauk. Just come back, would ya? Please.'

Those birds were lucky. Lucky they hit the ground. Their fall had a stop. And lucky for them Taukiri came and cupped them in his hands. But in the end they died anyway, alone, in box after box.

There was one who survived, though. I remember that one flew away.

Taukiri

Elliot dragged me back there, finally. Two girls and some guy who didn't seem to realise he'd been hardout friend-zoned wanted us two busker boys to take them to the beach. Elliot had promised me a beach that I could close my eyes and pretend was a river.

'Please, bro,' he'd whispered, 'these girls are hot. You'd be mental.'

'Well ...'

'Please.'

'Let's see.'

We carried on busking. Five people watching us. A real wasted girl with jet-black hair and ripped jeans danced, tripping over her feet, shouting. Her brother seemed pissed off when he realised he'd better take her home. 'I should just call Mum,' he said.

'*I should just call Mum*,' she laughed, then fell backwards, and he hauled her up. She swung her arm around his shoulder and off they went. Siblings. Got each other's back. Like siblings should, even when they didn't want to.

Then there were three. These two girls and a tag-along.

We sang some good stuff. Some of our best.

Only about ten bucks in Elliot's cap though. Didn't matter.

Elliot started clapping and singing Middle of the Road's 'Chirpy, Chirpy, Cheep, Cheep', and I worried he was not a real friend. That he had a mean streak. I looked at him singing to me like that, and he didn't stop. He stopped clapping and strummed the chords, looking right at me, singing the words. Not smiling with his mouth, but definitely with his eyes.

I didn't give him the satisfaction. Fuck him. I joined in. In fact I changed the words and made the song mine, all mine, *owned* it.

'Where's my māmā eh? Where's my pāpā eh? Farrr, Farrr away.'

By the end I was laughing, head banging, skipping around Elliot, singing the happy song. The happy, cruel song.

'Too much, bro,' he said when we finished. 'I think you're ready to go to the beach.'

I laughed. 'You smart cunt.'

The sea was calm. No foam. No roar. Only the quiet sound of pebbles – not sand – being tugged, rolled, by the lazy tide. The sea smell was there, but we lit joint after joint to cover it. Elliot kept fishing them from his pocket as soon as he saw my eyes start to widen again.

The friend-zoned guy had gone, and I hadn't even noticed when. Poor bugger. But here we were playing our guitars, doing our thing, being *those guys*.

And we wanted to be *those guys*. It was unoriginal – I could see that – buskers on a beach playing their guitars for girls.

One of the girls could sing. Jessie. Jessie's voice was nice-ish. Everything else about her was annoyingly intense. She watched my fingers move on my guitar, seemed to stare down my throat when I sang. Elliot walked away with the other girl, who had another name, maybe Sarah. Jessie came upon me like a wave, and the urge to push her away pulsed through me. She kissed me and I could hardly breathe. I felt the ghost sand rise in my chest and I turned away to cough. When I'd got all the sand up, I used the urge I'd had to push her to kiss her hard instead. Let her unbutton my jeans. Let my fingers unbutton hers. Let myself be seventeen. Let myself do what a guitar-playing boy on a beach, with a girl whispering, 'Fuck me,' into his ear would do.

The feel of it, on the early morning air, ghost-like, trying to find its way under my skin, woke me. I wasn't ready to be waking up on a beach.

The sun wasn't up, but it was already getting light. And there was all that sea, right there, where we'd slept. I shook her.

'Jessie, let's go.'

'Why?' she curled closer to me, rubbed her head against my chin, her eyes closed, 'It's nice here. Light the fire again.'

'No. I want to go.'

She sat up. 'Stay.'

I stood. 'I'm going.'

I started walking quickly up the beach, over the rocks to where the car was parked. Elliot and the other girl were asleep inside. I thumped on the window, then turned my back, leaned against the car.

Looked out at that sea. Got impatient. Thumped the window again. 'Oi. Wake up. Get your clothes on. Time to go.'

Jessie came running up the beach with her sandals in her hands, her hair all a mess. Straps falling off her shoulders.

'You would just leave me?' She was shouting and slapping me with her sandal.

'No. I told you … I told you I wanted to go.'

She drew the strap of her singlet back onto her shoulder. 'Typical Māori.'

I stepped towards her, my fists clenched at my side. Behind her the sea blended with her hair.

'What did you say?'

'Nothing.' She shook her head. 'I meant. Typical men.'

I leaned back on the car, looked out at the sea lighting up, 'This typical Māori has got a job to get to.'

Which was a lie. I had nowhere to go and nothing to do. But she didn't know that.

I punched the car window. 'Hurry up. Get dressed.'

I jumped in the driver's seat, put my head out the window at Jessie, her arms folded in front of her. 'Get in, girl,' I said, and I turned the ignition. Revved the car.

Jessie got in and slammed the door. I sped off as the two in the back rummaged for clothes.

'What's the hurry, bro?'

'Don't like sleeping on beaches.'

'What kind of surfer are you?' He laughed. 'Oh, right, you're one who just drives round with a board on his roof looking to score.'

I stared in the rearview mirror at him, said nothing.

Ārama

One flew away. I remembered that.

The last one we found died, like the two before, but this one was special, Taukiri said. It was a baby tūī. I thought it looked exactly like all the rest of the birds we found. With the same fluff over the pink body and the same pear shape and alien head, and the tiny soft-looking beak.

Mum had told Tauk to take me to the school playground. I was on the swing and he'd gone behind a tree, and I could see puffs of smoke in the air and knew he was smoking, which Mum would be really mad about. It was a cold day and my fingers hurt holding the metal chain.

I walked to Tauk. He dropped the smoke on the grass and stood on it. Then he saw something. He crouched down.

I ran up to him. It was a baby bird.

'A baby tūī,' Tauk said.

'How do you know?'

Its mother had been flying around, singing, he said. Searching for her baby. I wasn't sure I believed him, it sounded like one of his middle-of-the-night-and-go-back-to-sleep stories.

'How'd you know it was this baby's mother?'

Taukiri picked it up.

'I reckon this time we should try something,' he said.

'What?'

'This time we should say a karakia. We never did that before. It couldn't hurt to try.'

Taukiri told me to close my eyes, and put my hands together. And I did. Then he said: 'Dear God. Can you please help this baby bird get strong enough to fly, so he can find his mummy? Āmene.'

'It's not a karakia if you just add āmene on the end,' I said.

'Shall I say the karakia I know then, smart-arse? *Bless the food.* Then I'll eat its head right off, and you can have the rest?'

'Ewww.'

'Thought as much. Now shut up and pray.'

He said the same not-a-real-karakia again. Told me to keep my eyes closed but I opened them a little bit and peeked to the side to look at him.

I'd never heard him use the word 'mummy' before.

He kept his head down a bit longer, his hands still pressed together, and I looked from his face to the baby bird, and then he opened his eyes, so I quickly scrunched mine closed, and put my face down and he must've thought I'd been doing that the whole time.

Walking home the wind bit my face, made my eyes and nose water. My fingertips stung.

'The bird'll die,' I said. 'It's so cold today.'

'Maybe not,' Tauk said.

'Why don't we ask Nanny for a real karakia?'

'Look, Ari. Nanny's not magic, not as special as you think she is. If her karakia were so wonderful she would have found that stupid earring by now, don't you think?'

'I suppose. Sorry. The earring wasn't stupid though.'

'Forget it. If the bird dies, blame me. Like everyone else.'

He was quiet then, but he unzipped his jacket, opened it and pulled me to him, and we walked home like that. In Tauk's smokey jacket, the wind hurting my face and the baby bird in his hand.

Jade and Toko

One wrist bandaged, five stitches in her cheek, an eye swollen and shiny like an oil spill, a rib that only let her take in so much air before she felt something jagged might puncture her lung, a deep ache in her tail bone and a single plaster covering something on her neck, something she hadn't bothered to look at, Jade peeled spuds for the tangi. She cut pumpkin and shredded cabbage. She was working beside a kuia. And as they worked the kuia sang waiata and sometimes she wept. Every now and then she patted Jade on her arm, as if she were trying to move something inside her. Wake it.

Then she spoke: 'Auē! Te mamae hoki – kia tangi koe.'

Jade didn't understand the words but she could see what the kuia wanted in her face. Jade couldn't give it to her, really couldn't, though she tried.

The kuia had thick strong arms and short white hair and a face like a moon, and as she pounded the pāua, kneaded dough, split crayfish or snipped beans, she sang and she wept. And she sang and she wept as she washed dishes, as she dried dishes and as she made the apple crumbles. And Jade did not like to work beside anyone else. Even though others were also singing and weeping and snipping beans, Jade liked being near the kuia, who was Sav's great-aunt.

When Jade had arrived at the marae, she'd gone to the kitchen to avoid all the grief beside Sav's coffin. One woman had looked up but not into Jade's eyes and another had smiled meekly. It was then that the kuia patted a chopping board, hauled up a bag of spuds and said, 'I saved you a spot, girl.'

Jade found she belonged in the kitchen making the kai. And after sun had set and the sky had filled with stars, and smoke was drifting lightly into the night air like an incense cone from the hāngi pit, the kuia would set a plate for Jade beside her at a small wooden table close to the entrance to the marae kitchen and tell her to sit. She'd say a karakia mō te kai and tell Jade to eat all her mutton and earth-steamed vegetables and after that she'd pour cream over Jade's bowl of hot apple crumble.

'But I'm stuffed full,' Jade would say.

'Bit more. Āe. You must. Or how will you bear this kākahu whakatararatara?'

'What's that?' Jade asked.

'Can't you feel it? Can't you feel the heavy cloak of nettles on you now, girl?'

Jade couldn't. She could hardly feel a thing, just a throbbing in her tail bone. If she'd felt more, maybe she could wail too.

Early on the last morning of the tangi the kuia found Jade at the sink scrubbing potatoes. She stormed towards her, took Jade's arms fiercely and held them tight. She cried, 'Come on, girl, let it out.'

Jade closed her eyes and searched herself for the unshed tears. Then she remembered a story and told it to the kuia. It was about a road trip she once took with Sav – to a tangi they never got to. They'd put on a mix-tape Sav had made. REO Speedwagon's 'Keep on Loving You' was playing.

'Have this song at my funeral won't you, babe?' Sav said, her eyes on the coast as they drove.

'For who?'

'For Tommy.'

'Is Tommy singing the words, or you?'

'Tommy.'

'The funeral will be for us not *you*. When I die play "Peace Train", for you, from me.'

'And when I die, play *this!*' She shook a painted finger at the player. 'This heartbreaking song for me – from all the men that've ever loved me, to help them cry. So I can see. So I can see I existed. So I can see I was loved.'

'Stupid girl.'

'Watch the road,' she laughed. 'I wanna die old.'

Jade put her Cat Stevens cassette in the player and found 'Peace

Train'. So happy – the two of them – thinking about the good things.

'Call *me* stupid, you one stupid bitch, you were raised in the House, not a commune. Those commune hippies, we're lucky. I wouldn't trust them weirdos.'

They sang, their hair flapping as the wind blew in through the open window. They sped along the coast, and from a certain angle they knew they must have looked like other people with other lives.

'Ask him to come.'

'Who?'

'Tommy. Tell him when I die to come to my tangi. So I can see him cry.'

Jade put her hand on Sav's leg, 'Let's try and do a bit better than that – eh, babe? Let's try.'

'Yeah, let's try.' Sav tapped her foot to Jade's song, and when it was finished she put her mix-tape back in the cassette player and replayed 'Keep on Loving You'.

'This is more honest,' she said.

'Than what?' Jade asked.

'Than "Peace Train".'

'How's that?'

'Because, Jade, as long as there's love, there's never gonna be peace,' she tossed her black hair to one side. 'And really, love is the only thing we wanna dooooo.'

'I think you have mistaken love for other things – ' Jade started counting off her fingers held in the air '– money, fear, greed, hate.'

Sav shrugged, 'Whole lot of energy goes into getting our mack on, though. Recovering from the joys of love. So much useful energy. Play love is all we wanna do.'

When Jade finished telling the kuia the story, the kuia let go of Jade's arms and marched away from her. And Jade wanted to call her back and tell her she was sorry. Because all the waiata had been beautiful and Jade felt so forlorn. So numb and so dry inside and there were no tears to come. But she didn't call the kuia back, she just watched her leave the marae.

Jade was cleaning a bench when the kuia returned. She had a boom box in one hand and a brand new CD in the other. And she tore the plastic off the brand new CD: REO Speedwagon. She put it in the player, found the track and pressed play.

And Jade stared at her and she stared back at Jade, and when Jade didn't respond, she turned the music up louder. 'You cry, girl. I will not let you leave until you have. We will make the tangi go on forever if we must.'

Then the music was upon Jade and all the pain. She felt there must be something wrong with her that it had taken this Pākehā music to help her cry when all the beautiful waiata didn't. But when the song stopped the kuia played it again and she took Jade into her arms, and Jade howled into the old woman's soft neck and couldn't stop. The woman pressed her closer till her eye and her tail bone and whatever it was under the plaster on her neck throbbed terribly – and Jade was happy to feel the things she'd only seen when looking in a mirror, like they were illusions. The kuia played the song a third time and said: 'It's a perfect song for our Sav. It's a beautiful song.' And then the kuia sang it too. Sang it and wept.

The kuia scowled when the men in leather jackets and black sharkies arrived on motorbikes and in big gangster cars. But then she pinched Jade's arm and cackled. 'Sav'd love this. Oh, my little minx'd love this.'

Tattoos crawled out of clothes and onto necks and bled into the crevices of scarred faces. Hands, knuckles and shaved skulls. Up and onto chins, around mouths. Sav would have loved to see how many men were there, how they leaned over her coffin and kissed her cheek and wept for her.

Hash too.

And Tommy, his eyes covered by dark, dark glasses. Then Jade saw that boy from the beach. And he saw her. He came to her and he kissed her cheek. Then he kissed the kuia, and he handed her an envelope and said, 'Anei taku koha, ahakoa iti.'

And the kuia took it and hugged him. 'Māhea mai i tēnā.'

Jade went to the coffin before it was closed and knelt beside it and kissed Sav. She took her cold, stiff hand and sang quietly that she wanted to keep on loving her and she would forever and it was all she'd ever want to do. She wept and wept and hoped she'd be able to stop.

At the urupā Toko stood behind Jade as they lowered Sav's coffin into the ground, and he stepped up to stand beside her as the dirt was being thrown over it.

When the coffin was covered he touched Jade's hair and said, 'You want to come for a drive to Kaikōura?'

The kuia was standing close and she took Jade's hand and kissed it. 'If you don't, I will,' she laughed.

Jade left the tangi in the backseat of Toko's car. It smelled of bleach. Toko drove and Tommy sat in the passenger's seat. She struggled to breathe with the freedom blowing in her face through the window she'd opened. Then closed. It was like all the air she had ever missed was coming at her full force and her lungs couldn't take it. She could hardly believe she was just driving away, that she'd just got in a car and left, answering to no one. She touched the birds tattooed on her ribcage.

Sav had been with her the day she had them done because it was a birthday gift. Sav had stolen a wallet she saw in a car with its window down.

'It's a gift from the gods, not stealing, cuz,' she said. 'This was offered, because today is your birthday.'

It was one of those rare days that they had entirely to themselves.

'What do you want? Books? I know how you like those things.'

'No,' Jade said. They could be burned or ripped, pissed on.

'A necklace then?'

'No,' she said again. Could be stolen or sold, tightened around her neck.

'What then? A new pair of shoes?'

'To walk where?'

'Come on, girl. Think. Jeans, earrings, a mean feed?'

The mean feed appealed, but then she had an idea.

'A tattoo.' A tattoo, like a mean feed, could not be taken from her.

120

At the tattoo parlour she choose a bird. A bird in flight. Black, with a small white tuft at its throat. And a jewel! The bird should have a jewel, she decided. One of the jewels her father never had the chance to give her. One of the jewels he'd promised.

When the tattooist finished the bird, Jade loved the way it looked on her, raw and black, and she loved how the needle had burned and she didn't want to go home yet, so she asked to have two more. Sav pulled more birthday cash from her pocket. 'No mean feed then.'

And when he finished the two more she asked for two more. 'I want five,' she said.

'You can't afford five,' the tattooist said. He pulled his woollen beanie down a little, rubbed his hands together and folded his long arms. Jade saw the skulls etched into his knuckles then and wanted to be alone with her birds.

Sav walked over to him and touched his arm, pressed her body close, nuzzled her nose into his neck, took off his beanie, put it on her head.

'Hey,' he said and ran a hand through his curls.

'Come on, baby,' she said. 'Let my cousin have two more little birds. It's her birthday.'

And they went into a back room to have sex.

Jade could hear them, as she lay on the table waiting for the last two tūī to be inked into her side. As she waited she fingered away the tiny beads of blood rising to the surface of her fresh tattoos, and put them on her tongue.

Later that night at the House, Jade heard her cousin yelling at Hash, telling him she could do what the fuck she wanted when she wanted. Jade heard other sounds to the contrary. The next day Jade held Sav's hand, pressed a cold cloth against her swollen cheek. The tūī on Jade's ribcage throbbed. Throbbed like they'd been pressed into her wingless body, like they'd rather not be stuck on that skin.

Jade wandered Toko's small seaside house barefoot when they arrived. He brought in the single bag she had packed, though she had been tempted to leave it behind. She would never get the smell out, the smell of the House, and was sure she would be lucky to just get it out of her nose, her dreams. The smell of booze, cigarettes and pot. Vomit and urine, the metallic smell of blood. The metallic smell that made her wonder where the bullets and gun were kept. In a toy box? For playing gang?

She walked to his bedroom. His bed was unmade. The white sheets, pushed aside. He'd left in a hurry.

Jade sat on his bed and pressed her face into his sheets. She breathed in, and her whole body broke into something, something of a gallop, something of flight, but tethered by grief.

'Jade. What can I do? I don't even know you.'

Jade held her face where it was. 'Your sheets are beautiful,' she said.

She felt him sit on the bed. The way he smelled, like cloud and earth and soap, made her want him, but guilt welled in her heart, dousing it.

'What can I do?' He touched her shoulder.

'Can you throw out my stuff, get rid of it? The smell will get in here. In your house. Can you do that? And these.' She got up from the bed in a fury and undressed like a child would for the sea. She kicked the clothes away from her, and her swift movement caused pain that felt like pebbles and broken stones tearing up her spine.

He looked at her body, at the five birds with the tufts at their throats, in suspended flight up her ribcage. His pupils dilated.

'Please,' she said.

He picked up the clothes and walked out the door. From the window she saw him light the fire. She stood at his window watching the flames try to touch the stars, and she thought of a time when she had danced by a fire and Sav had been laughing somewhere close by and a blanket had been put over her shoulders.

She walked back to his bed, climbed between his sheets.

Ārama

Aunty Kat was taking me and Beth to town for school stuff. I told her we would need Duraseal, and she looked on the list and said it was an optional extra. Then she said we'd see.

She parked on the main street and we got out of the car. Outside the stationery shop there was a man with a shaven head and a long dark red outfit – sort of like a cape, but not. Sort of like a sheet. Like he was wearing sheets in the street.

'Would you like to buy a wonderful book?' he said, smiling at Aunty Kat. His skin was so warm and soft looking.

'Not today,' Aunty Kat said.

'What's it about?' Beth asked.

'World peace – how you can create world peace by creating it in your home.'

'How much is it?' Beth asked.

'Whatever you can afford or you'd like to give,' the man said. 'Preferably about five dollars to at least cover printing costs.'

Beth elbowed me. 'I reckon we could use a bit of world peace, huh, Django?'

I didn't have any pocket money this time round and so I didn't answer.

Beth looked at Aunty Kat. 'Can you buy it for us and we'll pay you back?'

'I would. I just don't have any change – or cash on me.'

The man reached into his pocket and whipped out a little thing that looked like a TV remote. 'You can pay with Eftpos.'

Beth clapped. Aunty Kat's face went a dull colour like a cloud had passed over and covered up the sun.

She rummaged in her handbag and started counting out coins. She

123

held a handful to him. He unzipped a bumbag and took the money and put it in. He handed the little book to Beth. 'Eternal blessings,' he said.

'Wow, look,' she held it out to me. The book was shiny and it had a picture of a sunset and a small boat and the people in it were rowing to an island with palm trees. They looked like they were escaping, which meant the world was probably not peaceful.

'Right,' Aunty Kat said as we walked away, 'I'm in charge now.'

'Eternal blessings,' Beth said.

We went to the stationery shop.

The Duraseal section was bigger than the last time. There were so many to choose from. I spotted one I'd had before with surfboards that Tauk had picked out for me.

I took a roll and ran back with it to Aunty Kat. She said it looked expensive and wanted to see the shelf it came from.

I took her to it and pointed – *$4.99*, the label said.

'Then sorry, but no.'

On the way home we stopped for dollar mixes, which Beth said she would definitely pay for this time. I didn't want to go into the dairy.

'Get me one, though, and check for two Eskimos at least,' I said.

I stayed in the car watching people walk by. Old ladies and old men. Mums. Dads. Families.

A little boy dropped his ice cream on the footpath when he came out of the dairy, and he started crying. A dog walked by, stopped to sniff the ice cream on the ground, licked it and snaffled it up. The little boy tried to kick the dog and fell over. I hadn't laughed when the boy dropped his ice cream because I felt sad for him, but by the time he got himself round to kicking the dog and landing on his butt I couldn't help myself. The little boy's mummy saw me laughing and gave me a mean look through the window, then she picked the kid up and stormed off with him as he went at her with his tiny fist. Why didn't she just go and buy the poor little guy another ice cream?

Aunty Kat and Beth were taking a long time in the dairy, but I was cool with watching all the people walk up and down the streets, in and out of shops, and my window was cracked down enough that I could hear people's voices. I heard bits of things. *Mashed potato and sausages for ... Do we need milk? No. What about bread? Did you take the dog ...*

Then I heard a voice that I thought I knew.

It sounded like Taukiri. I sat up quick in my seat and looked out the window. But I couldn't see him. I got out of the car and climbed up to stand on the car bonnet and get a better look. Turning into the park, over the street, there was a dude in a green hoodie carrying a guitar.

Could be, but I needed to get closer.

I jumped down from the car and ran over the road. A car screeched to stop for me. I didn't look, I kept running. I ran into a lady who batted me with her handbag and grumbled something. I didn't look. I kept running. The hoodie guy went into the park. There were a lot of trees and I couldn't decide if I should turn left or right. I turned left, which brought me to a bridge crowded with people throwing bread to the ducks. I zigzagged, under and through them all, elbowing and pushing when I needed to. I heard the sound of music being played. Guitar. I ran up a small path to follow the music.

My running was too loud. I couldn't hear. I started to walk.

The music was coming between so many other things now – ducks quacking, people talking, kids laughing, babies crying – that I lost where it was coming from. I stopped and closed my eyes. I heard it again. I opened my eyes and walked towards it. It got louder. My hands were shaking quite bad and I had a funny feeling in my tummy. When I turned the next corner I saw a group of older kids sitting together playing instruments. There were a lot of them. Some were smoking, some were lying in the grass. Two, sitting beside each other, had drums. A girl was singing. Three more were playing hackey.

Then I saw the green-hoodie guy, hunched over a guitar, with his back to me. I ran towards him. Ran like I never had before. Don't know why, but I started yelling Taukiri's name. My tummy was telling me I was right. The excited feeling in it was telling me I was right.

My brother had come here to get me but we hadn't been home. We had been in town buying books and here he was now and luckily I saw him in town because he might have left altogether thinking I was gone and it was so lucky I had found him and he would be so happy.

As I was running I yelled his name again but he didn't look up from his guitar. Tripping on my own feet I flew right into his back with a thud, his name flying out of my mouth. He turned and looked down at me. Everyone was quiet. Staring.

He had bum fluff and brown eyes. Pimples.

'Ouch, punk,' he said. 'Watch where you going. Shit.'

He rubbed his back, frowned at me. One of the boys who had been playing the drum stood up and gave me his hand to help me stand.

'Who's Taukiri, little dude? You lost?'

I shook my head.

'You okay?'

I looked down at my hands.

'You here with someone?'

Kept looking down at my hands. Everyone was quiet.

Walked away, looked back though. Saw drum boy hit green-hoodie guy on the back of his head.

'Hey. What's that for?'

'Being a dick. Just play, egg.'

The music started again. Drum boy was good, and nice, like Taukiri. Green-hoodie guy was shit on guitar. Taukiri was way better.

At the car Aunty Kat was looking around and stopping people walking by. 'Have you seen a boy wearing a …' Then she spotted me across the street, and she ran and hugged me real tight. It was the best hug she'd ever given me. Then she yelled. And that felt good too. I didn't say anything, just let her carry on at me with her arm around my shoulders as she crossed the road. Holding me like I was a little bit special.

I gave Beth one of my Eskimos for the ride back to the farm.

Sometimes the excited feeling in my stomach is right, like it was with that bird Taukiri made me pray for.

Tauk put me in charge of getting the box. 'A shoebox, or something.'

I found Mum. 'Tauk needs another box for another bird.'

'He must raid nests, the number of birds he's found.'

'And killed.'

Mum turned to me shocked then. 'He doesn't kill them. They die.'
She opened a cupboard, searched the shelves. No shoebox.

I remembered the chocolate box I gave Taukiri once. It had pictures
of stuff Taukiri liked glued to it. Waves and sun and me and him
hanging out.

I took it out to him.

'Perfect.'

He wanted to leave the golden foil in, because birds were used to
living high up close to the sun and might like the shiny foil. We put
bits of hay, old grass and weeds into the box.

'I have a good feeling,' he said.

The pink bird looked pretty much dead in its new home.

Taukiri fed it with a dripper at first, then after a week – the longest
he had ever kept one of our baby birds alive – he said to me, 'Needs
real food now.'

He took a yoghurt pottle outside and came back with it filled with
worms and other crawling things.

'You know what a mummy bird does?' he asked. I shook my head.

'A mummy bird would eat all this,' he lifted the pottle, 'and then
spew it back up, into the baby's mouth.'

'Really?' My mouth was already open wide, even before he lifted
the worm and dangled it over his mouth, looking at me out the corner
of his eye.

'No. No. Please. No.'

He closed his eyes, 'Sorry. Sorry. Don't look.'

'No. Don't do it.'

He lowered the worm to his mouth.

Then laughing, dropped it on the counter, picked up a knife, 'Look
away if you want.'

I didn't.

He lifted the pottle and shook out two little spiders, a worm, a
moth and a caterpillar. Before they could get away he slammed the
knife down flat on them then started chopping. He stuffed the bits
through the little holes in Mum's garlic presser. The caterpillar and
worm oozed through. He shook the oozy bits – the crunchy bits stuck
in the presser – and they oozed out onto a milk-bottle lid.

I spat into it. 'Might help,' I said.

Taukiri sang to the little bird. Just sang and sang. Every song I'd ever heard him sing or heard on the radio all mashed together like worms and spiders and bugs. The song about Alice, the one about gypsies, the rainbow one, waiata and Bob Marley ones, Justin Bieber and Tupac and 'Jingle Bells' and campfire songs.

The little bird opened its mouth. 'Ha, look at that,' Tauk said. 'It worked.'

Tauk built a sort of cage so that the bird was a bit safer in the chocolate box, but he left the top open, which I said was a dumb idea, and I was right. One day I took up the squashed-up worms and spiders for breakfast, and it was gone.

Today, I felt that buzz, like I was right about something.

About green-hoodie guy being Taukiri, and that things were really going to get suddenly better. Better big-time. Maybe better big-time was still on its way.

Mum had put the chocolate box into the rubbish. I found it. I took it out, laid it on my window to get sun. I sprayed it with Mum's perfume. The smell of hay and bird didn't come out, though, and the pictures had gone blotchy in places. I glued new photos of me and him on the top and under the lid. More waves. More sun. A picture of a tūī from a *National Geographic*.

'I saved it from the rubbish,' I said to Taukiri when I gave it back.

'Thank you, my man.' He held the box up. 'Wow,' he said.

Taukiri

I moved into Megan's attic and spent more time with her than I did with Elliot. Moving in meant I slept there and put my surfboard into the attic because I was pretty sure it was going to snap on my car roof soon. I'd drive over a judder bar and it'd just snap. So dry that it'd just snap like a wishbone left on a windowsill for a good couple of weeks.

Plus I was sick of the comments from people like, 'Drives round with the board on his roof but doesn't even surf. Legend.'

Me and Megan were sitting on her porch. I was smoking one of Megan's darts and I asked her, 'Can you show me a picture you've taken for work?'

'No,' she held out her hand, two fingers loosely parted, and I handed her the ciggy, 'I shouldn't.'

A plane was coming into the airport. We didn't talk over the roar, just watched. After it landed and it was quiet again she took out her phone.

'There's this,' she held it out to me, 'I had to take it with my phone when my camera was playing up.'

I looked at the photo. It was the bonnet of a car, squashed up like a paper ball.

'They survived,' she said. 'Jessie called again today. Left a message. She's added you on Snapchat, wants you to add her back.'

'I lost my phone.'

'I don't care.'

'Of course you do,' I smirked.

She didn't smile back. 'What're you going to do, Tauk?'

'Stay here, smoke all your darts. Talk to you when you free for me. Sell my board.'

She looked at her watch. 'I have to go back to work.' She stood and brushed her hands up and down her black trousers. She untied her hair, pulled it back tight, then retied it. She wasn't wearing any make-up. I looked at the freckle on her eyelid.

'If I had my phone, I'd take a photo of that,' I said.

'What?'

'That freckle. I want to have it,' I said.

'Sorry. It's mine.'

'Bring me back a picture. From work.'

'Nope. See ya. Go find a job, loser.'

She walked off. I heard her car start and drive away. The sun was beating down on me. I looked at it, then into it, and it burned my eyes and I closed them and there was Megan's freckle. Then lots of them, like a kaleidoscope.

When I went inside I saw Megan had left a note beside the phone: *Call Jessie you wanker!*

I picked up the phone and dialled Aunty Kat's number. After a few rings Uncle Stu answered with a grunt. I almost asked for Ari, then didn't. I hung up, walked out Megan's door. Drove off in my car. Because I could. I could just do whatever I wanted, whenever. And I enjoyed that, but still wanted to push against something, some boundary, and have it push back, or at the very least hold its ground. Like, as a kid, pushing on a wiggly tooth, you want it to fall out, but you're not sure if you want it to under your own pressing. Better an apple, better a string attached to a slamming door, better anything. Anything, but you, yourself.

I wanted someone to say, *Hey, Tauk, sort your shit out.*

Come here.

Do that.

Don't smoke.

Walk the line.

I liked that Megan told me to make a phone call, even if it was to the wrong person.

Tonight I could just go and buy myself some beers. I probably would. Or even some cheap top shelf, get myself shit-faced, like other boys my age were. Only the other boys my age could do dumb shit fearlessly. They knew there was a bottom to their fall. That if they

130

really messed up, someone would probably notice and stop them. The bottomlessness to my life was dizzying. The choices were as overwhelming as that terrible sea was.

Toothbrushes.

What time I should fucking go to bed.

Call Ari?

Look for my mum? Forget her?

Drink?

Just a few beers? Maybe a line of coke? Smoke some weed? Pop an E?

Decisions, decisions. I've made some shitty ones, shitty ones with terrible outcomes. Hard to completely regret though.

For example, that one when it was a terrible stormy night and Nanny came for dinner.

Nanny was here for dinner. She was wearing her favourite pearl clip-on earrings. Ari had asked about them. *Again.* I stopped myself from rolling my eyes.

'Why don't they stick through your ears like Mum's?'

'They're old-fashioned, like me,' she sipped her wine. 'From a time when it was uncivilised to put holes in your body.'

I wanted to gag. 'But your ears *are* pierced,' I said.

Nanny shot me an icy look. 'These are very special,' she turned back to Ari. 'My māmā gave them to me – your great-nanny. She was given them by a Scottish sailor.'

I stood up, took mine and Ari's plates to the sink. Mum patted my back and lowered her voice. 'Sit down, listen to your nanny's story. It means a lot to her. I'll do the dishes.'

'Lucky you.'

I walked to the table and slumped back in my chair.

Nanny put her hand on Ari's. Like she was about to tell the story just to him anyway. 'The Scottish sailor came to Aotearoa on a big ship,' she said. 'He had with him just a few coins, a change or two of clothes, and his late mother's pearl earrings.'

'Why was his mother late?'

131

Nanny took in a big breath.

I sat up, thought I could help. 'Dead, Ari,' I said, 'she was dead.'

He frowned. 'Oh, that's sad.'

Nanny squeezed Ari's hand. 'It is,' she said, 'but listen, this is a happy tale. One day the sailor was walking along the beach at Halfmoon Bay when he heard a woman singing a song. He could not understand the words but he knew it was a happy song.'

'She was singing in te reo Māori eh?'

'Āe, my moko.'

'What was she singing again?'

'She was singing a waiata that made him smile, because it was not pōuri – it was not very beautiful either – but it was bouncy and the woman was laughing as she sang it to herself. The Scotsman walked up the beach to her and said, "What is it you're singing that's making you laugh, woman?"

'She said it was a secret. And if she told him, he might get angry. She didn't trust his funny accent and, for all she knew, he could have been a Nazi.'

'What's that?'

'Ūpoko mārō.' She touched her earring then. 'And a coward.'

I wasn't sure why, but I liked Nanny very much at that moment, her expression had softened, she was holding the earring, and then she looked at me and smiled.

'A poaka,' I said, grinning back at her.

'A poaka,' and then she touched my hand like she'd touched Ari's. 'The Scotsman pleaded with the woman. "My curiosity will kill me, I need to know what has made you laugh here, singing to yourself by the sea." Your great-nanny trusted him and she didn't know why, but she told him: "A school in the north has been singing this song. My cousin wrote to me and told me about it. It's called 'Hītara Waha Huka, Ūpoko Mārō'." And the woman – my māmā, your great-nanny – started to sing it again, and she laughed louder and louder. "We could sing it to his face and he wouldn't even know!" she exclaimed to the Scotsman.

'She walked to him and stood very close, so their arms touched, and she leaned down and said into his ear, "It's about Adolf Hitler."

And then she began to sing the words about the pig-headed Hitler foaming at the mouth. "The song says we'll break his jaw, the bloody bugger, and that his buttocks are shaking with fear." The Scotsman urged her to tell him more still, so she did.

"'They are singing a softer version of this song at a hui, for the community," she said, "but in the playground the children put the mean words back in and the teachers are pretending they don't hear. These Nazis are like an animal pack, their gangster symbols on their skinny arms."

"'Sing it to me again," said the Scotsman. And your great-nanny did, and he danced, stomped his feet, slapped his thighs, skipping around her. When she stopped singing he drew the pearl earrings from his pocket and told her to try them on, and when he saw they looked perfect on her –' Nanny touched them again on her own ears '– these freshwater pearls that once upon a long time ago even Julius Caesar admired, invading countries to get them, the Scotsman, your great-koro, knew he was deeply in love and would be forever.'

Nanny broke into a roar of laughter. 'That's all it took to make that silly Scotsman fall in love with my māmā. And so here we all are.' Then her face fell dark like the night. 'I never met him. I only have stories. And my earrings.'

She clapped her hands together. 'Kia ora, my mokopuna, for listening to an old kuia prattle on. Āe. Give me a kihi.'

Ari went to her first. I stood back.

'Haere mai, tama.' She waved me close, pressed me to her chest, kissed my cheek. 'Pō mārie.'

I went to bed deeply in love with my nanny.

Later, I heard her speaking, but by then her voice was syrupy. 'He wouldn't've wanted *this*. He would've wanted his wife, his son's mother, to've stayed. I always knew she was no good for him. If it hadn't been for her.'

'Not this shit again.'

'I lost my son. Don't forget that. You've no idea.'

'I lost my brother. But I have Tauk – we have Tauk.'

They stopped talking. Running water, the clatter of plates. Nanny sniffed, then softer: 'It hurts. When I look at him, I see her.' Voice

133

wetter, and she mumbled something, and maybe if I'd heard what it was I wouldn't have left. Because maybe it was nothing. But it felt like it was something. Something hurtful.

'I'll drive you home,' Mum said.

My face was white-hot and my hands shook. My leg bounced up and down without my wanting it to. I heard them leave.

I went downstairs. Nanny had left half a glass of wine on the table. I sipped it. It was thick and sweet and yuck. It went somewhere and did something I couldn't pinpoint. I sculled the rest.

I go back upstairs and to my room. The lamp gives a muted light, making my bedroom seem cosy, the sound of the rain drumming hard on the roof. I pick up my guitar, sit on my bed and strum it, but there's no one around to hear me so what's the point. I find my phone and lie back on the bed.

Sandra's sent me a Snapchat. A picture of her tits. Pressed together. Her nipples are dark and hard.

She writes then: Your turn.

The sound of the rain ceases, like the cloud it's come from has hit the off button.

Instead of sending a dick-pic, I write: Meet me at the skatepark?

There in ten, she replies.

I go downstairs and load up my backpack with dad's beer and go out the door.

We meet at the skatepark. Other kids from school are there. It's cold but she's wearing a loose wraparound skirt and a low-cut green singlet. She has gold hoops in her uncivilised ears and her lips shine.

We pretend we aren't there to meet each other, and mix in with the others. Some are sitting on the edge of the half-pipe. Legs dangling, smoking darts.

We sit on the ramp and I take out a can of beer and hold it to her.

'I only drink gin, sometimes vodka,' she says, then takes the can.

Someone passes us a joint, and I take a deep drag on it, hold it in until it burns my lungs. My head lightens, and Nanny and all her shit is not a thing. Not a thing at all and never will be again.

The smoke feels so good in my blood. We lie back on the cold wooden skate ramp, slick with rain, and look up at the clouds moving, exposing bright, starry patches of sky.

'It's wet,' I say.

'Who cares,' Sandra says.

I take her hand, she lifts it and slides one of my fingers between her tits. The goose pimples on her flesh are hard, pulling her skin taut.

Sandra rolls onto her side, faces me. She leans close and says something, something I can't hear, blood hammering in my head. Something like, 'Come.' And she laughs too loud and says, 'Come with me, Taukiri.' She giggles as we stand, 'Come with me, Taukiri. That rhymes.'

Police sirens cut the night, but I have no blood left anywhere but my dick now, so I don't care. Hardly listen.

Behind the skateboard ramp is a bench. Sandra nudges me into it, lifts her skirt and puts a knee either side of my thighs. She kisses me and takes my hand and puts my fingers, like they are not mine they are hers, oh my god, into her underwear. She's wet like a dark and stormy night, and she takes my hand out and presses my fingers into my mouth.

'Taste that,' she says.

She unbuttons my trousers, takes something out from the waist of her skirt. I hear the sound of foil ripping. She spits into her hand, takes my dick, and she's putting the condom on, and should I watch?

I watch and watch.

And, fuck, she's standing then, taking off her underwear, and the cloud hits the on button and rain hammers down on us.

She is on me like a wave and oh my god there's nothing else. Oh my god there's just her just her just her, her face wet with rain now, my face wet with rain now, rain and her hands in my hair, running down my neck and just her, just her and the warm smell of pot and beer moving quickly, quickly in and out of our open mouths.

Mum, Dad and Ari were at the table when I got home. Ari had a blanket around his shoulders and was drinking Milo. His face was red and blotchy. Mum's too.

Dad stood up. 'You left your brother at home alone. We've looked everywhere for you.'

Ari cried. 'Sorry, Taukiri. I was scared and I called Nanny. I'm sorry. I'm so sorry. She's really mad.'

Jade and Toko

Though she'd woken in his bed every morning for a month, Jade still had to blink and blink and blink again until she believed it. She was certain one morning she'd wake to the dank colours of the House. On one hand that would mean Sav would be sleeping just a few doors down a dark hall, and Jade would be able to see her cousin again. But on the other hand they'd have still been two women dying.

Two sides to every coin.

Jade spent her first moments awake every morning doing three things. First, she convinced herself she was really there in Toko's bed. Second, she wished Sav was a drive away in Tommy's. Third, she listened to the sea.

The sound of the sea told her what day awaited her outside. When Jade heard a soft roar she imagined white cloud blanketing everything. From the mountain tops to the sea. Those days where the whole world seemed under soft cotton she felt the safest. Other days she heard almost nothing, just a quiet sound like a muted shell at her ear and she knew the sea would be its best. Blue and green and placid.

Today it sounded like they were covered by cloud.

Toko was beside her, sound asleep. She reached out and touched his warm body with her index finger, slowly tracing the long muscle running up his spine, to the nape of his neck and into his thick black hair. He stirred, rolled over and wrapped his arms, still heavy with sleep, around her. She almost felt perfect in them. In his lovely sheets and warm blankets.

She closed her eyes, slept, dreamed he hit her and he was sorry and said, 'Oh baby, you so hurt,' and he kissed her where he'd hit her. But then he hit her in her leg, harder this time.

She woke wet, wanting him.

Toko was no longer in the bed. He was taking things from his wardrobe and putting them into a suitcase. Jade sat up.

'Leaving me?'

He put down a T-shirt and over to her.

'Dad bought a new boat. It's docked down in Rakiura. I have to go with him to bring it home.'

'How?'

'Up the coast. Try her out. I packed some things for you – you can come. Have you ever been on a boat before?'

Jade remembered a ferry ride she had been on with Coon. And the ferry trips she had taken with Sav to attend funerals that they never got to. Their bags were always spiked with drugs. Even when Jade went with Sav, Sav would at least make sure she took some of Hash's business along with her, making him all good with her going. Jade spent ferry trips biting her nails to the flesh.

'No,' she lied.

'You'll love it.'

They picked up Toko's dad from the family home. He was at the door when they arrived, wearing a checkered shirt and jeans. He had a small duffel bag in his hand.

'Aha. Now it makes sense,' he said. He took Jade's hand. 'I'm Hēnare.'

Jade heard herself say something ridiculous like, 'Well, I can see where Toko gets his good looks from.' She immediately hated herself for pretending to be another sort of person.

Toko opened the car door, 'Jade's never been on a boat, Dad.'

The ferry rides. She lowered her eyes, wished the thought away.

She'd boarded the ferry once with a ticket Sav had pick-pocketed money to buy. And here she was saying things like: *Well, I can see where Toko gets his good looks from*. She made herself nauseous. She had no idea who she was. And neither did Toko.

'Never been on a boat! Really? Let's hope she finds her sea legs then.' Hēnare slapped his son's shoulder lightly and swung the duffel bag into the open boot.

A woman came out of the house, she had a plastic container in one arm and a bag in the other.

'Hello.'

She offloaded the container and bags to Hēnare, and went to Jade.

'I'm Colleen,' she said, and they hugged. Colleen took Jade by the shoulders and held her at arm's length. 'Lucky I put extra pata in the sandwiches.'

'Nice to meet you, Colleen.'

Nice to meet you, Colleen.

'Āe, and at last. We knew.' And she took her son in her arms.

'Hahaha,' Jade laughed.

Hahaha!

'Be safe, you hear. Thank you for going with your dad, Toko.'

'Of course, Mum. Jade has never been on a boat before.'

'Well … I was on the ferry, now I remember. Once or twice. Can't believe that slipped my mind.'

Can't believe that slipped my mind.

Colleen put a hand on her shoulder. 'So, you've never been on a boat then.'

'I suppose not.'

It was a long drive to Invercargill in the rental car, and from there they took a catamaran ferry to Rakiura. Hēnare, Toko and Jade all took turns driving but they still needed to spend a night on the way. They stopped at a small town and found a hotel. They went for dinner in a restaurant. Jade ordered mussel chowder, which was served with warm buttered bread. Hēnare said she would love Colleen's seafood chowder and Toko must bring her for dinner soon.

'That would be lovely,' said Jade.

She let herself talk nicely. In neat rounded words. 'That would be lovely,' she said again. And wanted to say it once more but didn't.

Back at the hotel, Jade busied herself. She picked up the pen with the hotel name printed on it and ran her fingers over the tea bags. Tea bags lined up in neat rows like sea-eye winkles. Ready for guests.

To make cups and cups of tea.

Toko watched her.

'Would you like a cup of tea?' she asked him. He smiled and shook his head. She flicked through the hotel information folder: 'Gosh, how much does it cost to stay here?' And then she realised what she'd done, questioning him like that.

No questions asked, shut the actual fuck up, box and lock.

Embarrassed, she stood quickly and elbowed a teacup from the bench. It smashed on the floor and she snapped her head up, eyes wide to Toko.

'Shall I see if there's a dustpan and brush somewhere?' he asked.

A horrible feeling come over her, that he might not really love her at all.

She told him no, she'd clean it up, and he seemed not to care either way, and she pretended the room hadn't turned to quicksand in wake of the revelation that she could move about freely in the world, question things and elbow things, break them, smash them, and want answers.

Toko wouldn't pounce to tuck her wings in for her.

He lay back on the bed. His feet touched the floor.

'What now?' she asked.

'Come here.'

It was a relief to be told what to do so she went to him.

He ran his hands under her T-shirt.

'You know what else?' she said. 'Apart from never having been on a boat before, I had never eaten in a restaurant before, until tonight. Or slept in a hotel.'

'First time for everything,' he took his hands out from her top and put them under his head, revealing the muscle on the underside of his arm.

She took off her T-shirt for him. It was one he had given her after she'd asked him to burn all her clothes. She had spent a few days after that either naked or shuffling about in his oversized shirts, until he arrived home one day with a small bag from his sister and a few things he'd bought from a store. Underwear, two T-shirts and a pair of jeans. All of them, except a soft cotton bra and packet of cotton underwear, were an ill fit, but she wore them anyway. Loved them.

Having clothes bought for her – that was something she saw happen to a woman in a movie once.

Sleeping in a hotel too.

Feeling pretty too.

She was glad the clothes only kind of fitted her, and that some of them had been worn before. She was glad to see a slight tear in the wallpaper of the hotel room. She was glad that the table to make tea was also the place for a phone and a writing pad. And was so close to the bed she'd knocked her knee on it twice already. Glad for the smashed crockery. Only she wished his nostrils had flared a little.

Jade ran her finger along the hemline of Toko's T-shirt until he sat up and lifted his arms and let her take it off. He wrapped his bare arms around her naked upper body. Her breasts pressed against his chest. The birds tattooed up her ribcage looked as if they were taking flight into the inky wave of his tā moko.

They kissed.

Coon had kissed her too. The night he found her at the bus station, and told her she should come with him, back to her home and he would keep her safe. He had kissed her. Her first kiss.

He had looked at her with a soft expression, head cocked. And she had thought that might be the real him, that maybe under everything else: the patched leather jacket, the drugs and even his eyes, the coldness of them, maybe none of that was him. With only almost enough money to get a bus she had decided to go back home, back to the House. She could leave another day, when she had enough money and a desire for something more than just a warm bed within familiar walls.

Back at the House he'd moved into the room she had once shared with her mother and father. The partition that Head had built for Jade had been smashed down. Otherwise he had kept everything. Even Head's and Felicity's blankets, even the red bed sheet now faded to pink. A rush of blood hit Jade smack in her head, dazing her. She couldn't take her eyes off the messy bedding, like a child's imaginary shipwreck.

Coon had shut the door behind them. 'Bed looks good, huh? I always knew behind that sweet face ...'

In the closed room she could smell him, nights of sleep unwashed from his skin and clothes. She heard his heavy leather jacket hit the floor behind her.

He put his hand on her shoulder, and she turned around.

At the train station he'd sat so she was on his good side, and the open air had swept away the smell of him.

'Maybe you go soon, maybe later. Let's see.'

Now she was on another island and the House seemed like it might never have been real, and Coon was locked away. Toko was kissing her in a hotel room. She could still smell this morning's shower in his hair, wine on his breath.

He was clear-eyed. Didn't look sleep-deprived. Love-deprived. Milk-deprived. He was brimful with the good stuff. His skin was bright with life and rough from work. She didn't mind that he stood up, lifting her as her thighs tightened around his hips.

He leaned and pressed play on a CD player he'd brought along especially for moments like this, when his hands were too busy to strum her a song. *Lie la lie, lie la la la lie lie … Lie la lie, lie la la la la lie la la lie.*

He kissed her hard, before throwing her down on the bed and removing her second-hand jeans without asking. And she didn't mind that she couldn't fight him off, because she'd never want to.

SONG

If only the boats that sailed, night and day to find these islands, had been filled with guitars instead of guns. Tambourines instead of opioids. More triangles, fewer Bibles.

See this: my twin brother, Toko, just a boy, finding birds fallen from their nests and trying to give them a chance to survive. He put them in shoeboxes and fed them from little drippers. Fed them cut-up worms or cat food with tweezers. More often than not they survived. It was his superpower.

Then it was Taukiri. The first time my brother's son came home, a bird in his hand, I wanted to send him back, stop him, say: 'Leave things be, Tauk.' He walked in the door and looked up at me. I saw his eyes bright, like his father's, with hope. And how could I stop that impulse, that desire?

I worried because Toko didn't stop at birds. There were stray dogs and stray kids and stray women with empty bellies too.

Toko introduced Kat to Stu. The farm boy, who always came to school with blue rings around his eyes and looked at Toko's lunch with envy. Looked at Toko's life with envy.

Toko's most loved guitar was trash.

He found it at the dump in a pile of black rubbish bags, a seagull perched on it.

I was sitting beside him in the backseat of Dad's car, and Toko had wound the window down and the smell outside had hit us in our faces.

'Dad,' he said, 'look.'

'What?'

'Wind up the window.' I held my nose. 'God, it stinks.'

'No, Aroha, look! Dad! Look. There!' Toko was pointing out the window, his eyes going back and forth from Hēnare's face to the guitar, back to mine, to see if we saw it too. When he saw we didn't, Toko opened the door and jumped out of the car, scrambling up and into the rubbish.

Dad yelled for him to get back in the car: 'Get out, Toko. It's dangerous. Come down now!'

But Toko went up and up. The squawk of seagulls was all around.

Toko grabbed the guitar.

He lifted it over his head. Dad banged on the horn.

It only needed two new strings. The scratches were superficial. He'd been given a new guitar only a year before, on our tenth birthday. We were given one each. But that guitar he'd saved from being pressed with tin cans and milk cartons, mouldy bread, bananas and bones – that guitar, which he restored with his own young fingers, became his first love, and when he rested it beside the flawless store-bought instrument, which had needed not a thing of him, he saw more clearly its beauty. Enjoyed it more. My brother was often wrong, but he never stopped looking for good where others wouldn't. And he loved damage. Adored it.

Taukiri

I strummed the scratched-up guitar Mum gave me.

People were dancing.

I opened my mouth.

I sang.

Elliot was tapping his foot beside me.

He howled: 'WOOOOHOOOOO.'

Everyone was looking, like Elliot was, at me. This moment was the only unscrewed-up piece of my life. Outside of here, people were dead and gone.

Disappeared abandoners.

The car crash was somewhere out there, and the wave which ripped us away from shallow water, like cold fingers. That too, continued. Somewhere it still rolled and ripped. And out there, was the unknown. Ari every age from then until forever, and how much of him would be good. How much bad. And of the badness, how much would be because I'd left him. But I was singing and strumming. And none of that was important.

It was drop-in-the-ocean small.

Felt no guilt for leaving Ari.

Had zero fucks left to give.

Used my pain to help me busk on Cuba Street. It was all that mattered.

It was good to have a beer with everyone at the pub afterwards.

Megan went to the bar for drinks. She brought them back on a tray then handed them out. Jason, Elliot, and then me. The cold wet glass felt good on my fingers. She took her phone out of her pocket.

'I have a picture to show you.' And she came close and tucked in beside me, almost in the crook of my arm.

'Oi,' Jason said, 'bit close, you two.'

'Just showing Tauk that crack-up meme you sent me,' she said.

'Oh, yeah. That's a goodie. Don't let Elliot see, he's all woke and easily offended.'

I looked down at the phone. The picture was of a woman. Her face was clear white and matt, like a hotel sheet, her eyes blue like faded denim. Her lip was swollen and there was a gaping cut in it. A welt on her head, shone like a purple water balloon, too full, bursting.

Megan elbowed my rib and whispered, 'You should laugh.' Then louder she said, 'Funny eh?'

Megan was standing close enough to me that I could smell moisturiser on her skin. I was looking at the cut lip and shining welt on the woman, and I felt the hairs on Megan's arm brush against mine and the tingling of them got me hard.

Jason was looking for my reaction to his meme, so I gave a little chuckle, still looking at the girl's split lip. 'Crack up. Good one,' I said.

'Funny-as eh?' he said.

'Real funny,' I said, still looking at the picture.

Megan went over to Jason. 'Where do you get them?' And she kissed his forehead.

'Just find them,' he said, like he was being humble but it was him who'd created it.

Jason went to the toilet and I asked Megan to show me the picture again. It was startling, the blood, the flesh inside her lip, the terrible paleness of her cloth-white skin, the welt shining like the skin had expanded as far as it could.

'That's why I don't wear make-up to work. What sort of a bitch I'd be rocking up with my foundation and lippy on.'

'What's her name?'

'I shouldn't tell you – but it's May.'

'Won't you get in trouble for taking this with your phone?'

'I'm trusted. I've never done anything to lose that. Before.'

'Boyfriend?'

'In court tomorrow.'

When Jason came back from the bathroom he and Megan left. Jason had some important shit to do, he said, and Megan was tired. Elliot was dancing with a girl, so I left and took a walk through the city. There was the smell of frying meat and onions. Windows were lit up but doors locked. A block away I heard the sound of glass breaking. Laughter. And then the pound of feet on the pavement.

Pounding feet. Feet pounding, running. I'd run home that dark night when Ari was home on his own.

While I am at the skateboard ramp Ari wakes from a bad dream. He goes to crawl into my bed, but I'm not there. Neither are Mum and Dad. Scared, he calls Nanny. She has been drinking, but still, she will go out again on a stormy night for Ārama. She will leave her and Koro's cosy seaside bungalow at Gore Bay and she'll be there in a flash.

Koro argues, tells Nanny that Mum is already on her way. No need to go out on a stormy night, but she insists. 'What if she doesn't go right home?'

'But you know she is,' says Koro. 'You just want to rub it in, woman.'

'No, Hēnare, I don't.'

She picks up the car keys and goes out and the rain starts again. Heavy, heavy rain as if Ranginui is crying for Papatūānuku.

The rain lashes at the car windscreen. Nanny is driving faster than she should on that twisting, narrow road. She wants to get to our house before everything sorts itself out. Or at least that's the version I tell myself. That she is pleased to be proved right. *He's trouble.* She wants to get there at the most climactic moment to say I told you so.

Her wheel hits a rock. She swerves off the road, crashes into a ditch. Not bad, she's a bit shaken. A fright, that's all. No harm done.

She isn't far from home, not really, and if she waits – well, she drank more than she should have and maybe she should've stayed home. If the police do arrive they might find she shouldn't have been driving in the first place.

So she walks in the rain and the cold and the dark. She trips on a rock, falls, but again, no harm done. Hurts her old knees, but she's tough. She dusts dirt from her trousers, brushes her hands against each other. A little blood, nothing a plaster won't fix. Just a scratch. This is what she tells Mum on the phone when she gets home, and Mum tells it to Dad and Koro.

But that's before she goes to the bathroom.

She calls Mum after she does, hysterical.

Because when she goes to wash her hands she looks in the mirror and realises something terrible *has* happened.

She gasps.

She reaches and touches the place where one of the earrings should be. For there is just flesh there now, a fleshy lobe. She pulls off the other earring, stares and stares at it in her scratched palm. A nothing now. Garbage. Because what's an earring without the other? And that, I imagine, was about the time she decided I was an actual curse on her family.

There are stories that need props and stories that need voids. As a kid, whenever Ari asked Koro to tell us the story about the how he lost his leg, he started many ways, like, 'If I'd known that octopus would fight back I never would've picked one.'

Koro's best story needed a void.

Nanny started her stories many ways too, like, 'Can I trust you – you're not a Nazi?'

Nanny's best story needed a prop.

Nanny hasn't told the story of her Māori mother and Scottish father falling in love on a beach at Rakiura since she lost that precious pearl clip-on on the road and never found it, although we looked and looked until all we could see were pearls everywhere trampled under our feet.

Ārama

Tomorrow the school bus would come and pick me and Beth up and take us to school. I wouldn't sleep tonight, and Beth neither. It would be harder for her. She reckoned classrooms were like boxes. Made her want out.

The lady who'd talked to Tom Aiken at the café, who'd helped find out about us getting a bus for school, came to visit today. To wish us good luck. She had pressies for us. Beth got a packet of rubbers which looked and smelled like strawberries. Plus a new yellow lunchbox and matching drink bottle with strawberries on them. I got rubbers shaped like rugby balls, and an All Blacks lunchbox and drink bottle. They were pretty cool. I was happier about mine than Beth was about hers. She was a bit grumpy when she said thank you and didn't try and impress the lady with funny stories and jokes, which was not really like Beth.

Back at home this afternoon, I put my All Blacks lunchbox on the kitchen bench. I opened it up so Aunty Kat would remember to fill it up for me for tomorrow. I went upstairs and packed the other things into my bag, and hoped this wouldn't turn out to be another bad story beginning with me packing my bag, like the last two times. I put in my Durasealed books. Clear, but with cut-outs from some surfing magazines Tom Aiken had found for me.

I packed my new rugby ball rubbers too. Right down deep into the bag I stuffed my toy lion. Then I zipped up my bag.

Without really thinking about it, I put my hands together and closed my eyes tight, and I said: 'Dear God, can you tell Taukiri to call me? I have news he'd wanna to hear. Thank you. Āmene.'

I really wanted to talk to Tauk today. I thought about him all day. I wanted him to know I was going back to school. I wanted him to

151

wish me luck. Asking God had helped before.

During dinner the phone rang, which didn't happen very often, and my heart leapt up, like it was a frog, leapt high and landed in the mashed spuds, got stuck in them and freaked out.

Uncle Stu got up from the table.

'Better not be that son of a bitch leaving me in the lurch again.' He picked up the phone. 'Hello,' he said. 'Hello.'

Uncle Stu slammed the phone down, came back to the table and sat. His chair squeaked and the table shook. Every time Uncle Stu moved or spoke, he made noises that made my heart lurch around like a scared frog stuck in hot mashed spuds.

'Fucken wrong number,' he said.

I was so sure it was Taukiri. My tummy told me it was, but just like I'd been at the park with that dickhead green-hoodie guy, I was wrong.

Uncle Stu didn't know much about lurches. I wished I was big enough to throw him one. A horrible *lurch*. I would close the lid, like on a shoebox. He could be a bird fallen from a nest. And although I tried to wish away the bad thought in my head, it didn't turn out for him the way it had for the one we prayed for. That tūī that flew off without saying goodbye.

It turned out for Uncle Stu how it had for the other birds.

And that might be the worst thought I've had.

He left the table, his fork and knife leaning on his plate, like he wasn't finished his meal. Like he wasn't grateful, like he thought he deserved something better for dinner.

Jade and Toko

They shopped for stores at Halfmoon Bay's only supermarket. Toko pushed the trolley and Jade filled it.

'Blood sausage,' Toko said. 'Dad loves it.'

Jade threw in two.

'Know how to make corn fritters?'

'I'll soon find out,' Jade replied tossing tins of corn kernels in the trolley.

'There's a freezer on board,' Toko reminded her.

So she loaded the trolley with chopped frozen spinach, ice cream, chicken nuggets, and reached for a packet of fish fingers.

'Nah, baby,' Toko said. 'We'll be eating kaimoana fresh from the sea.'

She put the fish fingers back.

Apples, cream, beans, kūmara, mutton, almonds, dried figs.

'Figs?' Toko asked

She shrugged. 'Never tried them.'

A box of beer, a bottle of red wine, a round of camembert, water crackers and a tin of asparagus. Butter. Bread. Eggs and milk. Lumps of sugar in a box, because Jade had only read about lumps of sugar in Enid Blyton books and had always thought they must be better than normal sugar.

They sailed out of Halfmoon Bay late that afternoon. Fridge, freezer and cupboards bursting like they were to sail around the world for eighty days.

In their cabin Toko unpacked his bag: a CD player, a book, a pair of blue overalls, a pair of boxer shorts, a toothbrush and a tube of toothpaste. He found places for those few things, pressed play on the little player, then lifted Jade onto the tiny bed and they kissed and kissed until they couldn't tell the difference between the sea's swell and theirs. And because they'd discovered that sex was something they were very good at, they had themselves some lovely afternoon sex as the boat dipped and bobbed, and the gulls cried, and the land disappeared from sight like it had been just an illusion.

'You're so damn beautiful,' she said to him.

'You are,' he mocked.

'Are ya?' she laughed. She could have stayed at sea forever.

Jade loved the galley. With it loaded like it was, it was an indulgent place. There was a large pan – a gimbal pan, Toko told her – designed to stay steady even with the ship's pitching and rolling. She fried eggs for breakfast and even when the waves lifted the boat up and dropped it again, the sizzling eggs only slipped a little this way and that. Just barely.

The cupboards had sliding doors on them. The sink was small and the bench had only enough space for one meal's worth of dishes. Three plates, three cups, three sets of cutlery and a pot if you were lucky. That first evening she made a feast, cleaning each dish she used as she went. She made Toko his corn fritters from the tinned kernels, flour, egg and onion. She sliced blood sausage and fried it in butter. Toko brought her a big blue moki fish and she baked it in the oven. She cooked frozen spinach in cream and garlic.

She set a plate with sliced dried figs and the camembert and water crackers. She put out cold beers and wine in the glass holders.

She called Toko to the galley. He made a plate for Hēnare and took it to him to eat in the wheelhouse. Jade and Toko sat together.

The boat hit a wave and the plate loaded with corn fritters slid across the table, slipped off, and smashed on the floor.

'Two-second rule,' he laughed, gathering the corn fritters and putting them alongside the creamed spinach. He picked up the broken pieces of plate and tossed them in the rubbish then sat back down. 'We might come up with a better system,' he said, looking at the feast.

Jade ate a fig and said, 'Mmm, yum,' but didn't take another.

Toko shovelled mouthfuls of baked fish into his mouth and washed it back with beer. He ate a corn fritter covered in creamed spinach.

'Fit for a king,' he said.

Jade took one of the corn fritters that had fallen on the floor.

She cut a small piece off and put it in her mouth. It was a little undercooked in the middle but she chewed it and didn't say anything. Then she felt something pierce her.

'Ouch,' she said, tasting blood.

She pulled a tiny shard of broken plate from her mouth.

Toko leaned and looked inside, 'Just a scratch,' he said and kissed her. He took a piece of fried blood sausage and held it up. 'Open up,' he said and fed it to her.

After dinner Toko took their plates to the bench. Jade stood and hit her head on the shelf behind her. She brought plates of leftover food to the bench, but stood there with nowhere to put them down and Toko was in her way.

He turned to her and saw her standing there, a plate in each hand, nowhere to put them, her stance wide, riding the sea.

'We'll find a better system, baby,' he said.

Taukiri

The moonlight through the attic window was keeping me awake. And awake I kept thinking and thinking, and wanting not to. Because Ari was waiting. As long as he waited, I wouldn't be free. That was fair though. Why should I move on, when I left him with promises I didn't want to keep?

I went outside and smoked a roach I found in Elliot's ashtray. Sipped on a beer. And thought on the promises I'd made. I went back to the kitchen and sat beside the phone. For a while I just looked at it. Then I dialled the number of the farmhouse, sort of hoping he wouldn't answer but knowing this was as brave as I'd get.

Just before I hung up I heard his voice: 'Tauk?' He answered the phone in the middle of the night with my name. I hated myself.

'Bud,' I said.

'Tauk! I *prayed* you'd call, you know, just like we did for that bird who flew away. And you did.'

'I did.'

'When're you coming back? Soon?'

'Ari.'

'Soon?'

'There's something I called for.'

'Yes. And I wanted you to call! To tell you I start school again tomorrow.'

My eyes stung. Water crept into my body. A murky, seaweedy tide.

'You do? That's great. You're happy – right, Ari? It's good there, isn't it?

'I miss you.'

'You're happy.'

'I suppose. But,' then he whispered, 'Uncle Stu.'

156

'Ari.'

I heard him start to cry. I heard him hear the words I couldn't say.

'Are you coming back?

'No, Ari,' I whispered, 'Not yet.'

'Why?' he asked, sobbing now.

I couldn't answer, because I didn't know.

'I'll call, okay.'

He didn't say anything. Just sucked back his breath and sniffed.

I waited. He waited.

'You'll miss me one day,' he said, then hung up.

I looked out of the window at the moon, and the night, sky now emptied of stars, and imagined Ari in his pyjamas crying, walking back to bed.

Climbed the stairs to the attic. Sitting on my bed I took out my chocolate box. Took off my bone carving. Took off my bone carving for the first time since Koro gave them to us. For the first time since we called ourselves the bone-carving warriors. Put the bone carving inside the chocolate box and shut the lid.

I shook some of Aunty Kat's pills into my hand and swallowed them in one dry mouthful. Then I put the box back under the bed and ignored the naked feeling.

The lightness of my neck.

It felt good. It felt like I'd finally coughed up every last bit of ghost sand. And I could get on with my life.

In the morning I drove to the city, and went to the Wellington district court. I parked close and stayed in my car.

May was the person I wanted to see, but not the first person I saw. I didn't know why I wanted to see her in person, see her out in the world – that woman in Megan's photo, her split lip. I needed to see that she was a real person and not just a picture or a story.

I'd tried to tell myself it was because I had too much time on my hands, but I knew it was more than that.

First, I saw a woman with short bright red hair. She was leaning on a brick wall talking to the second person I saw: a skinny man, his hair cut in a mullet. The red head was bouncing around him. She smoked, offered it to him. He shook his head and she hiffed it on the ground, walked back and forward. Talking, looking left and right. Leaning back on the wall, crossing her arms, hands in her pockets, hands out, lighting another smoke.

Then I saw May. The girl from the photograph.

She was sitting on a concrete wall near a glass door. Very still. Like a pile of damp sheets.

Her lip was stitched. She was wearing a white T-shirt with a print of a large scallop. I recognised it from working at the shelling factory. It was what the café staff wore. She was holding her left thumb tightly with her right hand. She started tapping her heel against the ground.

A young man came out of the court, and she jerked herself up, thumb still in hand. He walked right by her, and she followed him. He was wearing a grey shirt and black jeans and white high-top sneakers. His hair was slick with gel. She was talking to him, a pleading look on her face, but he didn't look back. They reached a beat-up blue Mitsi. He opened the driver's door, got in and started the car. She got in the passenger's seat, and put her face in her hands. He reversed out of the parking space quickly, his lips pouting, eyes steady and they drove off.

Ārama

After dinner I got ready for bed. It was still early, and I knew I wasn't going to be able to sleep anyway, but I decided I would rather go to bed than sit around with Uncle Stu and Aunty Kat. My mouth kept almost opening to say something like: 'I wonder what my teacher will look like?' or 'I wonder if the playground has a fort?' or 'I hope the kids like me.' But then I just closed my mouth and kept the words inside because it was better than saying them and no one hearing me.

Uncle Stu wouldn't hear because he never heard me, and neither would Aunty Kat, because she couldn't hear me when he was around, because even when he wasn't talking, he was loud.

I tried calling Nanny again, to tell her. But she still didn't answer. Ever. And by now her answer service must be packed full of messages from me.

'Hi, Nanny. How are you? Do you feel better yet? I still feel sad too. Maybe we can cheer each other up.'

'Hi, Nan … Where are you? I miss you. Call me.'

'Nanny. Do you know where Tauk is? I think you need to tell him to come back.'

'Nanny, can you call me?'

'Nanny, I know someone who will really cheer you up. My friend Beth. Can you call me so I can come over with Beth sometime?'

'Nanny, did I leave an old rugby ball at your house? Lupo put a hole in my new one.'

'Nanny. I forgot to tell you. Lupo is Beth's dog. You will like him. Can I bring him over?'

'Hi, Nanny, called to tell you Lupo ate another bee. You would laugh at his fat muzzle.'

'Nanny. Where are you?'

'Are you so sad, Nanny?'

'I love you, Nanny.'

'I watched *Django*, Nanny.'

'Uncle Stu said C.U.N.T.'

'I found your earring, Nanny.'

I thought those last three messages would get her here. Especially the lie, which I felt really so bad about – but it was for the best. I knew that adults lied *for the best*. So I could too. But she didn't call me back. Not once. And Aunty Kat said she didn't know when we could go and visit again.

Aunty Kat came up to read me a goodnight story. She picked up my big book of myths and legends.

'Would you like Māui tonight?'

'Yes.'

'Which one?'

'How he found his mother.'

I went to the box in my wardrobe and held up both copies of the same story. One was in Māori, the other in Pākehā.

Dad had bought the Pākehā version. To help us learn it. It hadn't helped. We just read that one instead.

'Which one?'

'Ha. English,' she said.

I liked the story, either way.

When Māui was born his mother thought he was dead and she cut off her hair and wrapped him in it and tossed him into the sea. The wave children of Tangaroa, the god of the sea, carried him on their backs. Tāwhiri, the god wind cooled him under the sun. When he found shore the seabirds wanted to eat him. Also the flies and even jellyfish. But his uncle came and his uncle didn't know he was his uncle, but he took him anyway. And he taught him things. Māui could turn into birds. Māui was sad that other children had mums, so he searched for his and he found her.

'Again,' I said.

Aunty Kat read it again, and I think her voice went quieter, almost embarrassed when she read about Māui's uncle teaching him things. Even though he didn't know he was his uncle.

'That's enough,' Aunty Kat closed the book. 'Are you scared for tomorrow?'

'A bit.'

'Me too,' she said. She stared out my window for a while. 'I miss teaching you and Beth. You know when I started it was holiday time anyway. No other kids were learning. I just wanted, I just thought …'

She stood up, tucked my blankets in and kissed me on the forehead. It felt very nice. Like I might get to fall off to sleep good tonight, because of those things. The story. Tucked in. Kissed. She must have forgotten I was too big for all that.

'Night, Ari. I love you.'

'Night, Aunty Kat.'

Aunty Kat had never said I love you to me before. I didn't say it back, it felt like I would be lying. I'd lied before, but it didn't feel good and that bad feeling would take away the good feeling, the feeling that would help me sleep tonight. The kiss on my forehead and the blankets tucked snugly around me, a story in my head. Even if it was a bit sad. It was still a story, a story someone had read to me.

'You're nice sometimes, Aunty Kat.' It was the best I could do, and at first I was okay with it.

Aunty Kat gave me a small smile as she turned out the light and closed my door.

I felt a bit bad afterwards that I hadn't said, 'I love you back,' to Aunty Kat. I didn't think she got those words said to her. And I probably did, I probably did love her.

The harder I thought about it, the more I felt it.

I loved her before I even moved here because she was my aunty. Sometimes I compared her to Mum, and then she was just like the sugar I ate spoonful after spoonful of when I really wanted a lolly. But sugar was still nice, on Weet-Bix or in lemonade.

It was funny I didn't say I love you to Aunty Kat because I thought it might be a lie and I wouldn't be able to sleep. And then I couldn't sleep anyway, because I should've said I love you. I decided I would go downstairs and tell her.

I got out of bed, and walked to the door. When I opened it I heard things. The sounds made my heart go frog in mashed spud.

There was a smash, and I heard Aunty Kat cry out.

'So you spent it, you stupid bitch.'

'I needed them.'

'Books?'

'For our nephew.'

I closed the door.

I wanted to jump out my bedroom window. But I couldn't.

I was scared to go running out in the world when no one might notice because they were too busy keeping themselves from being sucked down the plughole with the bathwater and they might even wonder if I'd even been there at all, because maybe I was just a ghost and why should they go wasting their precious time looking for a ghost.

'Dear God,' I said out loud, 'Tauk needs to call me. And you need to make sure it happens. You owe me it.'

I sat with my bone carving pressed between my hands, breathing slow. 'Āmene,' I said.

I climbed into bed and closed my eyes.

When I woke again it was late in the night, so late, morning would be coming, and I heard a sniffling somewhere in the house. It sounded like Aunty Kat. I thought about how sad Uncle Stu must have made her. I got out of bed and walked out of my room, towards Uncle Stu and Aunty Kat's room. I peeked in through the crack in the door. Uncle Stu was asleep on the bed, not under the covers, jeans on, shirt off, white belly hanging loose, snoring loudly. Aunty Kat was kneeling on the floor with her back to me, hunched over my schoolbag, a pile of my new books in front of her. On top of the books were the photos I kept tucked in one of the pockets of my bag.

She was holding one in her hand. One of her with my mum and Uncle Toko and Tom Aiken. They were all standing on a beach, a big fire behind them. I knew that picture. I've stared and stared at it. Aunty Kat was smiling in it like I had never seen her smile. Big and wide and toothy.

I knew. That had been her real life, not this one, not this one we were both in now. Living like ghosts.

I tiptoed downstairs and to the kitchen for a drink of water. There was a mess, a broken plate, some leftover dinner over the floor. My All Blacks lunchbox, too, broken in pieces.

It seemed like one of Uncle Stu's favourite things to do was to hiff food around. Like a kid. Worse than a kid.

I went to the phone and dialled Nanny's number.

'Nanny. I'm really scared.'

I hung up, then sat cross-legged in front of the phone and stared at it. Taukiri would call me, I thought.

I lay down beside the phone. I'd wait. I'd close my eyes for a minute, and wait there.

Jade and Toko

It was true, Jade realised quickly, her ferry trips were nothing like being at sea with Toko, sailing from Rakiura, up the coast and back to Kaikōura.

The last evening at sea, Toko filleted a blue cod for dinner. He slid the small knife slowly through the belly of the fish, up behind its gills and along the spiny back in one fluid movement, removing a translucent pink fillet.

Finished, he drove his knife into the cutting board, then thumped his chest, 'I am man. I hunt. You,' his smile was wicked, his white teeth shone and his dark skin glistened, 'you, woman. You cook this. You cook for me this. And then you do for me everything else I want.' And he grabbed her and pulled her to his overalls, and she could smell the fish guts and blood on them, and could feel the dampness – the sweat from his day's hard work – through her T-shirt. He smelled so earthy, so dirty, so masculine and good.

Jade saw there was another cod, set aside.

She pulled away from Toko and took up his knife. She snatched the fish up by its tail, and she pierced its belly and slid the knife along, splitting it, so its guts spilled onto the board.

She went to plunge her hand inside, but Toko touched her wrist. 'Hey there, little lady. You trying to put me out of work.'

His voice was light, playful, but Jade thought she heard a ragged edge in it.

She set the knife down, 'Ha. Yeah right. That's me. No way could I fillet it.'

'Do you want me to teach you?' he said.

'No, no. I'll leave that to you.' Then she added, for emphasis: 'Yuck.'

A wave hit the boat, and some of the loose warm guts slid from the bench and onto the deck.

'I'll clean that up,' Toko said.

'Thank you, baby.' She put her arms around his neck and looked up at his face, the sea and sky behind him creating a dipping and rising horizon, from two unblending blues. 'Everything you want,' she said. Then she took the fillets and ran off, ran along, skipped away with them to cook up for dinner.

Later, when she was resting in the cabin, she heard the door open. There he was. His face browner than it had been that morning. He smelled soapy. She leapt from the bed and a jolt shook up from her feet and into her spine when she landed but she didn't wince. She was upon him and she took down his jeans and took him in her mouth and she didn't stop until he came, just as the ship cleared a wave and she wondered if both their stomachs might be in their chests.

His because it felt so good, to feel so good, to be so lucky and loved. Hers because it felt so wrong to feel so good, to be so lucky and so loved.

They found a system. Jade cooked and she put the food on the plates, and she wouldn't make feasts at sea. She made simpler meals. Just fish or chicken nuggets with one serving of vegetables. No other plates in the centre of the table with other choices. Eat before you lose it. Take your plate up as soon as you finished, scrape it in that bucket. *I'm washing and get the hell out of my galley or I'll tan your behind.*

'I'll tan yours,' Toko would say, scraping his plate. Then, 'Good woman,' as he left her galley.

When they docked in Kaikōura four days after they'd set sail it felt like they'd been at sea for months. Jade took to the dock like a newborn calf. Her feet struck solid ground and she no longer needed to dance to get from A to B. But instantly she wanted to be back where the floor anticipated her next step and rode up to catch it, throwing and catching her, as if from a billowed sheet. The world didn't care where she placed her feet and didn't care how. The sea did, the sea demanded her attention.

Even driving seemed harsh now. The sound of gravel crunching under the tyres, the dust turned up. The speed the car could go at.

They pulled up at the house at the foot of the mountain, and Colleen was waiting in a white wicker chair on the front porch. A man was sitting in another white wicker chair opposite her. His scarred face, his hands, those hands in his lap, his leather waistcoat. Sitting close to Toko's mother he looked much uglier than Jade remembered him.

Colleen had packed a lovely lunch for them to set sail with. Across the garden her sheets, cold and white, were pegged on the line. She was wearing a cream woollen cardigan over a lilac shin-length dress. And there, on a Sunday afternoon, with her garden looking lovely and her sheets snapping in the wind, was Hash.

Jade saw Toko's jaw jut out and his hands grip the steering wheel tighter.

'Stay,' he said, opening the door. 'And lock it.'

Toko got out of the car, then Hēnare.

Jade cracked her window open, just a bit, so she could hear what was going on.

'Hi, Mum,' Toko said to Colleen. 'You can go inside if you like.' She did.

'Why are you here?' Toko asked Hash. His voice was loud.

'To see Jade.'

'She doesn't want to see you.'

'I was a brother to her. We both lost Sav. We both loved her. You know how it is, my bro.'

'I'm not your bro.' Toko sat in his mother's wicker chair. Hēnare stopped in front of them. 'Can I leave you, son?'

'Yeah, go catch up with Mum.'

Hēnare went inside.

Hash took a packet of smokes from his pocket, opened it and held it out to Toko. 'Smoke?'

'You're not welcome here,' Toko said.

Hash put a cigarette in his mouth, lit it. Took a long, not-a-care-in-the-world suckle of it. 'You and your bro show up. Nek minute my missus is kicked to death. I don't care if I'm not welcome. You owe

166

me. You and your mate. You and your little bitch.'

'We don't owe you. We were there to take her away, to save her.'

'None of your business, though, was it? And look what happened.'

'You blame us? Ha. Really?'

'Here's my equation, if you will, *bro*. Tommy plus Sav plus you equals she dead.'

Toko laughed. 'And here's mine – she stayed with you and she stayed with you and she stayed with you and she's dead. Blame yourself. Fuck, seriously, blame Coon.' He stood up. 'It's time to go … what was your name again? Hash? That's gangster, that name, gangster as. It's time to go, *Hash*.'

'I blame your mate, I blame Jade and right now, 'cause you so full of yourself and think yourself a hero, I feel like you owe me something too. I mean, you the only one who's come up trumps in all this. You owe me.'

'Nah, *bro*. Nah.'

Hash took another drag, then flicked his cigarette butt on the porch. Toko lunged out of the white wicker chair and shoved him down the steps.

Hash stumbled and landed face down in the dirt. Sprawled out, he lifted his chin and looked up, catching Jade's eye from the car window. He spat. He stood slowly, rocking on his feet, then dusted off his black jeans, his patchless leather waistcoat. He wiped his forearm across his mouth, smearing filth across his face. He walked towards the car.

Jade wound the window up. She wanted to leap from the car and attack him, bare her teeth, kick and punch him. Scratch out his eyes. Instead, she pressed her palms together and squeezed her hands between her thighs to hide her talons.

Hash came to her window and tapped on it. Jade saw Toko take the porch steps two at a time and sprint towards them. She didn't look up at Hash until he'd set a palm softly against the window, and then she wondered if he had something remorseful to show her, a nod maybe, or to mouth the words 'I'm sorry'.

So she lifted her face to him.

He spat.

Toko shoved him, and Hash's body moved like it might snap.

'Open the door, Jade,' Toko said, so she did. 'Get inside,' he said, so she started for the house.

Hash stumbled down the driveway. Toko followed him, turning back once to make sure Jade had listened. And she had. She'd gone inside to the kitchen window and was watching Hash walk slowly up the road to a car full of people. People she knew, perhaps cared for?

Colleen and Hēnare were sitting at the kitchen table. There was the smell of freshly ground coffee beans and baked scones. The table was set for four. In the centre was butter, a jar of jam, one bowl of sugar and one of whipped cream.

Colleen asked Jade, 'What've you got my son into?'

Toko came inside. 'Smells good,' he said.

They pretended there wasn't another smell in the air under the smell of Sunday's afternoon tea.

Hēnare said the karakia mō te kai and they ate English scones in silence. Until Jade spoke.

'Colleen,' she said. 'I love your earrings.'

They were the most beautiful earrings Jade had ever seen. Pearl and old. Very old.

Colleen shifted in her seat, sat up slightly, almost smiled. As she smiled the earrings shivered slightly, gleamed. 'Oh, these,' she said, setting her knife on the table and touching one with the tip of her finger, 'are from my māmā ...'

And she told Jade the story. And as Colleen sang the words to 'Hītara Waha Huka, Ūpoko Mārō', she had to grab Jade's arm to steady herself, to laugh louder and more wickedly, and when she did, Jade snuck an arm around the older woman's shoulder and laughed too.

Taukiri

I drove to the factory. I parked at the wharf and walked to the café.

Walking to the counter, I saw her in the kitchen in her scallop T-shirt, head down washing dishes. I ordered a coffee and a chicken sandwich and sat at a table by the window. I ate the sandwich, which was good and salty, then drank the coffee.

May came to take my empty plate. As she reached for it, I said: 'My name's Taukiri.'

She paused. There was a red mark on her wrist. She looked younger close up, but thicker in the waist, slumped in the shoulders.

'May,' she said.

'You just start working here, May?'

'Today.'

'It's gonna be a long one, girl.' Standing, I was close to her. 'You're too pretty to be serving fishermen and wharfies all day.'

She scoffed and grabbed the plate. I set my hand on it.

'Tell them, the wharfies and fishermen, you've got someone looking out for you. A big guy,' I puffed up my chest, 'with mean green eyes.'

'What the *fuck*? Who are you?' She pulled the plate away and picked up my cup, but her neck had coloured a blotchy red. She was looking around, nervous now.

This was a mistake. Who was I? Yeah, good question. And who was she? May with the split lip wasn't my long-lost hoebag of a mother. May wasn't my weak and stupid aunty Kat. I was wasting my time here.

'Enjoy your first day, May,' I said. 'Hey, that rhymes.' I smiled but she didn't smile back. I walked out of the café to the tinkle of the scallop shells that hung from a string on the door.

Ārama

Me and Beth were standing at the end of the driveway waiting for the school bus and something worried me. I was trying to work out if I had a bad dream last night. I was trying to work out if Taukiri called and said he wasn't coming back.

I didn't believe it but his voice sounded real, and I woke lying in front of the phone, and even though it felt like a bad dream it also felt like it was real. And Aunty Kat had looked at me like she was sorry.

It was weird for Beth to be so still, so quiet. I wanted her to tell me a story while we were waiting for the school bus. Sometimes she chose the absolute worst times to tell stupid stories and right now, when I needed one, she had nothing.

Her black shoes were shiny and she had her hands together in front of her, her feet were right under her knees, which were right under her not-swaying hips. I thought that maybe I should be a good friend and tell her something funny, but my brain was busy working out if Taukiri really called me in the middle of the night.

My lunch was packed into a bread bag because Uncle Stu broke my All Blacks lunchbox. He'd already gone to the cow shed when I woke up on the floor in the hallway in front of the phone. Aunty Kat had woken me up and asked me what I was doing. I told her Tauk called, and she looked at me like she felt really very sorry, the sorriest she has ever felt. She said I must have been dreaming. And now we were waiting for the bus and I was still wondering.

'Tauk will take us both to do really cool things when he comes back,' I said to Beth. 'And it will be real soon.'

She kept looking down the gravel road. 'Yeah?' she said.

'Yeah. He called.'

'Did he?'

'Last night. Said he's coming home soon.'

'I think he's up himself.'

'He is not.'

'Yeah, he is. And he's a dick.'

'No he's not!'

'Yeah, look, I've been meaning to tell you, Ari. I've always thought he was a dick.'

'He isn't!'

Beth laughed. 'Take a joke, Django. Geez.'

I didn't like her then, and I decided I wouldn't sit beside her on the bus even though we had promised each other we would.

Beth turned the toe of her shiny shoe in the gravel.

'I wanna show you something,' she said.

I pretended not to care. But I knew it would probably be very good.

She put her schoolbag down and pulled out the nice lunchbox with strawberries printed on it that the blonde lady had given her. It looked heavy and through the plastic I could see something dark inside. Beth put it on the ground and looked up at me. She opened the lunchbox.

Inside was the yellowist slop of cowpat I had ever seen.

I didn't want her to see my eyes go wide, but they did and she did.

'What will you do with it?' I asked.

She shrugged, and put it back in her schoolbag.

'I dunno know yet. You wanna help me think of something, Django?'

I swallowed.

We heard gravel being crunched on the road and saw a white van coming. It had a sign on it: SCHOOL.

I heard Tom Aiken's four-wheeler revving above us. Beth and I turned around to see him at the top of the driveway waving out with a big red face.

'Have fun,' he yelled, and Beth grinned up at her dad, and waved like she was swinging a banner back and forth.

'Bye, Dad. We will!'

I waved up at Tom Aiken too.

'Have fun, guys,' he yelled again.

'Bye, Dad,' Beth yelled back.

'Bye, Tom Aiken,' I yelled, and I kept yelling, 'Bye, Tom Aiken. Bye, Tom Aiken,' until I swallowed another word and a lump.

On the bus I almost thought of breaking my promise to Beth and not sitting by her, and then I remembered the slop of cowpat in her lunchbox, and I so really wanted to sit by her so we could think of something to do with it.

There were three other kids on the bus. One of them was a girl who looked about the same age as Beth. I paused, went to step past Beth and take another seat further down.

She got mad. 'Sit down here, you dummy, I can't let anyone else sit beside me.' She lowered her voice. 'They might smell my lunch.'

'Morning,' the bus driver grunted. 'Belts on.'

And we began our first ride to school.

The school was smaller than my old one. It was painted cowpat-yellow and had fences lined with trees.

When we got out of the bus there was a group of older kids waiting. A woman came towards us.

'Nau mai, haere mai,' she said, smiling. 'Welcome to your new school, we have prepared a special pōwhiri for you.'

Beth shot her hand up.

'Yes, dear.'

'What is a paw-ferry?'

The children behind the woman covered their mouths and giggled.

'A pōwhiri,' she said, 'is a Māori welcome.'

'Oh that's good,' Beth said. 'My friend Ari here is a Māori, though he doesn't look much like one, does he?' Everyone giggled again.

'Well, yes. He does a bit,' the woman said then shook her head, 'but that doesn't matter, anyway.'

Beth carried on. 'He's not as tough as most of the Māoris I know though. They pretty tough, the Māoris I know. One fella that is a friend of my dad's once tattooed his own arm. It looks like shit but he did do that. And didn't cry. Ari's not very tough.'

I elbowed Beth.

'Sorry,' she whispered, 'but you not … it's okay though.' She grabbed my arm, and whispered, 'You're still my best friend.'

Everyone was looking at us.

The woman was smiling – but not in a happy-happy way, more like a waiting-impatiently way. I wondered what everyone thought of Beth saying the 'S' word before she had even got in the gate.

The woman said, 'Would you like to see the pōwhiri?'

Beth looked around at the kids who had been on the bus. No one spoke. Then Beth squared herself up to the woman, clasped her hands together and straightened her scuffed-up shoes under her. She began nodding her head very slow and straight, up and down.

'Yes, ma'am. Yes, we would like to see this paw-ferry.' She made a big deal of saying it, like she didn't know the word. I'd seen pōwhiri before but all the strangeness of the day and night before made me feel a bit lost. Strange and jumpy.

The girls started the waiata. I knew the words but didn't want to show off so I kept my mouth shut. Some boys who had been standing at the back of the group started chanting and moving towards us on quick feet, and they twirled long sticks in the air and looked like they were angry.

One came forward pointing his stick. He did a good pūkana, tongue out, eyes real wide. Then the girls started shaking the leaves in their hands, and their voices were shaking like their fingers. It made the hairs on my arms stand up. It made my chest puff up too.

A tall boy danced over to us and placed something on the ground, and the woman moved her head like I should get up there. I was shaking a bit myself, but I started walking with my heart pounding. On the ground was a white feather. I bent down to pick it up and I walked backwards to my place beside Beth.

A small group that had been standing there watching the pōwhiri began to clap, and the woman looked at them like she didn't like the clapping much and so they stopped. One of the people who had been clapping was the woman who had given us the lunchboxes, one of them already broken, one of them in Beth's schoolbag filled with cowpat. Thinking of them made me feel happy and sad at the same time.

I twirled the feather in my hand and looked down at it, because everyone was quiet and I didn't know what to do.

'Well, that was scary!' Beth said, and looked around at us bus kids to see if we agreed.

A little girl nodded.

'It was eh?' Beth said. 'Nice, though. Real nice. Can we come in now?'

The woman started walking into the school and we all followed her and the children we didn't know yet. The school had a grass field with rugby posts at each end, and a tall fort. I had decided it had been just a bad dream – me and my bad dreams – Taukiri hadn't called at all. Of course he was coming back. I'd bet my new feather on it.

I will use words.

Forgive me if I am too vague. Too blunt. Too honest.

All those years ago, it is still beautiful to see two creatures under the spell of lovely things. Lovely thoughts, lovely wishes. Their own loveliness. But they're fools in love. Tangata whenua, we have myth and legend, not fairy tales. Have they forgotten who they are?

Wombs can blind. Love can blind. Kicks to the face can blind.

We roar, we shake at the world, we weep, but most of the time roaring and shaking and weeping only makes everything much worse.

Jade and Toko

After Colleen shared the story of her pearl earrings with Jade and they had laughed together, Jade wanted to go home and clean Toko's sheets for him and peg them out, and vacuum his floors and shop for crockery and bake something and invite everyone for afternoon tea, and who was Coon anyway, and had Hash even showed up there at all?

They drove back to Toko's house. Inside, Jade opened all the windows then took a shovel and cleaned the ash from the fireplace.

Toko checked the fridge.

'Let's go out later,' he said. 'Can't do much on scones.'

'Call Tommy then. I want to see him.'

'Like him?'

'I do.'

'You do, do you?'

'Jealous?'

'Never.'

'Never?'

'Hardly. Definitely not of that smelly farm boy.'

'Okay,' and she came close to him. 'By the way you still stink like fish guts.'

He grabbed her and pressed her close. 'Fish guts or cow shit? You choose, woman.'

'Choosing you. Guts and all.'

Jade pulled on jeans and dark blue singlet – if she moved a certain way her highest tattooed bird peeked out the top of it. Toko shaved his face, put on jeans and a black T-shirt, and they went to a pizzeria out of town.

At a small table, with the orders being called and the waitress bustling by and the couple near them leaning close to each other and Tommy not talking but heavy with words, Jade asked: 'Did you love her?'

'Yes.'

'She knew that?'

'If she did, why would she leave? Every time she left.'

Jade looked away from his eyes, knowing he wanted an explanation. Knowing she could never articulate Sav's reasons, which were also hers. And they all sat at the table, not speaking. Their bodies were nets and their words were silver fish writhing for escape.

On the drive back home, Toko pointed at one of her tattoos.

'Sav was with me when I had these done,' Jade said. 'She went out back to shag the tattoo artist, while I lay waiting on the table for them to come back.'

'Was it even Tommy's baby?'

'Yeah, it was. She loved him. Sure, she loved a lot of men, but Tommy was, well Tommy is Tommy.'

'Got it bad for him, don't you?'

'Adore him,' she laughed.

'Watch your mouth, woman.'

'Ha. You know why. He gave Sav her love story. In her tragic tale, she had this big, fucked-up, crazy love story. Every time someone she knew died, she packed her bags and pretended to go to the tangi. I mean, isn't that celebrating life in the wake of death to the extreme?'

'How is it you're not a complete mess?'

'I am, though. But I was loved. My mum and dad loved me. Sometimes it's enough.'

'I suppose.'

'Felicity was given a box full of kids books when I was a little girl. My school teacher brought them over. One day she arrived at our front door, and I was so excited. I wanted to show her my bedroom, but Felicity didn't look happy about me taking her in there, and I remember looking at both of their faces. So many things neither of them could say easily out loud.

'It was a wooden house, Toko. Did I ever tell you that? It was a normal wooden house. There was a high concrete fence, and no grass.

176

But behind the fence, barbed wire strung up above it, it was just a normal wooden house.

'My teacher came back after a wall was put up to make a bedroom for me. She brought the box of books. I loved Māui best, there were lots of those. I guess my teacher thought Felicity would like them, would understand them, but they were the ones she made the most fun of. I really wish she hadn't done that.'

In the middle of the night Jade woke with a start.

Of course Hash was there. Saw him with your own eyes. Fool.

Taukiri

'Bones Bay,' Jason said to me across our drinks. We were sitting at a bar. Jason had suggested it.

The bar was quite a dive – torn carpet, bar stools that wobbled, scratches over the countertop.

All the windows were boarded up.

But along the top of the far wall there was a row of small square stained-glass windows. They were random as. A dolphin, a lily, a sunset, the moon, a dragonfly. Amateur as. They made the bar look sort of, well, haunted. I liked them.

'Mr Kyle, long time no see,' the fat bearded bartender had said when we'd walked in.

'Has been, Blue.'

'Who's the young fulla then? Bastard kid?' he laughed. Ari would have called him a pirate. I forgave myself for thinking of Ari sometimes. Thinking of him made me feel less guilty because now he knew I wasn't coming back and I wasn't lying to him anymore. He wasn't waiting.

'Get us a coupla beers, Blue.' Jason said. 'You know, Taukiri, when Elliot told me your story, he mentioned Bones Bay. I gave it a Google search. Couldn't find it.'

I didn't answer. I stood up and walked over to the jukebox, scanned the tracks and found something good. Old school. Reminded me of Mum. Herbs' 'Dragons and Demons'.

I slipped a coin into the slot and punched in the track number.

I stayed by the jukebox to listen, my back to Jason and the pirate man at the bar. Outside the wind sounded as if it had picked up. The door opened then slammed shut, wind whistled through the boarded-up windows.

Blue yelled out, 'Good tune.'

'You wanna hear him play it,' said Jason. 'Now that's something.'

Blue bent down and pulled a guitar out from under the bar, 'I'm always on for a jam,' he said. His voice sounded gripped by something.

I walked over to them, took the guitar, began playing. Singing Herbs to a pirate and a drug dealer. I thought if this was my life now, it was magic and could only get better.

I didn't look at them. I sang with my eyes closed, not knowing if they were enjoying the song or not, just loving that inside a song there was no such thing as time.

When I opened my eyes Blue was white-faced and wide-eyed. Like he just saw a ghost.

I watched Taukiri enter the bar with a man.

I blew at the sides of the old building, I tried to rattle at the windows. There was a song playing, and I wanted to carry it all the way to Jade, somewhere, who should know I loved him. I loved her boy, my brother's boy, like he was my own. But now it is her turn.

The turn I took from her. Whipped away from her.

What I have done swells. Like the sea.

But look: they are all moving out of town. My māmā, my pāpā. The moving van is here and they have bought a little bungalow in Gore Bay. They won't have to drive past the Craypot anymore.

Ārama

Our first day at school was not going well. It turned out the blonde lady with red lipstick who got the bus sorted for us to get to school was going to be in the *Kaikōura Star* for making it possible. And everyone decided to make a big deal out of it. The pōwhiri was cool. And so far that had been the only cool thing about our first day of school. I had told Beth it was gonna be the coolest. Someone was taking lots of photos, and the blonde lady was busy straightening her hair and putting her lipstick back on all day. She wrapped her arms around all us poor little country kids for a photo. She called us darlings.

I could tell Beth wasn't liking it, and to be honest I wasn't either. This wasn't what a first day at school was supposed to be like. We just wanted to go to the fort and play. I ran out to the field where some boys were throwing round a rugby ball. 'Can I play,' I yelled. Then the photographer came behind me with the lunchbox lady and all the boys ran towards her saying they wanted to be in the paper. Forgetting their ball, the game, they didn't seem to hear me.

Beth came over. I saw she was thinking, thinking hard.

'You thinking about that lunchbox, Beth?'

She thumbed behind her at the blonde lady who was talking to someone. 'Her shoes are pretty.'

'Be a mighty shame,' I said grinning.

'Sure would, kid,' Beth winked.

And because we sounded like we were in a movie, we thought our idea was good.

Beth said I should go talk to the lady and I should ask for a photo with her near the school, beside the low window of the toilet block. She reckoned the window was low enough for her to reach, and she could tip the cowpat out easy enough.

'We are only going for the pretty shoes, though, right?'

'Of course, don't be a sook, I'm not going home with cowpat in my bag. It needs to be used. Unfortunately for blondie, she's the only one who's pissed me off today.'

'Me too.'

'You see.' She whacked my shoulder. 'You aren't easy to piss off. She deserves it.'

'Maybe she does,' I said.

Beth took her lunchbox from her bag and marched away like an angry dwarf with her swinging arms and legs.

I went over to the lady who was talking to the principal. The feather from the pōwhiri was still in my hand.

'Oh, Ari,' she said when I came over, 'Oh, dear Ari, how is your first day going?' She didn't wait for me to answer. 'Such a sweet boy,' she said turning away from me to the principal. And the blonde lady had an extra button undone on her shirt. I felt weird noticing her extra undone button.

I also felt peed off again when she called me a sweet boy. I probably was sweet. But she didn't actually know I was, which meant she wasn't being honest.

Suddenly I hoped I was right and Beth wasn't going for her pretty shoes but maybe her pretty hair. The wind whipped, brushing up the hair and blowing the feather out of my hand. It landed over near the window Beth told me I should take the lady to. I got an idea.

I touched her elbow, which was surprisingly wrinkly. 'Miss,' I said, 'I lost my feather, the one from the pōwhiri today. Could you help me look for it?'

The lady wriggled her boobs further up her shirt. 'Of course, sweetie.' She tilted her head, smiled at the principal. 'Where do you think it is?'

I told her I had been playing on the concrete near the toilet block.

'Okay,' she said, 'let's start there.'

My heart started beating louder and I was scared she could hear it. When she got close to the feather, she turned to where the principal was standing, to make sure he was still watching, then to me, 'I think I see it,' she said. I followed her.

The wind had carried the feather to the perfect spot.

She bent down to pick it up.

'Now,' I whispered, and hoped Beth would hear me.

Then I saw the lunchbox pop up at the window, and Beth's fingers holding the sides, and the yellow cow S.H.I.T. sliding down and landing all sloppy over the lady's bent-over bum, running down her legs and onto her shoes.

'Ahhhh,' she screamed. 'Is that …? Oh God is that … is that … shit?'

The whole playground was quiet, and everyone was looking.

I covered my mouth with my hands because I couldn't believe what we'd done.

They found Beth's lunchbox. She'd stuffed it into the rubbish bin.

They also figured I was in on it because when I'd whispered, 'Now,' it came out as a yell.

Aunty Kat and Tom Aiken came to the school together to pick us up. Beth and I were sitting in chairs near the principal's office. He put us there after being pretty mean. He told us we were the worst kids in the school. The worst! Then he made us sit on a bench near his office. I heard the school door bust open, and by the quick steps I knew Aunty Kat was here. I was pretty scared to see her. So I ducked down behind Beth.

I heard Aunty Kat tell the principal she was here for me.

She said, 'I've come to get my nephew.'

The principal started to tell her about our very, very terrible behaviour. And my aunty stopped him, stopped the school principal in the middle of what he was going to say. I peeked around Beth and down the hall. Aunty Kat had her hand up. And then she said again: 'I've come to get my nephew.'

The way she said it made me feel the safest I'd felt in ages.

I smiled when I saw Aunty Kat. But she didn't smile back. Neither did Tom Aiken. Aunty Kat gave my ears a solid clip, a real stingy one, and said the fish-and-chip trip to town at the weekend was canned. Which also meant no dairy for one-dollar mixtures.

But it didn't matter. I was hers. She came to get me.

All the way home in Tom Aiken's truck I thought of the pretty lady and felt a bit sorry her. She had cried. Even Beth felt a bit sorry. Probably only because we got caught. She wasn't allowed to go to the movies at the weekend – Tom Aiken had planned it as a surprise, and for me too – but it was out of the question. That's all we heard all the way home. Everything was out of the question.

At home I sat at the kitchen table. Aunty Kat was making me a snack. Which I thought was a good sign: she wouldn't make a snack for someone she was really, really mad at. Uncle Stu came home, and Aunty Kat said nothing to him when he came in. He walked real quick towards me and looked right into my eyes. He'd never looked me in the eyes. He grabbed me by my collar. Aunty Kat yelled at him.

'Leave him, Stu!'

'Left to finish cleaning the sheds, while you picked up this little shit.'

'Stu. Leave him. He's just a kid.'

I felt scared. Looking into his eyes was scarier than his hand holding my collar so tight my bum lifted out of my seat and my eyes burned.

'He sure is just a kid! A fucken dumb kid.' Uncle Stu's spit flew into my face and he threw me back into my chair, where I had been waiting for cut-up apple and a cheese sandwich. I fell backwards, the chair flipped back and my head cracked against the floor. I looked stupid. My legs up in the air, my eyes open trying to stop the room from spinning.

He grabbed his work boot and held it above my face. Then he threw it against the floor beside my head. It just missed. He walked away.

'Just a kid,' he said. 'Just a dumb-arse kid. An idiot, like his loser brother.'

'You could have hit him!' Aunty Kat yelled.

'If I wanted to hit him, I would've. I don't miss.'

Then he said three words to Aunty Kat and at first those three words hung, making the air all wet and cold and gluey, but they suddenly dried hard and tore into me, tore into my mouth like angry bees, down my throat into my chest where they buried their stingers

183

in my thump, thump, thumping heart.

He slammed the door, and above me the light swung. I heard his truck drive away. I had wet my pants. And I just looked up, not blinking, at the light swinging above me, and listened to the sound of my aunty Kat not knowing what to do for me.

Aunty Kat called Tom Aiken on the phone, and he came and got me. I went to their house and sat in the lounge staring at the TV, watching colourful pictures flitting on the screen, but the only thing I could feel was the bees stuck in my chest, making my heart sore.

Beth was so sorry, so sorry, for what we'd done at school, and Tom Aiken felt sad for her. It was hard for her, without her mum and school not being her thing. It was just too much. She didn't need to be punished – she was sorry.

'And you, Ari, well you don't deserve … you're just kids. You're just a kid,' Tom Aiken said, and it sounded so different from him, different from when Uncle Stu said it, but I just kept my eyes on the TV with my mouth closed.

I figured out Beth wasn't really sorry. And the reason I knew was because at school she called things she liked 'mighty fine', and things she thought were C.R.A.P. were 'a damn shame'. And she winked a lot and called everyone 'kid'. Even bigger kids got it. And she told the story of the cowpat in her lunchbox every time she was asked. Said that she had the whole thing planned out. And the reason she got away with all the winking and calling big kids kid without being told she was a D.I.C.K. was because everyone knew she was the little prankster farm girl. One who poured cow slop out the window, hitting the bum of a lady everyone said was running for town mayor. And Beth made her say the word S.H.I.T. out loud in a public school.

So Beth was cool, and could say dumb stuff that made her sound like she was born in some big country, where people used to ride around on horses shooting each other, and I was cool because I was her little sidekick, who yelled out, 'Now!' Kids sometimes call me 'Beth's friend' instead of Ari. Beth tried to introduce me as Django, but for some reason the nickname didn't stick.

It was the not-good version of actually being cool.

So, I was not cool. And now I was not only lonely in my new home but scared as well. Plasters-covering-my-belly scared. Pee-in-my-pants scared. Scared like Django wouldn't be. And scared of what Uncle Stu's bees, stuck in my heart, planned on doing next.

I am tired. And I am starting to accept this is no longer my job. To make things understood or help people see.

The world is but a grain of sand in my mouth, and yet my lips leave a perfect print on the cheeks of the ants I could kiss.

I am the worm, and the bird, and the ten thousand things which make a nest. I am the stone and the hand from which it is thrown.

If I had fingernails, they were still full of the dirt of my young years, digging. To China. For treasure. Animals' graves. My heart still pounds from the run we took up the hill.

But come, you need to hear something new, something happy.

See them: they're marrying each other. He is wearing a white shirt. She is wearing a cream dress, and under it her belly is growing. Only they know, and now I do too. I know so much more now that I don't need to, can't fix.

The church is by the sea and painted white, inside and out. It is weathered, so it is soft and lovely and the paint peels in places revealing a light brown wood underneath. There is no harshness.

The children are called in from the beach. The ceremony should start. Not Taukiri, nor Ari — not yet. These are other children whose names and the names of who they belong to are not important. These names would only make us tired.

The children come into the church flushed. Panting.

Oh, these words are so limiting, and I am tired.

This feels an impossibility, but I must try. It may be the last time. I brush the netted curtain aside, the white paint peels from me, outside I lap at the beach, and I am carried under their nails. I am the red flush of their cheeks. They're married then, and they are so lucky, they know that.

'I always wanted a sister,' she says to me, to Kat. 'Now I have two.'

Taukiri

Blue knew my father.

He knew Tom Aiken. He knew my mother. Blue used to own a bar in Kaikōura called the Craypot, until he decided to sell it. He couldn't live there anymore, he told us.

He swallowed as he spoke and chose his words carefully. This seemed to go against his nature. He was used to saying whatever he wanted. That much was clear.

'There were stains in the carpet, so much glass was broken,' he said, and looked at me to see if I understood the words behind those words. I looked from the tattoos that covered his arms to his small light goatee.

'It was a long time ago,' he stopped, again looking for the right words, 'Fucken hell, can't believe I didn't see it off the bat. Wasn't till you sung that song.'

'And my mother? Do you know where she is?'

He took a bottle down from the mirrored shelf behind him and poured whisky into a glass, 'Drink?'

I shook my head. Jason lifted his empty bottle. Blue sculled his drink, popped the top off two beers, then poured another whisky and put the bottle back.

'Shit,' he said. 'Do you know what happened to your dad, Taukiri?'

'A boat accident.'

'Fuck,' he said.

My mouth watered.

I wanted to be anywhere but this bar. I wanted my own room. I even – for the first time in forever – wanted Ari's head in my lap, while we watched a dumb cartoon. And I wanted not to hear words that meant there were other things to be said.

'Do you know where my mother is?' I felt my voice shake.

'I knew her.'

'Knew?'

'No idea where she is now.'

I didn't know what to ask next. I sipped my beer and placed the glass slowly down on the bar. I strummed Blue's guitar.

'Your dad used to play just like that, with you on his lap. It was unbelievable, you never moved a bloody inch, was like you were hypnotised. A tiny thing like you were, never saw any kid so small stay so still so long. I always thought you seemed a thousand years older than you were.'

I kept strumming, didn't look up. I didn't push Blue to keep talking. I decided to sing. Blue and Jason poured themselves drink after drink from a bottle which had stopped finding its way back to the mirrored shelf behind the bar. Blue and Jason left me not wanting to talk alone. That's what men did, I was learning. They left things alone. The two of them kept drinking, unbothered, as my mum or Nanny or any of my aunties would have been, by the open end of our conversation. I played. All I ever needed to do was play. Pluck and strum and sing. I could almost survive entirely off the energy music gave me.

It got late. I could tell, because the sun had stopped lighting a triangle at the feet of the people who opened the door. My fingers got sore, but I didn't give a shit about them, they could bleed for all I cared and I'd keep playing.

Jason's cell rang. 'Megan,' he said looking at the display. He slurred some crap into the phone, before passing it to me, 'Here,' he said, 'she wants to talk to you.'

I slid the guitar down between my legs. 'What?'

'Taukiri?'

'Yeah.'

'It's Megan.'

'I know.'

'Are you guys all right?'

'We're fine.'

'Okay, sorry. It was just getting late, and I wondered if you wanted dinner. I was also worried. Because, Jason.'

I didn't say anything.

'Should I send Elliot? To drive you home.'

'Sure, send him. Tell him to bring a drum. Blue's Bar, Cuba Street.'

I hung up and handed the phone back to Jason.

I wanted to tell them a story, so I started.

'Bones Bay,' I said, as I plucked the strings of Blue's guitar, 'is a place you can only walk to. Koro used to take me and my brother there. It was a good place for him to get pāua as he didn't have to go deep. My koro only had one leg, lost the other as a kid, about my age. Farm accident. He never told us about it really, whenever we asked he'd make something funny up.

'Anyway, at Bones Bay he could get his own pāua, easy. My brother and I would explore the rocks. One day we went there, and found a baby whale had beached. It was dead. Stunk something wicked. Seagulls were at it. We begged Koro not to tell anyone, so we could have a secret. I was still barely young enough for secrets to be important. For a long time the whale stayed there. And it did stay our secret – and I just loved my koro for giving us that. I just thought that was amazing, you know. Adults don't keep secrets for kids anymore. If something is exciting they want the likes.

'After a long, long time there were just bones, picked clean by the seabirds, and after an even longer time it didn't stink bad. There was a storm, and we worried the bones would be gone, but they weren't. The sea had just cleaned them up. And then they dried out and Ari and I would climb into them.'

I thumbed the guitar strings and they sighed heavily at me. 'I still can't believe Koro gave us that. No one else would.'

'But one day he asked us if we could share our secret. And we said yes. And we went with two other men and Mum and Dad and Nanny. They sang waiata and said karakia and one man took the jaw. My bone carving …' I felt for it, though I knew it wasn't there – it was in my chocolate box. 'They took a picture of my father's tā moko to a carver, and he made us carvings from the design. And Mum asked the carver to add us, Ari and me, together. Ari has one as well. We called ourselves the bone-carving warriors …'

Ari wouldn't have taken his off. Not once.

'Bones Bay,' Jason said.

'Bones Bay,' I said. 'I don't think that little bay even had a name. No one went there except us. It was only through a road on Koro and Nanny's land – before they moved to Gore Bay – that you could reach it. We called it Bones Bay. Just us three. Me, Koro and Ari.'

'And then?' Jason asked.

'I swam there. When we crashed. The sea sucked me out a way, then sort of dragged me south. I battled for shore, reached Bones Bay. And I was lucky. Lucky I was found at all. But Koro went there.'

Jason said to Blue, 'Two shots.'

Blue poured three. 'To Bones Bay.'

'To Bones Bay,' Jason said.

'Bones Bay,' I whispered.

Elliot arrived, and let more of the night in as he entered the bar. He had a wooden drum under his arm.

'Far out, bro. This is a dive.'

'Hey,' Blue said, 'watch your mouth.'

'Sorry. Megan's worried. Thought you sounded strange.'

'Let's jam on a stage, for a laugh.'

And I didn't sing Dad's or Mum's or whoever's song it was. I sang something that didn't remind me of anyone dead. Or just gone.

'You were holding back, I didn't know your name. You were gone too long. Nothing, na-uh, nothing, will be the same ...'

No one danced. No one clapped. The few people in the bar hung their heads over their glasses and stubbed out cigarettes, which Blue occasionally reminded them shouldn't be smoked in his bar.

The place emptied. Jason pulled out goodies. A wake-up, because he had important shit to do. Needed to get woke and get woke fast.

We snorted enough to go another set. Jason left. 'Shit to do,' he said. 'Talk about that job soon. You need one, right?'

'Sure do.'

'Lucky you found me, bro.' And he left.

Blue locked the door and went out back for a sleep. He wasn't into our shit.

'Boy, Toko Te Au wouldn't want his son snorting that crap. Do what you want though. Just can't be part of it. Gonna get some shut-eye.'

Me and Elliot snorted some more.

I strummed and hummed. Slapped and plucked at the strings. Buzzed up, fizzing.

It was when we were ready to go home, because morning had come, that someone started thumping on the door.

I went and opened it, and there was Megan.

She pushed past me.

'You ungrateful little bastard. You think you are awesome eh? Talk to me like that and just hang up.'

'Settle down, psycho,' I said.

'Oh, good. An insult. I haven't slept. Worried.'

'We've been here the whole time.'

She walked to the bar and sat down on a bar stool and looked at me, 'I'm trying to be your friend. You're too good for all this shit, Tauk. And you got no one to tell you so.'

'We were just having a jam in a bar. It was fun.'

'Yeah. Sure.'

'I'm sorry I was like that on the phone. It wasn't cool, you've done a lot for me. But we've been talking. It's been intense. Blue knew my mum.'

'Knew?'

'And my dad.'

'What else?'

'And I think I don't know the truth about what happened to him. And I think I always knew I didn't know the truth.'

Megan took my hand. 'I'm sorry for you.'

I wanted so bad to kiss her.

A shining clean Blue came out from the back room. His hair was wet and tied tight back. He was wearing an ironed dark purple collared shirt. He had on a pair of reading glasses, books under his arm.

'Jesus, go home already,' he said.

'Blue, this is Jason's girlfriend, Megan,' I said.

'Right.'

Megan's face hardened. 'You know where his mum is or not?'

190

'No. I don't. I'd tell her I was sorry if I did.'

'For what?' Megan asked.

'I was there the night he died. The night they killed him.'

When he said that, when he just let it out, just said it loud, not careful with his words, I felt so busted, so broken, like the moon had been plucked from the sky.

'Who's they?' I asked.

'There was one, one man who knew your mum. The other two were just a couple of animals. It was senseless. It was horrific. It was just so horrific. I can still picture your mum, fighting, howling ... I'm sorry.'

'My nanny said she was just a drug addict. Loved the gang life. Gave me up for it. *Just an addict.*'

'Na, boy. No one is *just* anything. And on that note, I'm off.'

'Where then?' I asked.

'None of your business, nosey shit.'

But he held the book up anyway.

'Leadlight design? What the fuck?' The windows. I looked up at them – the dolphin, the lily, the sunset, the moon, the dragonfly.

'Ever cut glass, boy? Makes you feel magic. Smashing glass makes you feel like an animal, cutting it makes you feel magic. There was so much glass broken that night, I been making broken glass into beautiful things ever since.'

He walked to the door, opened it and stepped lightly, whistling then, out into the morning.

Jade and Toko

Toko sold his seaside house and convinced his dad to sell him the boat. Jade brought a Moses basket and cotton sheets and the softest baby blankets.

They'd marry and live on the boat. Maybe one day, they'd buy a house. But for now the boat was all they needed. They'd fallen in love and they'd made a system so they could live together without breaking things, without breaking each other.

'Our baby will love it,' they said to each other in the little bed in the little cabin of the little boat that they'd named *Felicity*.

He or she would be rocked to sleep every night as they lay there listening to the sound of the ocean.

In the evenings Jade and Toko cooked fresh fish, crayfish or black pāua meat. Sometimes they mended nets together or rewired the craypots. Sometimes he would need to put on his diving suit and mask and snorkel. The big heavy tank too. And Jade would sit on the deck, watching the water, her hands on her small round belly until he resurfaced.

She wanted to fish too, with a rod, while she waited for him. But she didn't.

Once he took her to dive for pāua. He gave her a mask, snorkel and flippers and they leapt overboard. Together they dove underwater, and her hair spilled above her like kelp and her belly loosened from her spine. Toko pointed and took her hand. They took a deep breath in through their snorkels and swam down to a rock.

The shellfish hovered, he'd told her. You had to cut them away before they sensed danger. Once they sensed danger they'd suck against the rock and you'd need manpower. Cutting a scared pāua free was depressing, he said. On the rock she saw the shells, and they seemed stuck to it. But she looked at Toko and he nodded so she struck quick and slid the knife under it, felt it try and pull towards the rock but it was too late. She had it. The animal hadn't sensed the danger and now she had it. Hot in her hand.

They only took the one pāua that day.

Jade had only wanted one, and Toko decided it was best if they only cooked one.

'Then you know for sure that every mouthful, is what you brought home for us.'

Toko shucked it, and took out the hua to keep for Hēnare.

'You don't eat it?' Jade asked.

'Nah, I'm not as hearty as the old man,' he told her.

Jade pounded the meat. She sliced it then simmered it in cream with garlic and onion. It was tender to eat, soft, sweet, because it hadn't sensed danger.

Their system was always improving, fluid, like a tide. Only one thing was set. Only one thing was sure, only one thing made her feel more like a woman than anything else. When they'd finish dinner she'd say: 'Now get the hell out of my galley.'

She'd clean it alone. And she loved to, because she knew no one was coming back to party, no one was coming back to drink and smoke and throw food against the walls and piss in the corner.

She sprayed and wiped, happy knowing the next person along to make a little bit of mess would be her.

On warm nights they sat above the wheelhouse, legs stretched out in front of them and dinner plates on their laps.

And Toko would say a karakia mō te kai before they ate, and she loved him for it. She loved him for so many things. He was man. She was woman.

Ranginui. Papatūānuku.

Toko's sister Aroha was a midwife. She came and checked on Jade. She brought them things they needed and always used her visits to tell them they should come home. She told them they no longer had anything to worry about.

One day Aroha arrived early to pick up the morning's catch and take it back to her dad, who sold the fish for Toko.

When she got out of the truck Jade saw from the wheelhouse Aroha was carrying a large box in her arms. Jade recognised it. She remembered it being carried into the House years ago by Miss Matt, who was spurred on by her good intentions. She remembered shuffling through it like it was locked-up treasure, Head teaching her to read *The Little Mermaid* because that was Felicity's favourite.

'The police took this from the House. It's being knocked down. There wasn't much to keep. But they found this. Your name's on it. They wondered if you'd like it.'

Jade didn't thank Aroha. Nor did she smile. She took the heavy box below deck and shut it up in a cupboard that had a lock.

Ārama

We were going camping.

That's what Beth said when I went to her house, because my house was so quiet and Aunty Kat was nowhere around.

'Hi, Ari,' she said when I walked into the lounge. 'Dad said we're going camping. Today. He called your aunty too. You're allowed to come. In fact it's for the best if you do,' Beth said, her eyes on the TV.

That was weird. Hadn't seen Aunty Kat when I got up, hadn't heard her.

'Where's your dad?'

'Sheds.'

On the TV, Django, Monsieur Candie and Doc were in a room sitting at a big shiny table and there were candles burning and there was a statue of a man with his naked butt out. Monsieur Candie set a skull on the table. He said it was Old Ben's.

Then he took out a saw, like the one Tom Aiken used to cut down our Christmas tree, only smaller, and he used it to cut the skull, and the sawing sound he made sounded like our tree being cut while we stood on lookout for Tom Aiken's old mate. And when he had the skull open, he broke off a piece of it and held it up and said he could tell Old Ben was no Isaac Newton or Galileo, whoever they were, because of three dimples in his skull.

Monsieur Candie said something I didn't catch I was so busy looking at his yucky dark teeth.

'*Unbirded by genius*,' Beth whispered, repeating him, but it didn't make sense. Her eyes fixed on the TV, not blinking, mouth open.

And I thought of my skull then, like a room with candles burning, and Monsieur Candie was sitting at a table, sawing Old Ben's skull to bits.

'I'm gonna go back home then, Beth,' I said.

'Yeah, and pack,' she said. 'I'm packed.'

Walking home on the gravel road, I felt heavy like I did all the time now. Brain felt heavy in my skull.

I'd thought one day life would just get back to normal. No more Uncle Stu and Monsieur Candie and quiet mornings where I didn't know where anyone was.

I was starting to get it. It wouldn't go back. It just kept running forward, like a train with no driver, and people were falling off, and it didn't care. It had somewhere to get to.

The heaviness really started after I dreamed Taukiri had called to tell me he wasn't coming back and then I woke up to Aunty Kat looking sorry for me and my All Blacks lunchbox I'd left open on the bench, like I used to for Mum so she could fill it up, was broken on the floor. And Uncle Stu grabbed me and looked me in my eyes and threw me to the floor, and I still couldn't work out when it was I peed my pants. I'd told myself it was when he threw his boot but it was probably when he was finished with me, and said three words to Aunty Kat. The worst three words I've heard. And they flew into me and buried themselves in me and where had they gone now?

Were they still in my body, becoming something terrible?

I wanted to tell Nanny about them but Nanny didn't answer her phone.

I didn't really want to go camping, and that was the worst of it all. I didn't want to.

If Mum and Dad and Taukiri were going with me, I'd have had my bags packed already. I'd be ready for the adventure and the big starry sky around us. But now, even with Uncle Stu sleeping down the hall and the bad dreams – bad dreams that were getting worse, that sometimes had men wearing white masks coming to kill me and Beth or put us in the hotbox, and Monsieur Candie setting his pack of dogs on us – my bed in Aunty Kat's house was the only place I wanted to be.

But I'd go on the camp. I was brave. People didn't know that about me anymore, but I was, because I'd pack my bags and I'd go.

That was brave, even if people didn't see it.

196

When I got back to the house, I went into the kitchen.

Aunty Kat was stirring something in a bowl and she looked up at me.

She had a black eye.

And I just stared at it, because it gave me such a fright. Not just because it looked so ugly and so sore, but because I hadn't heard anything last night like I usually did. Not a sound. No yelling, no things getting smashed or broken. There was no food on the floor this morning.

Just a black eye. From a punch. Uncle Stu quietly punched my aunty Kat right in her eye and I slept through it. Like a person would if they lived in an apartment and they were in the bottom one or middle somewhere, so they didn't hear a storm outside.

I hated him.

When I thought I was starting to hate Taukiri that wasn't hate. It was just an angry feeling. This was hate.

I was supposed to pack my bags for the camping trip with Tom Aiken and Beth, but Aunty Kat was shuffling around in her pyjamas with a black eye and I didn't think it would be a good idea for me to leave her alone. Because I did love her. And I didn't want her to wonder if I did.

'Morning, Aunty,' I said then.

'Mōrena Ari. You're invited to go camping with Tom Aiken and Beth. I'm making you cookies to take. A recipe your mum gave me.'

Aunty Kat had never brought up my mum without me bringing her up first.

'Should I help?'

'That'd be nice. Get some choccie chips out the pantry would you?'

I found the packet and gave them to Aunty Kat.

'Would you get your muscles on this job a minute, Ari?'

She handed me the bowl and wooden spoon, I started mixing really hard. I could smell the smell butter and sugar made together.

'Your mum made these for you, huh?'

197

I kept mixing. Didn't answer.

'We don't have to talk about her. I'm sorry I haven't asked you how you're feeling. How *are* you feeling?'

'I don't know. How do you feel about having a black eye, Aunty Kat?'

'Shit.'

'Me too,' I said. 'Mum baked these for me.' I stirred the cookie mixture. Then I felt brave again. 'Why did Uncle Stu give you a black eye, Aunty Kat?'

'Because he's an arsehole, love. That's why.'

'He *is* an a-hole. Aunty Kat, could you come with us?'

'Where?'

'Camping.'

'Uncle Stu might need help.'

'But he's an a-hole, he should just do it himself.'

Tom Aiken's truck pulled up.

'Shit,' Aunty Kat said. 'Didn't even get them in the oven.'

'Come with us, Aunty. Please.'

And I saw for the first time that my sadness was a little bit magic.

'Okay,' she said, sliding the cookie tray into the oven.

Aunty Kat told Tom Aiken and Beth to come inside and sit at the table while the cookies baked and she packed. First, she made Tom Aiken a coffee.

'What happened, Kat?' Tom Aiken asked.

'Stu. One of his moods.'

Tom Aiken folded his arms. Beth and I stayed really still, the way we often did when we wanted adults to carry on talking and knew they wouldn't if they remembered we were in the room.

'Why do you put up with it?'

'I don't know. Why do people do all sorts of things?'

'I mean after what happened.'

'Come on, though, Tommy, that's different. Stu's no mobster. He's just a grump.'

'You're kidding yourself – he's a redneck, a self-entitled, can't-keep-his-hands-or-his-ugly-thoughts-to-himself prick. If Toko were here …'

Aunty Kat slapped her hand down on the table.

'He's not though. Everyone left, didn't they, Tommy? My own mum and dad, said, "Oh, Gore Bay is just up the road, Kat – we'll see you all the time." But do I see them all the time? No. And Jade walked away and Tauk left, and sure it's for the best, but does anyone want to stay here? No.'

I wondered who Jade was and Beth looked like she had at her house just before, secretly watching *Django*. Mouth wide open, like she could eat a whole big bowl of popcorn.

Jade and Toko

They were married in a small weathered church beside the sea. On Monday they came to Colleen and Hēnare's house under the mountain to tell them they were getting married, and on Saturday morning they woke as husband and wife. A bun already in the oven.

The small church was full with whānau. Tommy walked Jade down the aisle. Aroha and Kat stood opposite their brother and held flowers. Colleen and Hēnare sat in the front row. All Jade saw was Toko.

They hadn't left the boat for a long time and everyone asked Toko where he'd been. He said he'd been busy and now he was getting married.

'We don't even know her,' people said.

And they gossiped about Jade's round belly and the thin line Colleen made with her lips.

Toko and Jade were happy to get back to the boat, as husband and wife, away from the people.

For the honeymoon Toko didn't fish for a few days. They only got out of bed to cook and skinny dip.

Toko would tease her. He'd swim underneath the *Felicity* to the other side, and Jade would scream at him to stop playing games.

'Get your black arse out here! Stop being an arsehole!' and then he'd swim back under the boat, grab her feet – she'd squeal and kick – and pull her to him, against his tā moko, the curling black inky wave tattooed across his chest and down his arm. She traced it with her finger, and asked what it meant, and he told her it meant he was a warrior who would die an old man. That they'd make so many babies, who would grow up to be as strong as she was.

She laughed, 'Don't lie.'

'No lies, my tattooist knew I would meet you. Look here you are,' and he pointed to a shape that could have been a tiny bird flying towards the curl of Tangaroa. Toko grinned.

'Good,' she said, 'that's good.'

Above the wheelhouse they watched the sun set.

Toko played his guitar and sang. Sometimes a Māori waiata. Jade's favourite was a love song: 'Akoako o te Rangi'.

'Play it again,' she'd say.

He would.

'What does it mean?' she asked her smart husband.

'A Pākehā wrote it to be translated into te reo, so it's tragic.'

'Just tell me what it means, smart-arse.'

'It means that after I saw you, fell in love with you, and you left me, I crept under a tree stricken with love, and I wept for you, woman.'

'And then what happened?'

'I was alone forever.'

'Then?'

'Music came to me and said, "Awake, Toko, there is no darkness love cannot light."'

'So what did you do?'

'I stopped weeping for you. Went and got me another woman.'

She slapped him. 'After that?'

'You mean after the next couple or three?'

'Yeah, Romeo, after them.'

'Well after them, I needed a challenge, so I came hunting for you. Drove night and day for you. And I took you for mine. My challenge to make you a decent woman.'

'What'll you do with me when I'm decent then?'

'Oh, you'll never be decent. I'll make sure of it.'

And she stripped off all her clothes and leapt into the sea. Felt magic then, like a mermaid.

Toko's sister, Aroha, visited her on the boat.

Aroha was like her brother. Beautiful and sensible and smart. She was making her way in a Pākehā world, Jade thought. And she would help them bring their baby into the Pākehā world. Jade felt so safe with her, with her opinions, and her knowledge and her mana.

They took walks along the coast together, because it was good for the baby, Aroha said. They talked as they went.

Aroha once said: 'Kat's got this cute boyfriend.'

'Does she? I want to see her, sometime. Bring her to visit.'

Aroha laughed. 'Okay. Sure. Good luck with that. Hard to get that one to commit to anything.'

But Aroha did bring Kat for dinner on the boat, and Jade made a fuss. She was very pregnant by then, due any day.

Toko left them to it, no room for four on this boat, he said. He went to the Craypot to play pool with Tommy.

Kat arrived, the riot of the lot, taking nothing serious, free and easy, barely eighteen. She was wearing a pink halter-neck top that showed off her cleavage, and skin-tight pale blue jeans. Her hair was silky and ran straight down her back, almost to her bum. She wore eyeliner and blush and smelled like a pharmacy.

Aroha brought bubbles and orange juice and Jade had made a smoked-fish pie. Kat brought a box of beer. They crammed together in the tiny wheelhouse. Jade had to sit in the skipper's seat, Kat and Aroha sat on crates.

Jade turned over a banana box for the plate of cheese and crackers.

Aroha popped the cork and poured the drinks. Orange juice for Jade, bubbles for the sisters. And they made a cheers for finally being together and Kat sculled hers, 'Cheee-hooo,' she howled, 'Now that's what I'm talking about. Pop that baby out, Jade, then we can all go out and par-tay.'

Aroha poured her baby sister an orange juice, 'It'll be a while.'

Kat didn't pick up the juice, took a beer from her box, cracked one. 'Meeting my girls later. Ain't gonna drink juice, that's for damn sure.'

Jade went to her galley and brought over the fish pie. Aroha told her to sit. She'd get the plates and forks.

'No pie for me. Eating's cheating,' Kat said, and took a scull of her beer.

Jade asked, 'Still got that cute boyfriend, Kat?'

'Hell no, he was such a wet blanket.'

'Eye on anyone?'

'Well …'

Jade cut a piece of pie for her and one for Aroha.

'Tell us then,' she said.

'I already know what you gonna say, but try keep an open mind, all right?'

'Just tell us,' Aroha said.

'Stu.'

'What, as in Stuart Johnson?'

'Yes, Stuart Johnson. He's been making the moves. It's so sweet. He's well-off now he has his dad's farm. Says he's got so much money that if I marry him I'll never need to work. Can stay at home making him lovely dinners and painting my nails. Go lunching with my girls.' Kat laughed then, really laughed. 'I mean he was totally joking, like flirting, full on, you know. "If I had you. God, if I had you," he said to me. And shit, when he said that, well I went bloody weak at the knees. Never happened to me before. I mean no one has ever spoken to me so, so … what's the word?'

Jade offered: 'Brazen.'

'Yes! Brazen. Wicked flirt. It's fucken lovely.'

Aroha ate a forkful of pie. She chewed slowly, swallowed, took a sip of bubbles. 'Told Toko?'

'Hell no. And you bloody better not either. He'll ruin it.'

'I don't know, Kat. I mean, I have no real reason to dislike Stu – just I think it's pretty wrong of him to be after you. He was Toko's friend.'

'So what? They're not anymore.'

'And why's that?'

'Well, mostly because Toko is up himself.'

'Is that what Stu said? About your brother? And you're okay with that?'

Kat changed the subject. 'Jack? How's he then?'

'Great.'

'Course,' Kat said. 'He always is.'

After Aroha and Jade had eaten dinner and Kat had downed six beers, she had to get going. 'Time to go get my mack on with my girls,' she laughed, then sliced a piece from the round of camembert, put it on a cracker, chucked it all in her mouth. Chewing she said,

'Better line my stomach. Ha! Craypot gonna crank tonight.'

'Was cool to see you,' Jade said.

'Yep, sure was,' Kat said. 'I'll visit again when pēpē's here.'

After Kat left, Jade asked Aroha. 'Should we tell Toko?'

'No, she'll be over it before we know it. If we upset Toko he'll make a fuss and Kat will get stubborn. Want Stu more. He's harmless enough, I guess. Just a bit of a dickhead.' She cut herself some cheese. 'She'll find out.'

The next morning Jade discovers a light pink stain in her underpants. The contractions peak at midnight. And the pain comes so good. So deep and deserved. She is in the galley when her waters break on the floor. She gets disinfectant and a mop and cleans up her mess.

On the bed, Toko sits at the head so she can hold him. She has his arms in her grip and she claws into them and cries, 'Oh my god.'

Toko tries to get up.

'I'll get Aroha, now,' he says but she holds him, almost pins him to the bed.

'No,' she says.

'But the pain?'

'It's okay. It's okay.' But she's swept up in the thundering current of another contraction, and she screams and she wants him to just sit and let her hold him, but he can't. He climbs out from under her.

'We need Aroha,' he says.

'Fine. Get her. Go get your sister, Toko. She'll do it for us. She'll do it better.'

'What's your problem?'

Where's her cocky Toko? Her man who can do everything, needs no one, maybe not even her. 'Just go,' she says.

She wishes that their baby is born while he is out getting Aroha, then he'll be sorry.

While he's gone she must hold herself steady. Hold herself steady against three long, hard, punching contractions. And those contractions make her feel sorely abandoned.

When she sees Aroha running up the dock to the gangway, a bag in her hand, her hair back tight, wearing a cotton shirt and pale green pants, and Toko following with a gas canister, Jade wants to lock the door and hoist anchor, but she has no energy. Maybe tomorrow, she thinks.

'How's our mummy?' Aroha asks, putting the large bag on the bed, then correcting herself, 'Mummy-to-be.'

'God,' Jade says, 'if I wanted a hospital I would have gone to one.'

'We're not taking any risks. I have every scenario covered in this bag. Now, how's your pain?'

'Perfect.'

'And what does that mean? On a scale of one to ten.'

Toko stands back behind his sister. And Jade wants to scream at him.

Instead she sneers, 'Zero.'

And a contraction is upon her, a slow squeezing burn inside, and fuck it hurts. Oh God it hurts and, oh, this is beautiful, she thinks. Aroha is still standing between her and Toko, and she goes to take Jade's hand but Jade shakes her off.

'Help your wife, Toko.' she says. 'Come on, stop acting useless.'

By the time Toko gets to Jade the contraction is already falling away, giving out, giving up, and Jade resolves to leave him tomorrow at first light. And she'll leave with their baby and Toko will never get to see it again because he is a useless son of a bitch.

He needs to know that, so she tells him: 'Why don't you just go, Toko? Your sister's here now. She'll take care of this now. Off you fuck, boy.'

He seems stunned by her words, her language, the look in her eye. Jade hears Aroha console him. 'Don't listen to her. She's in pain.'

'I said zero,' Jade yells.

'Go to her, Toko,' Aroha says.

'Listen to your sister,' Jade growls as another contraction begins building a house in her womb, a big house from hot round stones.

He goes to her and he leans close to her and his sweat smells beautiful like it always does and the contraction rises up in her belly, and she squeezes his hand. 'Huh?' she says, her own sweat rolling down over her lip, down her chin, onto his arm. 'Why don't you just piss off.' And she takes his elbow. 'You shouldn't have bothered coming back.'

He cries now. 'I'm sorry.'

She screams, from the pain. 'You should just piss right off forever.'

'The pain now?' he says, and he kisses her.

But she can only howl.

Then Aroha tells them it's time for Jade to push.

Jade shuffles, then stands, she pivots and turns and roils like a cat. Is she going to turn inside out, is everything inside her going to fall out, her heart, her lungs, her tīpuna?

She squats at the end of the bed. Toko stands behind her and starts rubbing her back.

'No,' Aroha says. And she nudges him to the bed. 'Sit,' she tells him. Then softly, so softly nudges Jade to him. 'Hold her,' she instructs. And Jade thinks it's the best thing she's done, though it was not in her bag of tricks.

Toko takes Jade under her arms, and she holds his waist and rests her head against his belly. She pushes and he sobs. He sobs and sobs.

'Oh baby, you're so brave,' he says.

But then his sobs grow too loud, too base, and Aroha sounds as if she's getting bothered by him. She yells, 'Quiet down, Toko. I can't think.'

But he can't. He just doesn't. And Jade adores him for it.

Then Jade is angry with Aroha, because Toko is crying for her pain, he is sobbing for it, and he is feeling it. And nothing can ever replace that. No bag, no knowledge, no crisp white shirt.

And as Jade heaves their baby into the world, she resolves to never, ever leave her Toko. Not in the morning, not at first light, not with his baby. He's not a son of a bitch, never could be.

Aroha has their baby in her hands now, and they hear his soft cry and Jade licks a tear from Toko's face then she struggles up, to her feet, on shaky legs, and she rips her T-shirt off and takes her baby and presses that lovely silken baby to her breast, curls up at the foot of the bed.

Toko nestles behind her. 'I'm so sorry,' he says.

'You should be.'

'I am.'
'Sing your family a waiata then.'
Toko sings 'Akoako o te Rangi'.
Aroha goes to Jade's galley to boil water.

Taukiri

At Megan's we ate leftover Chinese food in the lounge. I took a pea from the fried rice and threw it at her. 'Here, princess.'

She walked out of the room.

'Hey,' I yelled. 'Don't be a precious princess.'

She came back with her hands behind her back. 'If I give you something, I want something in return.' And she brought an envelope out and held it in front of her.

'So what is it?'

'Pictures. Old ones. Of May – well, of May's brand new arsehole boyfriend. No one will miss them. I hope.'

I opened the envelope and slid out the pictures. There was a picture of a bat, lying in some grass. A picture of a smashed lock. And a set of skid marks on a road.

The pictures were cold and light in my hands. I could feel the oil from my fingers seep into them. I stared and stared and Megan let me, didn't ask what the pictures were making me think or feel or why I wanted to look at them, why I was still looking at them. Why I didn't blink.

She just let me be. The bat. The lock. Skid marks.

I set them on the coffee table.

'I want something in return,' she said, 'I want a story.'

'Why May? What is she to you?'

'She was my friend. Once. I stopped keeping up with her. First time I see her in ages is at the police station to take her picture. I'm wearing lippy and my hair's done perfect. She's a mess. Split lip, bad skin, put on weight. Dark circles. I saw how ashamed it made her to see me. After such a short time – just a year – and we were so different. What she went and did to herself.'

'Did?'

'Allowed? Accepted? I don't know. Took her hands off the wheel – just for a second. All it takes, Tauk.'

'She works at the factory – in the café.'

'How do you know?'

'Saw her in the street, saw her work T-shirt.' I felt bad for lying to Megan, but didn't want to lose her trust. 'Go see her.'

'Come on, Tauk,' said Megan. 'I gave you pictures so I could hear your story.'

'That's hardly fair.'

'Pay your rent then.'

'All right. I do have a ghost story,' I said.

'A real one?'

'Of course.'

'A sad one.'

'Terribly.'

And she stood up and flicked off the light and took a box of matches and lit a candle. 'Tell it to me good.'

'As I remember it,' I said.

She nodded and she put her head in my lap, and because I knew what I was about to tell her, her head in my lap didn't make me hard. I asked, 'What if your boyfriend comes home?'

'He won't. He's busy. Important stuff. Now tell me the ghost story, Tauk.'

I put my hand on her head. She closed her eyes.

'Once upon a time I'm a small boy tripping over my own feet. The boat rocks and my father has so many books spread out in front of us. My mother is sad. She doesn't want the books. I am crying because they have pictures. I want to look at the pictures and my father wants to let me, but my mother doesn't like something about the books. She says there's something smeared on them that will never come out.

'I steal one picture though. I rip one from a thick book. A beautiful picture of a mermaid with long green hair. And one day my father finds it under my pillow. He comes to me and he says, "Did you wreck one of mummy's books?"

'And I can feel that he is unhappy. It was a bad thing to do, rip mummy's book. And I feel like I am not his good boy anymore. So I tell him, I didn't. And he says that I must tell the truth always and I won't be in trouble if I tell the truth. And I believe him so I do. I tell him the truth. I tell him I did rip out the picture. And I'm sorry, and I cry. He says he has a great idea, and he wipes my face with his thumb and he says, "Come with me, my tama."

'And we go walking along the coast, and he tells me to pick sweet-smelling flowers. I pick at everything, grass, weeds, flowers, and thrust bunches at him. He takes them in his large hands. The sun blinds me when I look up at him. His face, his teeth and eyes, brilliant like a galaxy. And I grab a weed, but it bites me like a jellyfish. It stings me all over and my hand and arm goes red and lumpy.

'Dad says, "Oh, my tama, that was nettle." But he stuffs it in his pocket anyway, like he's too strong for nettle to hurt him, then kisses my hands and arms over and over.

'Back at the boat we put the flowers and grass and weeds, even the nettle, between the pages of all Mum's books. And I remember the smell. Smells are hard to remember, but I do. Because after, maybe a long time after, whatever a long time might be to a kid, my mother would read to me from them. And every time she did, the smell of flowers and weeds came out of the book, and they fell from between the pages. We didn't have to get rid of the books anymore, and I was allowed to look at the pictures whenever I wanted. And we taped the little mermaid back into her book. My mother called us her heroes.'

Megan opened her eyes. 'The end?'

'The end.'

'Thank you,' she said.

I pressed my thumb, lightly, against the freckle on her eyelid. 'You're welcome.'

I had another ghost story, but I didn't tell it to Megan. Me and my mother. Another smell – a sweet metallic smell. Birds bleeding.

The black ink birds on my mother were bleeding.

She was on the floor, with her eyes closed.

I painted her skin with so much blood.

Jade and Toko

They came back to the town. The whenua had long been buried under a tree along the coast. Like an anchor.

They stopped hiding on the boat. Enough time had passed and their little green-eyed boy was growing big and needed to move.

He needed to see other people. And they needed those people to see their beautiful boy.

They wanted to show him to the world.

And show him the world. The whole wide world.

All the stuff from before. Hash, even Coon, couldn't hold them captive any longer.

They went to town for ice cream.

They visited Nanny and Koro.

The line of Colleen's mouth stayed elastic. Bending to a joke, or joy at seeing her moko.

Toko, Taukiri and Jade walked together in town.

Sometimes they stopped at the Craypot.

For Taukiri a juice, or a sneaky fizzy from Bryan the bar owner.

Sometimes a beer for Toko.

He would bring his guitar, like he used to. And Taukiri would sit on his lap so still – so still – Toko could play a whole song. And Toko's little boy would move his eyes from his father's lips, to the moving fingers, and back again. As Toko tapped his foot, little Taukiri would look and listen, his mouth open – struck dumb by his daddy's songs. And everyone smiled at the two of them.

'Gonna be a musician, just like his dad,' they would say.

'Look at him, it's like he's hypnotised by the sound,' they would say.

'Spitting image.'

And when it was time to go home the bartender polishing glasses would ask Toko to play another song. 'One more for the road, Toko.'

Toko always had time to play one more.

People loved to see the Māori man sing his Māori songs. It was the south. People in the south often treated him like he was a souvenir.

Toko, Taukiri and Jade would climb into the truck and go back to the *Felicity*. Seagulls keeping watch. And not far off the peninsula the dark water of the Kaikōura Canyon was nothing to fear. It was not angry, and even though it could at any moment break pieces of the land to make islands, it didn't.

Jade had stopped having nightmares about yellow-eyed, yellow-toothed dogs living below deck. The pages of her childhood books were lined with flowers and weeds and flax so they no longer had the smell of the House in them and they no longer needed to be kept away. They always kept some in the box though. Some in, some out.

Like an anchor.

Taukiri

I had no money. None. I busked, I spent the coins, the odd note, I busked, I bought food, I busked. And now I had no money.

I opened the closet and I took out my board. I tried to open the bag but the zipper was stiff, and I had to pull harder. The board was stuck to the bag with wax, didn't slide out. Was dried out. Sad.

The board felt lighter than usual, and bone dry, brittle. There were bits of sand on it, and I realised that sand was from Kaikōura, and it was so dry it looked like prehistoric sand. Like it belonged in a museum. Like ghost sand.

I took it outside and I got a blunt butter knife and began peeling the old wax away. At first it spun away like cold butter, until the sun warmed it so it got soft like fresh-chewed bubble gum and came away in globs that got under my nails.

Jason came out of the house. He had on skinny jeans, white sneakers and a black bomber jacket. Freshly shaven too. But it looked like he hadn't eaten in a week. Despite the shit he was up to, he was a pretty decent guy. Was hard to hate him, even though I wanted to.

'Going for a surf, bro?' he asked.

'Nah, selling it.'

'Need cash?'

'Yeah, bro. I'm a broken arse. Fucked it up bad losing that job.'

'I got something.'

'What?'

'A run. Easy one too. No sweat. Just a drop off, pick up.'

'Dropping what?'

'Just an order.'

'Yeah, I get that. What sort?'

'A mixed order. Weed on top – all you need to know, if you prefer.

If it helps you, you know, morally.'

'How much?'

'One-hour drive loaded. Fifteen-minute stop, and a nice cruisey return, no load.'

'How much?'

'Three hundred.'

'When?'

'Tonight. Tonight'd be ideal, actually. Yeah?'

'I dunno. I dunno. Nah. Nah.'

'Good luck with the board then, mate.'

'Yep.'

And he left.

Once I got all the wax off, I cleaned out the bag, wrapped the leg rope around the tail of the board and pushed it back into the silver bag.

I secured it to the roof racks and headed to the nearest surf shop.

There were two second-hand boards outside, selling for four-hundred dollars and six hundred-and-fifty. Mine was better than both of them. I went in. There was a guy at the counter with long dreadlocks and those piercings that turn your earlobes into gaping holes.

'Selling?' he said, nodding to my board.

'Yup.'

'How much you want for it?'

'It was worth a grand when I got it new. I'd sell it for eight hundred.'

'Ha. Good luck.'

'Go lower?'

'Try seven hundy, give it a month, drop it if it doesn't go.'

'All right,' I said, and set the board against the counter.

'Open it up,' he said, and I did. 'Nice. Good nick. Should sell.'

'So you can give me the seven hundred?'

'Ah, no. Not exactly.'

'Ah right, sorry, what's your commission.'

'No, I mean, yeah we take ten per cent, but you don't get paid till the board sells. Sorry, dude. Still wanna sell it?'

'Yeah, I guess. Don't have much choice.'

'You could go on Facebook. There's a Buy and Sell Wellington page. It's easier. Get your money quicker.'

I could ask Megan or Elliot, I thought. Or I could sign into my own Facebook on Megan's laptop and do it, but I really didn't want to see the messages I might've got these past months. 'I'll leave it with you, bro,' I said.

I wrote down Megan's details on a square of paper, and left. Went to find Jason. He wasn't back at Megan's, so I called his phone from her landline.

He answered. 'Hey, babe.'

'It's me.'

'Tauk, what's up? Sell the board?'

'Nope. You still need someone for that job?'

'Sure do. Eight all G? I'll be there. At Meg's. Loaded.'

'All G.'

I went to the attic and I lay on the bed. Stared at the ceiling. It felt so empty in there. Was it that my surfboard wasn't in the closet now, was it that my life was about to change, and I was in that sad trough before I did something I never had and never thought I'd do – a run for Jason?

And 'weed on top', that's all I'd need to know?

Why was Megan even with that guy? I didn't like him. Hated feeling like I needed him. And why did I really? Why couldn't I just go and get a real job. What was I even doing in Wellington now – what was I even *doing*?

The board. I'd held onto it telling myself I'd never use it again, never go near the sea again. But I didn't really believe it. Mum and Dad bought that board for me. And Ari always told people his brother was a surfer and one day he would be too and I was going to teach him.

Now my board was in a shop like a loser reject no one loved.

I leapt from the bed and ran downstairs. I got in my car and drove to the surf shop.

The guy was still there. 'Ha! It's not sold yet, bro. Sorry.'

215

'Not selling anymore.'

'Good for you, bro, good for you. No price on happiness.' He gestured to the board and I took it.

My fuel light was on, but I headed out of the city centre. To the sea.

I took the bend around the bottom of Moa Street and found Lyall Bay, wide open like a big lovely smile. Beaming. Above the rocks, the waves were peeling. They bowed to the sky. They moved from left to right, stilling time in sublime slow motion, like they were in no rush and yet moved quicker than anything else ever had. A giant-like pace, quick, powerful, graceful.

I pulled in to watch the surfers. Left my car running. There were six or seven out. One surfer took a drop and made a smooth bottom turn, rode the clean wave all the way in, before lifting his arms in the air and springing off his board. And then there he was, up on it again, duck-diving the white wash, making his way back out quick, not wanting to miss a thing. My heart beat, my feet tapped, my hands slapped the steering wheel.

And a song with a quiet, deep, mournful beat came on. I didn't turn it off. Just listened, just listened and looked out at the broad open bay. When the song finished, I turned off the ignition and got out of the car. Stripped my clothes off and pulled on the bone-dry wettie, coarse and brittle now. Unstrapped the board and watched another surfer ride in. Cut back, cut back, cut back. Finally, placed my car keys on my front tyre, and with only the sound of the sea and a loud, '*Akaw!*' like a bird about to take off, I made a light-footed jog down to the ocean. My board under my arm.

The sea is not grey and the sky neither. The sun is high and the bay is open like a Cheshire cat's smile and the water is already bringing my brittle wetsuit back to life and sucking against my skin.

And the sea!

She kisses me like I've been missed.

She's like, 'Where've you been?'

She's like, 'Where did you go?'

She's like, 'What'd I do?'

I don't say, 'Don't you remember?'

It's in the past. All's forgiven. She's forgotten and, for now, so can I.

She's like the tongue of a giant puppy who did something a long time ago, something silly like chew up my shoes.

The saltiest sorry is gushed.

She's happy I'm back, and licks me sloppy, and wags her tail for me in perfect curls.

Forgive her. Drop down the face of the first wave, and turn quick, cut back, up, down. Forgive her. I forgive so much my heart swells full up, like she is, swelling up, swelling up over us being back together again.

Licked better, like an old bruise and she wants to make it all better now. And the blood in the bruise of me uncrystallises, and decides to swim about again, beneath my kissed-better skin.

Surf. Duck-dive. Surf, surf, surf, up down and swelling more now.

And let go, and swim away from my board and float. Leg rope on, though, so not separated. Not floating unowned, together still, even if just by a cord. Floating, and the sky so open above me that there's nothing but this. Wave crashes on me, pulls my board away, and I feel the pull at my ankle. Haul it back, jump on.

Sit with feet dangling under. Bird darts. Cloud moves. It's energy, pure hit. Smack. And into my blood.

Surfing for an eternity. Surf until thirst from accidentally-on-purposely drinking salt water, draws me to land.

Find a bottle in my car. Chug it back, so quenched now. So perfectly quenched now.

Feel me again. Taukiri. And for the smallest moment, looking out at the ocean, I let Taukiri miss Ari.

How is he? How's he doing?

After my surf I don't really dry off. My skin and hair wet I try to dress and the clothes are hard to pull on because I don't dry properly. I don't want to. I'm so happy I don't want to. I've been trying to dry my whole self out ever since I crawled out of the water and onto the beach at Bones Bay. But now, I want to leave the salt water on my skin.

⌐

In my car, turned the ignition and couldn't get it to start. No gas. Shit. Shit, shit, shit. The time. Eight. Jason.

I walked to a bus station. Waited twenty-five minutes, took it, shaking. Cold. Worried. I needed that money. Too late now. Unless Jason waited? Would he wait?

Got off the bus near the airport, walked to Megan's. At least an hour late. Would he be there? Weed on top, whatever it is underneath. No harm done?

Door locked. I knocked. No one answered. I sat on the porch. Jason would've been here, with the load. Hoped he wouldn't be mad. Needed some weed myself just thinking about it. About the money I'd lost.

A car pulled up.

Elliot and Megan came around the side of the house. Elliot ran at me, he ran at me and swung at me with both fists.

'Elliot!' Megan yelled and grabbed his arms, but he shook her off. He tackled me to the ground and clocked me in the jaw.

'What the fuck? What the fuck, Elliot?'

'You stitched him up, you narc.'

'What? What? What are you talking about?'

'You know what I'm talking about. You were running for him, he arrives, has to do the job himself, but what's Tauk gone and done? Called the po-po.'

Megan stood there. Pale, except for the skin on her cheeks that had gone a blotchy red, her eyes crimson-rimmed.

I walked towards her, my hands open in front of me.

'Yeah, there's your motive right,' Elliot sneered. 'There it is – right there.'

'Fuck up, Elliot.' I went to Megan. 'I didn't, Megan. Promise. I wouldn't. I needed that run. I've got no money. Went for a surf. Car ran out of gas. It's still there. Board probably nicked by now.'

Elliot laughed. 'Boo fucken hoo, you narc.'

I swung around and punched him in the guts. 'I didn't narc on him.'

Megan spoke, 'We're in trouble though, Tauk.'

Elliot doubled over, panting. 'No we're not. He is. Let them have him.'

Megan shouted at Elliot. 'But I know he didn't narc. I believe him. He wouldn't lie.'

'Of course he did.'

'No, Elliot. He wouldn't.'

'You know him so well? He's a fuckwit, left his own brother, just left him the way he did. Yeah, real decent, Tauk is.'

'He didn't do this.'

'Doesn't matter,' Elliot said. 'They would've decided who's to blame by now. And they'd be right.'

Megan pressed her palm against her forehead, walked to me. 'Jason's the front man, Tauk. He's the shiny store window. He's the weed covering the something else. The something else that's more sinister.' She grabbed my arm. 'Do you understand what I'm saying?'

I did. The people coming for me were not Jason. Not like Jason. Not at all like Jason.

'No,' I said. 'Fuck no.'

They don't know what they do.

They do not calculate moves, or have kills, which fall into their hands, planned out. Saying so would give them too much credit. When someone's time is up, it's just the wrong place, wrong time.

It starts with just a feeling, which transmutes to a need, which becomes a look, an angry word. Then: one hit, a blow, a boot. The gun might find its way to a hand. A gun that was only ever supposed to be a scare tactic, and the trigger just something to touch and wonder about. Like a woman's nipple.

Trouble finds them. It finds its way out of their veins, and out of their porous bones. Bones so weak, as if their mothers never gave them the milk they cried for.

She is pregnant again, but keeps it a secret. Her cheeks flush when she thinks of it: another strong child in her belly. The tattoo tells the truth, she hopes. He is a strong warrior, and will die an old man, after having many children as strong as she, as he, as they are, she thinks. As the sun sets, womb-gold light kissing her warm cheeks.

They don't know what they do, and yet, they bring into the bar the exact thing to do it.

Three men walk into a bar. But they are brandishing a shiny weapon, so you should know the end won't be for laughs.

Did you think I was telling a joke?

Did you prepare your laugh for the punchline?

A man with a bulldog tattooed on his neck is waiting for a load, and another man comes and says the load ain't coming. But the bulldog man's been trembling for that load, his bones have been itchy for it. Then, a name he recognises. 'Find him, kill him.'

He scratches his neck and feels three things. Fury, remorse, forgiveness. But he has forgotten which time has come. Is it fury time or remorse time? Is forgiveness time coming, or has it been? Where is he in the loop? Where is he on the wheel?

Is he the punchline, or the end?

Is he the beginning?

In the beginning there was darkness, he thinks.

Yes. I am the beginning!

And he leaves, looking for a bar as dark as he.

Ārama

Aunty Kat was in the passenger's seat, and Beth and I were in the back. Tom Aiken's car smelled like cow dung and warm cookies.

We were driving down to the Conway Flats to camp, and we were going to catch some eel. Tom Aiken would like to bring an eel back from our camping trip to smoke. He told us the only way to eat an eel was smoked, otherwise it tasted like water and mud. Beth said there was no good way to eat an eel because it tasted like S.H.I.T. Beth would eat a worm, so I trusted her opinion.

Lupo was at the window, his head out, his tongue wet, and the saliva ran off it in big thick globs. I ran my hand along his back. His fur was smooth and soft. I was so happy he was with us. I wanted him to sleep with me in my tent. But what I wanted more was for us all to sleep in one tent. Me, Beth and Lupo in the middle, and Aunty Kat and Tom Aiken on either side. Then I wouldn't be scared at all.

At the river we pitched our tents under the trees a little way back from the river. The water was low, but we hiked upstream to a small waterhole, not much bigger than a paddling pool. Tom Aiken and Aunty Kat sat on the rocks, and me and Beth stripped down to our underwear and swam, our knees knocking the rocks on the bottom. We were eels, curling between the large rocks, scraping over the stones.

In the runover, where Aunty Kat and Tom Aiken couldn't hear us, I decided to ask Beth something that had been bothering me.

'Do you know what a redneck is?'

'Yes,' she said, but her eyes also shot up into her brain like she was scrambling for bits and pieces to put together for an answer.

'What is it then?'

'A person who tries to hide their bad thoughts, but their skin is so white. Like white, white like mine is. But their thoughts are so ugly, you can see them. Just in their neck, making the skin there all red and angry. 'Cause you know all skin is actually exactly the same and their neck skin has actually had quite a gutsful of keeping their secrets for them. So it shows the world. Sort of like Rudolph.'

'You made that up.'

'I made some of that up.'

'I like it.'

'Me too.'

We had two tents, one for Aunty Kat and me. One for Tom Aiken, Beth and Lupo. Beth and I were disappointed, we wanted to sleep together so we could talk. And I wanted to sleep with Lupo.

We were both peed off, so Tom Aiken said, 'Fine, I'll sleep with your aunty Kat then,' and he winked at Aunty Kat, and Beth jumped up happy, but I didn't like that idea either. I would be scared if it was just Beth and me. Aunty Kat gave Tom Aiken a little shove, and said she wouldn't dare share a tent with him, he would probably fart and snore all night.

'Nothing you're not used to then, Kat,' Tom Aiken said, and Aunty Kat looked sad. Probably because it reminded her she'd left Uncle Stu on the farm, and she was probably worried how angry he would be with her when we got home.

Her black eye looked darker with her face sad.

Tom Aiken gave her a little jab to the shoulder, 'Cheer up, Charlie,' he said. 'I'll have a word to him.'

Aunty Kat clapped her hands together, 'Who wants a cookie then?'

Beth and I jumped up and down like we might not get one if we didn't show her how much we really wanted it.

'Me, me, me, me,' we shouted. And we all ate the cookies under the trees, with Lupo watching us, wagging his tail.

'I remember these,' Tom Aiken said, 'Colleen's recipe.'

'Who's Colleen?' I asked.

'Nanny,' Aunty Kat said.

I'd forgotten she had a real name. I always just thought of her as Nanny. 'Where is Nanny, Aunty Kat?'

'Gone to try bringing Koro home.'

'But she doesn't like to drive,' I said.

'I know. But Koro needs to come home.'

'Where's he?'

'Rakiura.'

'Why did he go there?'

'Because Nanny was making him sad, and he was sad enough.'

'What did Nanny do to make him sad?'

Aunty Kat didn't answer, and we all chewed on our cookies quietly.

Then I asked: 'She hasn't gone looking for her earring, has she?'

Aunty Kat laughed. 'Of course not.'

I felt the blood boil up into my face. It was a dumb thing to say.

Aunty Kat said, 'You are right though. A magpie could have taken it. It really could be anywhere now. But I doubt Nanny's looking for it. I mean, I hope not.'

'It was my fault, not Tauk's, that she lost it. I called Nanny.'

'It was just a *thing*.'

'Nanny said it was irreplaceable.'

'She shouldn't have.'

Then Tom Aiken stood up, and dusted the cookie crumbs off himself, 'We're going eeling, that's what we're going to do. And we're gonna be warriors of the river.'

Beth and I followed Tom Aiken to the car to collect the things we would need for eeling. Beth grabbed my arm and whispered in my ear, 'I know when he's lying,' she said. 'He had much more to say than "we going eeling and river warrior, blah, blah, blah". Ari, we gonna find out what it is he's lying about.' Beth squeezed my arm. 'Don't you worry, Django.'

Tom Aiken had a big hook-looking thing called a gaff. And a Tilley lamp, and we were waiting until it was dark and then we were going to walk up the river, with our lamp shining. Tom Aiken said we would hook the eels with the gaff, and spin them around and then bang them into the rocks, and if we had to we'd bang their heads with sticks until they were dead. Beth kept asking if it was dark enough to go yet, and Tom looked up at the sky and said not yet, and I had a yucky feeling in my stomach. I didn't want it to get dark. Firstly because we would go into the river with hooks, and secondly because it would be dark.

I wished Taukiri was here. He always made me braver.

Aunty Kat was stacking wood for our camp fire. Tom Aiken was chopping some of the pieces up. I heard him whisper to Aunty Kat: 'I used to go eeling with Toko, for your dad. Your dad loves smoked eel.'

Aunty Kat didn't look up. 'I know, Tommy.'

'Taukiri needs to come back, Kat.'

'It's too much anyway, though, Tommy. For Stu. They wouldn't get along and I'd be in the middle all the time. I just don't have the energy for it.'

'Fuck Stu, Kat. Fuck him.'

I felt so happy to hear Tom Aiken say that out loud, and in my head I said, *Yeah. Fuck you, Uncle Stu.* Then I changed it to just, *Fuck you, Stu.* And I wouldn't eat a worm for it, because it was only in my head and also, he deserved it. My aunty Kat, who looked more like my mum away from the farm, had a black eye.

Uncle Stu had punched Aunty Kat in the eye. I looked at her face, then just her eye.

I thought of the words he'd said and then I could hear his voice, and I heard him say those three words while I was staring at the ceiling, pee in my pants, and I had decided they were the worst words I'd ever heard and I've heard so many terrible things this very long summer, but now, as I looked at Aunty Kat I heard them again, just inside my head, like now he was walking around in my brain repeating himself over and over, saying those words, and he was making parts of my brain turn out their lights to pretend they were not home so he'd leave, and that he didn't leave, that he was okay walking around in the blackness of my brain, made my body feel so yuck, so heavy and the world so terrible, like a swamp, because in my brain he was tailing Aunty Kat, and she couldn't find her way in the dark, and she was falling, and sinking, and drowning, and he walked behind her saying those three words over and over again: 'You black bitch.'

'Fuck,' I said, like I was letting one small bee out of my mouth. 'Fuck him, the cunt.' Like I was letting out more small bees.

And because I'd let some out, more wanted out.

'Fuck you, Uncle Stu, you shit fuck cunt bastard. I wish you were dead, you cunt. I hate you, you redneck bitch fuck.'

No one moved. Like they were afraid of the bees now, like the bees were hovering now. And the air went like boiled honey, thick, too sweet, hurting your teeth, like the bees were feeling afraid out in the world now, and what should they do? Should they find another mouth? Should they leave now? But they just hung in the air, almost like they hoped no one saw them, but prepared to attack just in case someone did.

Beth turned her head slowly, as if she was afraid to disturb the creatures in the air and looked at Aunty Kat to see what she was going to do to me for saying those bad words.

A tear ran down Tom Aiken's cheek.

Aunty Kat's hand twitched. She looked up at the bees in the air and dropped the wood she was holding, and put her hands around her mouth and tilted her head up towards the hills behind the river, and she let some bees out too.

'Fuck you, Stu, you absolute cunt,' she yelled, and then Tom Aiken yelled, 'You bully dickhead,' and Beth screamed, 'There's a bounty on your head, Stuart Johnson.'

And then we all stood in a row, with our hands around our mouths yelling, 'FUCK YOU, STU!' at the hills.

And our army of bees swarmed the river's edge, the banks crumbling as they passed, and they swarmed over a sheep lying dead in the open field beside the river, and they turned and suddenly swung back around like a taniwha tail and came back to us, and we were not afraid. They buzzed around us, millions of them, their fuzzy bodies vibrating like they were giving us superpowered butterfly kisses all over our bodies.

Then they flew off.

And I wasn't scared for dark to come anymore, because the darkness wouldn't feel so lonely. We'd got some stuff off our chests. And the world felt less lonely when you got some stuff off your chests. The world felt less lonely with our army of bees in the world.

Dark's here.

I carry the Tilley lamp. Beth and Aunty Kat are on each side of me.

225

Tom Aiken has the gaff. We walk up the river. I am the river warrior, Tom Aiken keeps saying I am, and I'm not scared. We'll walk up the river in the dark and hook eels by their mouths and then swing them onto the rocks. Tom Aiken says he'll go first and then we can try. We can catch one each, he says, because Koro likes them smoked. When Nanny brings Koro back, he'll be happy if we have smoked eel for him.

'Watch the water carefully,' Tom says. 'Point if you see one.'

A bit of moon is high in the sky now, and the air is getting cold. Some water gets in my gumboot.

Tom Aiken turns to us, then puts his finger to his lips. Beth whispers to me, 'Can eels hear?' and I shrug, and Tom Aiken is creeping up the bank. Then I see the eel, swimming just ahead of us in the same direction we are walking. Tom Aiken turns to us again and gives a big grin before he takes a different grip on the gaff. He lifts it up over his head and swings it, letting it cut through the water, hitting the eel's head, then swinging it right up behind him and the eel is on the end of the hook, and Tom Aiken yells, 'Yeeehhhaaa!' and keeps swinging the eel around and around like a windmill, really fast, before he smashes it down hard on the rocks. The eel carries on moving a little bit, but not much. Tom gives it one harder hit on the head, while we watch, our mouths hanging open.

An eel has been hooked by its head and smashed onto the rocks, and I feel a buzzing in the bones of my hands because I would really like to gaff an eel too.

Tom Aiken puts the eel into the bucket Aunty Kat is carrying, and then lifts up the gaff, grinning, 'Who's next?' And everyone looks surprised when I step forward and say, 'Me.'

The gaff is really cold and more water gets in my gumboots, but I don't care. Holding the hook I feel like the river warrior Tom Aiken says I am, and river warriors don't care about water in their gumboots. And then I start to wonder about what shoes a river warrior would even wear, and without thinking I kick the gumboots off onto the side of the river, and I pull off my socks with one hand, the gaff still in the other. The socks have fire trucks on them. River warriors don't wear socks with fire trucks on them. My feet are bare now, and no one is saying anything to me about taking off my gumboots and socks. I see out of the corner of my eye Tom Aiken nudge Beth and Aunty Kat. He might have shushed them up.

I am in the front, leading the way with the gaff in my hand, and the only reason I need the light that shines from the Tilley lamp is so I can see the eels I am hunting.

That is the only reason.

I see an eel swimming ahead. I turn around and put my finger to my lips. In the Tilley lamplight I see Tom Aiken smile, and Aunty Kat and Beth's wide eyes. I turn back to the eel and start creeping, my feet getting all scratched up, and sometimes the way I step on the rocks hurts so bad I should cry or yell about it, but I don't. I am a bare-footed river warrior.

I creep up behind the swimming-slow eel. He turns fast towards a dark deep part of the river and I almost stop, but I can feel Tom Aiken right behind me, so I don't stop. I follow. I walk right into the deep dark part of the water. It comes up to the waistband of my shorts. Beth and Aunty Kat have stopped following us, and Tom Aiken has snatched the Tilley lamp from them, for me. To help me see. I search the dark water for the eel but I can't see him. And for a second I think of my bare toes, but I just grip tighter on the gaff and the thought goes away. Tom Aiken points and we see the eel coming up the other side of the deep dark water back into the shallow part. We creep through the deep part. My belly button is wet.

The water gets shallow again, and we still have the eel in our sights.

'There,' Tom Aiken says. The wind chills my wet legs. Tom is pointing. I think the eel must only be another small step away from me. It seems stopped. Like a bird gliding on wind, not using its wings.

'Lift slowly,' Tom Aiken says in my ear, and for a second his arms are on mine as he pushes the gaff down hard and I feel it hit something very hard and very soft. Both at the same time. Tom Aiken pushes my arm into a swinging motion.

'Keep swinging, buddy! Keep swinging! Swing all the way to the stones!'

I think I feel Tom Aiken's hands push my arm into more of a swing and as I pull the windmilling eel down to thump it on the rocks, I think I feel Tom Aiken's hands on mine, but when I look up, after I have smashed the eel hard, Tom Aiken is a few steps away from me with Aunty Kat and Beth, and his arms are folded.

Lupo was so excited when we got back to the tent. He licked all the eel blood from my fingers, licked the smile on my face, then went back to licking eel slime and blood.

We got warmed up by the fire. I warmed my feet and Tom Aiken gave me a pair of his big woolly socks to put on. His Swanndri too.

Aunty Kat pulled out a book. It was the one about Māui finding his mother. 'I thought we should get into some of the ones in the bottom of that big box you have stashed away, Ari.'

She opened it and a dried flower fell out.

She paused on some words and she read it slowly, but she read it all, every word, and it sounded so magic, this other language. Ours.

I imagined me and my aunty Kat in the kitchen doing dishes or something, and Uncle Stu would come in and we'd say: 'Hi there, ūpoko mārō.' Right in his face, smiling.

Then in te reo we'd tell him we'd like to break his jaw, clean him up, and he'd say. 'What are you saying?'

Me and my aunty Kat would be smiling and smiling, and she'd say, 'We hope you enjoy your dinner.'

She closed the book. 'My te reo might come back to me eh?'

I would sleep fine. After the eeling and the yelling out bad words and the story in the magic words beside the campfire. If I had to, I could sleep outside the tent on lookout. I was as big as the whole sky knowing what I knew now.

Jade and Toko

Jade told Aroha first. They were sitting above the wheelhouse, cross-legged, Taukiri asleep on a blanket beside them.

'We're going to have another baby,' she said.

And Aroha hugged her.

'I'm pregnant.' Jade said, and Aroha nodded.

'Have you told Toko?'

'No, not yet. I want to make it special.'

'It already is.'

Aroha was always so predictable, so level-headed. It was something Jade tried to love about her.

'Will you and Jack have kids?'

'I hope so. Hasn't come easy.'

'You'll be an amazing mother.'

'You think?'

'If anything happens to me and Toko, you have to take Taukiri, and …' Jade placed one hand on her flat belly, the other in Taukiri's black hair. 'Will you?'

'Of course I would, but I won't have to.'

'I know.'

Jade thought of how it might have been if Sav were alive. Her baby would have been just a little older than Taukiri. They could have, would have, played together.

But Smart-Jade knew if Sav were alive where they'd be.

I am tearing at things I shouldn't be. I rock things. I shake. I shake. I stir up waves. I pull and push and sweep.

I am the wind rushing down a narrow winding road. A moving truck is barrelling down it too. Because Māmā and Pāpā are moving to a bungalow at Gore Bay so they don't have to drive past the Craypot anymore.

'It's just down the road, Kat. We'll see you more often than you'd like to.'

Alone Māmā says to Pāpā: 'She's so independent. She doesn't need us. But we need to be away from that godforsaken place.'

And so they leave, and Kat feels so hard done by, almost abandoned, though she is old enough to look after herself, always has been – but still.

She moves in with Stuart Johnson, to make him lovely dinners and paint her nails all day long. He cares, and she's so hurt and she needs someone who understands now.

Who knows the history, the story, so she can share bits, snippets, and he can fill in the blanks. The cavernous holes.

'My mum is such a bitch, you know.'

'Do I what?' he laughs, and she does too. He rubs her back. 'She can be a bitch all right.'

And because Kat knows he's just trying to comfort her she laughs again. She is sure that he knows she doesn't mean it, is just getting it off her chest, loves her māmā, and that he doesn't mean it when he says it too. He's just making her feel understood. I see all of this, as I rush around them, a chilly winter wind, rushing in through the windows, rattling the door.

Hā.

He doesn't say he thinks her brother was up himself, because that would be inappropriate.

Under the circumstances.

Jack and me and little Tauk box up our things and pack them into a moving van too. We will go to live near Māmā and Pāpā.

In Cheviot.

They need us. They've lost enough. 'We're all just up the road, Kat.'

Now no one is dropping in to visit her at the farmhouse unannounced. Which is good, she and Stu decide. I hear her say that and him say that. And who am I to argue when I'm dead and this happened all so long ago, anyway? It's ideal actually. God they could be annoying, she says.

Arrive at the worst times, without calling first, he says.

But that is long ago now.

Now my boy is with her. And she has taken him to a river, to camp, to eel, to yell at mountains, to give him the childhood I can't. He kicked off his gumboots to hunt down an ancient fish, in a dark river. I wish he had hooked me by my mouth and smashed me upon those rocks, just so I could be the blood upon his fingers. Just in case he might decide to put me on a fire, cook me, take a bite of me.

Swallow me, please. Stop my fret, my fight.

Swallow me.

Jade and Toko

Aroha came to the boat to babysit. Kat was going to but then she was invited to a party instead, so couldn't. Toko and Jade were going out alone for the first time in forever. They left while Aroha was teaching Taukiri a brand new waiata, 'Tai Aroha'.

Jade stepped into the doorway of the tiny cabin. 'Sorry, just want to say bye.'

'You said goodbye already,' Aroha said, still strumming her guitar. 'Go. Have fun.' She waved Jade off.

'Bye-bye, Mummy.' Taukiri blew a kiss.

Jade kissed the top of his head, 'I love you,' she said into his dark hair that she let in her mouth, catching the strands in her teeth.

'Ouch!'

Aroha saw. Jade was afraid her sister-in-law thought she loved her son too much. But Aroha had no children – she had no idea. She couldn't understand the feeling of wanting to put your own child in your mouth, Jade thought. Of eating them up, keeping them safe forever.

'Love you, Mumma!'

She gave him another quick kiss then went back up to the wheel-house. Toko went to say goodbye too.

'Be good, buddy, love you.'

'Okay, Daddy. Love you. Me and Mumma make you pancakes for brekky tomorrow, K?'

'K, son.'

'For F's sake,' said Aroha. 'Get going.'

Jade could hear Toko give one more kiss. Then a tickle. 'Hang on,' Toko said. 'If Aunty's teaching you a waiata you need to be holding a guitar.'

Taukiri squealed. Jade knew he'd be thumping his feet on the bed and she closed her eyes. Toko would put his guitar in his son's lap and it would be too big and the boy would have to reach over the top to touch the strings. He'd hardly be able to see Aroha over the guitar, but he'd feel her and he'd listen and he'd be falling in love with music, waiata, te reo, his aunty.

From the wharf, star and moonlight shivering on the sea, the boat bobbing, Toko and Jade hear them. The guitar, singing, laughing.

At his truck she says, 'I'm driving.'

'My truck, woman.'

'Don't care, boy.'

'Is that right?'

'That's right.'

And on the road the air thickens because it's been so long since they've been alone.

Jade pulls the truck to the side of the road. She leans, loosens his belt buckle. She tears the fly of his jeans down. Takes off her underwear and climbs on him. Pulls her dress up. Can't get close enough. They push against each other so hard, so deep, no air between them. He squeezes. Arms tight around her back. Presses her close into his chest.

Can hardly breathe. Dull pain in her tail bone, from something, some cruelty, from once upon a time long ago. The pain rises, thunders. She cries.

He hesitates.

'Don't stop.'

Squeezes her harder then. Hurts her. Hurts her good, all of it. Might not know he's hurting her, but she pretends he does know. Bites into his shoulder to stay quiet. Pretends he knows how much he's hurting her. Makes her come.

'You know,' he lifts her shirt, touches her tattoo, 'there are five tūī here. Maybe we will have ourselves five baby birds.'

She bends and kisses his tā moko and warm skin and looks into his sea-green eyes.

233

'We're having another baby,' she says. 'We're going to have so many silky babies to read my books to.'

They make it to the Craypot in time to watch Tommy play his first game in the pool tournament. Who knows? They might go to the beach later. Collect some driftwood. Light a big fire. Night's young. Toko's left his guitar at home with Taukiri, but that's okay, Toko's hands will be free then.

Tommy howls, 'Cheeehooo, my bro's here.'

Bryan, the bar owner, thumps his fists on the bar. 'First round's on me.'

The bar crowds. Toko's got a glow on.

Turned from her, Toko's laughing at a joke, he's laughing and laughing, and Jade wants to know what the joke is, because she wants to know what's making him so happy now. But it's so loud.

And there's Kat! In a silky red dress.

'Kat,' Jade yells.

Kat waves, mouths, 'Back soon – we gonna par-tay,' and in a flash she's gone. Jade looks out the bar window, sees her running down the street with her friends.

Toko pulls Jade from her bar stool to his lap.

'I saw Kat.'

'Where?'

Jade points out the window, 'She was just there, she's gone now.'

'She'll be back.'

'Sing me a song while we wait, boy.'

'Boy?'

'Boy.'

'All right, girl.'

'Woman.'

'Woman?'

'Your woman.'

'My woman. Now don't that have a ring to it?'

Then the jukebox clunks and Tracy Chapman's singing about speed and escape.

Drunk. Fast. Car. Deal. Drive. Fast. Decision. Leave. Die. Drive. Fast. Car.

Toko sings and then Jade sings with her husband because she hasn't seen them yet.

Jade and Toko are hovering like pāua.

Toko laughs and whispers she's lucky she's beautiful and got a nice arse because she can't sing. Not for shit.

Then, Jade hears a voice behind her. 'She sure does. You right about the singing there, bro. Sorry, should I say, Toko. You fucken right about that.'

Jade feels Toko's fingers press into her belly.

There's three of them.

One has long wiry black hair threaded with beads, another has a long ginger goatee, colourless eyes, a slouched back, and fat pock-marked arms flecked with silver, like he's bursting at his seams.

The third is Hash.

Jade wishes she and Toko had stayed home. Why had they wanted more than they had on the boat?

'No trouble here, fullas,' Bryan says.

'Yeah, course not, Mr Bartender. Get us four bourbons please.'

Jade feels the air in the room begin to boil.

Car. Fast.

'Why're you here, Hash?'

'Business, Jade. Just business, don't you worry, wouldn't come all the way here just to see you fullas. Just thought we might kill two birds with one stone.' He lets out a dusty laugh. 'Reminds me, saying that, always liked that bird tattoo of yours. Hot number that was. So long ago it seems now, right?' Hash steals a look at Toko. Checks to see if what he is saying is hitting the right chords. 'Another skank's day out that turned out to be. You two had a lot of them, little ho days out. Playing the victim now, though, aren't ya?'

Jade feels sick listening to him. At knowing Toko is listening to him. Hash takes a sip of his drink.

'Hey. Congrats to the happy couple,' Hash lifts his glass. 'Good on you, bro. Fuck it, I don't care if you don't consider me a bro. We brothers all right. Good on you for making a decent woman out of her. Ha, Jade!' And he lifts his glass again, downing his drink in one gulp, before he slams it on the bar and asks for another.

235

'I don't think so, mate,' Bryan says. 'I'd rather you guys just left. Or I'm calling the cops.'

'Ahhh, the po-po. Slow bunch, aren't they?'

Jade feels the mistake Bryan has made, threatening them with authority. She feels it kick right in her pregnant belly.

Toko stands, a slight sway in his legs, 'Don't worry, Bryan, we're gonna head off.' He pushes Jade behind him. 'It's been a good night.' Toko is trying to keep the slur out of his words, but his trying makes it worse.

'Oooo-weee, had a bit to drink tonight there, bro. It's all good, us too. We been drinking too. You remember, Jade? Shit, good times. Good times.'

Toko looks at Hash's bros, then, with one finger, flicks the drawstring of Hash's hoodie. 'Where's your patch? Ahh, I see. Lost a few brothers after your mate did what he did?'

'You rude. These are my brothers.'

'Right, good for you. Given gang life the boot?' Then Toko laughs, 'Nah, nah, the other way around, wasn't it. Stink one.'

Jade has never heard her husband talk the way he is.

Hash stops him. 'Hey, where's your bro? What's his name – Tommy?'

Tommy comes towards them then, his pool cue in hand.

Hash thumps his glass down on the leaner. 'You.'

Tommy raises the pool cue, just slightly. 'Nah, bro, not me. I didn't kill her.' And he lowers the pool cue, just slightly. 'You know who did that. Look, we don't want trouble.'

'You should've thought about that, before you decided to root my missus.'

'Someone had to.' There's a sudden spike in Tommy's voice. Jade sees the man with the ginger goatee snigger. Almost like he's laughing at Tommy's one-liner, laughing at Hash. Allegiance to nothing, she sees. There's something unnerving about him. The glazed look, the bored way he leans against the bar. As if he doesn't know where he is, or why he's here, but that if something doesn't happen soon, he'll start it himself. He's hungry for something, something base.

Fast. Decision. Car. Die.

236

Jade says. 'Just go home, Hash. Why should anyone get hurt now?'

'I dunno, Jade. But I do wanna hurt someone. I need to hurt someone and because I don't like your boys – I really fucken don't – *they* who I wanna hurt. You know us, we don't let things go, not nothing.' Hash lifts his glass and throws it across the bar. It smashes against the wall.

'Who is *we* now?' Jade says. 'You've got no one.'

'Stop talking to him, Jade.' Toko steps towards Hash. 'You think you can hurt me. Look at the state of you.'

Bryan comes around from the other side of the bar. 'Settle down, guys. Cops'll be here any minute. Just settle down, all of ya.' But there's a weakness in his voice. Red cloth to bulls.

Jade tugs Toko's T-shirt, 'Let's go home, baby.'

Hash strides towards her. 'No one's going home yet.' He picks up the ginger beer she's set on the bar and throws it in her face, then he hurls the empty glass at the bar's fridge door and it shatters to pieces. Broken glass everywhere.

'Hey!' Bryan yells.

'*Ho!*' Hash yells back, cackling.

Toko lunges and punches him in the jaw. Tommy lifts the pool cue overhead and brings it down on Hash's shoulder. There's a splintering crack.

The man with the ginger goatee – like he's a robot and has just been switched on – whirrs to life. He tackles Tommy, and the man with the beads in his hair runs forward. They kick Tommy.

Boom, boom, boom.

Toko pushes Jade away, sending her into an armless, stumbling-backwards-with-no-control fall. Like a crowd-surf she didn't ask for, a joyless crowd-surf. A set of soft hands pulls her to a bosom.

Jade cannot see Toko.

She hears noises. A crashing and a smashing, an ugly crunching and a gasping, something spilling and something breaking.

Make her bare her teeth, the noises do, ready herself to claw out eyes. No way she'll let anyone hurt another person she loves. She tears the soft hands from her. Rushes from the crowd.

A thought comes at her, breaking her momentum, like a colourful beach ball tossed: tomorrow, she and Taukiri should make Toko pancakes. She hopes she has eggs in the galley. They should pick some up, on the way home.

On the way home.

They have to get home. Fast. Car.

They have to get home and to get home she must claw out eyes, so she pierces the floating thought with her talons and lunges.

Decision.

A bar stool has been lifted, high up in the air, so high it might bust the ceiling, might smash it open, let in the moonlight and the starlight and no one would want to punch anymore.

But good. It's her Toko who wields the bar stool and she runs towards her warrior, ready, if she must, to fight at his side.

Then she sees something and it is like she is watching theatre, she runs but she is running like she runs in dreams, sprinting and sprinting but gaining no ground.

Toko brings the wooden bar stool down and into Hash, knocking him from his feet. Tommy swipes at people with his pool cue.

What is harder and meaner than wood?

Metal.

From the jukebox Pat Benatar is singing 'We Belong', and behind Toko's head is an ugly grey thing and the ugly grey thing has a hook on it, and is metal so should be used to pry things, like boots and boxes open, and where has it been all this time? Where was it, not up his sleeve? In a box? No, perhaps behind his back, in the waistband of his dirty jeans. Perhaps there the whole time.

The man with the ginger goatee cracks the hook against the back of Toko's neck and there's a crunch. A soft sound like a fistful of bird's eggs being squeezed.

And he strikes again, as Toko falls back. Strikes again and misses, and he strikes again into the lovely dip where Toko's nose meets his eyes, where his eyes meet his forehead.

And when Toko thuds to the ground, the hollow sound of his breath busts from him.

And the man aims once more, now for Toko's teeth.

Jade hurls herself, wings behind her, vicious like a dog.

238

She pierces the white skin of his arms with her fingers, she kicks him, and she punches him, screams at him and spits in his empty eyes, snatches his long ginger goatee and twists it in her hand, but he sets a single palm on her head and takes a handful of her hair and scalp and he pulls her head down then lifts her up until she's lost the ground beneath her feet and he flings her to the floor and she sprawls. But quick like a dog, she kicks up and leaps, and Pat Benatar is singing out the last of her ballad. We belong. We belong. We belong.

And down the metal comes, down it comes, freeing the beautiful white teeth from Toko's open mouth. As Jade leaps forward, pieces of Toko spray out and land heavily on her, burning her skin, and she falls on the floor where Toko lies and takes her husband's face in her hands and she wishes she didn't look at his mouth, and now she will spend the rest of her life wishing she didn't look. She closes her eyes and kisses him better.

Kisses. His cheeks. Kisses. His neck. Kisses places. On his face that. Her lips don't. Recognise now.

Calls out something, calls out for someone to come and fix what's fucken happened in this godforsaken place. Love him to life! Love. You cunt of a thing. But she stops that talk. No. No. No. What did Toko say? Love. Love. Yes! There's no darkness love cannot light! You cunt of a thing. No. No. No. Love. It's all she wants to do. Love Toko. All she'll ever want to do. Wraps her arms around his shoulders, tries to lift him. Awake, my Toko! Remember, *there's no darkness love cannot light*, and she keeps loving him and will until he stands up, and takes her home, to their boat, to their bed. To their son and the other babies they haven't even had the fucken chance to make yet.

Had. A. Feeling.

Could. Be. Someone.

Toko's woman. Mother of Toko's babies. *Be someone*.

She looks up. On the street there's a face staring into the bar through the broken window, glass shattered on the street around her, red silk lifting from her body into the wind.

Kat screams, her hands fly to her mouth.

The jukebox makes a mechanical clunk. And Smokie comes on wanting to know where Alice has gone. He guesses she has her reasons, but he just doesn't want to know.

Taukiri

The surf had been amazing and being alone with Megan was more amazing. No one would find us here, where we were. She used her credit card, bought me a ferry ticket, and we got my car. The surfboard was nicked and I was sad for that. But we were alone in my car in the place I'd once parked, where I'd once lived. Between the abandoned house and the sea. And we were so safe. No one would find us here.

I was sitting in the driver's seat and she was in the passenger's seat, and she wanted us to call the cops.

'We should. It's safest. Tell them. Stay with them, then you get on the ferry and you go.'

'No,' I said.

'I'm calling, Tauk.'

'We're okay here, no one'll find us,' I said.

She picked up her phone.

'Please don't, not yet.'

'When?'

Then I kissed her, kissed her hard, so hard, so deep. Tasted her. And she kissed me back. Had my hands in her hair, then up her shirt, then held her chin. Everywhere, wanted to be everywhere. I took the hem of her T-shirt in my hand, said: 'Taking this off,' and she bit my lip until I did.

Unbuttoned her jeans and pulled them off and kicked away my shoes and my worry and all logic. Just wanted to feel her, because she was a sea, a rising swelling ocean. I kissed her freckle and she moaned. Just could've died like that, with that sound. Just could've died then when she moaned because it struck me as the most beautiful thing I'd ever heard. Could've died because, well, fuck. What I saw was the skin I hadn't seen, and oh my god was she beautiful. Was she what.

The water under the full moon is black.

Wind scatters everything. Everything, and everyone, and without hands, it is all so very hard to regather. Without a voice to call them home, herd them, warn them, tell them where they will be safe. The good seeds are scattered amongst the bad now, and only with the first unfolding of their leaves can anyone see their worth. Or worthlessness.

It is painful to only see through these watery sea-eyes of mine and hear what the wind – what I pull towards myself – will bring. The songs, the tiring words, which have begun to escape me. The jewels, the truest treasures: the lyrics, the poems, the ballads. The stories. They are the reddest, bluest, greenest jewels.

The real treasure at the bottom of the sea.

Not my bones, but what I did, and the aftermath of that, and how it will go, on and on and on.

Give me my mouth, give me my fingers and hands, so I might make something right.

I took him. I whipped him away, like the wind I am now, and told her I would take care.

She couldn't, people said. I should.

And I did. I watched her go, and I was glad, to see her back turned, her head down. I was glad to take him, and let her walk away with a child in her belly.

Taukiri's first day at school is the week the children are making Mother's Day cards. He comes home and puts his bag on the floor, and looks up at me and says: 'Hi, Mum.'

And I say 'Hi, son.'

And that is that. What's done is done.

Give me my mouth, give me my fingers. Let me fix this.

I am tired of toothing at the grey grit. At ghost sand. Biting and biting, saying nothing. Let me have one last, useless word.

242

Jade

They are alone on the boat.

She rewinds the song and plays it again.

They're crazy to have left her alone with him, she shouldn't be allowed near anyone, not ever, because they'll die. And for much longer than a mere moment she wonders if she should jump overboard with him. Drag him under and drown Toko's two fatherless babies at once.

The knife on the counter is the first thing that has smiled at her since Toko's teeth were smacked from his head. Her son is asleep on the little bed in the little cabin.

She takes the knife. The knife she gutted a fish with.

She lifts her shirt, and sits down on the floor. She aches.

Maybe we'll make five baby birds.

And she cuts into the highest bird in flight, deep in and under it, to the bone of her rib. This, at least, can go. This, at least needs to not be on her body anymore. She slices under and cries at the white-hot pain, as she frees the inked bird from her body, in a small babble of blood. And the pain feels good, like crying at a funeral, so she cuts the next, slicing it away like black pāua meat. She moves to the next one, taking a weak stab at it, but only making a pissy bleed before she passes out from the pain. Not the pain of the bleeding birds, but the many other terrible things. Does she slice at something else before she closes her eyes? She hopes so. She hopes she did a good job. She hopes she won't wake. She waits for Toko to find her. 'Toko, I'm here. I'm just here. Auē.'

Instead of Toko, she wakes to screaming, and she is tired of it. There is so much screaming, so much noise. So many words, everyday: 'How do you feel? What can we do?'

You can fuck off, she thinks. All of you.

243

Taukiri is crying beside her, his fingers on his mother's ribcage. He touches the open wounds and bleeding birds. He says, 'Mumma! Mumma!'

Aroha screams and swings Taukiri up. His hands are so bloody. Aroha whips him away like the wind.

A day later, or an hour, maybe just a minute, Aroha comes to the white room. The room where Jade has slept, drugged and bandaged up, for what seems to have been an eternity. The room doesn't rock. It doesn't glow gold. The motionlessness is harsh. Like being born into stark room from a warm blinking womb.

The door opens often, letting in more blinding light and blurry white-clothed silhouettes.

'Fuck off,' she says loudly – words from a past life – but they don't. They buzz around her like she has become their tagged property – an experiment in how much pain a person can take. The people seem busy making graphs about her like she is a statistical miracle.

'She's still alive,' they seem to say to each other. She wonders if they think she shouldn't wake.

Aroha comes to help her dress in black. 'E kare, it is the last day of the tangi,' she says. 'We need you there.'

She thinks of the apple crumble that might be there. And vomits.

Aroha cleans her up, and undresses her like she's a doll. Or like she is to be buried soon.

Aroha strips an old cloak of nettles, fused to Jade's skin now, from her. Dresses Jade, raw and wounded, in a fresh cloak of nettles.

But she won't be in the kitchen this time, to prepare the kai.

Her grief, oozing from her, could well poison the apple crumble.

When the dressing in black is done to Aroha's satisfaction, she walks Jade to the car, parked close. Special circumstances close. They walk to the car waiting in an ambulance zone, their arms linked like they are the sisters Jade thought they were. Toko made their sisterhood true. Linked them. Now he is dead. Aroha should have left her for dead.

'You need to be there. It will be harder for you, later, if you're not. You need the tangi and the tangi needs you.'

244

Jade almost trusts Aroha more than she trusts herself, because she seems to be in motion as the world around her is. She is like the sun rising as it always has. Some in, some out. Circular. Jade is tired of everything – the weather, the trees, her own beating heart saying to her, 'This has always been coming, pretty woman. Thought yours was a fairy tale? Good things are not to come. Get off the peace train, fool. The tracks ahead have been plucked away from the curving mountain like they are guitar strings.'

Even Aroha's composure says these things.

Aroha takes the gas canister out of the boot and sits back in the driver's seat. Both of them wearing black dresses. Sun shining in, hurting Jade's eyes, 'Why is the sun shining?' Jade asks. The light dizzies her.

Taukiri in the backseat. Hair combed.

Important? No.

'Mummy, where's Daddy?'

Foolish boy.

Aroha presses the mouthpiece against Jade's lips.

'Deep breath.'

Jade's head lightens. She could almost laugh.

But she asks, 'Is it okay? I mean for the baby.'

And Aroha gives her the sorriest look she's given her since she found her with the tattooed birds cut from her ribs and Taukiri's tiny hands, running across the open wounds, leaving lines like red finger-paint.

'Does that really matter?' Aroha asks, before pressing the mouth-piece against Jade's lips again.

Now, as Jade stands beside Taukiri in his pushchair, she cannot work out what those words meant.

Toko will be buried today. She cut the tattooed birds away from her ribs, and Aroha will take Taukiri for a while, just so she can rest, and she could almost laugh.

Under her black dress her knife wound is bandaged, and under the bandage she feels nothing, no throbbing, none at all. Her legs feel weak. Her heart seems to hardly beat. The soles of her feet are numb. She feels like she is floating.

245

Colleen's sparse tears don't bother her as much as Hēnare and his eyes. To look at them would require more medication, to look at them and wonder if they might have been Toko's one day would require more than gas.

The shiny black coffin her husband lies in looks small beside the large mound of earth. A man with dark glasses and a leather jacket comes to stand beside her, and says, 'Your kid?' and she looks down at Taukiri's sweet, sleeping face, turned against the side of the pushchair. Jade looks at him, his black eyes, as he says again, 'Yours? Going to be hard for him,' and he leans to whisper into her ear, 'now his arrogant father is dead.'

And she spins to face him and holds his sunglass-covered eyes with hers. Holds them long. Holds them for ransom. Holds them like she could have them if she wanted. Could rip them from their sockets. People claim her, she thinks. Why can't I take? She holds those sunglass-covered eyes the strongest she has held anything in days. She sees him try to breathe, but he can't.

'Not mine. Not his.' And she points to Aroha. Aroha's head bowed, an arm around Colleen, 'Hers.'

Jade steps away from the pushchair Taukiri is sleeping in, and away from the man. A last look, and Aroha is standing just a bit too far away from the fatherless little boy.

For one moment – with Jade a step or two away, and poised to flee, and Aroha, with her back turned, a step or two away, not poised to flee – neither of them were close enough. He was alone and yet to be claimed.

Jade walks away. Aroha would take him, that much she counted on. Aroha would not let her nephew down. She would not let her brother down.

Smart-Jade walks away and hopes they bury Fool-Jade with her foolish dead husband.

She wonders how long Taukiri is orphaned. Only seconds, which will never collect enough of themselves to make a minute.

But what's time?

He's been abandoned for an eternity.

A man with a bulldog tattoo on his neck has entered the bar, looking for a young man who owes him something.

I bang again at the windows and rattle the door. I find my way in through the cracks. Sun is outside. She doesn't even try to join me. It is too dark here, they hold her out, the walls and roof, and windows painted black. She could burn it all, but she leaves everything as it is. As it always has been.

A bearded man, tattooed down his arms, takes a bottle from the mirrored shelf behind him, pours himself a drink, takes a sip. I blow in his ear. It takes everything I have, everything I have, and I see in his eyes he hears the words I blow, the words of a song about a fast car he wished to never hear again. I see in his eyes, he knows something else is there. Me. He feels me. He doesn't blink. He turns to the man who stands at the leaner now.

'Looking for a kid. Kid named Taukiri Te Au.'

And the man behind the bar freezes up, tenses. We all see it – the man who's come with questions sees it too. 'Never heard of him,' he says.

'Don't lie now.'

'Haven't.'

'But I know you have,' he says. 'I know it.' And he leaves.

The light, the light that loses patience with me and my trying, splits everything open again, but doesn't swallow. Just splits or pierces or cuts. Again and again.

Taukiri

There's a thump on the window, almost splitting it in two, and Megan shrieks because she sees a man peer through the glass, then suddenly he is on the passenger's side and she goes to hit the lock but too late. He swings the door open wide. I leap from the car, pulling up my jeans and running, running around the car to get him, to stop him, and he is pulling her from the car and I lunge at him.

But smack. Crack. Then black.

Dream of her now. All of her, so beautiful. But the black. Just black. Sinking into the Kaikōura Canyon, muscle loosening from bone, hot blood running down my throat.

Kat has her secrets too.

The day after Māmā loses her earring, Kat drives to Gore Bay and finds me, Jack, Ārama, Tauk, Māmā and Pāpā walking the road, looking for something. She's driving Tommy's car. She pulls up, pulls over, gets out. She has been crying but has reapplied her mascara. Pinched her cheeks.

'Hi, Aunty Kat,' Ari says.

'Hi,' Tauk says, sullen, whakamā.

'Tēnā koe, Kat,' Māmā says, not looking up.

'Hey, sweetheart,' Pāpā says. 'Great to see you.'

I ask, 'Why have you got Tommy's car?'

'Borrowed it. So I could come and see Mum and Dad.'

Mum doesn't look up. 'We're having a really bad day here, Kat.'

'What's happened?'

'I've lost one of my pearls.' She looks at her daughter. 'You know, my lovely ones. From your nanny.' She goes back to searching.

'Oh, is that all?'

Mum snaps her head up, 'It's irreplaceable, Kataraina.'

'Yeah, I know, it's just,' a bubble of strange laughter comes from Kat, 'we've survived a lot worse, haven't we? At least some of us have.'

Mum doesn't laugh. 'You can't take anything seriously, can you? Don't care about anyone but yourself.'

Kat closes the car door, leans against it. 'I went inside and I saw Toko's teeth on the floor of the Craypot.'

Dad speaks up then. 'Kataraina, don't.'

'Yes, let's look for a fucking pearl earring. White like a tooth.'

'Go home,' Mum says. 'We don't need your self-pity here. Not now.'

And because I'm just wind, air, hā, blowing around people, being drawn into their mouths, lungs, thoughts, I know this now – Kataraina sees something. Something shiny.

Before walking to it, though, she thinks. She thinks about why she has come here. She has come here to tell her Mum and Dad she needs help. Because last night Stu got mad, and though he didn't punch her out right, which he has before, he was very angry because she'd put on a tight shirt and come down the stairs thinking she might to go to a friend's house while he went to pool.

She didn't, in the end. He made sure it wasn't worth it.

When he got home they argued in bed, and he lifted his arm and then he set his hand on her neck and applied some pressure to her throat, not much – and for a second she could not breathe. She would rather he'd punched her, or said something mean, pushed her in her back.

But, it was just a second. Just a second.

She feels silly then. There's no mark. Worse could happen when you hug someone too tight. What was she going to say to them? Stu pressed on my neck? They know he's done worse, and she's protected him.

And it's been a long time since he's hit her, really. Ages.

Things are going well.

She walks to the shiny thing, walks to it slowly, and steps on it, turns her foot, crushes it down into the gravel, walks back to Tommy's car, gets in and drives back to the farm.

Just a second. Nothing really.

She gets home in time to get a decent dinner on.

Ārama

Beth and I begged Tom Aiken to cook us a piece of the eel I'd caught.

Tom told us it would taste like muddy river water, but we told him about how we ate worms sometimes and this would be nothing. In the end he said of course, a hunter should eat what he'd hunted, and he cut the very end from the eel, and rolled it in some foil, and put it onto a hot rock outside the fire. It sizzled and juice rolled in oily lines down into the dirt.

The eel wasn't that bad, we ate it with our fingers, and even licked the juice off them. We felt brave and like real adventurers eating the eel I'd caught in the dark river at night. Lupo wagged his tail and his tongue was hanging out as he watched us. I held a piece of eel in the palm of my hand. He ate it. Then carried on sniffing and licking my hand until I gave him some more. Lupo was Italian for wolf, Beth had told me. Beth's aunty went to Italy once, and when she came back Beth called her on the phone and asked for a cool Italian name for her new dog and her aunty gave her one.

'Dad was pissed, though, he wanted him to be called Sav. And I was like, "Sav, like a saveloy. Dumb." He said, "No, Sav like savage," but all I could think of was savs, so, yeah, nah.'

Me and Beth would sleep with Aunty Kat and Lupo. Tom Aiken would sleep alone in the other tent. When we went to bed Tom Aiken winked at me and said, 'You look after the girls, river warrior. I'll sleep good knowing they are with you.'

'I don't need him looking after me,' Beth stamped her foot.

'Look after each other then.'

Tom Aiken was the best. He should be Aunty Kat's husband and there should be no Uncle Stu.

When we went to bed I could smell the campfire in our hair, and feel the dirt between my toes. I wished we could stay there forever, camping and running up the river, and smelling like dirt and fire when we went to bed at night.

'Does Lupo really mean wolf?' I asked Beth.

'Yup.'

'Uncle Stu has a gun,' I told her. 'One for hunting, one for pests.'

Beth shuffled closer to me. Lupo was squashing our feet. We were both thinking about Uncle Stu having a gun.

'Maybe my dad has one too,' Beth said.

That made us feel better.

Then Beth pulled out the book with the picture of the people rowing a boat to an island on its cover. The one she made Aunty Kat buy her from the guy wearing sheets on the street. The book about world peace.

She switched on her torch light.

'Read it to me, Django.'

'You can read now.'

'I know, but still, please.'

Beth hardly ever said please, so I read to her while she held the torch.

'*Sex is an ab-ab-surd thing. Imagine it. Imagine a man and a wo-man having sex without any ro-man-tic at-tach-ment. Imagine that they have no de-sire but to cree-ate an-o-ther human. Imagine people not fuu-elled by a story in their head. A story ex-plain-ing what they are bio …*' – I pointed to the word – '*bio, bio, bio-log-ical feeling.*'

'Give it,' Beth snatched the book. She read on, '*Im-a-gine that there is no ch-ch-ch-em-is-tree. How would hum-an-ity even ex-ist? Without po-e-tree, songs, hair gro-win' long and per-fuuume and gu-i-tars we would have become ex-tin-ct. There'd be no pee-oo-ple without love. And what's love? Would you have bot-he-red with love unless love made you feel like a child playing the most fan-tas-tic game? Cat and moo-uuse. Hide and seek. Without roo-ro-man-tic love, the world woo-uuld would just be trees and rii-vers rivers and ice-cap-ped mo-un-ta-ins mountains and birds now. Just an-animals. Yet ro-man-tic love is just an ill-ill-ill-loo-son.*'

Aunty Kat unzipped the tent. 'Hey. Lights out.'

Beth stuffed the book under her pillow. 'What are you and Dad doing anyway?'

'What do you think we're doing? Playing tiddlywinks? We're tidying up. Putting out the fire. Coming to bed soon. Go to sleep now.'

She zipped the tent back up.

Beth pulled the book out again. *'Pee-people are an-i-mals. They might write po-e-tree and let-ters and sing. But they are an-animals.'*

Beth closed the book.

'You've got real good at reading, Beth.'

'Like I said, I want to move to Auckland and get a job in my aunty's office in the big city. Smart car. Remember. Me and you. Husband and wife. No yuck stuff. No poetry. We are Django and Doc. Not Django and Broomhilda. Look at the mess those two made.'

'They lived happily ever after.'

'Did they? Sure we *saw* them ride off, but did they?'

Lupo came up to lick our faces, maybe get a bit more eel juice off our chins. And it might have been the wind, but outside it sounded like our army of bees was circling and circling, keeping watch.

Taukiri

Dream I'm singing to her. A love song, softest I've sung it.

You can make any song soft and yours. I make Pat Benatar's 'We Belong' soft and mine. For Megan.

We are kissing in my car and I'm teasing her, and I'm gonna do all sorts of things to her now, and she's laughing, she's laughing like there's so much more hope in the story, more than we thought.

'I want you – always will. Again and again. You ready?' I ask.

She laughs. 'You're too young for me.'

'Like the stars?' I say and bite her hair.

'How'd you find my attic, boy?'

I peck at her cheeks, over her nose, to the freckle on her eye. Most beautiful starfish I've seen.

'You brought me in from the rain,' I say.

'Wet bird,' she says.

'Let's go together. Let's go get Ari together.'

She climbs into the driver's seat. 'I'll drive.'

'Good. And I'll sleep.'

Dream that when I wake, we are almost at the ferry. So close now.

I wake for real, my head throbbing, taste blood in my mouth, sit up. 'Hey,' I say.

The voice is murky and black and my ears are ringing. 'I knew your mother,' it says.

I look into the rearview mirror.

In the moonlight his teeth look so broken.

Ārama

Tom Aiken thought it would be best to arrive home right on milking so that Uncle Stu wouldn't be home. I didn't want to go back. Wanted to stay by the Conway River and live there.

I packed my things back in my schoolbag. Real slow. Then I was worried I'd forgotten to pack my plasters, so I emptied everything out again. Found the plasters. Counted them. There were fifty-three left. Folded everything back up, rugby jersey, shorts, wet togs, even my underwear.

Toothbrush? Emptied everything out again.

'Hurry up,' Aunty Kat growled. 'Tom's got work.'

Stubbed my toe on a tree root walking to the car. Stopped. Emptied my schoolbag. Got the box of plasters. Put one on my toe.

Counted them again, carefully.

'You've got to be kidding,' Aunty Kat growled.

Only fifty-two left now.

Packed everything up again. Got in the car, tried to think of something we should do before we left, but before I could, we were off.

On the drive home Tom Aiken told Aunty Kat that she should just pack her bags and take me and go. We should find Taukiri and head down south to Nanny and Koro, and everyone could just start looking after what was left of this family. Aunty Kat was nodding but I could see her hands holding each other tight, like they weren't sure.

'You know, Kat, Stu ain't gonna change. He has been and always will be an arsehole. More than that, Kat. Actually he is more than that.'

'You don't know him like I do, Tommy. He can be sweet.'

'Really? Can he, Kat? I don't think so. And Ari,' Tom Aiken lowered

254

his voice, 'does Ari think so? Does Ari think he can be sweet? That's one thing Colleen was right about.'

'She was right about more.'

'Like?'

'Jade.'

'No she wasn't. She was not right about Jade.'

'If it hadn't been for her …'

'There'd be no Tauk.'

'Toko would be alive.'

'Stop it, Kat.' Tom Aiken was looking at me and Beth in the rearview mirror. Lupo was asleep between us, his head in Beth's lap. Bum in mine. And I hoped he wouldn't fart like he had all night after eating the eel. I had almost died from the stink in the tent, which Beth had tried to blame on me, because her precious Lupo could do no wrong. Just then he let out a stinker and I wound down the window and Aunty Kat was yelling. 'You stop it, Tommy. Stop telling me I should be driving off with my dead sister's son to go find my dead brother's … She's probably dead too! Like she wanted!'

'Kat!' Tom Aiken yelled.

Lupo woke, let out a growl, the hair along his back stood up. Beth patted him. 'He doesn't like yelling,' she said, 'that's probably why he doesn't like your uncle Stu.'

'He's not my uncle Stu.'

Tom Aiken turned up the radio.

Beth waved me close with her hand. I leaned in, 'I thought Taukiri was your brother?'

'He is,' I said.

'Who's Jade?'

'Don't know.'

'There were a lot of dead people in that conversation,' Beth said. 'Like a movie.'

The smell of Lupo's fart was gone and I wound the window back up and used my finger to write 'Au Feedezeen, Uncle Stu' into the glass.

Then the name 'Jade' over and over.

Uncle Stu's steel-capped boots were not at the door. And his truck was not in the drive.

We pulled up and Tom Aiken stopped the car.

'Go in and pack your bags, Kat. I'll drive you anywhere you want to go.' He sounded angry.

Aunty Kat didn't answer him. I took my bone carving in my hand and held my breath. I wanted her to say that she'd just pack our bags and we'd go. Tom Aiken touched Aunty Kat's face. He touched the black bruise with his thumb. The black eye Uncle Stu gave her. A tear ran down her cheek. I wanted to take a breath, but I couldn't because I needed to hear her say we were going, we were going right now.

'You're my family,' Tom Aiken said. 'Please, Kat.'

'I don't know.'

I was getting dizzy, needing air. But I held my breath. Beth's mouth was open wide. I heard Lupo pop another fart. I wouldn't smell it holding my breath. Then Beth snapped her mouth shut and screwed up her face, punched me. 'You're disgusting, Ari.'

I kept holding my breath.

'Do it for Toko, everyone has been through enough. I didn't do enough for him that night. Truth is, I made it worse. I know I did. I'm the reason he's dead. I need to be the reason you live. You're not living. Please.'

Suddenly me holding my breath and Tom Aiken's sadness made magic together, because Aunty Kat said: 'Okay.'

And I opened my mouth and sucked and sucked, and the breath rushed in, and I was a kite in the sky then, bees in my bones and a kite in the sky, and wind in my hair.

I almost felt sorry for Uncle Stu. But mostly, I was just spinning under the sun, beaming, buzzing, fizzing.

Jade

Jade never found her feet again. They hurt when she walked, like her tail bone did, and she was afraid she'd be forced to live for three hundred more years, feeling like she had shards of glass in all her smallest bones. Her head forever adjusting, trying to navigate life on land after too long at sea.

She'd only known life with a man.

Good man or bad man. She'd only known what it felt like to belong to someone. What it was like to have a system. Good or bad. Galley or gang house. Fresh cod or yesterday's fish burger.

She stumbled through life for so many years after burying her husband and deserting her son.

One day she received a letter.

She had stayed in one place long enough, for once, to be tracked down. Inside was a cheque. And a note: *Taukiri is happy.*

Jade hated herself for the way that made her feel.

The number on the cheque was not big enough for her to pretend she was more than who she was, but big enough to put down a deposit on a bungalow on Rakiura. An island Toko had once taken her to. A place they'd shopped for the ship's stores and bought a bag of dried figs.

There she stayed put.

A letter had come once before when she had stayed put long enough to be found. She almost hoped it might happen again. A letter, a call, maybe even a knock on her door.

She hoped for a chance to ask the only sister she had for forgiveness, for things no one even knew of: how she had wanted to jump from the boat with Taukiri in her arms. And other things. Other things she had done, other cuts she had made. What everyone had suffered over:

Toko dead. The fact that if she'd never come into his life he would still be alive.

But no letter came.

Jade's hair greyed, her face became lined.

The scars on her ribs, though, looked as if she'd cut herself only days ago.

When she thought of the baby who died in her belly because she'd bled too much and had too much pain to kill, she knew she deserved every version of loneliness and isolation there was.

Rakiura provided isolation, facilitated the loneliness.

Until. One spring morning Jade's phone rang. It was Aroha calling, Aroha calling her and asking: 'Is it too late to fix this?'

Jade didn't know.

'We might as well try.' And Aroha laughed.

'We might as well.'

Aroha would bring Taukiri down to Rakiura on the boat Jade and Toko had once lived on.

'Do you mind? Would you mind seeing her, seeing *Felicity*?'

Jade couldn't be sure, but she said, 'No,' like she was sure. 'I'll see my son. So what does a boat matter?'

'I took him,' Aroha said. 'I'm sorry.'

'I left him.'

When they didn't arrive Jade found some courage and called Colleen, and Colleen told her what had happened.

'They were coming here,' Jade said. 'To me.'

'Well, of course they were.' Colleen hung up the phone.

Jade decided she would kill herself. She walked to some cliffs, because she wanted to die flying.

She leaned over the edge and looked down. Something in her badly wanted to jump, and something didn't. Something wanted to smash into the white-toothed bottom below. Something wanted to suffer it out. That's what she deserved. She sucked her breath deep into her stomach. The wind picked up and made a sudden, human-like protest. She was pushed back. A cry. And again she was pushed away by the hand of the wind, pushed away from the wide open space at the edge.

She was wild then, wild at herself. And ran. Found herself sprinting, leaping logs and puddles and brooks. She charged through the paddocks and the twisting trail, wild at herself. She ripped a branch from a tree as she went, and hurled it like a spear through the air.

She arrived panting back at her little island house and took out pages from a closed square drawer. Pages and pages of scrawl she'd locked and boxed. She pushed them under her arm and walked out of the house and down to the bay.

At the water's edge she held the pages.

'I wrote our story, Toko,' she cried. 'Dumb-arse I am, I can write. You wouldn't believe it,' she laughed, 'but I can write.'

She sniffed. 'I couldn't write it all though.'

'In our story we met on a beach. That's what would have happened, if we'd been lucky. But we will – in another life, my Toko. In another life we'll meet on a beach. Where did we meet, baby? Right, it was the hospital. You came with Tommy. We went to the beach after, didn't we? But to tell my story it was beach first, hospital after. What's time anyway? I let myself believe we met there. You deserved that. You played your guitar, and I danced. It's a better way to tell a story. Because the beginning can be anywhere and for me it was beside the sea, you singing, me dancing.

'When I was little my mum and dad took me to the beach, and I always imagined that would be where I'd meet someone like you. One day. One fine day.

'I let myself believe I only said no once. To him. To that dog.'

She wants to stop crying but can't.

'In my story I felt as beautiful as you thought I was.'

Jade touched the scars on her arms. Her tongue ran along the gummy spaces in her mouth. She held her fairy tale, her tragic love story, her once-upon-a-time-and-fucked-forever-after in her hands.

'I learned to read for my mum. And when she couldn't listen to me, listen to how I was outgrowing her, and told me to fuck off, because who did I think I was, so clever now eh? I hauled books under my bed and read the words Head had taught me to read, and from those

I taught myself more and more. Felicity would come back though. 'Sorry,' she'd say. 'Tū meke, my girl, you are too much.'

'I wrote our story like I was writing about an island. I wrote like I was a bird. I wrote the good. In Head. In Felicity. Because there was good, there was good. I saw it in their faces. I saw it in their shaking hands. I saw the pain in my mother. There was so much good in them, and I absorbed it. They gave it to me, without realising. No one is *just* anything. Right, my Toko? You taught me that. "I'm *just* a gang slut," I said to you. And you said, "No one is just anything." And in my story Aroha found me with only my tattoos cut. Nothing else. No veins.'

She ran her fingers over the scar on her wrist, wild at herself again.

'Forgive me.'

She put her story just out of the sea's reach. On the stack she placed a rock. To keep it from being carried away by the wind.

She wanted the words swallowed whole, like only the sea could.

The sea touched the pages. Jade watched them go. Watched them taken away in a sad purple murmur. Sea the colour of a bruise.

Fool-Jade. Smart-Jade. Become Jade.

Taukiri

'I knew your mother,' he says. He lowers his head as I sit up, and I'm happy to not have to look at his broken teeth in the mirror anymore.

'A long time ago. I'm a man you should be afraid of 'cause I'm dumb. That's what people should be afraid of. Dumbness. And pack dumbness is the worst kind.'

'Megan,' I yell. I rub my head. Find blood on it.

'Sorry about that. But it's not the worst.'

'Megan?'

He has a bulldog tattoo on his neck. He has a face that looks like he's done bad things and paid for them.

'Ah, Megan,' he laughs. 'Boys always be getting themselves in trouble for a root eh?'

'Where the fuck is she?'

He spins and points a gun at me. 'I'd fucken watch it.' Then softer: 'You remind me of someone you do, tama. Anyway, offskies, you were. Why's that?'

'I'm going to see my brother,' I say.

'You got no brother.'

'I have a brother.'

He keeps driving. Gun in one hand, steering with the other.

'Know where your mother is, tama?'

'No. I don't.'

'I do. Was looking long. Found her. Faaarrr. Years. I find her, and you! You see, there was talk today. I was waiting for my load to turn up, I was waiting. Unhappily waiting. 'Cause, actually, lately I been thinking I want out, just there are some things I wanna do first, you know. Before I check out of the game, there's some rights I gotta wrong. Wrongs I gotta right.'

I search the car for a weapon. And he sees me searching.

'You scared, tama. You should be. You fucked up. And people are mad. Real mad. And when people fuck up like you have, someone gotta pay. Word is Taukiri Te Au is a narc, 'cause he wants to root Jason Kyle's missus. And fuck,' he laughs loudly then, 'I sure saw that was true.

'Anyway I was waiting on that load, and in that load is some stuff I been getting stuck into myself, you know, but as I said, I been wanting out. And the boss comes to me. "Know a Taukiri Te Au?" Fuck me, I think. *Taukiri Te Au.* Fuck me. Ain't life like a fucken box of chocolates? You should be scared, tama. I've killed people.' He pulls off to a side road and pulls up beside a boatshed, absolutely no one around.

'The story I'm about to tell you is going to come as a shock, tama.'

What the fuck is going on? I'm shaking, I can't stop my knees jolting up and down. I feel frozen to my guts.

'A real shock,' he says, tapping that gun against his forehead.

'I ordered this gun,' he spins round, points it at me, 'to your koro's head. The koro you ain't never met. I ordered him shot. Watched your mumma crying at his funeral.'

And he starts to cry now. The sound he makes is horrible, like he's never cried before. It's choked, constricted, pained. Like his lungs are full of black, black ghost sand.

'Was all good. Part of the life, you know.' He turns to face me. 'This also going to come as a shock … I got your pa done in too.'

His face suddenly brightens, beams, like a kid. 'So can you imagine my surprise, when my boss says to everyone, "Find Taukiri Te Au. And fucken kill him." And boy, if I don't want to get to you first, if I don't want to find you more than anyone else.'

I stop shaking then, and my body goes so empty and numb and hopeless, but he keeps talking. 'I sometimes thought of you over the years. You see, orphan too, tama,' he slaps his chest, 'orphan too.'

He breaks into a dry laugh, 'Look at the animal I am now. Faaarrr.'

His dry laugh becomes a cry again. He cries a while before suddenly stopping, and sucking air hard through his nose then wiping it with the back of his hand.

'You don't seem so bad though, tama. You look like you never hurt anyone. But you sad. I know that. I hear that. You sad. And she too. And me, but I don't deserve sadness, sadness is for ones who got a soul. You see in my eyes I don't got a fucken soul. That's why you scared. And you should be, we animals we change. No reason. Too stupid. Not like your mum, not like your dad. Faaarrr, even Head, your koro. Too smart for his own fucken royal boots.

'I like the dark now. In my pōuri.'

He reaches into the glovebox. When he opens it, I see the chocolate box Ari gave me. And I want that carving around my neck again. My heart is so exposed. My chest so unprotected. I feel so dumb for taking it off.

'Not much money, eh tama. Life is like a box of chocolates. But in this one there was fuck all! Beautiful carving though.' He lifts my bone carving out of the box and dangles it in front of his eyes. He becomes absorbed in the beauty of the bone. The ridges and intricacies.

Then he drops it. Snaps the box closed.

The lights of the Picton ferry were not far off, lights blinking in the distance, floating on the water.

'Megan?' I ask again. 'Please.'

'No harm. Promise. It's you I came for. But I made no promise to her. You owe me, tama. I mean if you ain't a root she remembers, if you ain't a man she remembers forever, I don't know what would be.'

And he's crying again, and saying things I can't understand. He's admitting to ten thousand wrongs, and they come out of him like murky water, flooded and full of debris, held back too long. I don't want to listen.

'Bad things. I'd do bad things, then get me some P. Or I'd get me some P, then I'd do bad things.'

Tears fall down his craggy face.

I don't know what to say, so I say nothing while he bangs his head against the steering wheel.

He bangs and bangs.

He gets out of the car. With his gun he gestures me out. 'Let me look at you.'

I get out slowly. It is hard to move my body. I stand, frozen. I

263

wonder if I should just try and run. Run and hope he won't shoot me in the back. He looks into my eyes for a long time.

'Beautiful eyes they were. Strong. Love to look in those eyes again.'

He runs the gun along his temple, cries more, then laughs. The sounds mix like he's an animal. Snot streams from his nose. He looks at the gun in his hand. His cheeks are wet like he's been in the sea.

'You know, this your koro's gun. Only one I ever seen or held. Heard bang. Pressed the trigger myself. A few times. Makes you feel atua eh, a gun does.' He looks up from smiling down at the gun, 'You wanna hold it?'

A trick question. Probably I go to take it and he shoots me in the face. I don't want to hold it. Or see it. Or know it exists.

'No,' I say.

'No, what?'

'No, thanks.'

He laughs.

'You know, I reckon what's in the chamber are the ones put there by your koro. A few are gone. One maybe two left.'

He touches the gun in a way that makes my stomach churn. He looks at it in a way that makes me feel ashamed.

He is not afraid of it. Of what it can do.

The numbness subsides and I'm white-hot now. It's the first time I have felt my organs, my bones and the skin on my little toes. I am acutely aware of my fingernails. My hands. Should I fight now? If I'm about to die anyway? Should I use this white-hot blood in me to fight?

He wipes his nose again, puts his free hand on his head, revealing the skinny underside of his arm, scabby and bleeding.

'We used to talk about her. And what we'd do to her if we ever saw her again. What we'd do to you.

'Then one day, faaarrr, I wake in hospital and there's a nurse. That nurse got eyes like your mother. Skin so smooth and dark, hair in a plait, she touches my cheek. "Kia tangi koe," she says. And she touches my cheek. I'm so lucky to be alive, it's okay to cry, she says. "You tried,

264

you tried in your sleep. Let it out."

'Her kindness, tama! Ever been treated so kindly it makes you wish you'd never been born? Ever since, I've only wanted to be dead. Dead, dead, dead. There are some things I gotta do first, though, like I said, couldn't just go out without them done. Because something in me woke when that nurse touched me. When she said I should cry. Wake. Boom. Faaarrr.

'I knew he'd shoot Head in his skull when I touched his shoulder and called him son. He pressed on the trigger like he'd only ever needed to hear that word. Son.'

He takes hold of my eyes, and grips the gun.

'Son eh? Ain't that word got some muscle, got some load.'

His story is broken. Like his teeth, and I can't follow him.

What is he telling me?

He snaps his head back down, cocks it.

'That fucker, I laughed and slapped his back. Fatherless fuck, I called him. And so he visited me inside, 'cause I'm his daddy now and I tell him, "Go to the tangi." I tell him to scare her, because she should never feel good in the world again. Never safe again. "Never again eh, son," I say to him. He visits me after the tangi, your dad's tangi, tama, and he tells me. Tells me he scared her good, and she walked away, and now you was a motherless little fuck. And we laughed. I thought of you, the way he described you sleeping in your pram, ya dad in his coffin. Hole dug up. Your mum walking away. And then we called you a fatherless fuck too. We said, he'll find us one day. He'll need us. And we laughed again. Fucken crack-up, we thought. And now, here we are. Need me now, tama?'

White-hot. 'No. Not at all,' I say.

'Cocky shit.' He waves the gun. 'This should really be yours. Bet you never touched anything he has?'

I don't answer and he doesn't care.

'We were Coon and Hash, our play names, because we were two dumb arseholes. Thinking we knew what we were doing, playing gang. You don't play gang. I know that now. Farrr. What I did to Sav... what I did to her. What I did to your mother, again and again.'

265

He turns and walks down over the rocks to the water's edge, and looking out at the sea he takes the gun and presses it to his head.

'This is your chance, tama. I'm letting you go. I got to you first and I'm letting you go. You get on that boat. You don't go looking for the girl 'cause then you're dead. You get on that boat, you hear me? You don't follow your dick around town now. You get on that fucken boat.'

The gun's at his head.

My lips are dry, my voice comes up from my chest caked in ghost sand and I don't know why I say it, but I do.

'No. Please. Don't.'

He storms back towards me, pointing the gun at me, and I cower. 'Your compassion for me is an embarrassment. Did you not hear me? I have destroyed your life.'

'Maybe you haven't,' I say.

He looks to the stars and laughs. 'I'll tell you another story then, tama, and then you stop me. Just one more story. Ha, you got time. And this is a killer. We make friends in prison we do. We all make friends. People need people. A man nicknamed Sunset needs me. Sunset's a monster, a white monster, who shaves his head every morning, but lets his ugly ginger goatee grow long. Loved hurt. Loved to hurt, loved to be hurt. But, more than anything, to hurt. Feels it oozing in the air around him.

'I help him. Mostly I get him razors and belts and plastic bags, the odd bit of glass. Once a knife, which he was kind enough to pull on himself. I take these things to him and so long as I keep doing that I'm not the one he uses them on. Day he's getting out, fuck knows how, he comes to me: "Who you want hurt? I might miss it here," he says. "If I do, who you want hurt?"

'And I tell him, tama, I tell him I want your mum hurt, but don't touch her. "Find Hash," I say. "Hash won't be done either, and youse do it together. I want her hurt," I say, "so hurt *him*, that Māori she with now. Hurt him bad."

'He laughed. "Now that's cheeky," he said. "That's two for the price of one. That's two birds with one stone," he said.

'And I said, "You a big stone, Sunset." I knew Sunset would miss it

266

inside, all that pain, all that pain simmering and glugging under one roof.

'Whakamā. That's all I feel now, in my bones like cancer. Whakamā killing me. And that's the end.'

He takes one step back and presses the gun to his temple.

'So go on. Now you've heard that story. Stop me.'

I don't move, or speak.

'You get on that boat, boy. You tell your mother you met Coon.'

Then. A crack. Slits the world in two. Head explodes. Shatters. Skull shatters. And oh no, the spray, the foul, foul spray. Gulls shriek. A body, just a sack. Empty thud on the ground. Move. I can't. Move. No. No. No.

Walk to him. No. Walk to him. Legs bent like a doll. I vomit.

I vomit. I vomit. I vomit.

The blood, the bone, the brain. Fuck. The whakamā.

He's lying there, his whakamā pooling around him, glugging from him, drenching the air now.

I recognise that word. Nanny used it. To describe the way other people should feel, never herself. Shame.

But I'm standing there, a dead man on the ground, and yes, there's his blood. A droplet on my shirt, one burning my face like acid. And one there, right there. Right on my palm.

The gun glints in the moonlight.

You wanna hold? Bet you never touched anything he has.

No.

Touching the gun now. Taking the gun now. My koro's gun.

Taking the gun now. Running now.

Drop the gun!

No. No. No.

Get to the car. Get in the car.

Throw the gun out the window.

I put the gun in the chocolate box. Blood. His blood, brains and bone on me. Changing my clothes now. Quick.

Got the gun? Got the gun. What the fuck am I doing?

Bet you never touched anything he has.

I open the door and vomit. I close the door.

267

I take the bone carving out of the box and put it around my neck. The heaviness a sudden comfort.

Get on the boat, back to Ārama. I turn on the engine, and go, go, go. The smell of him smeared thick in the car.

Koro's gun in the glovebox.

Go, dog, go.

Ārama

Aunty Kat sent us to play, we should stay off the farm and not tell Uncle Stu anything if we saw him. Tom Aiken was going to help Aunty Kat pack.

We took Lupo to the river, to throw sticks and stones. It was a bit close to the farm, one of Uncle Stu's paddocks ran along it, but it was hot and there was nothing else we felt like doing.

Beth was really quiet. We sat on a boulder while Lupo ran up and down the bank barking at the water. Sometimes he was really dumb. Beth threw a stone into the river. Beth pulled something out of her pocket. It was the wishbone from when I went to their place and we had roast chicken sandwiches for dinner.

She held it out to me. 'Let's make a wish.' Her finger was curled around the dry bone.

I hooked my pinky around it too. We closed our eyes.

I wished for Tauk.

Beth probably wished for her smart car in Auckland. We pulled. It broke quickly. Beth held up the longest piece.

'Good,' she said, tears in her eyes.

'What's wrong?'

'Aren't you sad?' She was frowning.

'No, I'm getting away from Uncle Stu. He gave Aunty Kat a black eye. And he's not nice.'

'And me. I'll be alone here again. Be just me and Dad again. And I really like being your sister. And your best friend. No one else could be as good as you are at playing Django.'

'Come with us like we planned, and we can still go to Auckland and buy our smart car and get a puppy for Lupo to play with.'

Beth puffed out her cheeks and closed her eyes. I put my arm around her and she elbowed me in my ribs.

'It's a mighty shame …' she said.

'Sure is, Doc.'

The sun got bright in my eyes, and stung them.

Beth saw. 'You are the sookiest Māori I ever met, Django.'

I wiped away the tears, 'And the whitest.'

'Yeah and the whitest! Is it bad I am sometimes a little bit happy your mum and dad died?'

I thought about it. 'That's bad, Beth.'

'Only because then you came to the farm.' Beth actually cried then. 'I'm sorry, I'm sorry I was happy.'

'I forgive you. My mum and dad would too. They'd want you to be happy. Not about them dying maybe, but they'd want that.'

'Maybe God did it on purpose.'

'Don't you think he could find a better way to make us be friends? I mean we were already were, kind of.'

'No. We weren't. I thought you were boring, until I got to know you.'

'Hey!'

'Sorry, but see, maybe God did do it, for us. So I'd stop thinking you were boring.'

I laughed. 'Nanny says he works in mysterious ways.'

'He or she.'

'He!'

'Maybe she,' Beth whacked me in the rib again, sending me flying off the boulder. I fell into the water and made a big splash. Hurt my bum on the rocks. Beth cracked up. Then she patted the rock again, and I went and sat beside her dripping wet.

She asked: 'What was the funeral like? For them?'

'It was a tangi,' I said.

'What's a tangi?'

'It's a really, really sad, really, really happy funeral. I think.'

'Like how?'

'Food like for a king's birthday, but people crying like every single queen in the world is dead.'

'What else?'

'And it goes on forever, but feels over real quick.'

'What else?'

'Laughing and laughing and playing with my cuzzies so much that I sometimes forgot that I should be sad and crying, then I'd realise and I'd be mad with myself. But then someone would say "you're it" and I'd be off again. Lots of crying, big crying, not like me crying or that time you cried over the dead rabbit.'

'I did not!'

'Yeah, you did. Like, if I took you to a tangi you'd see how crying can really get. You remember when I told you that time that cows make fifty litres of saliva a day?'

'Yeah?'

'Well at a tangi, it is the rule for everyone to make fifty litres of tears a day.'

'Really! Do they measure it?'

'Sure,' I said.

'How?'

'Invisible fairies flying around catching people's tears in little pots, and bringing them to the kuia in the kitchen and the kuia in the kitchen decide who can leave and who has to stay at the tangi forever – or at least until they've cried enough.'

'Wow. But what if you are not a cryer, like me?'

I tried not to look up into my head, so Beth wouldn't see I was making things up, partly because I sort of believed myself, and partly because making up a story felt like a plaster, one that covered the sorer places not on your skin.

'They have songs for people with your problem. If the songs don't work, the kuia in the kitchen will put a spell on your food to force the tears out. Sometimes those spells get out of hand and then you end up not being able to stop.'

'Ever?'

'It depends how clogged up you are.'

'I bet I'm a bit clogged up.'

'Laughter gets measured too, the fairies can tell if everyone has laughed enough. That's quite an important one, because it's just as dangerous to let a person leave a tangi if they haven't laughed enough.

271

'That's impossible to measure!'

'Nope. It's easier. Because laughing is how fairy hearts keep beating. If a fairy can survive off a person at a tangi then that person laughed enough. Tangi laughter is strong. And that's why fairies like a good tangi.'

My story was so good, I started to believe it myself, started to wonder if that was where Nanny had been all this time. Forced to stay at the tangi, until she'd cried enough, until she'd laughed a little. Until she let her face twist and all her soreness rip out of her in dog howls.

'Dreaming, Ari?'

'Just thinking about the tangi.'

'Can I tell you something and you promise not to be mad?'

'Yeah.'

'I lied to you. My mum didn't die. She just left.'

'Oh.' I hiffed a stick in the river. 'Well. She's an idiot.'

'You're not mad?'

'I don't think so.'

'Tell me more about the tangi.'

'Hopefully I can take you to one, one day. But you'd have to cry fifty litres of tears, reckon you could?'

Beth stood up. 'Of course. If I really had to. Because I am God,' and she thumped her chest and howled.

'That's Tarzan not God, you dummy country kid.'

'God can do whatever *she* wants!' Beth jumped down into the water. 'And anyway, don't call me a dummy country kid, sooky townie,' she said, and she splashed me.

I stood there with my legs really wide, my hands on my hips.

'You wanna fight the river warrior?' I chased Beth up the river and splashed her and she screamed.

Jade

Hēnare arrived, a bottle of whisky in his hand, at my door.

'Please,' he said, 'I can't take all their talk. The words make me tired.'

'Come in,' I took his hand.

We walked inside together, rolling with his fake leg.

Sitting in the house, the sound of the sea at the door, I didn't say anything, and only moved to fill his empty glass. How could I comfort him? What words would help?

He said, 'They say so many foolish things – "if Toko were alive" and "Aroha would want this" – and it makes me so tired to hear them constantly speak for dead people. They're dead.' I re-filled his glass. 'I found Jack dead on the beach. And Taukiri alive. That boy was alive on the beach.'

The old fisherman sobbed.

'He sang at their funeral, Jade. He sounded just like his father,' he said. 'Colleen didn't shed a tear. I just wish she'd stop talking. Stop talking for the dead, who have no use for foolish words, and cry.'

I poured two more drinks. And avoided his sea eyes.

'No one knows you're here, Jade.'

'That's safer,' I looked out at the dark night, the stars creating a sky above the horizonless black water.

The next evening I served him oily, salty mutton bird snared on the Tītī Islands. He ate it slowly. It was his first meal in days. He had, he told me, not managed to be sober since he'd lost Toko, and Colleen had constantly found ways to remind him who was to blame. For Toko. For Aroha.

He wanted to shout at her, 'No one's to blame. Blame has no place here. You need to know that.' And he took another bite, chewed then swallowed. 'She's only seen the side of herself she wanted to, the loving grandmother, who at least one of her grandchildren could always depend on. But she has failed, even there. We are terrible failures, Jade.'

Each bite Hēnare took of the small bird revealed a small bone.

I drank. And didn't talk. I let him eat and sit at the table I wished to have, just once, shared with his son.

When the old man was finished he cleaned his oily hands on a napkin. I avoided looking at the bird's carcass on his plate.

'Stu punches her, Jade,' Hēnare slurred. 'That's what hurts now. Him hurting her.'

'I should have brought the boat here. Aroha, she never even said goodbye. Just left. Angry. Hating me.'

Hēnare stopped talking to take another sip of his drink.

See-sawed back to Stu. 'What is he for a man?'

He finished his glass, 'My Kat. Beautiful, happy kid she was. I should have driven the boat, did I tell you, Jade?'

'Yes.'

'But Aroha said no. She wouldn't let me. I'd only had a drink or two.' The old fisherman put his head onto his arms on the table top. I touched his thick grey hair.

'My Kat, a beautiful little girl she was. Life of the party, drove us nuts with worry. Good worry, though, that we couldn't pin her down. That no one ever would. Do you know when Colleen fell in love with me?'

'No.'

'She'd deny it, but I tell you, I was leaning against a bar in some pub and she came to me – no small thing in those days – she came to me and asked me if I'd dance with her. I lifted the hem of my trousers and showed her my fake leg. "You'll have to take the lead," I said. Now, she'll deny she fell in love with me at that moment, but I saw it,' he sighed then, a forlorn sigh from his belly, 'and those twins took after her.'

Hēnare fell asleep slouched at my little table for two. He had finally been allowed to spill his own words into a wide open silence. Empty, he was tired. He had a book with him and he had a bookmark keeping his page. That comforted me. It meant he still cared what page he was on. For tomorrow.

Colleen arrived. She would like to see her husband, she said. I told her to be gentle, to try. He was getting better. Wasn't drinking as much.

'Oh. You fix him do you?' she said, angry. 'After destroying my family, it's you who fixes my husband. That's what you telling me? You're fixing my husband?'

'We're all hurting. We all hurt, Colleen.'

'Are we? Aren't your kind used to this type of thing? You people with your bad tattoos – your tattoos that show no respect for your tīpuna. People dying all the time. Sorry, it was new to us!'

'Doesn't get better.'

But, oh, it cleaved me open to be called 'you people'. So sudden, like I was a pāua and life was a rock and those words a blunt diving knife. I'd found my people. And Colleen was one of them.

She scoffed, 'Toko would be disgusted in you for deserting his son.'

'Do you know that? Do you know that, or is this what Hēnare talks about, you putting words in the mouths of the dead. Speaking for them.'

Toko's mother just stood and stood and looked and looked.

I took her arm. 'Our Toko.'

Her lips trembled, her legs went slack under her. She clutched her chest. Her eyes filled, and tears flooded her head, drowning the words. Washing them away.

All the tiring words.

There was nothing that could be said for what had happened – there were not enough words in the world.

As Colleen's legs gave out beneath her, I took her into my arms.

Hēnare and Colleen were sitting on the verandah of my little seaside house. The comfort it gave me to have people in my home was frightening.

Toko would have liked the house. Each day since this became my home, I have wished to wake here beside him. Uncountable times I'd wondered how it would feel to see him arrive in the doorway, his body blocking the view of the sea. Blocking a sun I'd have been happy to never see again if I could have had him back. I'd have stayed in his eyes. Lose myself in the depths of his voice.

Out there in the world was a child, though. Our child. He might look grown by now, but to me Taukiri was new, just hatched.

Our son's nanny put her hand on the stump of his koro's leg. An old Māori woman and old Māori man. Finally she was crying. Inside, I left a note on the table. *I'll be back as soon as I can. Stay here. I'm sorry, Jade.*

Before I went I picked up Hēnare's whisky, unscrewed the lid and took one long draw on it, shuddered.

There was a distance and uncertainty between here and where I wanted to go. Who I wanted to find, and who I would find. But for the first time in forever I was hopeful. I had fight in me. I let the window down.

I let it all rush in.

Go, Jade.

Go to them.

It is your turn.

The turn I took.

But Taukiri is in a car that speeds like he's drunk.

She thinks the winds have risen and she thinks it's strange that it could pick up so sudden.

She is tangata whenua, and she is the most important person alive.

And she must wake up, wake up and see that.

She is tangata whenua. 'Most important person alive. Wake up and see that,' I screech.

I am ashamed. I saw her whakamā and used it to steal from her.

Blow about her now, twist around her, trying to loosen the disease from

276

her bones, and muscle and skin. And Tāwhiri-mātea must help her now.
Must arm her now. Because she must fight now.

Taukīrī

This is what happened. I was standing at the bow of *Felicity*. Named after a woman I knew nothing about and probably wouldn't ever.

It was still dark. The sky was emptying of stars and the moon was pulling into the sky, but the birds were waking, singing, calling up the sun.

We were waiting for Koro because we were taking a trip to Rakiura. Me, Mum, Dad and Koro. Ari was staying with Nanny. There was a storm coming, but nothing to worry about. Koro was a good skipper. At least he used to be.

Koro finally arrived. He pulled up, got out of his car and walked over to us like he was already at sea.

'Mōrena, Aroha,' Koro said.

She was waiting for him, her arms folded. She growled at her father, my koro. 'You promised. You promised you'd be okay to leave this morning.'

'I am,' he said, as he tripped, just barely, on a pebble.

He blamed his walking stick, his fake leg. Which was partly true, they were partly to blame.

'No, Pāpā. No, you're not. We wanted to take the boat for her. Tell him, Jack, tell him. Help me out.'

My dad walked over to my mum and held her hand, and he looked at Koro, sorry for him. 'Let's take the boat tomorrow,' he said.

Mum stormed away. 'No, Jack,' she said. 'We'll let her and Taukīrī down. We'll drive. Tomorrow will be the same bullshit anyway. Ka pai, Pāpā. Ka pai.'

They spoke like they were trying to keep and reveal a secret at the same time. And I didn't put two and two together – maybe I hadn't wanted to. How was a special boat trip to Rakiura going to be a special boat trip to Rakiura if we drove Dad's car?

Mum looked at me, saw my brain working. 'The point is to go, son. It doesn't really matter how we get there.'

Koro stumbled away from the wharf, heading to his car. 'I'll go off home then. I'm sorry.'

'Bye, Koro,' I said. 'I would've got seasick anyway.'

Mum said nothing. She didn't even look at him. No goodbye, no forgiveness. Let him walk away. Like that was easy for her.

He hobbled on, slouched over his walking stick with his head hung like a dog. I ran to him and I took his shoulders in my hands and I pressed my nose to his, sharing his breath, spiked with whisky.

Koro looked at me. 'The last man who gave me a hongi was at your father's funeral.'

Mum was waiting in the car, in the driver's seat, Dad next to her. I got in the back and wound my window down. We drove off before Koro had even hobbled to his.

'He shouldn't drive,' I said to Mum.

She didn't answer. She just let him go. Just set her lips in a line like Nanny's and let him go. If anyone was going to drive off the coast road and into the sea, you'd have expected it to be Koro.

Mum and Dad argued. Her eyes on the road. Music off. Her window up. Hands at ten to two. White knuckled. Shoulders up around her ears as she went, got it all under control, everything under control, the day, Koro, the car, its passengers, her thoughts, her feelings, the journey. Now she was in the driver's seat, it had probably turned out for the best.

That's what her shoulders were hitched up for, telling herself she'd done the right thing, and then she said it: 'It's all turned out for the best, I reckon. Road trip. Quicker. Better.'

'We should've left tomorrow,' Dad was saying quietly. 'On the boat. Talked to your father, given him another chance. He'll be kicking himself.'

'If he could,' Mum softened her grip on the wheel, 'poor bugger.'

She tapped a finger, and I saw her take her eyes off the road for a second. 'See that. That's probably the colour it is for babies in the womb, you know. That smudged colour on the horizon there.'

279

Dad laughed, 'You think you know everything.' He turned and winked at me, and thumbed at Mum, 'Midwife with a God complex. Just drive, woman.'

'Hun,' she said, 'we're having another baby,' and as quick as she said it, decided she didn't like the way it sounded. She changed her words, 'I'm pregnant again. Finally.'

She smiled at Dad, then in the rearview mirror at me. He squeezed her knee. We looked to see what it was the baby might see. But the colour had already gone. Those purple clouds covered it, like bruises.

Mum turned up the radio just slightly. Easing into softness after being so hard on Koro.

'Would have been rough,' Dad said.

The sea was lashing at the rocks below. Whipping up like it wanted to say something. Like it had a terrible tale to tell.

'Wind up your window, Taukiri. That wind! I can't hear.'

'Just leave him,' Dad said. 'You know he likes it.'

I could hardly breathe with the wind in my face. Yes, I liked it.

Mum wound her window down too. Placed her hands at twenty to four.

As we took a sweeping bend another car burst into view, cut into the wrong lane.

'Watch out!' Dad yelled.

Mum swerved and the car spun like a coin. She tried to cut back and away from the narrow strip of grass between the road, the rocks, the sea. As she cut back we fish-tailed towards the other car. We were in slow motion and we were in slow motion and we were going way too fast, the wrong way.

Windows smashed. Bonnet busted. Whiplashed. Not thinking, I unclipped my belt. We had to get out. Get out. The car smacked into the sea. It filled quick. Water gushed into our open windows, turning the car to a solid steel sinker.

As I meddled, I was missing things.
Sun shines down on them. A little girl and my little boy in a paddock.

Blood flows down the river and is spilled on the rock. The eels who have tucked themselves in for the day, into their weedy beds along the riverbank, are woken by the smell of it.

But they will wait for night.

More blood, on another stone.

And there is a man I know. That man moves towards the house, his gun in his hand, as my sister looks into Tommy's eyes. He is pleading with her.

When the man arrives, he watches them through the window, and her looking into his eyes and him pleading with her crazes him.

I have been blowing wind in the wrong places.

Banging on the wrong doors.

I am my mother's daughter.

I blow at the house. My sister is crying and Tommy is holding her hand, and she looks up at him. I blow, I tear.

I am tearing.

Ārama

Uncle Stu was up the river. He was splashing water on his face. We froze. He shouldn't see us, Aunty Kat had said so, because then he'd know we were home and Aunty Kat was packing our bags to run away.

We crouched down behind a boulder.

Lupo started to chase a bee.

'I told you,' I said to Beth. 'I told you we shouldn't have come up here.'

'Come here, Lupo,' Beth whispered.

'You know he's not gonna listen, Beth, he wants that bee.'

'Lupo,' she said again, but he was so close to Uncle Stu now.

'Lupo,' I yelled.

We ducked back down behind the rock, Beth poked her head out again.

She slapped me. 'I think he heard you, you idiot. But the good thing is he'll probably stop Aunty Kat from leaving, and then you'll have to stay too.'

'You're very selfish, Beth.'

'Big word. Whatever.'

'What should we say to him?'

'Well he's not gonna talk to us anyway, so don't worry. Let's just stay hidden a bit. He'll go back to work.'

Lupo saw the bee again, started chasing again. We saw him scrambling up the bank, then Uncle Stu spun around and he said, 'Oi, mutt.'

Me and Beth came out from behind the rock. Uncle Stu looked right at us but turned away.

Lupo was bounding off into the paddocks, where the cows were

282

munching grass and looking over their cow noses at him like he was the most boring thing they had ever seen.

'I knew we shouldn't have come to the river,' I said again.

'All right, all right. I get it. Told you so. I get it.'

I saw Uncle Stu reach into the back of his truck. Lupo was on the bee's tail, a few cows jumped at seeing him, then moved.

Beth started running. 'Lupo, get back here! Stop chasing bees.'

Uncle Stu still had his back to us but I could see he was pointing something across the paddock. It took me a moment to work out it was his hunting gun. It took me an even bigger moment to work out where he was pointing it.

Beth had worked it out too; she started sprinting.

'Lupo, get back. Hey, hey! Put that gun down. He's just chasing a bee.'

I chased Beth. 'Beth, Stop!' I yelled.

The gun went off. Uncle Stu laughed, aimed, shot again, dirt sprayed up. Lupo ran. He ran and he ran.

Crack. Another bullet thucked into the ground. So close to Lupo. He yelped and then another bullet, and then one more.

Like a game, like Uncle Stu was playing a game with Lupo, but Lupo didn't want to. He wasn't having fun.

Another. *Bang!* Just to the side and Lupo ran into the bushes.

The saddest tail I ever saw between his legs.

Uncle Stu marched across the paddock.

He yelled back at us, 'Oi, kid, your dog was fucken chasing my cows!'

'Her name's Beth,' I said, a fat frog in my throat, so it was hard to speak. Pee nearly in my pants.

And Uncle Stu stood in front of the bushes and aimed his gun into them. And bang. Yelp. Another shot. No yelp, no nothing. Just Beth running, screaming, tearing towards Uncle Stu.

He put down his gun and reached into the bushes, dragged Lupo out by his dead legs, dragged Lupo like a sack. Beth was screaming and screaming. And where were our bees now, where was that army of bees now we needed them?

Then I saw. Pulling up from the river like a taniwha, swooping into the paddock and sailing behind Beth. And she must have felt those bees, felt that taniwha. I ran to catch up, but I tripped and fell and grazed my knee and it bled.

With the bees behind her, Beth went at Uncle Stu. She balled her fists and punched him in his guts. She kicked him in his knee.

'You!' she yelled. 'You absolute redneck wanker.' She punched him again and again and the bees were swarming and she was screaming. 'Bounty on your head, Stuart Johnson, the ugliest wanker in the whole damn town.'

Uncle Stu didn't see the bees and he swung his arm and drove it back hard. The back of his hand hit her face and Beth went flying backwards and smashed to the ground. The taniwha of bees shattered into a million pieces, spinning like splinters up into the air.

I got up. Blood ran down my shin, but I ran anyway.

Uncle Stu got his gun. 'Your dumb-arse dog was chasing my cows.'

I yelled. 'My brother's gonna smash your head in when he comes back to get me.'

He laughed. 'He ain't coming back. Never was. Wish he would take you. And he could try, he could try to smash my head in.' He laughed again. 'He could try.'

Uncle Stu dragged Lupo to the edge of the riverbank and slung him off. There was a splash. A bad, bad, empty, empty, dead, dead splash.

Uncle Stu walked back to his truck, got in and drove off.

Beth wasn't moving. I walked over to her. She was lying in the grass and her eyes were closed.

There were no bees then.

Just the sound of Uncle Stu's truck moving away, and when it was finally gone, just the river and cows munching grass. *Rip, munch, munch, rip, munch, munch, rip.* Like they'd just seen the most boring thing.

But it wasn't the most boring thing, it was the most terrible thing, because I've heard Uncle Stu say he was a good shot. Never missed. And he definitely didn't like to play games.

As I meddled, I was missing things.

I have been blowing wind in the wrong places.

Banging on the wrong doors.

I am my mother's daughter.

I blow at the house. My sister is crying and Tommy holds her hands.

I blow, I tear. But all is static. They stand as if they are being married. As if it is their wedding photo. I blow – but nothing moves. Only the blood down the river. And footsteps. Heavy footsteps.

I can hear those footsteps. I can hear them as Taukiri pulls me from the car. Wrenching me through the window. He pulls me from the water, brings me to the surface. We gasp for air.

'Hold this', he says, and sets my hands upon a buoy.

'I'm going for Dad.'

When he comes up for air the first time, I'm still there. 'Good, Mum. Good. Stay.'

He takes a big breath and goes under again.

When he comes back up a second time I'm still there. Clinging to the buoy.

He presses his hands upon mine, like he's anchoring me there. 'Good, Mum. Just a little longer. Hang on. I'm getting Dad.'

I already know he's not getting Dad. His dad is already dead.

Both of them.

I can feel it in the sudden chill of the sea. The way it starts to move like it is holding someone against their will. But I say nothing. Just let him go. Let him go. Like I have done to others before, would do again.

He disappears a third time. The sea rises up like a billowing sheet, only dense, only weighty. Only packing a punch. Punch enough to knock me from my miracle buoy. When Taukiri comes up for air a third time I have slipped from the angry swell to the calm dark depths below. An undercurrent sucks me towards the Kaikōura Canyon, so I will never be found.

I can feel him search and search for me. And as he does the sea pulls him further into her, further, so that soon he might not see land. Like she is trying to trick him. 'Forget about that place. Stay here, stay with me.'

I try to scream. 'Go. Go. Go …'

But he prays and cries and searches, diving deeper and deeper after every breath.

I watched Jade walk away, I watched Dad limp away, I watched Taukiri swim away and now I am drowned.

How will I ever be forgiven, when I am drowned?

How can I stop those heavy, heavy footsteps, when I am drowned? What I have done swells. Greater than the very sea we are all dead in.

Taukiri

The ferry had a map of the world on the wall in one of the passenger lounges. On the map, the water between the North Island and South Island of New Zealand looked like such a thin line, like you might be able to throw a stone from one to the other. Skimmed, it would reach on its third, maybe fourth, bounce. The water between the South Island and Rakiura looked like you could step across it in one easy stride. That I couldn't see the South Island or the North Island from here, halfway between, was what I thought about as I looked out the window.

All my money was still in the chocolate box. Along with other things. A crumpled five-dollar note and a handful of coins. Lint and bits of paper, a smoke filter, a bit of tobacco. He had just emptied it all out, all he had in his pockets. Maybe all he owned.

Before he shot a gun into his own head.

And he'd left me a note. *Your mum lives at 20 Beach Road, Halfmoon Bay, Stewart Island. Give this to her.*

He'd written three words on the back.

I felt shot in the chest when I read them. Shot by his handwriting, and the three words and what they meant. Hit hard. Squeezed his crumpled last dollars and bits of tobacco, and filter – and the note – in my hand.

I had my koro's gun, and what the fuck had I gone and done?

I was trying not to worry about Megan. I believed him – that he hadn't hurt her. I believed she was home now. I'd call her as soon as I got to Picton.

I read my mother's address again. People had addresses. Ghosts didn't, and she was real and she was somewhere with a house and a bed and a life and alive. I went outside and watched for land.

It had started to rain. When the South Island finally formed on the horizon, it was a relief. The morning had made everything look like Bones Bay, and the raindrops falling were Koro's tears, his face above mine, blocking the sun, as I woke all that time ago from one nightmare, to the next.

Am I alive, Koro?

You are, my moko, you are.

In Picton, I bought a phone card from a dairy and found a payphone. I called Megan.

'Hello,' she said.

'Hello,' I said.

'You're okay?'

'I'm okay.'

'Where are you?'

'Picton.'

'Go,' she said. 'Get to your brother.'

'Thank you for everything, Megan. I'm sorry.'

'Till soon,' she said.

'Till soon.'

I tried to take a nap in the back of the car before I started south, but couldn't. The wind blew at the car, and something else, something nagged at me, not letting me rest. Pushing me on my way, hurrying me on my journey. I turned the radio to Magic Mix FM, because I wanted old school. Because old school was what Coon might have heard, as a kid, in the pub with his aunty, eating chips from a small bag, drinking raspberry and coke, before his life turned to shit. That's what I imagined at least. That there was a time when all was good for Coon.

Chips and raspberries and coke.

It made me feel better. And so did Magic Mix FM.

The road. This road. Roads. I kept both hands on the wheel, taking the bends like a boss. Reaching Ward, soon I'd see the sea.

But first rocks like teeth, prehistoric.

Then all the water, almost smooth, never quite. The bull kelp, gulls, white sun. A seal, leaping! And I looked, I looked, and my grip on the steering wheel loosened, just for a second.

All it takes, Tauk.

I set my eyes ahead.

Magic, a stone cold classic, David Bowie: 'Heroes'.

Heart thumping with the song. At how soon I'd be at the farm.

Ari. So close now.

Another seal, and a black cloud, and the day darker, nicer, easier, slower. And then the cloud sailed on and I was moving forward and forward and forward, the road in front of me, unravelling and then reknitting itself to the shore.

And the gun. In the glovebox.

I couldn't put my finger on what was strange when I arrived. Was it that Tom Aiken's dog hadn't barked at me, or that Tom Aiken's truck was there at milking time?

Or was it just that I was there?

I turned my car off, and got out. Flies were buzzing around the back of Tom's truck. There were two dead eels. One of them had an end cut off. A steel gaff was lying beside them. A Tilley lamp, a tent.

They must have gone camping. I couldn't wait to see Ari so he could tell me about it.

A gun shot. Short. Sharp. Open field echo: *Hello, hello, hello. Is anybody home, home, home?*

Another shot. Another. From up the river.

Gun shot. Again. Shit. Guns. Shit. Coon's skull. Blood.

Should I grab the gun now? Koro's gun.

No, no way. Just a hunter. Just someone *hunting*. Leave the gun where the fuck it was. I picked up the steel gaff from the back of Tom Aiken's truck, though. There was blood and slime on it. Eel.

The shot had come from up the river.

Uncle Stu's truck. My guts froze. It pulled up on the other side of the house, I crouched, the cold steel of the gaff in my hand. I heard his boots, his heavy boots crunching on the gravel, and he stopped.

Stu. I lay on the ground beside Tom's truck, the gravel pressed against my cheek. I tried to find his feet. He was facing the house, standing still, as if he were watching something.

The butt of a rifle beside his boot. Blood on it.

A sudden wind lifted dust and dropped it. The back door of the farm house rattled, I couldn't see Uncle Stu's boots or the butt of his rifle anymore.

Where was Ari? Where was my baby brother?

I saw him. Blew about him, wanted to bully him, but I was just a light breeze on a summer day. Tāwhiri-mātea, in and out, of mouths, lungs, thoughts.

And I saw him watch the clock.

My brother-in-law had looked inside himself and felt embarrassed by his actions. He shouldn't have broken the lunchbox. He shouldn't have beaten her. Why did he have to hurt? And when he found they weren't home, he'd driven to town, and he'd bought fish and chips and a brand new lunchbox, because, well, fuck. He could do better couldn't he?

He sped home so fast that the fish and chips were still warm and the house still empty. And he put the food on the table, set the table for three, and sat down.

When the fish and chips cooled, he did too. They went soggy and his resolve did too. For warmth, he poured a glass of whisky and sculled it.

He ate a piece of fish, cold now, and the cold fat stuck in his throat so he washed it back. And he washed it back, and he washed it back, and when he found himself still waiting, sitting at the table in the dark, with the table set for three and a new lunchbox and the dinner he'd fucken bought.

He washed all that back too.

At midnight the monster reared up out of him, stomped pussy-Stu to sleep now, gutless wonder. I saw it, I saw the beast rise up and berate the man. And the beast took the food and threw it into a wall, took the new lunchbox and snapped it in two, and went to town for another bottle, because, well, fuck being made a fool of.

Stu slept at the table.

The only thing that was really different the next morning was that he found his lunch hadn't been made for him. So he took the bottle instead. Headed to work, feeling like the punchline.

Ārama

Beth was tiny, but when I tried to lift her, I couldn't. She was so heavy.

'Help,' I yelled.

But no one came. I could feel her breathing, and even though her eyes were wide open before, she had closed them. They stayed closed.

We needed plasters, both of us, we needed so many plasters. And Lupo, plasters for Lupo.

Pray? Like I did for the bird? Like I did when I wanted Taukiri to call me?

Okay. Pray.

I prayed like I was speaking to my mum, because I needed to speak to Beth's god and Beth's god was a girl.

'Hey, pretty God,' I said. 'You smell lovely like flowers but you are strong like a taniwha. Can you help us? Can you make us birds or can you make me strong to carry her? I gotta get to Tom Aiken. And God, we're getting a smart car and an apartment and Lupo's coming, so please. I owe worms,' I said. 'I'll live on them. Eat them for breakfast, lunch and tea.'

God told me I was brave. I heard it. It blew in my ear.

Beth was right. God was a woman.

I was right. God was a man.

I picked her up, and I took a step. It was all I could do. One step. Then I stopped. And I put her down. Then I picked her up, and took another step. Then I stopped.

I always knew I was brave. Even when people didn't see all my braveness, I knew I was the bravest. Beth's head hung over my arm. Her legs and head hung.

I was every kind of warrior. Bone-carving warrior. River warrior. Paddock warrior.

Anything anyone needed, I was the warrior of it.

I took another step. I stopped again. I put her down. And I picked her up. I did it again and again.

I did.

Me.

Ari.

I did that.

And even when I tripped I didn't fall. My arms were so strong. And even when Beth's body felt like it was full of a river and got heavier, I didn't fall. And even when I couldn't hold her, I did. Even as the blood rolled down my leg, I didn't let her fall.

Taukiri

I crawled along the gravel, to the front of the truck and looked out to the paddocks of the farm, and there, in the closest paddock, I saw Ari with Tom's girl in his arms.

Was that blood in her hair?

Ari stopped. He put her down. He put his hands together then he picked her up again.

Ari slumped to the ground, wiped something from his leg. Then his face, then her face.

I wanted to shout out to him, tell him I was there, everything was okay now. But I knew I shouldn't. Should stay quiet.

Then he ran. Hadn't seen me. He couldn't because he was searching for something? Someone? For help?

When he saw me crouched in beside Tom Aiken's truck, his face twisted, his body sagged, his chest lifted. So much pain in his face and so much relief in his torso.

I crawled towards him. I crawled to my brother. I crawled like I deserved to. For leaving him. I crawled towards his eyes, bright as limes, crimson-rimmed, like I'd crawl into them. Even if they were the wide open sea and I'd never be allowed out.

I pointed towards a tin fence. He went to it, and crouched behind it. And I kept crawling.

I crawled to him.

I wouldn't have been able to forget him. Not if I'd tried for ten thousand years. Not if I swallowed all the pills and smoked all the pot in the world. They made me believe I could forget him, but something stronger stopped it. And there he was.

He touched me, making sure I was really there. 'Tauk,' he said. 'Tauk.' Sounded just like he had when he answered the phone in the middle of the night. Just Tauk – nothing else. So sure, so sure of me. Like he never doubted me, but at the same time like I might not be real.

I wanted to go watch a movie or something. Do stuff brothers who haven't seen each other in an eternity should. But we couldn't. There was trouble here. I'd left thinking I was the trouble but all along the trouble was here.

He said: 'Beth.'

We crawled through the grass to her.

Her face was white, her hair sticky with blood.

'Uncle Stu hit her, and she hit her head on a rock.' He swallowed. 'Is she gonna die, Tauk?'

I put my head against her chest. She was breathing.

'He shot her dog, Tauk. He shot Lupo,' Ari cried. 'He shot him and threw him in the river.'

Then he said, like he had changed so much since I left him, like he was older now, 'Tom Aiken said dead animals in rivers can kill cows. Make them sick. Uncle Stu is a bad farmer. A bad person. The worst, Tauk, the worst.'

I grabbed him. I grabbed my brother fiercely and hugged him. 'It's going to be okay,' I said, holding him tight, as tight as I could.

I didn't want to, but I let him go. I carried Beth to my car and put her on the backseat. 'Stay here with Beth,' I said to Ari, 'Don't you move for nothing!'

He took Beth's limp hand, 'Tauk's here,' he said, 'Everything's gonna to be good now, Doc. Tauk's here. I told you he'd come.'

Stuart Johnson threw a dead animal into his river. Just left a little girl, her head split open, to bleed in a field. As if he didn't give a fuck about anything anymore. Just emptied out his pockets, but in the worst kind of way.

Jade

I didn't want to stay.

I wanted to find the people and the things I came for. Then leave. And I'd never come back here again. I'd always wondered how it would feel to return to Kaikōura, the place I fell in love, place I fell in love with.

It was worse than I thought it'd be. It stung my skin, blurred my vision. It pulled out my nerves and veins, laid them on the earth to be mistaken for worms by birds and curious children.

I'd thought of collecting the box of books, the ones Miss Matt once gave me and I'd used to escape. The ones Toko and I read to Taukiri, after he had folded sweet flowers, nettle and bitter weeds between the pages to hide the smell of my past. The books Aroha said she read to him too. I'd had to fight the tears when Aroha told me on the phone that Taukiri read them to Ari. He liked to hear them from Taukiri best.

'You'd be proud of what a good brother he is.'

I hoped the box of books was in the car with them.

Hēnare had told me that he saw the tyre marks on the road, the other car wrecked in the ditch. There were police cars by then, and he'd heard the ambulance bolting up the coast. He helped the people search the notch of land below, praying it wasn't the car he knew it was. Nothing was found. Not right away, at least

Just around the next bend was Bones Bay, which no one knew about but Hēnare.

Maybe it was because he was a little drunk and not thinking straight that he went there.

And there Taukiri was. His miracle boy washed up on Bones Bay.

I wanted to take that boy – my boy – and his brother and Kat back to their grandparents. Give them back. Scavenge what was left, and give it all back.

We could hide away together.

I pulled up the driveway. When had I last seen Kat? What would I say to her? Would I see Taukiri? Would I recognise him? Would he know me?

The gravel crunched, and the sky was vast. Two pūkeko were standing at the side of the road. They were taken by something, concerned with something. Then I saw. In the middle of the road was a hawk pecking at a dead pūkeko. The other two stood in the grass, watching the dead one be picked at. Just watching. One cocked its head, then the other. Blinking, blinking.

I got close in my car and they flew off. First the hawk, finally the pūkeko, up into the cloudless sky.

Taukiri

A car pulled up. The door opened. Beautiful woman there then, right there. Hair long and black. Eyes dark and round. A woollen cardigan on, despite the sun. Her lips purple like she was cold.

And smack! I couldn't breathe then. Who was this? Was this her?

It was her. The way her face looked was like how a boat can sway you to sleep.

The steel gaff suddenly hot in my hands.

The woman walked to Ari sitting in the backseat of the car. And Ari said to her, like he didn't have a child's head bleeding in his lap, 'I have a photo of you in my schoolbag.'

In the sunlight her hair was streaked with grey.

'I've waited a long time to meet you, Ari.' She touched his arm. She touched Beth's head. 'What happened to your friend?'

Ari was holding Beth like he was scared someone would try and steal her.

'Uncle Stu pushed her and she hit her head on a rock.'

'And where is Uncle Stu now?'

I opened my mouth to speak. Nothing came out. Gaff hotter now, chest bursting now, because, well. I tried again. 'He has gone into the house,' I said, though it felt like I couldn't really be talking to her. It felt like I was talking to the tooth fairy.

The words sounded like they'd been glued to my throat.

'He has a gun,' I said.

'He shot Lupo,' Ari said.

He looked like he wanted to cry again but stopped himself, 'Lupo is in the river. We need plasters.'

'Is anyone else in the house?'

'I don't know, probably Aunty Kat. And Tom Aiken's truck is here.'

She pulled a cellphone from her pocket, 'I'm going to call an ambulance, and the police.'

She punched in III.

She held her cellphone up in the air to find a signal.

A shot came from inside the house. Gun shots in closed places sounded much different, not like a farm.

Run. I couldn't. Legs like gum now. Then not. I ran.

Ran towards the house and she screamed: 'Stop, Taukiri, stop.'

The gun. Take the gun. But if I turned back for it, would lose the courage to go inside. Gripped the gaff tighter and ran faster.

'Stop,' she yelled again.

My whole life I've wanted my mother to tell me what to do. Didn't stop me though. I ran.

Inside there are dark sounds. Movement upstairs. Then she's behind me, close. My mother is behind me. Close behind me. I open a door slowly, quietly, close it behind me, behind us. In the kitchen there are fish and chips over the floor. Empty whisky bottle on the table and a lunchbox broken in two. Table set for three. One plate dirty, two clean.

I can still feel her behind me. Makes me dizzy. Almost want to tell her to fuck off.

Into the hall, start up the stairs. Gaff held in front of me and hands white from the squeeze.

Then: a muffled cry. Someone speaks through their teeth.

Hurt.

Hear that: the fear. The spit. Gritted. The hurt.

Uncle Stu's voice now. 'Run away? Ha. With you eh. *Tommy*? Ha. Had your bags packed. Haha.'

Soft, dark, fleshy sound. Then Aunty Kat.

'I'll shoot,' says Uncle Stu. 'Stay there.'

He laughs. Sounds sad. 'Now look what you did. Look. Look. Did that to yourself.'

Soft, fleshy sound again. Aunty Kat sobs. 'You did that, Tommy.'

The gun? Go get the gun.

Aunty Kat screams. Dark. Flesh. Sound. A moan. 'Stu, I wasn't running away.'

'Your bag was *packed*.'

And *thuck*. Aunty Kat screams.

My mother grabs my elbow. The touch whips through me.

I shake her hand from my arm. 'Don't,' I say.

'I'll go, Taukiri. I can't let you,' she says, 'I can't. Not again.'

I don't listen. Everything I've missed out on.

To not listen to my mother. For the hell of it?

Inching closer now. Towards the door where the sounds come from. Then she sucks too loud on dead air. Gets a bellyful of it. She takes all the air from around us. I stand close to the doorway, and I see him, swaying, gun. Blood on his boots.

He turns.

Pull back now, we pull back, press our backs to the wall, opposite each other in the hall, just a gaff, just us and a gaff.

I lift the gaff. My mother, eyes wide then, widen and widen.

Not with fear. Decision. Fast decision.

'It's me, Stu.'

She chooses to draw him out, away from Aunty Kat, away from me. To her.

Her voice is blood, and he's a shark.

Uncle Stu moves with I-don't-give-a-fuck-anymore steps, and then he is in front of us. Gun raised. Like a slippery grey fin.

Ārama

Going inside for plasters now.

She still won't wake up. I say to her, 'Doc, I got lollies. Eating them all now, Doc. If you don't want me to, you'd better wake up.'

She doesn't wake.

Going for plasters.

Find an old blanket on the truck floor. Put it over her. Kiss her cheek. She doesn't say, 'Eww, townie weirdo,' so I'm going.

'Stay there then,' I say. 'Going for plasters.'

The lady who said she is my aunty Jade left me the phone and told me to keep dialling 111. And I did, and someone is coming.

But I'm going in, gonna tell Uncle Stu, right to his face, he's not my uncle Stu. I might tell him, 'Hate you.' Then I'll grab the plasters and I'll grab Aunty Kat and take her right out the door with me.

He'll be stunned. He won't know what to say. He'll just stand there feeling embarrassed about himself.

I run to the house, open the door and walk in.

Step on a piece of fish, keep walking. Treading it through the house now, because who cares? We leaving. Grabbing our stuff and we leaving.

Taukiri

She doesn't look scared of him. She just wants him to look at her, and not at me. He points his gun in her face, touches her nose.

'It is you. What are you here for, Jade?'

'Kat. The boys.'

'Tommy here too, you know. Being a useless fuck. Thought he was a hero.'

I raise the gaff. He still hasn't seen me, just sways in his boots like the dickhead he is.

Gun steady on my mum. My mum. And have I brought this on us? For the hell of it? Is he going to shoot her in the head in front of me now?

She looks right past his gun, right at him. Like she has seen worse. And he must see her fearlessness. He must feel challenged by it.

Holds his eyes for ransom. Only chance I have.

I lift the gaff.

Behind me I hear soft footsteps.

As light as.

Ari steps up beside me.

'Ari. Get back. Get back now.'

But my little brother walks towards the man with the gun pressed against my mother's nose.

Stands in front of him. Between them. The gun above his head. Looks up at Uncle Stu. Smallest he's ever looked. And though I know I should do something, all I can do is nothing. Nothing. Not a thing.

'You are not my uncle Stu,' Ari says.

'Ha. Nah, you're right there, kid.'

'I'm getting plasters. And Aunty Kat.'

No one moves. Uncle Stu presses the gun harder to my mother's nose. Her neck twists slightly from the pressure he applies.

Ari between them.

'Come to tell Tom Aiken you've hurt Beth. And Lupo. Come to tell you to stop it. I've come to get plasters.'

Uncle Stu lowers the gun now, presses it between Ari's eyes.

Ari's legs are shaking.

Then Tom Aiken is moving into the doorway behind Uncle Stu, who's surrounded, but he's the only one with a gun in his hand.

'Come to get Aunty Kat,' Ari says again. Words like a river, trembling, shaking like there's an earthquake thundering up inside him.

Ārama

And that's when I pee my pants.

Second time Uncle Stu has made me pee my pants. He's holding a gun between my eyes. He presses the gun into my skin. Just the way Beth does with sticks.

But metal is different.

The me on my forehead is thin – baby-rabbit-skin thin – and the gun's open mouth is so close to my brain it makes it vibrate. When I speak my words shake out.

The bees are swarming again, and they are trying to bust in the windows. The windows are rattling, and the doors, and the walls. Everything is shaking. The house is being wrapped up in a twister of bees to be spun up into the sky.

Bees angry then, angry that the windows are shut, trying to smash the glass, twisting around the house, loud. Find the door, sweeping up the steps, sweeping up into the hall, tearing the wallpaper from the walls, and the lights from the ceiling, splitting the house in two.

Beside me now, roaring beside me now, roaring and twisting and ready for a fight: a big bad taniwha.

Beth.

Has a gun. Blood in her hair. A gun in her hand.

'Hey, Django. I wished for you to get your wish. And I see you did.'

Taukiri

Beth got the gun. Beth got Coon's gun.

Ari says, 'I've come to get Aunty Kat.'

Beth walks up beside him.

Uncle Stu says, 'Here's the tough girl.'

She adjusts her grip, raises the gun an inch, 'Name's Doc.'

'What?'

'You heard.'

My mother: 'Beth … Beth … honey, come to me.'

Ari holds something out to Beth. 'Dutch courage,' he says.

And she takes it, but I can't see it, and she drinks from it, but I can't see it.

'Don't worry, Django. I got you,' she says. 'Get Broomhilda now.'

Ari steps forward. 'Getting her.'

Uncle Stu presses the gun harder against my brother's head.

Can't comprehend his recklessness.

I speak then. 'Throw down the gun, Beth.'

Uncle Stu lifts the rifle.

There is a red mark on Ari's head and a dark patch between his legs. 'Go on,' he says. '*Collect* the bitch.'

'Monsieur Candie,' Beth says.

'Someone get that gun off this crazy kid.'

Ari walks towards Aunty Kat. Uncle Stu grins and points the rifle at her now.

Tom leaps at Uncle Stu from behind the door. His hands strike the rifle like two open-mouthed snakes. He takes Uncle Stu to the ground. The rifle fires, a bullet *thucks* into something.

Uncle Stu rips the rifle from Tom's hands and smashes the butt into his nose.

White-hot. The gun pressed into my little brother's face makes me white-hot. Aunty Kat not moving makes me white-hot. The pee stain on my brother's pants makes me white-hot.

I lift the gaff.

'Don't do anything, please, Taukiri,' my mother says.

I swing the gaff and hook it into Uncle Stu's leg. Right to bone. And I pull it free. He screams.

Quickly I swing to his flesh once more. He cries out.

I pull the gaff away.

He lunges, takes aim at me with the rifle.

Strange words then, strange words for a little girl.

'*Auf wiedersehen*,' Beth says, and she shoots her gun and flies backwards. Uncle Stu crumples to the ground in a dreadful heap.

Ari steps over Uncle Stu and runs to Aunty Kat.

'I came to get you, Aunty Kat,' Ari says and kisses her bloody face.

I drop the gaff.

Ārama

Beth's aunty from Auckland flew here. And she walked into the quiet special room for waiting quietly at the hospital looking like an angry queen. Like she wanted to yell, 'Off with their heads.'

She stormed in, heels clicking, black rivers running down her cheeks. She yelled at Tom Aiken. '*Django*? Seriously! Tommy, I told you I could look after her. Could take her. Could help.'

'Shut up,' he said.

'Shouldn't've left her with you.'

'Who then? Her mother?'

'Running around wild. Hardly been to school? Well done.'

Her voice echoed in the special quiet room for waiting quietly at the hospital. She was clean, apart from make-up running down her doll face, and her hair was perfect and combed and her heels were high, and Tom Aiken had dried blood under his nose, and his eyes were sagging and his clothes were smelly and dirty from camping. He stunk of fire and eel and blood.

She smelled like perfume and washing powder. I didn't know that for sure because I didn't want to get too close – but I reckoned that was how she smelled.

'*Django*?' she yelled again and stormed away, thundered through the swing doors, only one allowed to see Beth now. Even Tom Aiken is stuck here in the special waiting place. Clock ticking. Floor shining. Magazines sitting.

'Why won't they let us see Beth?' I asked Tauk, 'She's allowed.'

He didn't reply. I grabbed his arm. 'Tauk?'

He answered, in a voice that wasn't his: 'She's in trouble.'

'He hurt her first.'

'I know.'

'Real bad.'

'I know.'

'I'm glad.'

'Don't say that.'

'I am.'

'I said don't say that, Ari.'

'I'm glad.'

'Me too.'

I looked out the big window. It was getting dark. I tugged Tauk's shirt again.

'The eels are gonna eat Lupo.'

'Let's go then,' he said.

Taukiri

Tired. So damn tired. Needed a bed. Wanted an attic. Ari had a room in a house. A house with stains on the floors. And bullet holes in it. He lived there this morning but that felt an eternity ago.

Couldn't imagine packing up Ari's room again. Couldn't imagine abandoning another house. Couldn't imagine setting all his stuff up somewhere else and pretending it's the same stuff, so it's the same life. Couldn't pretend – like I did last time – that all it took was to put some of his books on a shelf and a cover on a bed and line up the toys and you got yourself a home. Same, same, just a little different.

Leave some of the books in the box, because that's how it was. Some in, some out. Some words in, some loose. Some love in, some given. Some anger in, some free.

We'd leave it all. We might as well stop pretending having the same stuff means we're the same people.

Uncle Stu pressed a gun to my little brother's head, and that made my throat so dry.

Coon emptied his tired pockets into that chocolate box before he shot himself in the head. Then my uncle beat my aunty to a pulp with a gun to her head, and Tom tried to stop him, but he kept saying, 'Come near us and I'm shooting her, Aiken. Now watch what you've made me do.' And now I was sitting here. And I didn't know what to make of any of it.

That woman cried, yelled. Looked perfect. Probably wasn't.

I wished she'd shut up. Just shut her mouth up.

Ari pulled at my shirt and reminded me Beth's shot-dead dog was still in the river. I'd rather go pull that dog from a hundred hungry eel mouths than sit there and listen to that woman say another word. We all wanted to yell and cry, but her yelling and crying meant we

309

couldn't. There was no room for more than her in the bright, bright waiting room.

'Let's go.'

I walked to Tommy first though. Blood and fish and ash on him. 'I'll go get Lupo out,' I said.

He barely looked up. 'All right,' he said.

Ari hugged him.

I took the note from the man who shot himself in the head out of my pocket and handed it to my mother.

I took Ari by his shoulder. 'Let's go get you some fresh pants. And Lupo.'

We walked out the door.

Jade

The piece of paper had my address on one side, written in child-like handwriting. I unfolded it, and on the other side I read three scribbled words. Just three words.

Please forgive me.

I don't care who it is from, it could be from Coon or Hash. Any one of those dogs.

It is dark. There is just moonlight.

The boys are walking up the river.

Taukiri tells Ari to stay, to sit in the grass.

'Stay, you shouldn't see it,' he says, as tears fall down his face.

But Ari follows his brother.

'I can help,' Ari says.

Taukiri goes into the river, and disturbs an eel. It moves away in a fluid motion.

He pulls the dog's body up onto the bank.

They dig a hole and bury what's left of Lupo.

I feel the smallest piece – a mere speck of me – find shore.

There is Ari walking out of the whare mate. In the sunlight he blinks, and he blinks and he closes his eyes, holds his face to the sun. Then he runs chasing his second and third and fourth cousins into the trees behind the marae, laughing then, laughing so loud, laughter enough it could almost make a dead heart beat again.

Soaring then. I soar on the wind of his voice. His laughter.

And a small bone alights upon the beach.

311

Then, Jade reads a note: **Please forgive me.** *And to her, it doesn't matter who it is from. It's from anyone and everyone. It's from them and him and me and her.*

'I forgive you.'

And the light opens, swallows me.

Swallows me whole.

Taukiri

Time to teach Ari how to play the guitar I bought him for Christmas. We had time. I wasn't going anywhere. I called Megan the other day, and apparently Coon left a note for his boys. Told them he was a narc, and that he'd had an epiphany. He could save the world from that single load, so that was what he did. Megan had seen the note. Photographed it and would show me one day. Maybe.

Called da po-po, Coon wrote.

Savin' da world from you cunts.

Sorry not sorry.

Peace out.

She had heard talk though. That the gun wasn't with him.

The gun that was with the police. My koro's gun.

Bet you never touched anything he has.

I had touched things he had. I knew that now.

Books.

'Your koro taught me to read this,' Mum said, running her hand over the mermaid's green hair.

Didn't need to touch his gun.

I didn't tell Megan that I knew it wasn't with him, decided not to put her in that position. I was afraid of what she'd think of me, that she wouldn't know what to say.

She'd been to see her friend, the one from the picture. 'You know. May. I picked her up and took her for a drive. We drove and drove, Tauk … Just drove. We talked about going backpacking together. Europe maybe.'

'Wow,' I said. 'Cool.'

I haven't called her since. She hasn't called me either.

Me and Ari were sitting on the bed that we shared in my mother's house at Rakiura. He brought it to me still wrapped. Just a little rip in the Christmas paper.

Clanking in the kitchen. Nanny setting the table. Koro had gone fishing. Aunty Kat was probably sleeping. My mum would be walking around the house, making sure, just making sure. That Nanny was sorting food and Aunty Kat was breathing and Koro had left a bookmark in his book, and I'd washed my face and made my bed and brushed my teeth.

All those things meant we were still here, that we were not going anywhere.

He dropped the guitar to the bed with a clunk. 'I can open it now,' he said.

'Go on then.'

He tore into it. 'I knew it, I knew it. A guitar. I thought, maybe it wasn't, maybe it was a trick, but wow. A real guitar.'

'It's not new.'

'Good. Like yours?'

'Yeah.'

Beth stepped into the doorway. She was here from Auckland while her aunty got some things sorted. She wasn't with Tom Aiken anymore because he was an unfit father, as defined by three easy questions from one or two important people wearing bad shirts and decent shoes from the Ministry for Children or something. *Django Unchained*? Really? And hardly been to school? Seriously? And knows how to keep house? Honestly?

It might not be permanent.

Sad she was without him. Like a small pebble now, the smallest bone. White and soft and soundless. Like something you could put in your pocket.

Ari was struggling with new Beth, though sometimes he seemed to enjoy being the talker. Being the brave one.

Until night came.

He was still a sook at night. It was lucky we were sharing a room for now.

Playing now, strumming now. He was a natural. I could hear that, though no one else might.

Beth leaned to listen. Then she moved, one step, stop, one step, stop. She sat on the edge of the bed, tucked her hands under her tiny thighs.

'Look what I can do, Beth.'

He strummed.

He plucked but didn't make a song. He was just learning and didn't know a chord. But he strummed like he did know. He slapped the shiny rosewood and nodded his head and tapped his foot like he did. He heard something no one else could, the song before it was a song. Ari felt the guitar play itself.

We stopped. My brother grinned at Beth, a grin that said, *You hear that?*

'Uh huh,' she said.

Beth fished in her pocket. Slow, like she was now. Probably not from the head knock, but the trauma of the bad things that happened the day she shot a man.

Beth pulled out a shell. Then a coin. A stone. Half a wishbone. A might-be-pearl.

Beth tossed all the things from her pocket in front of Ari and clapped for him.

And when Ari saw the might-be-pearl he gasped, grabbed it, lifted it, turned it in his hand, held it up to the light.

Then looked at me, already knowing. I shook my head. 'It's gone, Ari.'

He won't ever stop looking. He and Nanny go to the beach some-times and he drives her wild with his looking. Pointing. Lifting. Checking.

For a moment all was quiet, so quiet, just the guitar humming still under our breathing.

She said it again, though, out of nowhere. Just said it. Like it was a little animal that needed out, a little animal that got trapped inside her, so she freed it, but another one grew in its place, so she let that out too and round and round it went.

Some in, some loose.

Sometimes she said it over and over like there was a swarm, some-times she said it just once. Three words. Slow, singing. Ragged. Broken.

She could say them sad or angry, even happy: 'Shot him dead.'

Sing it high, sing it low. Let them know.

'Shot him dead.'

Then Ari would run off to get his box of plasters. 'Where's it hurt now, Doc?'

Beth touched a place on her that didn't look hurt. Looked fine. Not a scratch, not a bruise, not a blister.

And Ari tore open the plaster, and unstuck it, and covered where she was sore.

There was the smell of herbs and of fish being crisped, hiss and bubble from the kitchen.

'Haere mai ki te kai,' Nanny called.

At the round table: Koro beside Nanny and Aunty Kat beside Koro, Mum beside Aunty Kat, me beside Mum, Ari beside me, Beth beside Ari and Nanny beside her, and Nanny said the karakia mō te kai, and she said, 'Āmene,' and we opened our eyes and I looked at her and saw it then, shining.

I just looked and looked at it, and I looked at Ari, and I didn't want to be the one to tell him, I wanted him to see it first, for himself. But he was into his kai now, hard out, not taking a breath, gobbling down the fried potatoes and crispy blue cod.

'Homai te pata,' Nanny said.

Aunty Kat took the butter and passed it, and then I saw her see it too, and she looked at Ari, then me.

Ari was wolfing down his kai.

'He inu māu, Ari?' I said.

We'd had a family meeting, and Nanny had asked us all, 'How are we going to do this? How do we survive now?' And Ari had put up his hand and said: 'We will need a secret language, Nanny.' And she'd laughed and said, 'Āe, Ārama, let's start with our reo. We've lost enough.'

He didn't stop eating when I asked him the question. 'Nope.'

'You need one though. Nanny, pass him the L&P.'

Ari looked up. 'There's L&P?'

'I can't see any,' said Nanny. And as she turned, looking for it, confused, turning this way and that, Ari saw it too.

'Nanny!'

'What, my moko?'

Ari pointed. To her heart. To the shiny thing on a silver chain.

'You made a necklace with the pearl, Nanny. With your earring.'

She touched it, and smiled. 'I did, Ārama. So you can stop looking for its other now.'

Ari set down his knife and fork. 'It's not garbage?'

'Ehara, ehara,' she touched it then. 'Does this look like garbage?'

'Tell us, tell Beth, the story.' He elbowed Beth. 'You gonna love this. It's just your thing.'

She kept chewing but looked straight at Nanny.

Aunty Kat put down her knife and fork. 'Tell us, Mum.'

Nanny sipped some water, cleared her throat. 'Āe, āe. Whakarongo mai, whānau.'

Koro, grinning wide, touched Nanny's cheek. Her chin quivered.

My mum winked at my aunty Kat, who tilted her head.

Ari grabbed my hand, then Beth's.

Acknowledgements

Mum, you bought me typewriters, pens and books, and made me believe that the ghost stories and fairy tales and sad poems I wrote as a kid were the very best in the world – that I was a writer. Thank you for being the most supportive and kind māmā there ever was.

Maddox and Siena Manawatu, my beautiful children, you have inspired me to write using as much magic as I could muster. You didn't (seem to) mind that I was not always managing what other mums might have been managing, and you stepped up and helped pāpā keep our whare running.

To my sisters, Tami and Nicole, you made sure I always remembered that my blonde hair and blue eyes didn't mean I wasn't 'Māori enough'. I miss you.

To my dad, thank you for all your quiet support and generosity, for keeping the home fires burning and catching and cooking kaimoana. For our trip to Rakiura. For adventures collecting pāua, mussels, hauling up the odd octopus.

To my little brother Kodie, thanks for being the guy we all look up to and for being one of my best friends.

Tina Makereti, thank you for your thoughtful assessment and the tautoko you gave me as part of the 2016 New Zealand Society of Author's manuscript assessment programme. I'll always treasure that first hard copy that arrived back to me in the post, your sound advice scribbled in its margins.

Headland literary journal and The Maisonette Trust, thank you for the grant which funded the trip for me to spend the day with editor and publisher Mary McCallum at Mākaro Press.

Penny Howard, the images on the cover could not be more ātaahua, nor more perfect.

My tutor Cliff Fell and fellow students at Nelson Marlborough Institute of Technology, that class was choice, inspiring, challenging, and where I scratched out some of *Auē*'s best bones.

Lee Scanlon and Teresa Wyndham-Smith, I'm very privileged to work alongside two amazing journalists, who have much knowledge and such a wide-ranging vocabulary, as well as the ability to see and the desire to find stories. This book would not be what it is if I hadn't learned from the pair of you before the edits. I'm grateful for your support and patience over the past two years.

Te Miroa Maxwell and Emma Walker, thank you for letting me be a cheeky little wahine during our weekly te reo class, asking sneaky questions to make *Auē* better. You helped me ensure my limitations weren't my characters' limitations. Any mistakes that remain are my own.

Tokohau and Desiree Samuels, thanks for being all pai. (To the whole whānau, you're all pai too.) Ngatai whānau, thank you for letting me use the bach at Mōkihinui to work. The Frankfurt Writers Group – thank you for the inspiring meetings at Club Voltaire, and for encouraging me to let *Auē* have a ghost.

Paul Stewart for the wonderful typesetting and the tough job of proofreading, and to Carrie Wainwright for kindly checking the reo. Both Scotty Morrison's *Māori Made Easy* and Te Wānanga o Aotearoa's tikanga course resources were fantastic. Osho's book *Intuition – knowing beyond logic: insights for a new way of living* inspired the text of the book Beth and Ari read together in the tent.

I also want to acknowledge Emira Maewa Kaihau (Ngāpuhi, 1879–1941), who composed 'Akoako o te Rangi', the song Toko plays and tells Jade, wrongly, that it's written by a Pākehā. More on this talented wahine at www.folksong.org.nz.

Louise Leung Wai, you drove me across Wellington hungover (little Amelie and Ruby not so keen in the back) so I could hand my manuscript to Mākaro Press in person. I needed to do that.

Renée, thank you for seeing the potential of *Auē* and for championing it, rough as it was in those early stages. Thank you too for opening up the dialogue between Mary and me on the title, which opened up so much more, and for replying to my worried emails with kindness.

Mary McCallum, thank you so much for your amazing mahi, for your taumauri when I needed to make *just one more change*, add one more line, cut one more word, and for telling me when to stop. Thank you for planting seeds, never pushing me, but nudging me towards making some bigger changes. The best of this book was written from those nudges.

Auē would not have been written without the tautoko my husband, Tim Manawatu, gave me. Getting the kai on the table, hanging out the washing, making the endless pots of coffee. You dealt with the ups and downs of living with a person who was writing a novel. Well done, we survived it. And thank you for taking me to Kaikōura, and teaching me how to eel with a gaff.

This book was written in memory of our precious Glen Bo Duggan (1983–1994). An artistic, funny, kind, smart, handsome boy, who needed a taniwha to come and rip through his front door and tear down the walls of the house so everyone could see what was going on behind them.

Glossary of Māori terms

āe – yes

āmene – amen

Aotearoa – the country of New Zealand

atua – god

auē – to cry, wail, howl; interjection showing distress

Auē! Te mamae hoki – ooh, the pain

ehara, ehara – to the contrary

e kare – dear friend

Eskimos – old name for a sweet shaped like the Inuit people, now called Explorers as the term 'Eskimos' is offensive

gaff – hook to fish with and catch eels

hā – breath, essence

haere mai – come here, welcome (a greeting)

haere mai ki te kai – come to eat

hāngī – earth oven to steam/ cook food

he inu māu? – would you like a drink?

Hītara waha huka ūpoko mārō – song title, means 'pig-headed Hitler foaming at the mouth'

homai te pata – pass the butter

hongi – the practice of pressing noses to share breath as a greeting

ka pai – good

kaimoana – seafood

karakia – prayer

karakia mō te kai – grace, or prayer before eating

kei te pēhea koe? – how are you?

kei te pai ahau, Nanny – I'm fine, Nana/Gran

kia tangi koe – you can cry

kihi – kiss

kuia – elderly woman

kūmara – sweet potato

māmā – mother

manu – bird, (in this context) to curl up the body to make a water bomb when you jump into the water (colloq)

marae – area in front of the main tribal meeting house for Māori, the buildings around that area too

Māui – the great culture hero and trickster of Māori mythology, who performed many amazing feats

Māui catching the sun – Māui slowed the sun by catching it in a giant net, lengthening the day to make everyday tasks possible

moko / mokopuna – grandchild

nanny – grandmother

nau mai, haere mai – welcome

offskies – out of here (colloq)

on the mish – on a mission (colloq)

Pākehā – New Zealander of European descent

pāpā – father

Papatūānuku – Earth, the Earth mother and the wife of Ranginui – all animate and inanimate things originate from them

pāua – abalone

pēpē – baby

pīwakawaka – fantail

plasters – bandaids

pō mārie– goodnight

poaka – pig

po-po – police (colloq)

pōuri – sad, dark

pōwhiri – welcome ceremony

pūkana – to stare wildly, dilate the eyes, done by both genders when performing haka (ceremonial challenge) and waiata (songs) to emphasise particular words and to add excitement

pūkeko – an Australasian swamp hen, large deep blue/black bird

Ranginui – god of the sky, husband of Papatūānuku – all animate and inanimate things originate from them

'Tai Aroha' – song title, means 'tide of love'

tama – boy, son

tā moko – traditional tattooing

Tangaroa – god of the sea and fish, one of the offspring of Ranginui and Papatūānuku

tangata whenua – people of the land, indigenous New Zealanders

tangi – to cry, to grieve, a funeral

taniwha – a water spirit, monster or guardian that usually lives in the sea, lakes, rivers and caves and can take on many forms but is often represented as lizard-like; can be a spiritual guardian, a guardian of those who live nearby, or a malignant force; also describes a chief or leader, something or someone awesome

tarakihi – a type of fish (in this context), a cicada

Tāwhiri-mātea – god of the winds, clouds, rain, hail, snow and storms, one of the offspring of Ranginui and Papatūānuku

tēnā koe – hello (to one person)

te reo – the language, often used to mean the Māori language

Tilly lamp – oil lantern

tino pai rawa, my moko – very well done, my grandchild

tīpuna – ancestors

tūī – native bird with a white throat tuft and distinctive songs (depicted on the cover)

tumeke – to be surprised, shocked, frightened, startled

ūpoko – head

ūpoko mārō – pig-headed

waiata – song, to sing

weka – bird

'Whakahonohono Mai' – song title, means 'to join together'

whakamā – to whiten, to feel ashamed or abased

whānau – family (includes nuclear and extended family)

whare mate – the house of mourning

whakarongo mai, whānau – listen up, family

whenua – placenta (in this context), land